Death By DNA

John S. Shaw, III

This is a work of fiction. While this book is informed by real scientific developments and research, the narrative is essentially fiction. The story itself is the author's invention, and the book should be understood as a fictional account, not a scientific one.

For Carolyn, Carson, and Kendall

CHAPTER 1

911 Operator:	*Hello, this is the 911 operator. Do you have an emergency?*
Female Voice:	*Not really. There's nothing you can do now. It's probably all for the best anyway.*
911 Operator:	*What do you mean?*
Female Voice:	*I was afraid this might happen.*
911 Operator:	*Ma'am, I don't understand.*
Female Voice:	*That's okay. There's nothing you can do. Just tell Ryan I love him.*
911 Operator:	*Do you need any help?*
Female Voice:	*Not anymore.*
911 Operator:	*Do you want me to send an ambulance? The police?*

[Nineteen seconds of a constant rumbling sound]

911 Operator:	*Ma'am. Do you need any help? Shall I send the police?*
Female Voice:	*If you want.*

[End of recording]

1

The truth was buried somewhere in Lexi's despondent 911 call. Sarah just had to find it.

* * *

"Step on through, counselor!" barked the burly sheriff's deputy.

As Sarah proceeded slowly through the jailhouse security scanner, it sounded a sharp alarm.

"Any metal on you, Mrs. Wong?" inquired the deputy, somewhat annoyed.

Sarah had forgotten about her necklace. She removed it quickly, accidentally dropping it on the floor. Under the watchful stare of four male deputies, she got down on both knees and reached under the table next to the metal detector.

As she knelt on the floor, the distinct smell of vomit enveloped her, an odor she had encountered all too frequently at the Central Jail. When she started law school almost ten years earlier, she had envisioned glamorous positions at prestigious law firms, with the attendant trappings of power; she had never imagined that one day she would be groping for her necklace on the smelly, cold concrete floor of the Santa Felicia Central Jail. Finally, she found it, breaking the clasp in the process.

"Let's keep it moving, Mrs. Wong," ordered the deputy.

She tossed her necklace into the battered gray bin on the x-ray machine conveyer belt. She mused that it was probably harder to get *into* the county jail than break out of it. While waiting for an escort to the attorney interview room, she plopped down on the nearby bench, put on her belt and shoes, and stuffed her necklace into her suit jacket pocket.

At last, a tall gangly female deputy motioned silently for Sarah to follow. She tried to make small talk, but all she could elicit were a few uninterested monosyllabic replies. They passed through two large metal doors, shut by the taciturn escort with an unnecessarily loud bang, and after walking along a narrow hallway lit only by overhead fluorescent lights they arrived at the attorney interview room, a rectangular space faced by an entire wall of glass.

In front of the glass were four round metal stools, and Sarah took the one farthest from the door. The stools reminded her of the type often found in '50s-style diners, only these had no padding and didn't swivel. As she sat down on the cold, unforgiving metal, she couldn't help but long for the reclining padded leather chairs that cradled the backsides of her corporate-lawyer colleagues. On both sides of the glass, six-foot-high metal dividers between the stools gave the illusion of privacy, but there were no tops or backs to the dividers, and voices reverberated loudly in the bare, concrete room.

While she waited, Sarah reviewed the case against her latest client. Only nineteen years old, Lexi Conway was charged with first-degree murder in the killing of her three-week-old baby girl, Anna. On Monday August 11, just four days earlier, two police officers had responded to a 911 call at 42 Windmere Place where they discovered Lexi Conway unconscious in the driver's seat of her car, which was running in her closed, exhaust-filled garage. After one of the officers dragged Lexi out of the driver's seat and on to the driveway, he started CPR immediately while the other officer called for an ambulance. They reported that just as the ambulance screeched into the driveway, Lexi had started coughing and wheezing. It was only after the ambulance had taken Lexi to the hospital that the officers made a grim discovery: Lexi's baby daughter Anna was lifeless, strapped into her car seat in the back of Lexi's car. The officers had done everything they could to revive her, but it had been no use.

The preliminary autopsy report on the little girl was dry, clinical and straightforward — Anna Conway had died from acute carbon monoxide poisoning.

3

The district attorney would probably allege one or more special circumstances, which would make Lexi "eligible for the death penalty." Sarah detested that phrase. It made it seem as though the death penalty were some sort of prize with strict eligibility requirements. Even if the DA didn't seek the death penalty, Lexi still faced life in prison if she was convicted.

Sarah pulled out a copy of a written statement Lexi had given to two detectives while she was still in the hospital. The handwritten declaration filled two pages of notebook paper and was signed by Lexi at the bottom. Stapled onto the front of the statement was a half sheet of paper on which was printed the standard Miranda warning, and the signature on it matched the signature at the bottom of the two-page statement. It looked like the detectives had done everything right.

Statement of Lexi Conway

Monday was just a normal day. I just did my usual stuff. While Ryan was getting dresed, I fed Anna and played with her a little bit. I took her on a walk around the block like we did evry morning. Then we all got in the car, and I took Ryan to work at the R&B Paint Store.

Then I took Anna with me while I did some errends. I went to Pete's, the Donut Shoppe, and the Sunoco gas station. I think I went to the Donut Shoppe first, but it could have been the other way around. Anna seemed fine, just a little sleepie.

But when I got out of my car at the gas stattion, I noticed something was really wrong with Anna. She wasn't moving or nothing. I poked her and pinched her and nothing happened. I called her name, I shook her and shook her, I even pushed on her chest, but nothing worked. I really tried to help her, but she was already gone.

I didnt know what to do. For sure, I wasnt going to tell Ryan. He would never ever ever understand and he would be mad at me forever. I was panicy. I knew it was my fault that Anna was dead.

I figured I would kill myself. At least that way I would be with my baby in heven. So I drove home and pulled my car into the gerage, shut the gerage door and just sat there. I didn't know what to do. I had no idea how long it would take. Eventually I started feeling a little dizzie. After that everything is fuzzy. I think I made a call, but I'm not sure. Maybe I called Ryan, maybe I called my mom. I'm pretty sure I called somebody. Next thing I remember is that I woke up in the hospital and there were two police oficers in my room. I asked them what hapened.

Thats all I have to say.

Lexi Conway   *August 13*

Just as Sarah finished rereading Lexi's statement, a door at the back of the room on the other side of the glass opened and a slight woman shuffled in, her feet shackled by a short chain and her hands cuffed in front of her. She stared down at her feet as she shuffled forward.

"Lexi Conway here to see her attorney!" boomed the robust female deputy accompanying her.

Sarah raised her hand and motioned to the deputy, who guided Lexi to the seat on the other side of the glass. Lexi sat down awkwardly and didn't look up, even when the deputy handed her the phone. Sarah took the receiver off the hook on her side.

"Lexi, my name is Sarah Wong. I'm going to be your attorney."

Lexi looked straight at Sarah. "I don't have 'nough money for a lawyer."

"That's okay. The court appointed me so you won't have to pay."

Lexi's sparkling green eyes contrasted sharply with her disconsolate, sallow face. She had jet-black hair that fell just below her chin on the left side of her face but that was shaved close to her scalp on the right. Lexi appeared to be a couple of inches taller than Sarah — maybe five four or so — and she was thin, probably not more than a hundred pounds. Her left arm was covered with tattoos, most of them in black ink, but a few had color. All Sarah could make out were abstract designs, a few hearts, and a large sunset. There were also a few scattered Chinese characters on her right arm and one on her neck. Nothing demonic or evil.

Overall, Lexi's appearance evoked a wannabe actress who never made it and instead had settled into a tougher life. Her striking green eyes were filled with fear, not anger or defiance. Given a more flattering hairstyle, a few more pounds, and a new outlook on life, Sarah believed Lexi could be transformed into a beautiful young woman. But as she sat on the metal stool, lit by the harsh fluorescent lights of the Central Jail, Lexi looked right at home behind bars.

When the court clerk had called Sarah on Thursday to see if she would represent Lexi Conway, Sarah had said yes immediately. Although Sarah's law firm was financially stable, business had been a little slow over the past few months, and capital murder cases paid more than other types of criminal cases. Besides, Sarah hadn't had a juicy criminal case in a while, and she was growing ever more tired of nasty divorces and testy landlord-tenant squabbles.

All the clerk had said over the phone was that it was a capital murder case. What she hadn't told her was that the young woman was accused of killing her own baby. Had Sarah known that, she probably would have declined the case right off the bat. But now she was stuck. In any case, Lexi Conway was entitled to an attorney under the Sixth Amendment.

Lexi looked oddly familiar to Sarah, although after seven years of representing criminal defendants, almost everyone in the standard issue orange jump suit tended to look familiar.

"Have I represented you before?" Sarah asked. "Have you ever been in trouble?"

"No, ma'am. A couple of traffic tickets and a bar fight about a year ago. That's it."

"All right," replied Sarah, still not convinced.

She began by inquiring about Lexi's family and background, and she learned that she came from a loving family. Although her dad had died when she was about five, she had a pleasant enough childhood, living with her mom and older sister in a lower-to-middle-class neighborhood. Throughout their conversation, Sarah noticed that Lexi was sniffling and her eyes frequently welled up.

"Are you okay? I can see that you're really upset about all of this."

"Of course I'm upset! My baby's dead. What d'ya think?"

"I'm sorry," replied Sarah. "It's just that your eyes are all red."

"I've got a really bad cold or the flu or something. I've had it for about a week. They won't give me anything for it in here."

Maybe she's not really upset, thought Sarah. She considered probing Lexi further about her emotions, but decided to move on instead. She told Lexi what she was charged with — first-degree murder with special circumstances.

"The police say you killed your three-week-old baby."

"Yes, ma'am."

Sarah sat in silence. What did Lexi mean by "Yes,

ma'am"? Did she mean that she understood the charges against her or that she admitted killing her baby? Sarah was tempted to clarify Lexi's response, but she let it go for now. She summarized what was going to happen over the next few weeks and months, explained general court procedures, and talked about the presumption of innocence and the burden of proof. It was a lecture Sarah had given hundreds of times before, and as she droned on Lexi managed a few barely audible acknowledgments. Mostly she just stared down at the counter.

Lexi looked up, her green eyes full of despair. "You're not really going to help me, are you?"

"Lexi, I'm going to do my very best. That's why I'm here. Our first court date is next Wednesday when you'll be formally arraigned."

"What does that mean?"

"That's when the judge will tell you your charges."

"Will he set bail? I don't have much money, but maybe Ryan can bail me out."

"I can ask, but the judge probably won't set bail. This is a capital murder case."

"What's capital mean?"

There was no way to sugarcoat the next bit of information. "It means that this is a death penalty case," Sarah told her. "If you're convicted, you could be sentenced to death."

Lexi sat in silence for a few moments. "Maybe that's what I deserve."

Sarah decided not to press her any further. There would be plenty of time for that in their future meetings. She gathered up her papers, stuffed them back into her briefcase, motioned to the deputy on her side of the glass that they were done, and left.

After retrieving her phone and laptop from the locker, Sarah stepped out of the jail and squinted in the bright sunlight. It was hot out, even for an August afternoon in

Santa Felicia. She took off her suit jacket as she headed out to her car. This case was going to be a year-long headache for her, and her temples were already throbbing. Sarah and Matt had been trying to have a baby for almost five years, and here she was, representing a young girl accused of taking the life of her own child. It just didn't seem fair.

Suddenly, she looked at her watch.

Damn! I'm late.

She flung open the car door and sat down on the hot, sticky, black leather. Starting the ignition, she slammed the door shut and screeched out of the parking lot.

Matt's going to kill me.

CHAPTER 2

Sarah was almost always late for their appointments at New Beginnings Fertility Clinic. She rushed in and sat down next to Matt, who seemed to be more exasperated than usual at her tardiness. She could guess what he was thinking: *She doesn't really want to have children. That's why she's always late for our appointments.* But she knew that wasn't the truth. The journey to having a baby had been long and painful, both physically and emotionally, and she wasn't about to give up now.

They had been trying to have children from the day they got married over five years ago. For the first two years they had been "unofficially" trying to get pregnant. What that meant to Sarah was that they weren't telling anyone they were trying; what it meant to Matt was that the sex was for recreation, not procreation. Either way, they were spontaneous, playful, and affectionate. Sometimes their lovemaking dissolved into fits of laughter, and on weekend mornings they cuddled in bed, often not getting up until noon.

But eventually the sex became less enjoyable and less frequent. Steadily but almost imperceptibly, they shifted from unofficially trying to officially trying. Sarah told her parents they were going to start a family and Matt talked about boys' names (and a few girls' names, just in case). They bought pregnancy kits almost every month, Sarah using the tests if she was even one day late. After a year of procreational sex and a dozen pregnancy kits, Sarah had started to get worried. It wasn't quite panic, but it was heading in that direction.

On the night of their third wedding anniversary, they had booked a table at Ocean Cove, their favorite seafood house, and were determined to have fun—either recreational or procreational—that night when they got home. Sarah had worn her sexiest outfit—a red silk top over a short black skirt, three-inch spike heels, one strand of pearls, and her most alluring perfume.

They started with clams and moderately expensive champagne and, as the evening progressed, their conversation turned to kids, as it always seemed to those days. They both wanted more than one child—Sarah wanted two and Matt three—and they were getting increasingly frustrated by their lack of progress. As they lingered over a shared Death-by-Chocolate dessert, they made The Pledge—they promised each other that Sarah would get pregnant before their next wedding anniversary.

Despite Sarah's tantalizing appearance, the bottle and a half of champagne, and The Pledge, nothing happened that night when they got home. Nothing at all. Not even a kiss. By the time they got home, Sarah was almost asleep and Matt wanted to check the late scores on Sports Center. Tomorrow night for sure, they had agreed.

The next day came, and they were both too tired again. The tomorrows stretched into weeks and the weeks stretched into months. They did have sex occasionally during the Year of the Pledge, but rarely was it spontaneous, and never was it satisfying, either physically or emotionally. Most importantly, it never led to a pregnancy.

After the Year of the Pledge had come and gone, they decided to turn to fertility treatments and chose New Beginnings Fertility Clinic, a world-renowned facility less than an hour from their home.

They had gone through the usual panoply of testing that all fertility-challenged couples experience. For reasons that were never explained to Sarah, the doctors at New Beginnings worked on her first. After three ultrasounds, a complete blood work-up, and too many uncomfortable pelvic exams to count, her ovaries, fallopian tubes, and uterus had all checked out fine.

Then it was Matt's turn. It hadn't bothered him when all of the testing had focused on Sarah and all he had to do was show up for the appointments, but now that *he* had to go under the microscope, it was a whole other matter. In fact, it seemed to Sarah that he was ready to back out entirely. It took a great deal of pleading from Sarah to convince him to submit his semen for analysis.

He had two choices for producing a sample: he could do it at home or at the fertility clinic. Neither option was appealing. The first time, he gave it a go at the clinic. He was led into a small, plain room — labeled the Production Room — by an attractive technician in a slightly too-tight white blouse and gray skirt. She may have been employed to help prime the pump, but her presence actually had the opposite effect on him. She handed him a small, clear plastic sample jar with his name printed on the label and told him she would see him in about five minutes. Five minutes? Five hours would be more like it, Matt thought. He locked the door and took a look around. On the only table in the room were a TV and a VCR, several videotapes and numerous adult magazines.

He gave it a perfunctory effort, but it was no use. There was no way he was going to be successful with nurses, technicians, and other patients just a few feet away on the other side of the wall. After about twenty minutes, he emerged with an empty cup, which he handed sheepishly to the technician in the white blouse as he mumbled his apologies.

From then on, Matt produced his semen samples at

home, but even that had its problems. In order for the sample to be fresh enough to be used in fertilization procedures, he had to get it back to the clinic within an hour, and they lived about forty minutes from New Beginnings. It was a tight, but doable schedule.

Matt had submitted two semen samples for analysis, about two weeks apart, from his home-based Production Room. The first sample was too small for the lab to work with. He had been assured by the technician in the white blouse that this happened to everyone and he wasn't to worry, that he would be successful the next time, but her confidence in him made him even more nervous. So he was greatly relieved when his second sample was deemed large enough to be analyzed.

However, his elation lasted only until the lab sent him his semen report card. He had read enough of the brochures Sarah had given him to know that the results were not good. Morphology and motility, shape and swimming ability — these were the problem areas for his sperm. He had enough of them — sixteen million per milliliter, which was on the low end of the normal range — but the quality wasn't great. Many of his spermatozoa were deformed, and most of them swam sluggishly or not at all. No wonder Sarah couldn't get pregnant — at least, not under the usual circumstances.

Because Sarah had no apparent fertility problems and Matt had an adequate number of viable sperm, they were prime candidates for many of the usual fertility treatments. The myriad possibilities were dizzying. None were guaranteed and all were expensive. The most advanced techniques cost $10,000 or more for a single attempt, and their insurance didn't cover any of it.

First, they had tried artificial insemination. After Matt had done his part, his sperm were washed and injected directly into Sarah's uterus. She wasn't sure exactly why they washed his sperm, but it certainly seemed appropriate, given that fertility treatments were as far removed from dirty sex as one could get. Everything was washed or sterilized—the syringes, the speculum, the examining table—so why not Matt's sperm?

After three rounds of artificial insemination, all failures, they faced an important decision. Should they keep on trying, utilizing ever more invasive and expensive fertility procedures, or should they just cut their losses and stop? After all, neither of them was completely infertile, and they could just keep trying the old-fashioned way. They had both heard stories about couples that had conceived naturally after years of failed fertility treatments. But Sarah and Matt were not quitters, so they agreed to push on. The next eighteen months had been filled with an alphabet soup of treatment options, including IVF, GIFT, and ZIFT. Sarah did her best to read up on each procedure they tried, while Matt was content to leave the technical stuff to her and Dr. Svengaard, their fertility doctor.

In vitro fertilization and zygote intra-fallopian transfer were just variations on a theme. Sarah went through two weeks of hormone shots so she could produce as many eggs as possible, and Dr. Svengaard retrieved them with a long needle in a *very* painful procedure. Then Matt supplied his fresh sperm sample, and Dr. Svengaard mixed the eggs and sperm together in a petri dish. After that, everyone waited. If any of the eggs were fertilized, the resulting embryos were transferred into Sarah.

No matter what procedure they used, Matt had only two jobs: inject Sarah daily for about two weeks and provide a sperm sample on egg-retrieval day. Matt's reward for his relatively meager contribution was the embarrassment of arriving at the clinic with a brown paper bag, inside of which was a small container with a teaspoon or so of his semen. Each time he walked into New Beginnings with his precious cargo, everyone knew why he was there—the receptionist, the nurses, even the other patients in the waiting room. He might as well have been wearing a sign that said, "My Sperm is in This Bag."

But after two cycles of IVF and one of ZIFT, costing Matt and Sarah over $25,000, they had nothing to show for all their time, pain, and money.

* * *

On July 11, just five weeks before Sarah took on the Lexi Conway case, Sarah and Matt had met with Dr. Svengaard to discuss their options.

The doctor got right down to business. He was clearly a busy and important man, and he never wasted time with pleasantries. He wasn't completely cold, but his demeanor was lukewarm at best. To Sarah, he seemed more suited for technical scientific research than the practice of medicine. Sarah wondered why he wasn't peering into a microscope finding a cure for something instead of dealing with anxious fertility patients. Of all the medical specialties, fertility seemed an odd choice for Dr. Svengaard. Fertility patients were very demanding, and it took a special breed of doctor to skillfully navigate such emotionally rugged terrain. Dr. Svengaard was clearly not that kind of doctor. His posture was always erect—almost rigid—and he didn't even pretend to get to know his patients or understand their fears and hopes. He seemed to view fertility medicine as a scientific endeavor in which patients were a necessary, but annoying, inconvenience.

"In my professional opinion, further attempts at IVF, GIFT or ZIFT will not be fruitful," Dr. Svengaard said with his usual bluntness. "It's time to consider other options."

Sarah felt a rush of conflicting emotions. Although she was grateful that there *were* other options, at the same time she was disappointed that there was more work to do—more hassles, more embarrassment, more expense. In some respects, it would have been easier if Dr. Svengaard had simply said "That's it. There's nothing else I can do for you. Good luck."

"What other options are there?" Sarah had asked hesitantly.

"Your eggs and Mr. Wong's sperm are clearly adequate since I've been able to create five viable embryos in the past year or so."

Dr. Svengaard's emphasis on his "creative" role in the process infuriated Sarah. Sure, he had worked his technological magic, but Sarah and Matt had done their part too. Couldn't he at least share some of the credit with them?

"The problem, of course, is that you haven't been able to sustain a pregnancy for more than a few days."

So it was all Sarah's fault! Her personal opinion of the doctor, which had not been very high to begin with, plummeted even further.

"What other options are there?" she repeated.

"Surrogacy, donor eggs, or donor sperm," replied Dr. Svengaard brusquely.

She had never really considered any of these. Sure, she had heard about them, but she had never thought they might be appropriate for *her*.

"Let's talk about surrogacy first," began Dr. Svengaard. "Your eggs, Mr. Wong's sperm, somebody else's uterus. Interested?"

Wow, he really does get straight to the point, thought Sarah. In some respects, surrogacy was appealing to her because the baby would be all theirs, genetically speaking. They would just be borrowing somebody else's uterus for nine months — sort of renting a baby oven.

Without waiting for a reply, Dr. Svengaard plowed ahead. "There are two ways you can go with surrogacy: you can use a relative or you can pay a stranger. Most people choose a relative if one is available. A sister, sister-in-law, cousin — even occasionally the woman's mother."

Sarah remembered reading about a forty-five-year-old woman who had been a surrogate for her twenty-three-year-old daughter. In effect, the woman had given birth to her own grandchild. That was a little too icky for Sarah, who imagined how she might ask her own mom to be a surrogate.

"Hey mom, how's it going?"
"Fine, honey. How are you and Matt? Any news?"
"Well sort of."
"Really?"
"It looks like Matt and I are going to have a baby."
"That's wonderful! I knew you could do it!"
"But there's one small catch."
"What's that?"
"You're going to carry it for me."
"Of course I'll carry your baby! I'll take it to the park, on long walks, whatever you want."
"No mom. I mean you're going to carry it during the pregnancy. I want you to be my pregnancy surrogate."
"Let me put your father on the phone."

Sarah was jolted back to reality by Matt's voice.

"Hey, wait a minute," Matt said quickly. "Do I have to have sex with this other woman?"

"Hon, the baby would be all yours and all mine. Just like with regular IVF, your sperm would be mixed together with my eggs. But instead of putting the embryos back in me, Dr. Svengaard would transfer them into another woman. You wouldn't have to have sex with anyone."

"That's a relief."

"Not even with me." Sarah added under her breath.

"Do you think your sister-in-law might do it?" Matt asked.

"No. She's got her own family. My mom's too old, and there's really no other family members who could do it." She turned to Dr. Svengaard. "I guess we could consider paying a stranger."

"How much does all this cost, doc?" Matt asked.

"The going rate for a surrogate is about $20,000 plus all medical and other expenses. That would be in addition to the usual IVF charge. Of course, the surrogacy fee is payable up front in cash and is completely non-refundable. Even if the surrogate miscarries after a week she gets to keep the money."

"Wow!" said Matt and Sarah almost simultaneously.

"Oh yes, I forgot to mention there's a $5,000 administration fee, payable in cash to our clinic. This fee covers our costs of administering the surrogacy program. So what do you think?" Dr. Svengaard asked impatiently. "We have several outstanding surrogates on retainer here at the clinic. They're all in excellent health and have superb references."

Sarah wondered what sort of references a surrogate would have. Would they comment on the health of the surrogate's uterus? How she looked in maternity clothes?

"This is a big decision, doctor. Matt and I will have to think about it," she said. "How about you explain the other two options."

"All right. Donor sperm or donor eggs. You carry a baby that's produced from your eggs and someone else's sperm, or a baby created by Matt's sperm and someone else's eggs. Using donor eggs is becoming more and more popular, but good eggs are hard to find. Women who donate eggs go through the same hormone injection regimen you've been doing so that they will produce multiple eggs in one cycle. After we harvest the eggs from the donor, we use standard IVF procedures and transfer the embryos into you. Very routine, very safe."

Sarah winced at the word "harvest." It made it sound like Dr. Svengaard was bringing in the fall wheat crop instead of performing a delicate medical procedure.

"The price for one set of four or five eggs from a single donor is currently about $6,000. We have quite a long roster of egg donors, or you can find one yourself. Some people use relatives, but many prefer to pay strangers. If you find your own donor, it will cost you $2,000 to have her eggs retrieved here at New Beginnings. We want the eggs to be as fresh as possible, so we require that the harvesting be done here."

"Okay, and what about donor sperm?" Sarah asked.

"Given Mr. Wong's sperm problems, that's probably our best option. We have our own sperm bank here at New Beginnings. The cost of the sperm is negligible, only about $1,500, and then the usual IVF fees apply. Of course, there are dozens of sperm banks across the country, and you can use one of those if you prefer. Although fresh is always better, frozen sperm work quite well. If you use sperm from another sperm bank, a nominal transfer fee of $1,000 would apply."

Matt jumped in. "Absolutely not. I'm NOT going to allow some other fella's little guys to swim inside of my wife. End of discussion."

"Hon, there wouldn't be any sperm swimming in me — not yours, not anybody else's. Dr. Svengaard is talking about using sperm in an IVF procedure. Fertilization would occur in the lab, and then he would transfer the embryos into me."

"I don't care where fertilization occurs — it's not an option."

"You didn't seem to have any problem with using someone else's eggs. What's the big deal with using someone else's sperm?"

"Well ... it just wouldn't be my baby. Plus, my sperm are just fine!"

"Then why can't we get pregnant?" Sarah knew she had gone too far as soon as she said it.

Dr. Svengaard closed his folder. "Why don't you two go home and talk about this and let me know what you decide. Tell Allison you need to see me again in about a week."

Sarah jumped up and rushed out of Dr. Svengaard's office. She just wanted to head home without making an appointment, but she forced herself to stop at the front desk. Matt kept his distance, seemingly disinterested.

Allison laughed. "He tells everybody to come back in a week. Let me see what I have." She scanned the appointment calendar on her screen. "You like late afternoon appointments, right? My next late afternoon slot for Dr. Svengaard is on October 14 at four forty-five."

"But that's three months away," Sarah exclaimed. "Dr. Svengaard said he would see us in about a week."

"That's really all I have in the late afternoon. Would you like me to check for something earlier in the day?"

"Okay," replied Sarah with a sigh.

After two minutes, Allison looked up. "The best I can do is Friday, August 15 at two in the afternoon. That's five weeks from now."

"We'll take it," replied Sarah immediately, without checking with Matt.

While Allison wrote out two appointments cards, Sarah entered the appointment in her phone. She saw that she had a deposition that afternoon, but she could move that.

On the way home Matt and Sarah hadn't say a word. She was still mad at him. She couldn't believe how close-minded he was being about this, and wondered if he was just scared of all the new technology or if he was really that chauvinistic.

The weeks after that mid-July appointment had been a very painful time for Matt and Sarah. She really wanted to talk about all the options Dr. Svengaard had given them, but he avoided the topic at all costs. He started staying at work later and later, claiming he had to work longer hours because of his new responsibilities as the project manager at the Pointe Verde Office Complex, but Sarah knew better. Construction work started early and ended early, especially in the middle of summer, and she knew Matt was just avoiding her.

One morning before work in early August, Sarah had googled surrogacy and surrogate mothers, and what she found frightened her. Some surrogate relationships ended in heart-wrenching litigation between the biological parents and the surrogate mothers. After carrying the baby for nine months, some surrogate moms decided they wanted to keep the baby, even though they had no legal right to do so. Although the baby was almost always returned to the biological mom and dad, the litigation was often lengthy and highly contentious.

One way to avoid such heartbreak was to use a trusted relative as a surrogate, but Matt and Sarah had already eliminated every female relative who might possibly agree to serve in that capacity. The other two possibilities, donor eggs and donor sperm, didn't sit well with them either. They both wanted to have children who were completely biologically theirs. Otherwise, why not just adopt? Although they hadn't agreed on much during that tense five-week period between fertility appointments, they did agree that they wanted to have a child that was completely biologically their own.

Despite her reservations about donor sperm and eggs, Sarah perused several sperm bank websites. She really did want Matt to be the father of her baby, but she was more than a little curious about what else was out there, even if she did feel a tad guilty about browsing through online sperm-daddy catalogs.

Some sperm banks provided only sparse information about each donor, while others had full biographies, including pictures. A few websites even included a baby picture of the donor so prospective clients could see what the donor's baby might look like. There were many intriguing candidates, but one donor seemed especially attractive. Donor 148 from the Fort Worth Sperm Bank was thirty-five years old, six foot three, one hundred and ninety-five pounds, Chinese with medium brown hair and brown eyes, an Ivy League graduate and a Varsity baseball player. There was no picture, but she didn't need one. She was attracted to him because he was a smarter, more educated version of Matt.

She toyed with the idea of using Donor 148 behind Matt's back. Maybe she could arrange with New Beginnings to use Donor 148's sperm instead of Matt's during an IVF procedure. Matt would bring in his sample as usual, and he'd never have to know that the lab used Donor 148's sperm instead of his. Would Dr. Svengaard go along with the ruse? Probably not, but she had wanted to find out, just to satisfy her curiosity.

At the beginning of the second week of August, Sarah had gone to New Beginnings for some routine blood work to get ready for their upcoming appointment on August 15. Matt never went to those sorts of visits, so Sarah was alone with Grace, one of the older nurses whom Sarah trusted. On the spur of the moment, she jokingly asked if the clinic would be willing to use donor sperm without the husband knowing about it. Without hesitation Grace calmly replied that it depended. Sarah dropped the conversation immediately and never broached the subject again, but she wondered what exactly would it depend on? How much they liked her? Whether she would be willing to pay an extra "fee"?

On the way home, a more palatable alternative occurred to her. Why not use a donor she already knew? That's what happened in the *Big Chill*, one of her favorite movies, although in the *Big Chill* the sperm was "donated" the old-fashioned way in the cottage bedroom. What about Matt's brother, or one of her old boyfriends from college?

A few days before their August appointment at New Beginnings, Sarah had finally gathered the nerve to ask Matt about using his brother as a sperm donor. After all, she explained, if they used his brother the baby would be about seventy-five percent theirs. Not quite one hundred percent, but better than fifty percent if they were to use an anonymous donor.

Matt's reaction was no surprise to Sarah. No. Not ever. Not even with his own brother as the donor. It was just as well she had not mentioned old boyfriends. If Sarah couldn't have Matt's baby, she wouldn't have anyone's baby. They would keep trying with their own sperm and eggs.

* * *

While waiting to be called back to see Dr. Svengaard, Sarah scanned the calendar on her phone. She could hardly believe it was already August 15.

"Peter and Jacklyn, we're ready for you now."

Sarah looked up. The couple across the room got up slowly and headed into the inner sanctum of the clinic. They were both young, probably no more than eighteen or nineteen. The girl was skinny, with a slight slouch in her shoulders. Her face was covered with acne, and her long, straight, brown hair hung down over her face as she walked. She wore small, tight black shorts with a teal crop top that ended just above her navel. As she walked, she clung tightly with both hands to the arm of her male companion.

This young couple definitely didn't fit in at New Beginnings. In contrast to the thirty-something, forty-something, and even fifty-something men and women Sarah usually saw in the waiting room, these two seemed much too young. How could they possibly be having fertility problems at their age? Even if they were having trouble getting pregnant, why had they turned to fertility treatments? They had plenty of time to give it a go the old-fashioned way. And what about the expense? Sarah and Matt had already spent over $30,000, money that was supposed to be a down payment on a house with a yard and a driveway, and they had nothing to show for it. How could these two kids afford to spend so much money on fertility treatments?

Sarah knew she would never learn the answers to her questions because fertility patients *never* talked to other patients. It was an unwritten code that the denizens of fertility clinic waiting rooms avoided any and all personal contact with each other — there was rarely even any eye contact, much less conversation.

The waiting room at New Beginnings Fertility Clinic was surprisingly Spartan. There were six sofas — two along each of the long sides of the room, and two facing each other in the middle. In addition to a few floor lamps, there was one pitiful potted plant in the far corner, near the receptionist's window. The magazines scattered on the three rectangular tables had been carefully chosen. No baby magazines, no parenting periodicals, nothing about family or home to remind patients why they were there. There were some travel and sports magazines, *Fortune*, *People,* and *Time,* and a year-old edition of *SkyMall.*

After the teenage kids went into the clinic there was only one other couple left, sitting on the far side of the waiting room. They were roughly the same age as Matt and Sarah, maybe five years older, and they barely talked to each other. They simply flipped through magazines as they waited their turn. As Sarah gazed at them, she felt like she was looking in a mirror. Is that how she and Matt appeared to others?

She flipped through *SkyMall* while Matt read *People,* although "reading" wasn't quite accurate. He was gawking at an article called "The 25 Sexiest Female Celebrities." As best as Sarah could determine, it wasn't really an article at all — merely a collection of bikini pictures of impossibly thin models and actresses. Sarah was proud of the way she looked, but she could never attain the airbrushed perfection of those magazine beauties.

She had turned thirty-one over the summer—one year older than thirty, as her mother kept reminding her. Her bi-weekly visits to the gym and her neighborhood runs with Matt kept her in good shape—her legs and arms were well-toned—and she worked diligently at improving her posture so that, at five foot two, she looked as tall as possible when she appeared in court. She never had a problem staying thin. In fact, she could still fit into her wedding dress, something she verified a few weekends before when Matt had been out of town at a homebuilders' convention. Her hair was described by some as strawberry blonde and by others as dirty blonde (a term she hated), but in truth it was just plain blonde. It had just enough natural curl to make it easy to style, but not so much that it frizzed up on one of Santa Felicia's rare humid days.

Her personality matched her fit, youthful appearance. People thought of her as smiling, upbeat, and friendly— except when she was in court, where she transformed into a tiger, so much so that Matt had started calling her Tiger right after they got married. She was an optimist by nature and was usually able to see the bright side of almost any situation. No matter how hard she tried, though, she couldn't see the bright side of their fertility struggle.

The treatments were expensive, embarrassing, painful, and time-consuming. Sarah and Matt fought all the time about it, and the hormone injections didn't help matters. They were constantly pressured by their families about having babies—subtle hints from Matt's parents and not-so-subtle jabs from Sarah's—which led to even more stress. Where was the silver lining in all of this?

Matt tolerated the fertility treatments with more equanimity than Sarah. Of course, what did he really have to do? Give a sperm sample every couple of months and go to the clinic appointments. That was about it. As she reflected on all the sacrifices she had made—personal, professional, physical, and emotional—she could feel her anger toward him boiling up. But what had he done wrong? It wasn't his fault she had to do most of the work.

She glanced over at Matt. He was just as cute as when she married him five years ago, and he had grown even sexier over the years. His deep-brown eyes weren't quite smoldering, but they were close. His chocolate-brown hair was usually messy, and no matter how closely he shaved each morning, by the afternoon a dark shadow would reappear on his angular face. He was a full foot taller than Sarah, and she had to stand up on tiptoes when they kissed. As a construction foreman, Matt was outside almost every day, and he maintained a moderately dark tan all year round that complemented his brown eyes. As if all of that weren't enough, he had a small sexy scar right in the middle of his chin. They were indeed an attractive couple; at least, that's what everyone told them.

As Sarah watched Matt pore over *People* magazine, scanning every actress-adorned page as carefully as a set of construction blueprints, it occurred to her (a psych major in college) that they were engaging in what developmental psychologists would call "parallel play," which is how toddlers play with each other — building their own separate Lego towers, rather than working together on a single structure. Whether solving Sudoku puzzles at the beach or reading magazines at New Beginnings Fertility Clinic, Sarah and Matt's play was almost exclusively parallel. Of course, that hadn't been the case when they first got married.

She wondered when their cooperative play had morphed into parallel play. Had it happened suddenly or gradually over several years? A rush of sadness washed over her as she pondered their lack of emotional closeness. She reached over to hold Matt's hand and noticed that they were sitting on two different sofas, an armrest between them. There was plenty of seating in the office, all arranged so that couples could sit together as they waited to be called, but they were not even on the same sofa.

Sarah decided right then to do her best to rekindle some of the magic with Matt. She got up and sat down next to him, so close that she was pressed up against him. It probably looked strange to the other couples in the waiting room, but that didn't matter to her.

"Anything interesting happen at work today, hon?" she asked.

"Not really. We're still pouring slabs for the Pointe Verde Office Complex. Ralph fell into one of the freshly poured slabs, and he was mad as hell. Not mad that he fell in—mad that we all laughed at him. Even Gary laughed, and Gary never laughs at anything."

"Interesting," replied Sarah, who thought it was anything but. So while she had been interviewing a new client on a death penalty case, Matt and his pals were making fun of a guy who fell in some wet concrete. She had to fight off the temptation to say something condescending.

"Want to hear about my day?"

"Sure," replied Matt, looking up from his magazine. "You told me this morning you've got a new case?"

"Yeah, her name is Lexi Conway."

"What'd she do?" Matt smiled. "I mean, what is she *accused* of doing?"

"She's charged with killing her baby."

"The one on the news a couple of days ago?"

"That's the one."

"When we saw her on TV, didn't you tell me you'd never take a case like hers?"

"Yep, but it looks like I was wrong."

"How could you represent *her*? With everything we've been through?" Matt's voice rose with each question. The other couples in the waiting room looked at them. "I can't believe you took her case!"

So much for an intimate, caring conversation, thought Sarah.

27

"Hon, I'm not happy about it either, but it's my job."

"I know," said Matt. "It's your job to defend the Constitution, blah, blah, blah. I've heard it all before. But couldn't you have chosen another case ... something less ... something less horrible?"

"You know how it works. I don't choose the cases — they sort of choose me. When the court clerk asked me to take the case, she didn't tell me exactly what it was. She just said it was a homicide. I said yes, and when I found out the details it was too late to change my mind."

She would have preferred any other case too, but she couldn't let him see that now. Just as it appeared their discussion might escalate into something more contentious, her phone rang.

Despite the ubiquitous signs asking patients to turn off their cell phones while at New Beginnings, Sarah always left hers on so she wouldn't miss any calls from the office. She pulled out her phone and saw it was Nick.

"Hon, I've got to take this. It's the office."

"Sure, whatever." Matt turned back to the bikini-clad celebrities in his *People* magazine.

Sarah stepped quickly out into the hallway. "Hey, Nick."

"The jail just called. Lexi Conway tried to commit suicide right after you left."

"What? But how? When I saw her she was handcuffed and shackled."

"They told me she tried to hang herself with a ripped bed sheet."

"Is she okay?"

"Seems to be. They've sedated her and put her in four-point restraints in the jail hospital."

"I'm going to go see her right away."

"You can't. They said no visitors for at least twenty-four hours. Not even her family."

Sarah turned her phone off, went back into the waiting

room and sat down beside Matt. She reached out and held his hand. She couldn't stop thinking about Lexi.

"Mrs. Wong? ... Mrs. Wong"

Suddenly Sarah realized the nurse was calling her name and looked up.

"Mrs. Wong, we're ready for you and your husband."

Sarah and Matt were only at the clinic for a consultation, so they were escorted directly to Dr. Svengaard's office. There would be no procedures—no stirrups, no ultrasounds, no needles. For this, Sarah was grateful. She was tired of all the prodding and poking.

They had been in Dr. Svengaard's office several times before, but Sarah was still astounded by its opulence in contrast to the simple, almost stark, waiting area. It was lavishly decorated, and dominated by an oversized burnished cherry desk as big as a conference table. There were three leather chairs, one much larger than the others. Dr. Svengaard's chair faced the two smaller chairs across a small round glass table, which held a pitcher of water with lemon slices floating on top and a ceramic pot of freshly brewed tea. On a long narrow table along the far wall were two sculptures—a bronze eagle in flight and a porcelain rendition of the Madonna with baby Jesus.

Before choosing a fertility doctor, Sarah had done her homework. From a variety of websites, she learned that other patients praised Dr. Svengaard's extraordinary record of success but didn't seem to particularly like him. One comment: "Cold but efficient." Another was even more to the point: "Dr. Svengaard is condescending, abrupt, and arrogant. But we got pregnant!"

She had also discovered that three complaints had been filed against Dr. Svengaard with the California medical licensing board. All three made similar allegations—that he had been too aggressive in his treatments and that he was unwilling to listen to his patients. The most serious complaint alleged that he proceeded with a ZIFT procedure on a young couple without obtaining their consent. None of the allegations resulted in public sanctions against Dr. Svengaard, but the most serious one elicited a private letter of reprimand that was placed in his state licensing file.

Sarah had pulled every lawyering trick she knew to try to obtain a copy of that letter, even calling in favors from colleagues in the medical malpractice field, but she found the cloak of privacy that shielded doctors' licensing files truly impenetrable.

While they waited in Dr. Svengaard's office, Sarah got up and walked around looking at the many diplomas, awards, and pictures. Much as a hunter might display mounted heads of moose, bear, or elk, two walls in Dr. Svengaard's office were covered with his own professional trophies — countless photographs, awards, and plaques, all exhibited in ornate cherry frames that matched his showpiece desk. One wall was consumed entirely by pictures of Dr. Svengaard accepting an award or posing with scientific dignitaries. There was no question he thought highly of himself, but maybe he was entitled to such self-indulgence. As an internationally renowned expert, he had pioneered many advances in fertility treatments. Eventually she found his med school diploma as well as two diplomas from graduate schools — a PhD in genetics from UCLA and some sort of graduate degree in genetic engineering from Stockholm University.

Suddenly Dr. Svengaard burst through the door, breathing heavily. "Mr. and Mrs. Wong, how nice to see you again."

"Nice to see you," Sarah replied stiffly. Everything about their meetings with Dr. Svengaard was so formal — the office, the language, even the refreshments.

"What have you decided — surrogacy, donor eggs, or donor sperm?"

For the first time in all their visits to New Beginnings, Matt spoke first. "None of those are for us, doc. We want our own baby."

"I see. Well, that puts us back where we were five weeks ago."

"Isn't there anything else we can try?" Matt asked. Sarah was enjoying watching him take the lead for once.

"There's really only one weapon left in our arsenal," said Dr. Svengaard. "We can try intracytoplasmic sperm injection."

"Intra what?" asked Matt.

"Intracytoplasmic sperm injection," repeated Dr. Svengaard. "ICSI."

"I've read about ICSI," said Sarah. "Isn't that where you inject sperm with a hormone to make them swim faster?"

"Not quite," replied Dr. Svengaard. "Basically I take one of Mr. Wong's sperm and inject it directly into one of your eggs. The technical details are probably a little too complex for you, so I'll just leave it at that."

Sarah was not about to let that statement go unchallenged. "We understand more than you think. Go on."

Somewhat reluctantly, Dr. Svengaard went into considerable detail about ICSI, even pulling out some pictures showing the moment of conception as a single sperm was flushed out of the microscopic needle to fuse with the waiting egg.

Sarah understood most of his explanation, but one thing puzzled her. "Why would this procedure work any better than the ones we've already tried?"

"Two reasons. First, fertilization is virtually guaranteed with ICSI. We don't need to worry about whether Mr. Wong's sperm can swim or not, because I inject his sperm right into your egg. Second, with ICSI, I can preselect which sperm and which eggs are to be united. I choose the very best of both, which greatly enhances the likelihood of a healthy embryo. Given Mr. Wong's motility problems, this is a very good option for us."

Sarah turned to Matt. "What do you think, hon?"

"I guess it sounds okay. Are there any risks, doc?" Matt asked.

"No more than in any of the other procedures you've done. Usually we perform ICSI on four or five eggs. Then we transfer the best looking two or three embryos. Do you have any other questions?"

"I think I'm good," said Sarah. "How about you, hon?"

"I'm willing to give it a go."

"Then it's all set," said Dr. Svengaard. "The general procedure is the same as before. At the beginning of your cycle, we commence the twelve-day injection protocol. Then I harvest your eggs and inject each of them with one of your husband's sperm. Then we wait three to five days, and I'll transfer two or three embryos into your uterus. I'm sure Allison can fit you in in a couple of months, so you can work with her on the scheduling on your way out."

For the first time in a long while, Sarah felt optimistic about their chances. "Thank you, Dr. Svengaard. I've got a good feeling about this."

Sarah grabbed Matt's hand as they got up to leave.

"Of course, we still have one remaining problem," Dr. Svengaard said when they were halfway to the door

"What's that?" Sarah turned toward Dr. Svengaard.

"You haven't been able to sustain a pregnancy, Mrs. Wong. Implantation has never been successfully completed."

Hearing once again that it was her fault, Sarah squeezed Matt's hand so hard he let out a yelp.

Dr. Svengaard continued. "However, there might be something we can do about that."

"Such as?" replied Sarah sharply.

"I've been experimenting with a technique to fix embryos so that they are more likely to implant in women like you, Mrs. Wong."

"What do you mean, *women like me*?"

"I'm sorry, I didn't mean to offend you. Why don't you

and Mr. Wong have a seat so we can talk about this? Would you like a cookie or a scone?" the doctor inquired politely. "Or how about some tea or sparkling water?"

Sarah couldn't remember him ever being so civil. She wondered where he was going with this.

"Here at New Beginnings we've been working on ways to enhance our fertility treatments. Like you, many women have implantation difficulties. Most fertility experts believe that implantation problems are due to a defect in the woman's uterus or hormone production. The theory is that some women's bodies reject embryos in the same way that transplant patients reject new organs. However, my research has demonstrated that implantation difficulties sometimes occur due to a problem with the embryo itself. It seems that some embryos are less amenable to implantation than others."

"Does that mean our embryos are genetically defective?" Sarah asked.

"I wouldn't say that," replied Dr. Svengaard, leaning forward in his chair. "Your embryos are probably perfectly healthy, except for one very minor genetic problem. My studies have shown that there is a gene linked to implantation success. Embryos that have a defect in this gene, which I've named the BS1 mutation, are less likely to implant than embryos without the defect. I've taken the liberty of testing one of your embryos from your last IVF procedure and it does indeed have the BS1 mutation. I'm virtually certain that's why you've been having implantation difficulties."

"You did WHAT?" yelled Sarah. "I never gave you permission to do that!"

"Actually you did," replied Dr. Svengaard calmly. "When you signed the consent form the first time you came to New Beginnings, you gave us permission to check your blood, tissue, eggs, and embryos for a variety of genetic markers."

"Let's go, Matt!" Sarah leaped out of her chair, knocking it backward. She turned and glared at Dr. Svengaard. "You are rude, obnoxious, condescending, and just plain unethical!"

"I'm sorry you feel that way, Mrs. Wong," Dr. Svengaard said with an even tone. "But I do have some very good news."

"What's that? You've given my eggs to some woman in Brazil and she's just had triplets?"

Dr. Svengaard ignored Sarah's sarcasm. "The good news is that I can fix this genetic defect, and you can have a baby."

Snorting with anger, Sarah stared at him.

"If you will sit back down, I can explain this," he said.

"I'll stand, thank you." Sarah's voice was still full of fury.

Matt had started to sit down, but now he wasn't sure what to do. He stood in a half crouch while Dr. Svengaard began his explanation.

"I first identified this genetic defect about five years ago, and I've been working on fixing it ever since. First, I created an analog of the mutation in mice, then in chickens. Next—"

"I don't care about any damn chickens. Get to the point," Sarah snapped.

Matt sat down.

"I'm sorry. Here's my point. I've developed a technique that can fix the BS1 mutation so the embryo will implant. My success rate with this exciting procedure is eighty percent."

"How do you do this?" Sarah's curiosity was slowly overcoming her anger.

"I insert a fully functioning gene in place of the defective BS1 mutation in the embryo. I've experimented with several ways to do this, and I've finally identified the technique that works best. I use a viral vector as the delivery mechanism. It carries the normal version of the gene and inserts it in place of the BS1 mutation."

"Wait a minute—are you talking about genetic engineering?" Sarah asked.

Dr. Svengaard beamed. "Why, yes I am. I'm the first scientist in the world to perform this type of genetic engineering on humans."

"You want to genetically engineer my baby?" Sarah sat back down.

"Why? Does that interest you?"

"Well, I don't know." As she spoke, she couldn't believe she wasn't walking out the door. There was nothing wrong with asking a few more questions, was there?

"Is it safe?"

"Yes, absolutely."

"What I mean is, is it safe for the baby?"

"This procedure has resulted in almost two dozen live births in the past three years."

"How many times have you done this procedure? On humans, I mean."

"I can't give you an exact figure, but it's almost thirty."

"So the success rate is eighty percent?"

"About that, yes."

Sarah tried to do the math in her head to figure out how many had failed, but everything was coming at her too fast.

"I don't know about this. I'd like to talk to some of the couples who've done this to see what they think," she said.

"I can't give you any names. All of the couples signed confidentiality agreements. I'm sure you understand."

"I guess."

"So, what do you think?" Dr. Svengaard was looking directly at Sarah with just a hint of a smile.

She looked down to avoid his gaze. "I just don't know. Genetic engineering seems so scary, and I don't know anything about it." She turned to Matt. "Hon, what do you think?"

"I don't know. I really don't know."

Sarah looked back at Dr. Svengaard. "We're definitely going to need some time to think about this."

"I understand. Would you like to hear a little more about what else I can do?"

"What do you mean, *what else*?" She was definitely more than a little curious now.

"I've been working on other types of genetic engineering. I'm starting to learn how to make better babies."

Sarah suddenly felt a little lightheaded. What on earth was Dr. Svengaard talking about? It took a few moments, but she finally gathered herself and was getting ready to ask another question when Matt spoke up first.

"That's enough, doc. We're not interested in that kind of stuff at all. In fact, we don't need any more time to make a decision. We're not interested in any of this. It's time for us to go."

Sarah tugged at Matt's arm as he stood up. "Hon, don't you want to hear about better babies?"

"No."

"Just for a few minutes? Then we can go."

"Oh, all right." Matt slumped down in his chair. "Five minutes, then we're leaving."

Given this tiny opening, Dr. Svengaard dove right in. With great excitement, he explained his groundbreaking work on genetic engineering. He gave them a quick overview of his work with animals and then explained positive and negative genetic engineering. A full fifteen minutes passed before Sarah interrupted with her first question.

"Let me make sure I've got this right. In negative genetic engineering, you try to cure or prevent a disease or undesirable condition, and in positive engineering you attempt to enhance the individual in some way."

"That's basically it."

"Are these engineering techniques essentially the same?"

"Not in all cases."

"Can you explain?"

"Sure. In many cases, what we call negative genetic engineering isn't really engineering at all. It's simply a form of genetic selection. We test early-stage embryos for the presence of certain alleles and choose those with the alleles we want."

"Alleles?" interrupted Sarah.

"Allele is the term for a variation of a gene. Instead of saying someone has a gene for brown eyes, it's actually more accurate to say that they have the allele for brown eyes."

"I see."

Dr. Svengaard continued. "Genetic selection is nothing new. We've been doing it for decades. It's called pre-implantation genetic screening or pre-implantation genetic diagnosis — PGS or PGD for short."

"So that's what you would do to solve our implantation problem? Just select the embryos that don't have the BS1 mutation, right?"

"If there are any embryos that don't have the BS1 mutation, that's all I would have to do. If they all have the BS1 mutation, then I would have to use genetic engineering to insert the normal version of the gene."

Sarah would have to read up on genetics before she could possibly agree to any genetic engineering on her own embryos, but she had a few more questions.

"Can we go yet?" Matt butted in.

"Just a few more minutes," pleaded Sarah. "I want to hear a little more about this." She turned back to the doctor. "Can you give us a quick rundown on what sorts of things you can do with your genetic engineering?"

"Sure. I can do quite a bit. Let's start with negative genetic engineering. I can identify many genes in embryos that cause diseases such as cystic fibrosis, Huntington's disease, and even conditions like male pattern baldness. Once I figure out which embryos have these genes, I can just get rid of them. It's really quite simple. And if all of a couple's embryos have the undesirable genetic marker, I can use a viral vector to insert the normal allele."

"Have you done this sort of negative genetic engineering for other patients here at New Beginnings?"

"Yes."

"What about positive genetic engineering? Can you give me some examples?"

"This is where it gets really exciting!" said Dr. Svengaard, becoming even more animated. "I'm doing things no one else in the world is doing."

"Like what?"

"Without getting too technical, some traits are easier to engineer than others. As we've known for quite a while, some traits such as eye color are controlled by just a few genes, while others, such as the ability to read a map, are likely affected by dozens or even hundreds of genes. The fewer the genes, the easier it is for me to engineer them. I've been working on perfecting the technique for engineering traits with five or fewer genetic components. I've successfully used positive genetic engineering to change the eye color and hair color of an embryo, increase its lung capacity and metabolism, and even enhance its cognitive abilities."

Sarah's eyes grew wider with each of Dr. Svengaard's claims. "I ... I don't understand. How can an embryo have eye color or lung capacity?"

"I'm sorry. I got a little ahead of myself. What I meant, of course, is that I have been able to change the genotype of the embryo, which will result in concomitant changes in the phenotype of the baby when it's born."

Sarah resisted the temptation to ask about genotypes and phenotypes, making a mental note to look them up later. Then the skeptic in her emerged. "I didn't know anyone was doing this sort of thing on humans. Can you give me some more details?"

"All right. I'll try to keep it simple."

Sarah edged up in her chair and prepared to take as many notes as she could.

"First I begin with the usual IVF protocol, using the same drugs as always to stimulate your ovaries. I retrieve all of your eggs, and I put two of them aside. I'll explain why in a moment. I inject the rest of your eggs with Matt's sperm, using the intracytoplasmic sperm injection technique I told you about a few minutes ago. Once the embryos have started dividing, I take one cell from each embryo and screen that cell for twenty-two genetic diseases and defects, including the BS1 mutation. If one of the embryos is completely clean, I use that one for the next stage. If there are no clean embryos, I use the one with the fewest genetic defects."

Dr. Svengaard was talking fast and Sarah was doing her best to keep up. She didn't like his use of the word "clean" to describe the embryos without genetic defects, as it implied that those with genetic defects such as Huntington's disease or cystic fibrosis were "dirty," but she kept that to herself.

"Next comes the exciting part," the doctor went on. "The actual genetic engineering. I take stem cells from the selected embryo and start growing them in a petri dish. Then I use a viral vector to deliver the new genes to the embryos. Basically, these viruses infect the stem cells and deliver their genetic payload, including the genes you've selected. These vectors have been prepared ahead of time, so they're ready for use whenever I need them."

"Infecting stem cells with viruses? That sounds dangerous." Sarah looked at Matt to see if he shared her concern, but he was staring at Dr. Svengaard's plaques and awards.

"The viruses I use are just variations of the adenovirus, the virus that causes the common cold. By itself, the adenovirus is not very effective for germ-line genetic engineering because the desired gene is just inserted, free-floating, into the cell nucleus, instead of in its proper place in the host cell's DNA. When the cell divides, the new gene doesn't appear in both the daughter cells. Are you with me so far?"

"I think so," replied Sarah. She looked down at her notepad and saw nothing but unintelligible scribbles. She put her pen down and decided to just listen the rest of the way.

"This brings us to my great breakthrough, my grand achievement! I have developed a technique to engineer the adenovirus itself so that it acts more like a parvovirus, or even a retrovirus, while still retaining the basic genetic profile of a typical adenovirus. I can use this hybrid adenovirus to insert the desired genes directly into the host cell's DNA at precisely the right spot! I've engineered three variations of these hybrid viruses, and all three of them are perfectly safe." Dr. Svengaard's voice rose with delight. "Nobody anywhere in the world has been able to do this except for me. Nobody!"

Sarah didn't know whether to applaud or run from the room screaming.

Sensing her fear, the doctor looked directly at her. "The bottom line is that my viral vectors are just variations of a simple adenovirus. The entire process is safe, very safe."

"If you say so," Sarah replied, unconvinced.

"The final step is quite simple really. Remember the two eggs I put aside at the beginning of the whole process?"

"Yes."

"Here's where they come back into play. I take the nuclei out of those two eggs and insert a genetically engineered nucleus into each one. This is quite similar to the last step in cloning. Then I transfer the two engineered

40

embryos into you, and I'm done."

"Do you always use two?"

"Not always. I used to transfer only one, but now I've started to transfer two to maximize the chances of success. From beginning to end, the entire process takes about five days—sometimes a little more, sometimes a little less. During that time I'm in the lab about sixteen hours a day. It's a very intense time for me."

Who cares how intense it is for you, thought Sarah. What about me!

"This is a lot of information for us to digest in one sitting, Dr. Svengaard. Where can we read up on all of this?"

"There are a lot of theoretical articles about how to do genetic engineering, some better than others, and there are many studies on animals such as mice, rats, and even monkeys. I can give you a list of excellent references, although most of them are quite technical."

"What about humans? Genetic engineering on humans."

"There are numerous articles of somatic cell engineering on humans, but none about germ-line."

"Why not?" Sarah began to get suspicious.

"As I said, I'm the only person in the world doing this."

Sarah took a deep breath, then another. She glanced at Matt, who had checked out of the conversation long ago and was staring out the window.

"Do you think you might be interested in any of this?" Dr. Svengaard looked directly at Sarah.

"I don't know. I ... *we* need a lot of time to think about everything. Before we leave, though, can you give us some specific examples of the kinds of genetic engineering that might work for us?"

"Sure." Reaching into the top drawer of his desk, the doctor retrieved a small silver key and walked over to a massive filing cabinet that took up much of the far wall. He unlocked the top drawer, pulled out two pieces of paper, and placed them carefully on the desk in front of Sarah and Matt.

The first page was labeled "Diseases and Conditions." On it was a list of diseases and undesirable conditions, twenty-two in all. The first entry was the BS1 mutation, which Dr. Svengaard had just explained. Most of the other entries — cystic fibrosis, Huntington's disease, Tay-Sachs, BRCA1, BRCA2, and male pattern baldness — were familiar to Sarah. A few others, such as Fragile X Syndrome and Klinefelter Syndrome, she had heard of but didn't know much about. And there were a couple she had never heard of.

Nowhere on the piece of paper was there a reference to genetic engineering or specific procedures — no explanations or descriptions. The only other words on the page, centered at the bottom in small print, were "Results Guaranteed."

Sarah looked up quizzically. "What exactly is this?"

"This is the list of diseases and conditions that I can prevent by using genetic selection or by genetically engineering an embryo."

"Wow! Hon, take a look at this." Sarah shoved the paper toward Matt.

"Pretty impressive, doc," he muttered.

"It's more than impressive — it's unbelievable!" Sarah said brightly.

Matt squinted at the bottom of the page. "What does it mean, 'Results Guaranteed'?"

"It means that I guarantee that these procedures will be one hundred percent successful," Dr. Svengaard replied. "Pretty exciting, isn't it? Now take a look at the other form."

The second form had the same format as the first, but the list was shorter — only fourteen items in all. The list was titled "Genetic Enhancements" and included many things that Dr. Svengaard had already mentioned, such as eye color, hair color, lung capacity, and cognitive processing speed, as well as some others, including slow-twitch and fast-twitch muscles.

Sarah stared at the list, mouth agape. *Surely Dr. Svengaard is playing some sort of practical joke on us. He can't possibly be doing this. This is the stuff of science fiction, not the work of a fertility doctor in Santa Felicia.*

"Honey?" was all she could say.

"What?"

"What do you think?"

"Hmmm. I don't know."

"What do you mean you don't know?"

"Doc, it doesn't say on *this* page that the results are guaranteed. How come?" Matt asked. "That's a good question, Mr. Wong. Although I've had very high success rates with these enhancement procedures, they don't work one hundred percent of the time. Nothing serious, but I just can't guarantee they will be successful every time."

For a few moments, Sarah was speechless, astonished by what she had just heard and read. But eventually she was able to put a coherent sentence together. "This is a lot to absorb, Dr. Svengaard. We're going to need some time to discuss this at home."

"I understand. But we are only offering this opportunity to a few specially selected couples, so we'll need your decision as soon as possible."

Sarah didn't like being pressured, especially about something as important as this. *What's the rush? We're not buying a washing machine; we're talking about genetically engineering our baby.*

She took the two sheets of paper from Dr. Svengaard's desk and was about to put them in her briefcase when, in one swift motion, he threw himself over his immense desk and snatched the papers out of her hand.

"I'm sorry. You have to leave these here," he said stiffly.

Sarah was baffled. "We just want to take them home so

we can talk about this. It's a big decision."

"I can't let you take these home," the doctor said firmly. "What we're doing here is highly confidential and cutting-edge, and I can't risk the possibility that one of my competitors might find out about it. These have to stay here."

He quickly put the two lists back in the filing cabinet and locked it.

"Let's go out front and schedule your next appointment," he said, gesturing toward his office door.

When he handed their file to Allison at reception, he told her to be sure that she accommodated their preferences for their next appointment. Sarah noticed the bright-red sticker the doctor had put at the top of their file.

"It was great talking to you today, Mr. and Mrs. Wong. See you soon," said the doctor, shaking their hands and heading back into his office.

As soon as Dr. Svengaard left, Allison spoke up. "I can fit you in next week on Wednesday, Thursday, or Friday."

"Whoa. We need more time than that," said Sarah. Usually it took months to get an appointment. This was definitely happening too fast.

"Okay. How about Tuesday or Thursday of the week after that?"

"I've got a lot on my plate at work right now. Can we go into September?"

Allison peered at her computer screen for a few moments. "Unfortunately, Dr. Svengaard won't be available until the end of September. How about Friday, September 26 at ten o'clock?"

"That sounds better," said Sarah. "Let me check my calendar. Okay, I'm clear all day on the twenty-sixth. Is that day good for you, hon?"

"Sure."

Matt gently took Sarah's hand as they went out to the hallway, but Sarah pulled away from him abruptly, plopped down on the sofa nearest the door, and started scribbling as fast as she could on a legal pad she had retrieved from her briefcase.

"What ya doin?" asked Matt.

"I'm writing down as many of the things on those lists as I can remember."

Within a minute she had written down thirteen of the twenty-two items on the "Diseases and Conditions" list and eight of the fourteen items on the "Genetic Enhancements" list. She wasn't sure they were all exactly right, but she was pleased with her effort.

She put her legal pad in her briefcase and stood up. "That's all I can think of now. Let's go home."

As they walked out the door of the waiting room, Matt took Sarah's hand again and looked into her eyes as he spoke. "So are we going to make a better baby?"

CHAPTER 3

After all the excitement on Friday, the weekend provided a welcome respite for Sarah. She and Matt went for their usual Saturday morning run and spent the rest of the weekend relaxing. It was just the three of them, Matt, Sarah, and Chloe, the mixed-breed cat they had adopted from a shelter a couple of years ago.

On Monday, Sarah got up at five o'clock and was out the door by five fifty. Her drive to work was only about fifteen minutes, just enough time to get ready for the day ahead. Three years ago, she had moved from her first tiny start-up office to the eighth floor of a new ten-story building at 17 West Regency Avenue in Santa Felicia. The top two floors were already taken by an insurance company, so the eighth floor was the highest she could go — for now. One day she planned to be in the penthouse.

She almost always arrived before the security guard, who didn't come on duty until seven. She rode the parking lot elevator up to the main lobby, an impressive two-story space with floor-to-ceiling windows on two sides. Inspired by the atrium of Trump Plaza in New York, the interior wall nearest the tower elevator bank featured a waterfall that extended three-quarters of the distance up to the ceiling.

No matter how early Sarah arrived, the waterfall was always in operation, cascading softly over ersatz boulders embedded in the lobby wall. As no one was usually in the lobby at such an early hour, she had developed the habit of leaning over the small catch basin at the bottom and running her hand under the falling sheet of water as she made her way to the tower elevators. It had become a sort of daily good-luck ritual. Even on days when she arrived after the lobby was open to the public, she still performed her customary water touching; she just did it more discreetly.

This particular morning, Sarah spent more time than usual letting the water run over her hand, feeling that she needed all the luck she could get on the Conway case. After exiting the elevator on the eighth floor, her sleeve wet from her morning ritual, she walked down the hall to Suite 805. Once inside, she turned on the lights and the copy machine, and threw her briefcase on the small chair in her office.

She had come a long way since she had clerked with the Santa Barbara DA's office between her second and third year in law school. That summer she had sat in on victim interviews, read police reports, and attended court hearings and trials. She even got to view an autopsy of a mutilated homicide victim, although she lasted only a few minutes before racing outside to throw up in the hallway. Sarah had watched several autopsy training videos to get ready for the real thing, but nothing had prepared her for the smell — a mixture of formaldehyde and death.

She had learned an important lesson that summer: many of the bad guys (and girls) were not really that bad at all. Quite a few were simply regular people who had made terrible choices or who needed some sort of help. They needed someone in their corner, and Sarah thought it would be rewarding to be that person.

Near the top of her class at UC Santa Barbara, Sarah had been pursued by many of the best law firms and corporations in the western half of the United States, but by mid-January of her third year in law school, she accepted an offer from the Santa Felicia County Public Defender's Office. As the eponymous seat of Santa Felicia County, Santa Felicia was one of the fastest growing cities in California. It had a thriving cultural life, a vibrant downtown, and a growing crime problem. The small-town ambience coupled with big-city crime made it a perfect place for her to cut her teeth as a trial lawyer.

In many ways, Sarah was an odd fit for the Public Defender's Office. She had never broken any sort of law herself, save the one time she had been caught drinking beer at the beach with her high-school boyfriend, and now she was representing people accused of all sorts of horrible crimes. She came from an upper-middle-class family, yet her work at the PD's office meant she had to deal with people from the other end of the economic spectrum. It was taxing work, emotionally draining, and only occasionally rewarding.

During her time with the PD's office, she acquired the well-deserved reputation as an exceptional cross-examiner. She had an uncommon ability to elicit information from adverse witnesses, especially crime victims, with her compassionate, yet persistent style. In fact she won some cases she probably shouldn't have. There were quite a few criminals — even one or two killers — who were out on the street because of Sarah's exceptional trial skills.

Sarah and Matt frequently discussed the ethics of representing criminals. She would talk about democracy, the Constitution, fairness, and the presumption of innocence, and he would counter with victims' rights and descriptions of some of the horrible crimes perpetrated by her clients. He could never fathom how she could sleep at night knowing that she was helping robbers, rapists, murderers, and child molesters. To be sure, some of her cases *did* cause her to lose sleep.

After two years at the Public Defender's Office Sarah decided to set out on her own. Her first office had been located in a strip mall in suburban Santa Felicia, about fifteen minutes from the downtown courthouse. Sandwiched between Dora's Nail Emporium and a Rite Aid, her three-room office suite comprised a small waiting area and two offices, each about the size of a child's bedroom.

Sarah thought her private practice would consist mostly of non-criminal cases. Yet criminal defense work was her first love, and she kept returning to it, despite her safe, comfortable law practice. She had only one employee then: Nick Fargo. Nick worked thirty hours a week as Sarah's receptionist, secretary, office manager, and legal assistant while completing his paralegal degree at night. He was incredibly bright, and after he finished his degree she was delighted that he wanted to work for her full-time.

Sarah had intended to work in Santa Felicia for about two or three more years and then move to a big city — maybe on her own or possibly with an established law firm. But the time passed quickly, and she continued to build her small practice in Santa Felicia. She liked being a middle-size fish in a middle-size pond, and Matt was doing well in his job at Harbinger Construction, one of the fastest growing construction companies in Santa Felicia.

Instead of moving to a different city, she decided to move to a bigger office with a more prestigious address, hoping it would help to attract new clients. Her new office at 17 West Regency Avenue, a three-room suite on the east side of the building fronted by a moderately sized waiting area, had been more than big enough when she and Nick had moved in three years ago. She occupied two of the rooms, one for meetings with clients, and the other where she kept all her files. Nick spent his time alternating between the waiting room and the third office in the back.

An unexpected benefit of the upscale location was that she received referrals from other tenants in the building, including the insurance company on the top two floors. A small trickle at first, these referrals gradually grew into a steady stream of new clients, enough to keep her young law firm afloat. Within six months of moving into 17 West Regency Avenue, she was able to add a part-time office assistant, Maggie Hodgkins.

Maggie was a loyal employee, but only competent at best. She was pleasant enough, but her organizational skills left a lot to be desired. Her scheduling sloppiness had caused Sarah to miss two court appearances and one filing deadline. Sarah had been able to rectify the mistakes and decided to keep Maggie on, since her positives outweighed her negatives.

Thirteen months ago, Sarah felt ready to add another attorney to her small firm. She sought someone who was good in business law (not her strength), a lawyer who was familiar with the tax code and securities law. Some of her small business clients had grown along with her, and they increasingly needed legal advice about complex business issues, matters that were beyond her expertise.

She preferred not to take on a brand new lawyer, as she didn't have the time or inclination to train a newbie, so she had put out feelers with her friends at large law firms in LA, San Francisco, and Santa Barbara. Although none of them were interested in leaving their big-city law firms and big-city salaries, she did get a couple of names of young associates who might be willing to move to a small firm.

One of those was Conrad Blair, who had graduated as a member of the Order of the Coif from UCLA Law School. He had been working for a large law firm in San Francisco for a little over a year, and two of Sarah's acquaintances at the firm told her he might be ripe for a change. Apparently he had engaged in a fleeting romance with one of his fellow associates that had ended badly (and publicly), and he wanted to get a fresh start in a new city. His expertise was in personal injury litigation, not tax and securities law as Sarah had hoped, but he assured her that he was a quick study. He seemed to get on well with Nick and Maggie, so Sarah had offered him the job.

Now that Sarah had three employees, her once spacious suite was much too small. She had her eye out for larger spaces in her building, but nothing had opened up. Although the three offices in Suite 805 were cramped and untidy, Sarah made a concerted effort to make the waiting area comfortable and inviting. Two matching leather couches with deep-brown buttery-soft cushions, a large embossed cherry table, soft recessed lighting, and several original watercolors of the Santa Felicia coastline greeted clients as they walked in the door. The couches faced the floor-to-ceiling windows that framed an impressive view of downtown Santa Felicia, about three miles due east.

The nicest desk in the whole suite belonged to Maggie, who was situated at one end of the waiting area, near the hallway that led to the three small offices. In Sarah's, Nick's, and Conrad's offices, out of sight from the waiting area, the furnishings were sparse—metal desks with laminate tops made to look like real wood, but which fooled nobody, and inexpensive swivel chairs with gray fabric cushions—with filing cabinets lining two walls in each of the three offices.

After Sarah made a pot of coffee and put out some lemon cookies on the credenza next to Maggie's desk, she went back to her office. She was just about to turn on her computer when the phone rang. Sarah was the only one in the office, so she answered the call herself.

"Sarah Wong, attorney-at-law. May I help you?"

"Are you Lexi Conway's lawyer?" whispered a barely audible male voice on the other end.

"Client information is confidential," replied Sarah. "May I ask who's calling?"

"Ryan Stoudt."

"Your name is familiar, but I can't place you. Do you know Lexi Conway?"

"I'm Lexi's boyfriend."

Sarah was a little embarrassed about not recognizing Ryan's name; she had seen it several times in the police reports. This was a tricky situation: Ryan could end up being a witness in the case, or he might even turn out to be a codefendant. She plowed ahead tentatively.

"How may I help you?"

"I want to bail Lexi out of jail. How much is her bail?"

"Lexi doesn't have any bail. She's facing a capital murder case."

"What does that mean?"

"That means that the state may seek the death penalty if she's convicted."

"What? But she didn't do anything wrong!"

"How do you know that, Ryan?" As soon as she spoke Sarah knew she had gone too far, especially over the phone. How did she know it was really Ryan Stoudt on the other end? What if it was a police investigator posing as Ryan hoping to get some inside information about Lexi's defense? Cops had stooped to such tactics before.

"I just know that Lexi didn't kill our baby," insisted the man. "She could never do such a thing. I just know it."

Sarah took a deep breath. "Why don't you come in to my office and we can talk about this some more." As an afterthought, she added, "Are you represented by your own attorney?"

"No. Why would I be?"

She was stumped. What should she say? If she told him that the police might consider him a suspect too, that *would* scare him into getting his own attorney and she would never be able to talk to him.

"It's just a question I ask everyone, Ryan. Can you come to my office this Friday at eleven?"

"Can we make it one or one thirty instead? The detectives are interviewing me again at eleven. They want me to take a lie-detector test, and I said sure. I ain't got nothin' to hide."

"All right, one o'clock on Friday it is. My office is at 17 West Regency Avenue. You can park in the lot around the corner on Spitz Street. Check in with the guard in the lobby and tell her you have an appointment with me. We're in Suite 805 on the eighth floor, and my receptionist Maggie will be here to greet you."

"Can you pay for my parking?"

"Sure," replied Sarah.

"How about lunch?"

"I don't think so."

"That's okay. Just thought I'd ask."

"See you on Friday."

Sarah left a note for Maggie to clear her calendar for Friday afternoon. In the meantime, she had to think carefully about what to ask Ryan. It might be her only chance to talk with him and she didn't want to forget anything.

Lexi's case would be all-consuming over the next few months, so she spent the rest of the morning and early afternoon tying up loose ends on other cases and leaving notes with things to do for Maggie, Nick, and Conrad.

About two o'clock, Sarah decided she could do with some fresh air and went to the deli across the street to get a coffee. As she was paying for her order, the cashier congratulated her on being famous. Sarah thought he must have her mixed up with someone else, but he pushed a copy of the *Santa Felicia Observer* in front of her and told her to look in Section 2. She paid for the paper along with her coffee and hurried out the door.

As she crossed the street to go back to her office, she opened the *Observer*. She found Section 2, and there was her picture right below the headline that spanned the entire width of the page: "Sarah Wong to Represent Accused Baby Killer." Although excited about the publicity, she was none too thrilled about having her name and the words

"Baby Killer" in the same headline. She stuffed the paper under her arm and hurried back to the office so she could read it carefully.

"Sarah Wong to Represent Accused Baby Killer." At least the headline was factually correct. She skimmed the article quickly. There was no picture of Lexi, which was good. After reading the article more carefully, she was satisfied that it wasn't too bad. About half of the article was about Sarah herself — her education, her background, even the name of her law firm — and the rest was about the crime. Nothing too vivid or sensational; just the basic facts as outlined in the police report.

She put Section 2 in a folder labeled "Change of Venue Motion." As she would be making a motion to move the case out of Santa Felicia County, she needed evidence that pretrial publicity had made it impossible for Lexi to get a fair trial in Santa Felicia.

She was about to call Matt to tell him about her new celebrity status when she noticed the message light on her phone was blinking. She punched in her security code and the robotic voice replied, "You have nineteen new messages." How could that be? Sarah wondered. Her voice mailbox had been empty when she came in, and she hadn't heard her phone ring all day except the one call from Lexi's boyfriend. Only then did she remember that after Ryan's call she had set her phone to route all incoming calls directly to her voicemail so she wouldn't be disturbed.

She listened to the first message: "Hi, this is Kevin from the *San Francisco Examiner*. I'd like to talk with you about the Lexi Conway case. Call me at 555-876-9271." She jotted down his number and listened to the second message. "Good morning, Mrs. Wong. My name is Brian Kilmer from NPR and I'd like to interview you about the Conway case. Please call me as soon as you have a chance."

Wow, NPR! How did they find out about Lexi's case?

She quickly listened to a couple more messages. They

were all the same — reporters wanting to talk with her about the Conway case. She jotted down the details. It was an impressive list: *Los Angeles Times*, *Denver Post*, *Tampa Tribune*, Channels 3, 7 and 9 in Santa Felicia, two TV stations in Santa Barbara, and radio stations in Detroit, Provo, and Seattle. Some of the reporters had called twice, and Kevin from the *San Francisco Examiner* had left three messages.

She couldn't possibly return all the calls right then, but decided to contact Kevin since he had called three times already. The phone rang a few times and Sarah was about to hang up when a gruff voice spoke.

"Kevin here."

"Hi, Kevin, this is Sarah Wong. You called me about a case I'm handling."

"Oh yeah, you're down in Santa Felicia, right?"

"That's me."

"You're representing the baby killer!"

"The *accused* baby killer," said Sarah. Even that didn't sound right. "Just say that I'm representing Lexi Conway in a homicide case."

"So how does it feel representing a baby killer, you being a woman and all?"

"*Accused* baby killer," she said sternly, disliking the sound of the phrase even more the second time. "What does my gender have to do with anything?"

"Women are supposed to have babies, not kill them."

As sexist as Kevin's statement was, Sarah silently agreed. Women weren't supposed to kill babies. They were supposed to nurture and love them. That's what *she* wanted to do. But she felt that the interview was going nowhere fast.

"Thanks for your interest, Kevin, but I've got to run. As you can imagine I've got a lot to do."

"But we just started."

"I'm sorry. I'll have my assistant call you and set up

another time to talk. I've really got to go."

When she hung up, she wondered if she'd received any email inquiries about the case. She checked her email. Thirty-one new email messages, twenty-seven of which were about Lexi's case. Some of the senders' addresses she recognized — *New York Times*, *Newsweek* — but some she didn't. The *Intelligencer*? Where the heck was that?

Then it hit her. Lexi's case was going to be a big deal — a really big deal. If she won, and maybe even if she didn't, she would be famous far beyond Santa Felicia. Would this be the case that would elevate her from the ranks of the very good to the ranks of the elite? She thought about calling Matt, but he could wait. Lexi's case could not.

She pulled out the autopsy report and took a glance at the accompanying photos. No matter how many times she saw autopsy pictures she never got used to them.

She had never represented anyone charged with killing a baby, so she was unprepared for the emotional impact of the photos. She usually didn't allow herself to feel sorry for the victims, as she was afraid such emotions would compromise her ability to advocate vigorously for her clients. But try as she might, she could not help but shed some tears as she looked at Anna Conway's autopsy photos.

She was immediately struck by how small Anna was. According to the autopsy report, Anna was nineteen and a half inches long and weighed eight pounds seven ounces when she died, no bigger than a medium-size teddy bear. She appeared peaceful as she lay on the large chrome table in the county morgue, looking a bit like a life-size doll.

The medical examiner had not found any signs of trauma on the tiny body — no signs of beating or strangulation or any gunshot or knife wounds. There were no marks or abrasions on Anna's neck or face, no bleeding anywhere.

Sarah read through the autopsy report from start to

finish, stopping to highlight important passages. The first thing that caught her eye was near the top of the first page:

| *Date of Death:* | August 11 |
| *Time of Death:* | Unknown A.M. |

She wondered why the medical examiner had not been able to pinpoint the time of death more exactly. All the indications were that Anna had been dead for less than an hour. Then she homed in on the bottom of the page:

| *Cause of Death*: | Acute Carbon Monoxide Poisoning |
| *Manner of Death:* | Homicide |

It bothered her that medical examiners included the manner of death in their autopsy reports as if it were an established fact. Although they were undoubtedly experts in the cause of death, Sarah felt that establishing the manner of death was a complex matter that usually depended on more than just an autopsy and toxicology analysis.

The world of forensic science had changed immeasurably since the arrival of CSI and its legion of spin-offs and imitators. In the fictional world of television, medical examiners solved complex crimes, some of them decades-old cold cases, by examining a single bone fragment or a strand of hair, all in a one-hour show. Jurors had started to demand Hollywood theatrics in real-life murder cases, and medical examiners were all too happy to oblige. Instead of being pushed into the background of criminal investigations, medical examiners now occupied the limelight, with some landing reality television shows and even developing cult-like followings. Dr. Vijay Prakeesh, Santa Felicia's chief medical examiner, was far from a Hollywood celebrity, but even he had adjusted to the changing times by including increasingly dramatic language and more speculative conclusions in his autopsy reports.

The first section of his report described Anna's exterior appearance, noting that there was no evidence of any external injury. He described Anna's skin as being a pinkish-red color, which, he explained later in the report, was characteristic of carbon monoxide poisoning. Sarah looked at the autopsy photos again. She was unable to discern the pink hue of Anna's skin, but she figured that was probably due to the harsh lighting in the morgue and the camera's bright flash, which washed out many of the finer details on the child's body.

Dr. Prakeesh reported that rigor mortis was moderate, noting that it had impacted the neck and jaw muscles but had not yet spread to the larger muscles in Anna's body. He observed some deep cherry-red livor mortis in Anna's legs and lower back that was unfixed, which was consistent with her position in the car seat at the time of death. Based on the moderate amount of rigor mortis and livor mortis present in Anna's body, Dr. Prakeesh tentatively estimated the time of death at some time between nine and eleven a.m. in the main part of his report, but he qualified that estimate in the final section, noting that the coloration caused by the carbon monoxide poisoning made the livor mortis evidence difficult to interpret. His time frame for Anna's death was earlier than Sarah's own calculations — somewhere between eleven and eleven forty-five — but she knew that time of death estimates were often inaccurate.

The next section of his report described Anna's musculoskeletal system. Several of Anna's ribs were bent and cracked, which Dr. Prakeesh said was consistent with injuries caused by the forceful CPR performed by the police officers at the scene. The absence of bruising around the damaged ribs indicated they had been broken postmortem. In addition, Dr. Prakeesh identified a barely detectable bruise on the left side of Anna's face. It appeared to be a very recent injury, and he estimated that it had occurred about an hour before Anna's death. There were no other broken bones or soft tissue damage.

All of Anna's internal organs, including her brain, liver, kidneys, heart, and lungs were weighed, examined, and described in the report. All were within normal limits of a healthy three-week-old infant, except for her lungs, which exhibited all the telltale signs of carbon monoxide poisoning.

The rest of Anna's anatomy, inside and out, was described as unremarkable. In fact, the word "unremarkable" appeared over a dozen times in the report. Sarah found herself thinking how very remarkable Anna Conway had been—a beautiful baby girl with a promising life that would never be lived—and she imagined her playing with her friends in kindergarten, shopping at the mall in middle school, and going to the senior prom with the cutest guy in high school.

"Afternoon', Sarah!" said a cheerful voice.

"Nick! How long have you been standing there?" Sarah asked.

"Just a few seconds. How was your weekend?"

"Fine, I guess."

"Are you okay?" he asked quickly when he saw her face.

"Yeah, I've just been working really hard on the Conway case," Sarah said gruffly, a little embarrassed that he had caught her crying. "It's going to be a tough one."

Nick knew not to push further. "Let me know if you want me to do anything," he said and walked down the hall to his office.

Sarah got up and shut her door. She returned to the autopsy report and circled the next entry:

> *Toxicology*: Samples of blood from the heart and left femoral vein were submitted for toxicology analyses. Results pending at this time.

Then she skipped to the "Conclusions and Opinions" section at the end of the report. Sarah had read more than a dozen autopsy reports prepared by Dr. Prakeesh, and they almost always had succinct, even terse, summary statements at the end. But not this one: the final section was two and a half pages long.

After an initial statement declaring that Anna Conway died of carbon monoxide poisoning, Dr. Prakeesh went into considerable detail explaining how carbon monoxide kills. He noted that carbon monoxide poisoning from car exhaust was much less common than it used to be since the advent of catalytic converters, which eliminate most of the carbon monoxide from exhaust fumes, but there were still occasional cases stemming from cars left running in small confined spaces like garages.

He explained that infants, even healthy ones, are more susceptible to carbon monoxide poisoning than adults because babies breathe more rapidly, have a faster metabolism, and possess less mature lungs than adults. This could explain why Anna died from the effects of the carbon monoxide while her mother survived, Dr. Prakeesh explained. At the very end, he stated that he would file the final version of the autopsy report once the toxicology results were available.

Sarah flipped back to the first page and stared at the two lines near the bottom of the page again.

Cause of Death: Acute Carbon Monoxide Poisoning
Manner of Death: Homicide

She spun her chair around and gazed out the window toward downtown Santa Felicia. It certainly looked like Anna had died of carbon monoxide poisoning, but years of experience told Sarah not to settle in on the cause of death too quickly. She needed to eliminate all other possibilities first. She mentally ticked off a checklist of the usual prospects.

Gunshot? Stabbing? Strangulation? Blunt force trauma?

There were no wounds, no physical injuries, no other signs of trauma on Anna's body, save the broken ribs apparently caused by the police officer's efforts to revive her.

Accidental fall? Suffocation? Drowning?

Maybe Lexi rolled over and smothered Anna in her sleep. Maybe Lexi dropped Anna on her head, or Anna drowned in the tub while Lexi talked on the phone. Any of these *could* have happened. And if Anna had died accidentally, Lexi might well have blamed herself, which could have caused her to try to commit suicide. There was one big problem. There was no evidence supporting any of these.

SIDS or other natural causes?

Two pieces of evidence ruled out SIDS as the cause of death. First, the autopsy report contained multiple symptoms of carbon monoxide poisoning that would not have been present had Anna already been dead when she was put in the car. Second, a witness, Madeline Truex, who lived three doors down the street from Lexi, told the detectives she was absolutely certain she had seen Anna Conway alive on the morning of August 11, snuggled in her little carrier.

It was time to get more details from Lexi.

Sarah decided to visit her first thing on Tuesday. She felt bad that she had not tried to visit her over the weekend, especially given her suicide attempt on Friday afternoon, but she would make amends with her in the morning.

CHAPTER 4

On Tuesday morning, Sarah went to the office extra early to prepare for her interview with Lexi. After filling five sheets of paper with notes and questions, she was ready. Before setting off, she called the jail and found out that Lexi had been moved to the Forrest A. Spencer Jail. Although the New Jail, as it was usually called, was further from her office, she preferred interviewing clients there because they had more privacy than at the Central Jail.

Until two years ago, all attorney–client conversations in Santa Felicia jails were monitored electronically by the Sheriff's Office "for security purposes," but that had changed as a result of *Wong v. Santa Felicia County Sheriff's Office*. That case was the pinnacle of Sarah's career so far, as she had fought for the right to privacy in jailhouse attorney–client conversations. The California Supreme Court ruled that the right to effective assistance of counsel, as guaranteed by the United States Constitution, provided that attorneys should be able to converse with their clients privately and that the right was not diminished just because a defendant was incarcerated. As a result, the Sheriff's Office was no longer allowed to monitor attorney–client communications in the jails, or in the holding cells in the courthouses.

Because attorney–client interviews at the New Jail were face to face, the attorney screening procedures were even more rigorous than at the Central Jail. After putting their personal belongings in a metal locker, attorneys first had to pass through a standard metal detector. Then they had to go through a second scanner, an Orbitron 6000, one of the new scatter x-ray scanners being used at most major airports.

The New Jail was only the third jail in the country to use a scatter x-ray scanner. Sarah had seen pictures of its scans in the newspaper and on the Web. They showed every curve, every nook and cranny of the person's body, and depicted a ghostly outline of the person's underwear as if those garments were completely transparent.

Remembering her necklace mishap at the Central Jail the previous Friday, Sarah made sure to leave all her jewelry at home this time. When she got dressed earlier that morning, she had chosen her underwear carefully, annoyed that her choice was being dictated by the x-ray scanner at the New Jail.

Later, as she stood with her hands above her head in the Orbitron 6000, she was certain she could feel a slight tingling on her skin.

"You're done, Mrs. Wong. You're all clear to go in."

Sarah took her place in Interview Room 1, a ten-by-ten glass-enclosed cubicle with a square table in the middle. On each side of the table was a sturdy metal chair. She placed her legal pad and pen on the table and waited for Lexi.

She hoped Lexi wouldn't be mad that she hadn't visited her for four days, but she was ready to apologize just in case. She wasn't sure what she should say about Lexi's suicide attempt, but she thought she should say *something*.

One thing that had not changed with the move to a different jail was the waiting time. Sarah still had to wait almost fifteen minutes before Lexi was ushered into the interview room. When she finally arrived, Sarah could see immediately that she was more relaxed than she had been the previous Friday. Although still shackled, the restraints seemed looser and she wasn't wearing handcuffs anymore.

Lexi sat down quietly and extended her hand to greet Sarah.

"No physical contact of any type, ladies. Jailhouse rules," the deputy barked before leaving to take up his position outside the door.

"Good morning, Lexi. How have they been treating you?" Sarah asked.

"Not too bad. The food's pretty good, and I had my first shower yesterday — with soap, shampoo, and everything. It felt so good that I stayed in too long and the guards had to yell at me to get out so the other girls could get a turn."

"Where are you being housed?"

"In the hospital. It's really nice. They say I tried to kill myself last week, so they brought me over here."

"Did you?" inquired Sarah tentatively.

"Did I what? Try to kill myself? What do you think?"

"I don't know, Lexi. I'm just glad you're okay."

"Thanks."

"Have you had any visitors?"

"Nope. I called Ryan twice, but he wasn't home. I'd really like to see him. Can you send a message to him?"

"Actually, Ryan's coming to my office on Friday. I can give him a message then. What would you like me to tell him?"

Lexi banged her fist on the table. "Why is he coming to see you? What's he coming to talk to you about?"

"Ryan called me yesterday and told me he wanted to talk," Sarah said calmly. "I've no idea what he wants to talk about. Do you know what he's going to tell me?"

"No, ma'am!"

Sarah decided to back off. "Lexi, we need to talk about what happened to your baby. I know this is going to be hard for you, but it's really important that you're completely honest with me. That's the only way I'll be able to help you."

"I don't want to talk about it."

"Why don't we start by getting to know each other a little better? Is that all right?"

For the next forty-five minutes, Sarah and Lexi talked about family, friends, and common interests. By all accounts, Lexi had a normal upbringing—no abuse, no alcoholic parents, nothing unusual that Sarah could use in arguing for a more lenient penalty; certainly nothing that foreshadowed what she had done to little Anna. Then the time came to talk about the events of Monday, August 11.

"Why don't you tell me what happened the day your baby died?"

"I already told the cops."

"I know, but I need you to give me more detail than you gave them. Tell me everything that happened. Go slowly, and tell me as many details as you can remember."

"I woke up. It was just like any other day. Anna was fine. She was a little fussy 'cause she had a cold, but nothing unusual. I'd been sick for a couple of days too, and she probably got it from me. We just did our usual morning stuff. Ryan got ready for work, I changed and fed Anna and put her in her little bouncy seat while I ate breakfast."

"Did you and Ryan argue that morning?"

"Nope."

"Was there anything bothering you at all? Were you mad at anybody?"

"No!" Lexi's voice rose. "What are you trying to say?"

"Nothing. I just need to make sure I completely understand what happened. Go on."

"While Ryan was getting ready for work, I took Anna for a quick walk around the block, just like I did every morning."

"Did you see anyone on your walk?"

"I'm not sure. Maybe Madeline."

"Do you know Madeline's last name?"

"No."

"Then what happened?"

"After we all got ready, I got in the car to take Ryan to work. He works at R&B Paint Store. He starts at nine a.m., but he always likes to get there a little early, so I dropped him off about a quarter of. Ryan kissed Anna goodbye like he always does ... like he always did." Lexi stopped and looked down. She started to cry softly.

"I keep thinking this is some sort of horrible dream and I'm going to wake up any minute now and Anna's going to be fine and everything ... It's not a dream, is it, Mrs. Wong?"

"No, Lexi, it's not. Can you tell me more about what happened?"

"I'll try. After I dropped Ryan off at work, Anna and I went on some errands. I think I went to the Donut Shoppe, to Pete's Market, and to the gas station."

"When you went into the Donut Shoppe and Pete's, did you leave Anna in the car?"

Lexi became agitated. "Are you crazy? You can't leave a baby in the car in the summer! It gets way too hot. OF COURSE I brought her in with me!"

Sarah realized she had a lot to learn about being a parent. "Did you carry her in your arms or put her in a stroller?"

"Neither. I have one of those car seats that converts into a carrier and I just took it with me. I take her everywhere in that. I mean I *took* her ..." Lexi's voice trailed off and she started crying again, louder than before. "I don't want to talk about this anymore. I want to stop."

But Sarah had to push on—this might be her only chance to hear Lexi's version of what had happened that day.

"I understand how upset you are, Lexi, but we have to talk about this. I need to know everything that happened if I'm going to be able to help you. Can you keep going?"

"I'll try, Mrs. Wong. I'll really try."

Lexi sat straight up, grabbed the sides of her chair with both hands, and took two long, deep breaths. Her eyes narrowed and the tears stopped.

"So what happened in the Donut Shoppe?" Sarah asked.

"Just the usual stuff. I went in and got my juice and bagel, said hi to everyone."

"Was Anna with you?"

"Yes, I already told you she was."

"Do you know the names of the people who work there?"

"Only James. He's the cute guy behind the counter."

"Then you went to the grocery store?"

"Yeah. Pete's is just a small place, not a big grocery store. You ever been there?"

"I don't think so."

"I bought apples, melons, grapes, and some cereal. Probably some other stuff too, but I can't remember now. I was in Pete's for about thirty minutes. Anna was real quiet. I thought she was sleeping."

"Did you check on her?"

"Sorta. I looked down, and she looked peaceful and all, so I just let her sleep. I was hoping she'd sleep a little longer so I could get all my errands done."

"Do you know any of the people in Pete's Market?"

"Not really."

"Then where did you go?"

"To the gas station on Lassiter Street. When I got there, all the pumps were taken, so I had to wait 'bout five or ten minutes for one to open up. I remember it was really hot. My air conditioning doesn't work too good, so I had my windows all the way down, but it didn't help much 'cause the air was so still. After a while, a pump opened up, and I pulled up and started gassing up the car. That's when I knew something was wrong."

"What do you mean?"

"While the pump was running I opened the door to play peekaboo with Anna. The books say she's too young to laugh, but she always looks at me when I play peekaboo." Lexi's voice started to falter again, but she took another deep breath. "I knew something was wrong. She wasn't moving or anything. I poked her a couple of times and she still didn't move. Then I shook her and yelled at her, but she didn't respond at all."

Sarah was writing furiously to make sure she got every word exactly. "What did you think?" she asked without looking up.

"I knew something was really wrong." Lexi's voice was barely above a whisper.

Sarah looked straight at her. "Go on."

"I realized she was dead."

"How did you know she was dead?"

"I just did."

"But HOW did you know? Maybe she was just sleeping really soundly."

"I just knew it, okay? You wouldn't understand."

"Try me."

"I SAID you wouldn't understand!"

Sarah swallowed hard. It felt like she was one question away from finding out what had really happened.

"You can tell me, Lexi. I'm your attorney. I won't tell anyone."

"I SAID YOU WOULDN'T UNDERSTAND!"

At the sound of Lexi's shouting, the guard moved toward the cubicle door, but Sarah waved him off.

"So what did you do then?"

"I got back in the car and drove around for a bit, trying to think about what to do."

"Did you call Ryan?"

"No."

"Why not?"

"I knew he would be mad as hell that his little girl was

gone. Besides, there was nothing he could do."

"How about your mom?"

"No."

"Why not?"

"Because I KNEW Anna was already dead."

Sarah could tell Lexi was hiding something, but she didn't know how to get her to open up. "I still don't understand why you didn't get any help—why you didn't try."

Lexi stood up. "Did you ever have your own baby die?" she yelled. "Do you have ANY idea what I went through that day? If you don't, then just shut the hell up!"

The deputy burst into the interview room and grabbed Lexi by the arm. "Let's go. Interview's over."

"Deputy, I'd like to talk with her a little longer."

"Are you sure, counselor?"

"I'm sure."

The deputy pulled Lexi around so she was looking right at him, their faces only a foot apart. "Conway, if you yell or cause a fuss one more time, you're done here. Understand?"

"Yes, sir."

Lexi sat back down, and the sheriff exited the interview room, leaving the door slightly open.

"Officer, please close the door," Sarah said firmly.

"Are you sure?"

"Yes."

"Very well." The sheriff pulled the door shut but stood right by the handle, ready to enter at the slightest disturbance.

"I know how hard it must be for you to talk about this," Sarah said, hoping to calm Lexi down.

"Damn right it is. Why are you being so mean to me? How do you know what *you* would have done? I was scared and mad that my baby was dead. There wasn't nuthin' I could do about it. What should I have done? Call my mom and say, 'Hi, Mom. Guess what? Anna's dead'?"

Sarah decided to press on. "What did you do next?"

"I drove home."

"Do you know what time it was then?"

"Maybe eleven or eleven thirty—I'm not sure."

"Why did you go home?"

"I wanted to kill myself."

"What happened when you got there?"

"I pulled in the garage and just sat there."

"Was the engine still running?"

"Yes. I told you, I wanted to die so I could be with Anna."

"Where was Anna?"

"Still in her car seat in the back."

"Did you make any calls?"

"The cops told me I called 911, but I don't remember."

"Then what happened?"

"I woke up in the hospital and the cops asked me a lot of questions."

"Anything else you can remember about that morning?"

"No. That's it. That's everything."

Sarah looked down at her notes, then back up at Lexi. "I have to ask you the next question if I'm going to be able to help you. Before you answer, remember that I'm your attorney and I won't tell anyone what you tell me."

"Okay."

"Did you kill Anna?"

Lexi didn't reply.

Sarah decided to try a different tack. "Do you know how Anna died? What happened?"

"She just died, okay? I don't know exactly how, but she just died. That's all I know."

Lexi and Sarah stared at each other across the small metal table. Lexi's chest was heaving and her hands were shaking.

"I have one more question before we wrap up, Lexi. Do

you think there's any possibility, any possibility at all, that you killed Anna and you've just blocked the memory out of your mind?"

"GUARD!" Lexi screamed.

* * *

Back at the office, Sarah stared out her window toward downtown Santa Felicia. There were many things about Lexi's story that didn't make sense. Why would a healthy baby die suddenly? Why hadn't Lexi taken Anna to a hospital? Why hadn't she called Ryan? Or her mom? Or somebody? If she didn't kill her baby surely she would have done *something*.

For some reason she believed Lexi—or maybe she just *wanted* to believe her. Either way, she was determined to find out exactly what had happened to little Anna Conway. She decided to ask the judge to appoint an independent autopsy expert. Maybe the expert would see something that Dr. Prakeesh had missed.

Sarah stuck her head outside her office door. "Nick, you got a minute?"

When he came in, Sarah started up before he even got to sit down. "Lexi claims that Anna was already dead before she drove home to her garage. She says she went home to commit suicide to join her baby in heaven."

"You believe her?"

"I think so. Problem is, the autopsy is crystal clear that Anna died of carbon monoxide poisoning. There's no evidence of any injuries, trauma, or anything else that might have killed Anna. I'm going to have a medical expert appointed to make sure, but the autopsy report looks pretty solid. I'd like you to see what you can find out about Anna Conway's medical history. See if she had any injuries, illnesses, hospital visits—those sorts of things."

"Okay. When do you need this by?"

"How about tomorrow?"

Nick smiled. "No, seriously."

"I am being serious." Sarah smiled back. "Just see what you can find out in the next day or so."

* * *

Sarah arrived at court especially early on Wednesday morning. She wanted to get Lexi's arraignment done first thing before the court got crowded. She had even called the clerk the day before to make sure that Lexi's case would be first on the docket. In and out before anybody noticed – at least, that was the plan.

Like many well-thought-out plans, this one never had a chance. When Sarah walked in, a full fifteen minutes before the judge was to take the bench, the courtroom was already three-quarters full. There were newspaper reporters, radio reporters, TV reporters. Sarah recognized some of them, but most were strangers. Arraignments were routine affairs, usually taking no more than a few minutes, so she was puzzled by the large media contingent.

As Sarah had requested, Lexi's case was first up.

"State of California versus Lexi Conway," announced Judge Isherwood. "Will the defendant please rise?"

Lexi, seated with about a dozen other defendants behind a tall, clear Plexiglas barrier, stood up quickly.

"Is Ms. Conway's attorney here?"

"Yes, Your Honor. Sarah Wong, representing Ms. Conway." Sarah moved swiftly over to where Lexi was standing.

"Are you ready to proceed, counselor?"

"Yes, Your Honor."

"Ms. Conway, you are charged with the first-degree murder of Anna Conway, Section 187 of the California Penal Code. In addition, you are charged with a special circumstance in committing this murder pursuant to

Section 190 of the Penal Code. The district attorney alleges that the murder was especially heinous, atrocious, or cruel. Do you understand the charges against you?"

"Yes, Your Honor."

"How do you plead?"

"My client pleads not guilty, Your Honor," Sarah butted in loudly before Lexi could answer.

"Very well. I will set this case for preliminary hearing on—"

"Your Honor, we waive our right to a prelim," interrupted Sarah. The burden of proof in preliminary hearings was so low that virtually all defendants are bound over for trial, and it wouldn't help Lexi to have the details of Anna's death discussed in open court.

"Your Honor, I ask the court to set bail at $25,000 with a ten percent bond in this case," Sarah went on. "My client has no criminal record whatsoever, and she has strong ties to the community. She has lived in Santa Felicia all her life, and she is not a flight risk."

The DA started to object, but Judge Isherwood held up her hand.

"This is a capital murder case. The request for bail is denied. Anything else, counselor?"

"Yes. I have two other requests. First, I ask the court to appoint an independent medical examiner to conduct a second autopsy on Anna Conway. My understanding is that the body is still in the county morgue."

"And the reason?"

"To get a second opinion on the cause of death."

"Very well. Do you have anyone in mind, counselor?"

"No, Your Honor."

"All right, I'll appoint Dr. Bridget Gowell. And your other request?

"That the court appoint Dr. Peter Broussard to examine my client and prepare a confidential report for the defense."

"For what purpose?"

In truth, Sarah wasn't really sure. She wasn't considering an insanity defense at this point, but she knew she should cover all the bases in a capital murder case.

"To examine the mental health of my client as it relates to criminal intent and competency to stand trial."

"So ordered," said Judge Isherwood. "Would the prosecution also like an expert appointed?"

"I ... I guess so," replied the DA, who looked like he was still in high school.

"Is there anyone you would request?" asked Judge Isherwood.

"Can I call my office, Your Honor?"

"That won't be necessary. I'll appoint Dr. Martin."

Judge Isherwood had appointed the most pro-prosecution psychiatrist in the county. Sarah was not surprised. Oh well, tit for tat, she thought.

"He'll be fine," said the DA in a more confident voice.

"Dr. Martin is a *she*," said Judge Isherwood before turning to Sarah.

"Anything else, counselor?"

"No, Your Honor."

"The Conway case is assigned to Judge Burt Sandoval and is set for pretrial motions in Department H in the Superior Court of Santa Felicia County on Friday, September 26 at nine a.m."

Sarah glanced at her calendar and saw that that was the same day as her next fertility appointment at New Beginnings. "Your Honor, I have a conflict that morning. Could we set the hearing at one in the afternoon?"

"Yes, that will be fine. The defendant is remanded back into custody and is ordered back to court at that time."

Judge Sandoval.

Sarah was hard-pressed to think of a judge who would be more prosecution-oriented than Burt Sandoval. To make matters worse, he was a showboat and liked to be the center of attention.

It was going to be a long trial.

CHAPTER 5

Sarah was glad when Friday finally arrived. Had she really only been representing Lexi for a week? It felt more like a month. It was far more stressful than she had imagined. How was she going to make it through the next six months or so?

It was only eight fifteen a.m. and Ryan's interview wasn't until one o'clock, but already she was nervous. She had no idea what he was going to say, but he could turn out to be the most important witness in the whole case.

She realized this might be her only chance to talk to Ryan, so she and Nick spent most of the morning getting ready for the interview. After discussing several possible strategies, they decided that Sarah would ask most of the questions and Nick would take notes. If Ryan seemed skittish or hesitant, they wouldn't ask about recording their conversation, but if he appeared to be at ease they would see if he would let them use a recorder. Sarah contemplated recording him without his permission, but Nick talked her out of it.

He brought up the possibility that Ryan might say something incriminating. "What if *he* killed Anna? Or what if Lexi confessed to him?"

"Given how upset Lexi was when I told her about our interview with Ryan, he probably does know something about Anna's death. Let's just make sure we proceed carefully," said Sarah as she began to tidy her desk. "By the way, what have you been able to find out about Anna's medical history?"

"Nothing yet. I haven't been able to track down any medical records for her," Nick said. "It seems that Santa Felicia hasn't made it into the twenty-first century. Almost all their official records are still on paper. I'll let you know when I find something."

* * *

By one ten, Sarah was starting to get apprehensive. Clients and witnesses were late for appointments all the time, but she had a bad feeling about this one.

At one twenty, the phone rang. Sarah picked up on the first ring. "Sarah Wong, attorney-at-law. May I help you?"

"This is Ryan — Ryan Stoudt."

"Hi, Ryan!" Sarah tried to sound as upbeat as possible. "Are you having trouble finding us?"

"I don't think I can make it."

Her heart sank. "Why not?"

"My uncle has a friend who's a lawyer and he told me not to talk to anyone, not even you."

"How come?"

"I dunno, but that's what he told me."

"Is he representing you?"

"Sort of, I guess."

"If you change your mind, you know how to reach me."

"Okay. I do have one question. How much is Lexi's bail?"

"Lexi doesn't have any bail, Ryan. She's going to be in jail until her trial."

Without another word Ryan hung up.

* * *

First thing on Monday, Sarah went to see Lexi again. She spent over an hour peppering her with questions about her pregnancy and about Anna's general health. Lexi's shackles had been removed and she seemed a bit more at ease than in their previous encounters, but she was still quite guarded.

Sarah learned that Anna had been a full-term baby and Lexi didn't smoke or drink during her pregnancy. Lexi was very vague about the details of Anna's birth. She and Ryan had used a midwife, but she wasn't sure of her name. Labor went pretty well and she didn't need any drugs during labor or delivery.

Lexi hadn't been getting along with her mom for quite a while, so she and Ryan were on their own in taking care of the baby. They took Anna to a free clinic for a checkup when she was about a week old, but she wasn't sure of the name of the clinic. She didn't think Anna had a heart condition or anything like that. Anna had a cold on the day she died, but nothing serious. Just a case of the sniffles.

That afternoon, Nick told Sarah that he still couldn't find out anything about Anna's medical history and he had run out of places to look. The county clerk had told him it wasn't unusual to come up empty when looking for information on newborns because it often took a while for everything to get into the system.

* * *

On Wednesday, exactly a week after Lexi's arraignment, Dr. Gowell's autopsy report arrived. Although Sarah hadn't been optimistic about the report, she was still disappointed there was nothing new — no wounds or trauma, no evidence of suffocation, no underlying medical conditions or diseases. Dr. Gowell had reached the same conclusion as Dr. Prakeesh: Anna Conway died of carbon monoxide poisoning. Dr. Gowell noted that her report wouldn't be final until she saw the results of the toxicology analyses that would enable her to rule out other types of poisons.

Other types of poisons! Sarah hadn't considered that before. Maybe Anna had been poisoned, either intentionally or accidently. Poisoning didn't always show up during an autopsy, so it was still an open question. She didn't have to wait long for the answer.

While going through the mail on Thursday afternoon, she came across a letter from AccFirst, an outfit she'd never heard of. She tore open the envelope carelessly, partially ripping the three pages inside. Then she realized that it was Anna's toxicology report.

The lab had tested for the usual panel of drugs and toxic substances, including alcohol, amphetamines, antifreeze, arsenic, and bleach, as well as a laundry list of commercially available pesticides and animal poisons. There were no traces of any of them in Anna's blood.

The last page of the lab results was more telling:

Carboxyhemoglobin (COHb) Analysis:
Conducted via standard chromatography techniques.

Analytical Results:
Carboxyhemoglobin (COHb) Blood Saturation:
27.2% (averaged for two samples).

In non-smokers, the typical level of carbon monoxide in the blood was only three percent. If there was any doubt about the cause of death before, there was none now: Anna had died from carbon monoxide poisoning.

But Lexi still might be telling the truth, Sarah thought. Maybe Lexi believed that Anna was dead at the gas station and went home to kill herself in despair, and Anna's death was just the tragic consequence of Lexi's mistaken belief. She called Nick into her office.

"Nick, I need you to pound the pavement for me on the Conway case. Lexi claims that Anna was already dead when she drove home to kill herself, but it's clear from all the medical reports that she was still alive at that point. So either Lexi honestly, but mistakenly, believed that Anna was already dead ..."

"Or she's lying to cover up her murder of Anna," Nick interjected. "How will we ever know?"

"That's where you come in. I need you to find out as much as you can about Lexi. Is she peaceful, truthful, likable? Those sorts of things. I also want you to find out what happened on the day Anna died."

Sarah gave Nick a long list of witnesses to interview, including many of Lexi's family members and the employees at the Donut Shoppe, Pete's Market, and the Sunoco gas station. She also asked him to subpoena Lexi's school and employment records and any available medical records, and to canvass Lexi's neighborhood, interviewing as many neighbors as possible, including those the police had already talked to. She told him to obtain videotapes from surveillance cameras at the places Lexi visited on the day Anna died. She wasn't sure if any of these tapes would help, but they might provide some evidence of how Lexi was acting that day.

"Do you still believe her?" Nick asked as he got up to leave Sarah's office.

"I think so. But I'm not sure a jury will. That's why we've got to find out as much as we can."

It was time to go home. Sarah gathered her papers and took a quick look at her weekly planner to see if she had anything on tap for the next few nights. There, at the bottom of Thursday, August 28, was an entry in red: "Dinner with Matt at 6:30." She had completely forgotten! She called him on his cell, and it turned out he had forgotten too, but they agreed that a nice quiet, intimate dinner would do them both good and they arranged to meet at Olivia's, the trendy new Italian place on 26th Street.

* * *

Sarah got to Olivia's first. It wasn't quiet and it wasn't intimate; it was large and noisy. The tables weren't tucked away in dimly lit recesses; instead they were jammed together in one large room only a few feet from the open kitchen.

She was told she'd have to wait about a half hour for a table, so she grabbed the only vacant seat at the small bar and ordered a glass of Merlot. After fending off two college guys for ten minutes, she was relieved to see Matt walk through the door.

"Not quite what I was expecting," yelled Matt and kissed her on the cheek.

"Me neither, hon, but let's just make the best of it."

After waiting at the bar for almost forty-five minutes, long enough for two glasses of Merlot for her and two beers for him, they were led to a narrow table in the middle of the room. Sarah tried to steer the conversation away from work, but pretty soon Matt asked her how the Conway case was going.

"Okay, I guess."

"What?" shouted Matt.

"I said, it's going okay!"

"Do you want to talk about it?"

"No."

They looked at the menus silently and another fifteen minutes passed before the waitress arrived.

"I'll bet this case is really hard on you, Tiger," Matt said after she had taken their order.

"Actually it is." Sarah paused. "We're trying SO hard to have a baby, and here I am representing someone accused of killing her own baby." There was a tremble in her voice. "It's not fair. It's just NOT FAIR."

Then Sarah burst into tears—full-out, body-shaking wails. The last time she had cried like that was when she found out her dad was dead—and she had *never* cried like that in public.

"I'm sorry, Sarah. I really am."

She couldn't speak she was crying so hard.

"Why don't you just drop the case?" Matt suggested gently. "Let someone else handle it. The judge will understand."

"But Lexi needs me. She has no one else to turn to." Sarah wiped the tears from her cheek with her napkin, but they kept coming.

"Well, I need you too, and I don't want you to keep going like this."

The food might have been delicious, but Sarah couldn't tell. She was totally numb. For the rest of the meal, she shut out everything—the clatter of dishes, the loud babble of other patrons, the smells emanating from the kitchen, even the sound of Matt's voice.

After finishing their meal, they drove home, hopped into bed, and said good night. Matt was asleep within minutes, while Sarah stared at the ceiling until well past three.

CHAPTER 6

Over the next two weeks, Sarah saw Lexi three more times. Each interview followed the same pattern: Sarah probed for more details about Anna's health and Lexi's past, and each time she came up empty. Lexi barely talked, and when she did it was only to say, "I don't know," or "I don't remember." Given everything Lexi had been through the previous month, Sarah was willing to cut her some slack, but her evasiveness became increasingly exasperating.

Even more disturbing was Lexi's temper. Sarah had caught glimpses of it during her first couple of visits to the jail, but now her outbursts were more frequent and more violent. On two occasions, the guards had to interrupt interviews to restrain Lexi, taking her down to the floor and restraining her with plastic ties on one occasion. By the last of these three visits, Lexi was once again handcuffed and shackled. Sarah asked the jailers why, and they told her she'd got in a few scuffles with other inmates—nothing real serious, but enough to cause them to shackle her.

Except for the interviews with Lexi, those two weeks passed uneventfully. There were a few routine court appearances on other cases, a couple of depositions, and numerous client meetings. One thing that had changed was the influx of potential new clients to Sarah's practice. Almost every day, people contacted her about representation. At first, she was giddy at the prospect of growing her small firm with a stable of new clients, but she quickly realized that most of them were not the type of clients that she wanted to build her practice around. Since she was now known as the baby killer's lawyer, people who had done all sorts of terrible things sought her out. Many of them were already in jail or prison, and virtually none of them had the ability to pay her. She even got a call from a man who was thinking about killing his wife and wanted to know, before he went through with it, if she would represent him when he got arrested. He hung up before she could get any identifying information, sparing her the agonizing ethical decision about whether to notify the police.

The calls and emails from reporters, almost constant in the days immediately following Lexi's arraignment, tapered off slowly in the subsequent weeks. Sarah granted two brief phone interviews to reporters from small-town newspapers in Northern California to see how her words would look in print. But she did no more when the second interview, full of inaccuracies, was picked up by the wire services and appeared all over the Internet.

Less than two weeks after Sarah received the toxicology report from AccFirst Lab, the county's final autopsy report arrived. She pulled out Dr. Prakeesh's first report and compared it with this latest one. She could find only one difference between the two: He had noted in his first report that the toxicology results were pending; he now wrote that they had been completed, and he included the report from AccFirst as an appendix.

* * *

First thing on Wednesday, Nick knocked gently on Sarah's door.

"It's done."

"What's done?"

"My investigation." With a ceremonious thud, he

dropped a thick report on Sarah's desk. It was nicely bound in a black leatherette cover with gold lettering. "After you've had a chance to read it, let me know if you have any questions."

After Nick left, Sarah opened the report. It was meticulously organized, carefully written, and included a table of contents, a timeline of all the interviews, and even an index for key phrases and terms that appeared in the interviews.

He had interviewed Lexi's mom, sister, and two cousins. Lexi's childhood had been filled with the usual ups and downs, but for the most part it was unremarkable. Her dad died of a heart attack when she was five, so she was raised by her mom and older sister. She had been an average student in school and was involved in several clubs and activities. She was a little "spacey" (her sister's words) and fairly shy. Never the life of the party or the center of attention, Lexi didn't have a lot of friends, but she always had one or two close buddies.

Both her mom and sister said that Lexi had become quite combative in her teens, often lashing out and saying hurtful things, but they added that she was always quick to apologize and make up. Lexi fought with her sister on occasion, sometimes physically, and she had had a brawl with another girl in tenth grade (over a boy, of course) that garnered her a five-day suspension from school and a month of detention. Other than that, they said that Lexi never got into any real trouble. Evidently neither of them knew about the bar fight Lexi had mentioned in her first interview with Sarah.

Lexi had met Ryan when she was fifteen, and right away they talked about having children. She moved in with him and her grandmother during her junior year in high school, and fell out of touch with her mom and sister. For almost two years they never saw each other. But Lexi had reconnected with her mom as she awaited Anna's birth.

Lexi's mom said Lexi had frequent mood swings during her pregnancy, which intensified as her due date drew near. For the most part, Lexi said that she really wanted Anna, but there were a few times when she talked about it being "just another big mistake."

Sarah was discouraged by the tenor of these interviews. There were several signs of regret—not overwhelming, but clearly there. Maybe Lexi was afraid she wouldn't be a good mother. Or maybe the regret ran deeper than that.

Nick had tried to interview Ryan, calling him twice at his mother's house, but Ryan refused to speak to him, telling him that his uncle's friend was still instructing him not to say anything to anybody.

The next section of Nick's report contained interviews with employees at the Donut Shoppe, Pete's Market, and the Sunoco gas station. No one at the gas station recognized Lexi's picture or remembered seeing her on August 11, but two employees at the Donut Shoppe and another two at Pete's Market recognized her picture right away. Both clerks at the Donut Shoppe said she was a regular who came in almost every day. One of them, James Bayne, had especially nice things to say about her, and Nick surmised that James had a crush on Lexi. The other clerk said that Lexi had a bit of a temper, that she would get really upset if there was anything wrong with her order. He recalled one time when she threw a full cup of coffee at the cash register, yelling that there was too much cream in her coffee. Nick had asked them to think carefully about the morning of August 11. They both remembered seeing Lexi and Anna that day, but neither could remember anything unusual. The two employees at Pete's Market also remembered seeing Lexi on the eleventh, but they were vague about any specific details.

The third section of the report included interviews with Lexi's neighbors. Much like a door-to-door salesman, Nick had knocked on every door on Lexi's block, a total of twenty-six duplexes and small starter homes. Most of the neighbors refused to talk because they didn't want to get involved, while others said they didn't know anything. Several added that the whole thing was a shame because Lexi seemed like such a nice young girl. All told, six neighbors agreed to speak with Nick, and all six said more or less the same thing: Lexi was a loving mother who showed off her new baby every chance she got. Nobody had ever seen her drunk or using any sort of drugs. She didn't even smoke cigarettes.

Two neighbors commented that Lexi seemed overprotective and somewhat anxious, and they both had seen occasional flashes of anger from her, like the time she yelled and swore at a stranger who let his German shepherd get too close to Anna, and another time when she threw something at a car that was speeding through the neighborhood. But they characterized those episodes as the understandable overreactions of a nervous new mother, not signs of anything more serious.

Nick had asked all six neighbors what they knew about the events of Monday, August 11, the day Anna died. Three of them had been at work all day. The other three heard the ambulance, and one of them, Madeline Truex, had gone over to Lexi's to see what was wrong. Mrs. Truex said she saw Lexi pull into her driveway sometime between eleven and eleven thirty. She heard the police siren about a half hour after that and dashed down the street to see what was going on. She tried to get the attention of the police officers after the ambulance had sped away, but they just ignored her. Madeline also said she had seen Lexi and Anna on their daily walk that morning and everything seemed fine.

The fourth section of the report consisted of a single page on which Nick stated that he was still unable to obtain Anna's medical history. The final section contained a summary of his attempts to get surveillance videos from

August 11. Unfortunately, there were none to be had. The police had already obtained the videos from the Sunoco gas station, and the ones from the Donut Shoppe and Pete's Market had been taped over in the weeks since August 11.

That was it. All in all, the report depicted Lexi as a generally likable, somewhat high-strung new mother with a bit of a temper.

The report from Dr. Broussard, the psychiatrist who had examined Lexi, arrived in the mail later that morning. His report was nine pages long, and at first Sarah had trouble locating his opinion. She eventually found it on page eight:

> Based upon my three interviews with Ms. Conway, as well as my review of the police reports and other relevant documents, it is my expert opinion that Lexi Conway was legally sane when she killed Anna Conway on August 11. Furthermore, Ms. Conway is legally competent to stand trial.

Dr. Broussard had visited Lexi three times and had administered all the standard tests and psychological assessments. He considered all the usual mental illnesses, including depression, bipolar disorder, schizophrenia, antisocial personality, even postpartum depression. Sarah was not surprised by Dr. Broussard's conclusion, as she hadn't seen any signs of mental illness herself, but she was initially taken aback by his repeated assumption that Lexi had killed Anna. As she thought more about it, though, his assumption seemed reasonable given that psychiatrists are usually appointed only in cases where the responsibility for the crime is clear and the primary issue is the sanity of the defendant. Dr. Broussard's report was clear and unambiguous and Sarah was impressed with his thoroughness.

Later that afternoon another letter arrived, this time by courier. It was marked "Urgent and Confidential: To Be

Opened Only by Addressee." Sarah knew exactly what it was—the death penalty letter from the DA's office. She placed the envelope gingerly on her desk and just stared at it for a while before opening it, carefully and slowly. It was only one paragraph long. The DA was going to ask a jury to execute Lexi Conway. A surprising calm engulfed her. She had known the letter was coming and thought it would upset her, but now that it was here, it was something of a relief.

All in all, she had learned nothing particularly surprising that day, but it was discouraging nonetheless. And she wasn't any closer to a viable defense.

She decided to visit Lexi again on Thursday morning. Maybe she would be more forthcoming about what happened the day Anna died. Also, it was time to broach the idea of a plea bargain.

* * *

"There are a couple of things we need to talk about, Lexi," Sarah began.

"Like what?"

"First of all, I got a letter from the DA about your case. It's not good news."

"What did it say?"

"The DA is seeking the death penalty in your case—if you're found guilty they will ask the jury to recommend that you be executed."

"Okay."

"What do you mean by okay?"

"Nothing. Just okay."

"I think we should talk about the possibility of a plea bargain."

"Why?"

"I think I might be able to get the DA to offer some sort of lesser charge, like second-degree murder or maybe even manslaughter. If they agree, you might get out of prison in ten or fifteen years."

"Let's just have the trial. Whatever happens, happens."

"Don't you want to see what kind of deal they might offer?"

"No."

Sarah was taken aback by Lexi's response but plowed ahead. "We need to talk about how Anna died."

"But we've already talked about it a million times."

"But you've never really told me what happened to her." Sarah pulled out a sheet of paper from her folder. "Let's start with your statement to the police."

"What statement?"

"The one you wrote in the hospital."

"I don't remember writing anything."

Sarah shoved the paper in front of Lexi. "Is this your signature?"

"I guess so."

"Well, is it?" Sarah's voice rose just a little.

"YES, it is!"

Sarah pointed to a paragraph in the middle of the statement:

> *I didnt know what to do. For sure, I wasnt going to tell Ryan. He would never ever ever understand and he would be mad at me forever. I was panicy. I knew it was my fault that Anna was dead.*

"What did you mean when you said, 'it was my fault that Anna was dead'?"

"I don't know! What do YOU think?" Lexi screamed, her face turning scarlet.

"I don't know, Lexi. That's what I'm trying to find out. Now let's take a look at your 911 call." Sarah placed a transcript of the call directly in front of Lexi. "Do you remember making this call?"

"Not really."

"Let's go through it together now." Sarah read the entire transcript out loud while Lexi stared down at her feet.

911 Operator:	*Hello, this is the 911 operator. Do you have an emergency?*
Female Voice:	*Not really. There's nothing you can do now. It's probably all for the best anyway.*
911 Operator:	*What do you mean?*
Female Voice:	*I was afraid this might happen.*
911 Operator:	*Ma'am, I don't understand.*
Female Voice:	*That's okay. There's nothing you can do. Just tell Ryan I love him.*
911 Operator:	*Do you need any help?*
Female Voice:	*Not anymore.*
911 Operator:	*Do you want me to send an ambulance? The police?*

[Nineteen seconds of a constant rumbling sound]

911 Operator:	*Ma'am. Do you need any help? Shall I send the police?*
Female Voice:	*If you want.*

[End of recording]

"What were you afraid might happen? Were you afraid you might kill Anna? That Ryan might kill her?"

Lexi sat stony-faced.

"Lexi, I'm your attorney. I need to know everything."

"What do you want me to say? That I killed Anna? Is that what you want me to say?" Lexi punctuated each sentence by stomping her feet.

"I just want you to tell me the truth so I can help you."

"Okay, okay. Yes, it's my fault that Anna died! I killed her just by having her. Are you happy now?"

"I don't understand, Lexi. Are you saying you killed her?"

"I never should have had Anna. Then none of this would have happened. I just want to die so I can be with her in heaven." Lexi clasped her hands on top of her head and slammed it onto the table.

Despite repeated efforts over the next ten minutes, Sarah couldn't get her to utter another word. In the end she gave up and told the guard they were finished. Lexi didn't look at her as she was led out of the interview room back to her cell.

Lexi may have given up, but Sarah had not.

* * *

Back in her office on Friday morning, Sarah took a fresh look at all the evidence in Lexi's case to see if she had overlooked anything. First she thought about the cause of death, rereading both autopsy reports, the toxicology report, Lexi's statement, and her own notes. It didn't take her long to reach the same conclusion as before: Anna had died of carbon monoxide poisoning.

That brought her to the next issue: Who killed Anna? Lexi was the prime suspect — the *only* suspect — but Sarah had to consider other possible culprits. Maybe someone had tried to kill both Lexi and Anna by knocking Lexi out and leaving them both in the closed garage to die. Ex-boyfriends and lovers were always a good bet, the motive usually being revenge or jealousy. By all accounts, though, Ryan was Lexi's first and only serious boyfriend.

Sarah pulled out her stack of police reports to see if there were any other possible suspects. Police detectives had interviewed almost a dozen witnesses in an attempt to track Lexi's activities on the morning of August 11. They talked to five neighbors, two of whom had seen Lexi on her usual early morning walk with Anna. Both confirmed that Anna was with Lexi and seemed fine.

The detectives had talked to three employees at Pete's Market, two at the Donut Shoppe, and the manager of the Sunoco gas station. Two of the workers at Pete's and both of the clerks at the Donut Shoppe remembered seeing Lexi on August 11, and they all reported that she and Anna seemed fine. The manager at the Sunoco station didn't see Lexi herself, but she did give the detectives several videotapes from the station's three security cameras.

All the witnesses confirmed the timeline provided by Lexi in her written statement. After dropping Ryan off at work at the R&B Paint Store at about 8:45, Lexi went to the Donut Shoppe, arriving at approximately 8:55 and leaving at about 9:10. Then she went to Pete's Market, where she shopped for about forty minutes. The date and time stamps on the videotapes from the Sunoco gas station placed her there between 9:58 to 10:20. The only time unaccounted for was between 10:20, when she was seen at the Sunoco gas station, and 11:47, when she called 911 from her garage.

The detectives had interviewed Ryan twice, and he provided them with complete details of his whereabouts that morning. They had verified his alibi with his boss and two coworkers that Ryan was at the R&B paint store all morning, and they ruled him out as a suspect. They had asked Ryan if Lexi had been acting strangely or talking about hurting herself or the baby, and he emphatically said that Lexi could not and would not hurt their baby.

Sarah tried as hard as she could to come up with any other possible killers.

Lexi's mom or sister? Hardly.

An unknown thief or robber? Unlikely.

Although she had to try to keep an open mind, she was

certain that Anna had died at the hands of her mother.

But was it an intentional killing or a tragic accident? That was the question that would determine Lexi's fate.

Maybe Lexi hadn't really wanted her baby. Such killings occurred far too often — terrified teenage girls hiding their pregnancy from everyone until they gave birth in a mall bathroom, at a friend's house, or at home, and then killing the baby by drowning it in the toilet or suffocating it in a garbage bag.

Lexi had said repeatedly it was her fault that Anna was dead, which certainly pointed toward an intentional killing. And sprinkled throughout Nick's report were indications that Lexi regretted having Anna, a theme echoed in the jailhouse meetings with Sarah. If Lexi had indeed killed Anna on purpose, Sarah's only recourse would be an insanity defense. Yet as Dr. Broussard's report made clear, there was not one scintilla of evidence that Lexi was insane.

But if Sarah could argue that it was a heartbreaking accident, she just might have a chance. After all, Lexi claimed that Anna was already dead at the gas station and then drove home to kill herself so she could join her baby in heaven. If a jury believed her, they might return a verdict of involuntary manslaughter, or even not guilty. However, accident cases involving infant deaths were notoriously difficult to win, as evidenced by the guilty verdicts in many recent hot-car infant deaths where moms or dads "accidentally" left their children in a car in the broiling summer heat.

Sarah wanted to believe that Anna's death was just an accident, but Lexi continued to send mixed messages about what happened. After five full weeks of representing Lexi, Sarah had nothing to go on other than Lexi's vague, uncorroborated claim that she thought her baby was already dead before she tried to commit suicide.

Sarah felt more confused than ever about what had

really happened on August 11. Exasperated, she scribbled a quick note at the bottom of a legal pad:

*Colonel Mustard in the Conservatory
with the Candlestick*

CHAPTER 7

It was four forty-five on Saturday morning, but Sarah couldn't sleep. For weeks she'd done her best to cajole Matt into talking about genetic engineering, but she'd been largely unsuccessful.

Genetic engineering. Those two words conjured up vivid images from horror movies and sci-fi novels. As she lay still, her mind raced. *Wasn't Frankenstein's monster a product of genetic engineering? Or was he was just stitched together with parts from a bunch of dead people. Is my baby going to be a monster?* Sarah shuddered at the thought. *What are we getting ourselves into?*

She got out of bed as quietly as she could, tiptoed out of the bedroom with Chloe following, and silently shut the door behind her. They headed down the short hallway to her home office, which was really just a second bedroom. Like Sarah's office at work, the room was piled high with case folders and legal papers. After her computer booted up, she stared at the background image on the screen, a picture of her hiking with Matt on their honeymoon in Costa Rica. They were tanned, relaxed, and happy. Instead of looking at the camera, they were gazing at each other. It seemed so romantic and so long ago. No baby worries, no fertility stressors; just two newlyweds enjoying each other. She couldn't remember the last time they had gazed into each other's eyes.

Sarah typed "genetic engineering" into the Google

search bar, and the results were both enthralling and horrifying. She sat there transfixed as she scrolled through page after page of terrifying pictures of deformed animals and weird hybrid plants. She figured that many of the images had probably been doctored, but they were scary nonetheless.

Her voyeuristic urges satisfied, she started browsing scientific and educational websites looking for reliable information about human genetic engineering. It was hard to know where to begin. There was a lot of information about genetic engineering for animals, but hardly any on humans.

For almost two hours, she searched and read. She learned about transgenic animals and discovered that one of the first transgenic primates was a rhesus monkey named ANDi, who had been created by scientists in Oregon in late 2000 to show that genes from one species could be genetically implanted into the DNA of another. They had inserted the GFP gene from jellyfish (the gene that makes the jellyfish glow) into the genome of rhesus monkeys.

The research team claimed they had used the glowing jellyfish gene because it would make it easy to see if their experiment worked, but Sarah suspected it had more to do with the wow factor. How cool it would be to create a glowing green monkey! That would definitely make the cover of *Time*. Even the name of their monkey was whimsical, for ANDi was a backwards acronym for "inserted DNA." She read about many more genetically engineered animals, including some that held great promise for medical and scientific breakthroughs. The thing that stood out was that it took many, many tries to get these procedures to work. Often, hundreds of embryos were sacrificed for a single success. For ANDi, the scientists had started with 224 eggs and ended up with only one live monkey that had the glowing jellyfish gene. *No wonder they don't do this stuff on people.*

As Sarah continued to read about genetic engineering, one term kept popping up – CRISPR. As best as she could tell, CRISPR was the newest genetic engineering technique, and it seemed to hold great promise for altering genetic traits in humans. The scientific journal articles about CRISPR were too much for her, but Sarah found reports in *National Geographic* and *Time* that she could understand. CRISPR seemed to be the wave of the future, and Sarah wondered why Dr. Svengaard hadn't mentioned it.

Just before eight, Matt shuffled into the office, almost stepping on Chloe who had curled up by the door.

"What ya doing, Tiger? You shouldn't be working on that baby killer's case on Saturday. Come on back to bed."

"I'm not working on the Conway case, hon. I'm just doing a little research."

"For one of your other cases?"

"No, for *us*. On genetic engineering."

"Really? What'd you find?"

She didn't dare tell him about the monkey with the jellyfish gene. The truth was, much of what she had found scared her. "I found out there's a lot more we need to know about genetic engineering. Did you sleep well?"

"C'mon. You can tell me more than that."

"Hon, I'm tired of looking at this stuff. It's all just a jumble to me right now. How 'bout we go for a run and talk about it afterward?"

Sarah was surprised by her response. For weeks she had been gamely trying to get Matt to talk about genetic engineering, and now she was the one avoiding that very conversation. He had given her the perfect opening and she had just slammed the door in his face.

They pulled on their running clothes and set off. After about an hour, Matt slowed to a walk.

"That's enough for me. Let's go home," he said.

Sarah reluctantly stopped running too. As they walked home, they chatted about work, friends, and family, and they gossiped about one of their neighbors who they thought was having an affair with the divorcee who lived three doors down. After a while Sarah finally found the courage to talk about what was really on her mind.

"Hon, what do you think about all the genetic engineering stuff Dr. Svengaard told us about?"

"I don't want to do any of it," replied Matt quickly. "It's just too scary."

"I know it's scary, but wouldn't it be fantastic if we could guarantee ourselves a healthy, happy child?"

"Could genetic engineering really do that?"

"Well, I'm not sure, but Dr. Svengaard did say that he could use genetic engineering to choose some basic traits for our baby such as eye color and hair color, and he could even eliminate some undesirable traits like baldness."

Matt nodded.

"Hon, don't you want us to have the very best baby we can?"

"What do you mean, Tiger?"

"Don't you want our baby to be the cutest, the smartest, the most athletic?"

"I guess, but really anything will do. You know what they say — ten fingers and ten toes. That'll be fine with me."

"But what if we can make our baby just a little bit better. Don't you want to give it a try?"

"Better than what?"

Matt's question made Sarah stop and think. What *did* she mean by better? Were blue-eyed babies better than brown-eyed ones? Of course not, but Sarah wanted a blue-eyed baby anyway. Were taller babies better than shorter babies?

"Better than average, I guess," she said. "How about eliminating diseases? You wouldn't want our baby to have cystic fibrosis, would you?"

"Of course not."

"How about Huntington's disease?"

"Sarah!" Matt was clearly exasperated now.

"Well then, why shouldn't we use genetic engineering to eliminate those genetic mutations if our baby has them?"

"I guess that would be okay. But I need to think more about this. I don't really understand how genetic engineering works and what the risks are."

"That's why I was researching it this morning," Sarah said. "But to be honest with you, I'm more confused now than ever. I'm not sure what to do next."

They let themselves in through the front door, grabbed some water and plopped down at the kitchen table, dripping sweat everywhere. Sarah wanted to keep talking so they wouldn't lose momentum.

"I really don't know what to do," she said.

She did know she had a lot more to learn about genetics before she and Matt could make an intelligent decision. She remembered some of what she had learned in college, but that was almost ten years ago. When Dr. Svengaard started explaining how viral vectors were used in genetic engineering, she had been completely lost.

As Sarah got up to take a shower, Matt said, "I know, why don't you call one of those DNA experts you use on your cases? They might be able to help."

"That's actually a great idea!"

"I do have good ideas every once in a while," Matt shot back.

Sarah used two DNA experts on a regular basis. Dr. Phillip Joyce was certainly well qualified, but he was rather gruff and Sarah had never warmed to him. He reminded her of Dr. Svengaard — excellent credentials and eminently qualified, but cold and distant.

In contrast, Dr. Candi Markowitz was much friendlier and seemed more likely to help Sarah with a personal issue. The name Candi sounded more like the stage name of a stripper than someone who had a PhD in genetics, but Dr. Markowitz had told Sarah that that was the name her parents had given her and she kept it to honor them.

After she had showered, Sarah called Dr. Markowitz's answering service and left her name and number. To her surprise, Dr. Markowitz called back almost immediately. Sarah explained her situation in general terms, and before she had finished Dr. Markowitz agreed to an informal meeting with her. Sarah stressed that her questions did not concern any of her cases but were strictly about a personal matter. Dr. Markowitz said she understood and suggested they met at the Cheesecake Factory.

"They have excellent margaritas there," added Dr. Markowitz. "Can you meet me for lunch today?"

"Sure. I can probably get there by about twelve thirty."

When Sarah hung up, she told Matt that Dr. Markowitz could meet her for lunch that day.

"Today? Wow, that's great! We can all talk about—"

"Hon, I didn't say anything about you coming. I kinda thought it would just be Dr. Markowitz and me. You've never even met her before."

"But I want to go. I'm just as curious about all this genetic engineering stuff as you are. I really think I ought to go. What if you forget to ask her something?"

"I won't forget anything," Sarah shot back.

"But I really want to go."

"If it's that important to you, I can call her back and ask if it's okay. But I don't know if she'll be comfortable talking about these things with you there. You know—fertility, artificial insemination, all that stuff."

"Okay, okay. Go ahead without me."

"I'll have to leave about eleven thirty. Why don't we talk about the genetic engineering stuff over breakfast before I go. I'll make pancakes."

Matt went for a shower and came down just as Sarah was putting the pancakes on the table. He took four, covered them with syrup, and dove in before Sarah had even sat down.

"Why do you want to try genetic engineering?" Matt asked, his mouth full of pancake. "It seems so dangerous to me."

"At the very least I want to try the procedure where Dr. Svengaard engineers our embryo so that it will have a better chance of implanting."

"How does that work again?"

"Dr. Svengaard uses some sort of virus to insert a good copy of the gene to replace the BS1 mutation. He said it was perfectly safe."

"I guess that seems okay to me," said Matt.

"I'll be sure and ask Dr. Markowitz about this, but if she says it's safe, are we in agreement that we'll allow Dr. Svengaard to fix the BS1 mutation?"

"Fine with me."

"Now we get to the tougher stuff. Do you think we should try any of the positive or negative genetic engineering he talked about?"

"No. Absolutely not."

"Don't you have any hopes and dreams for our baby?"

"Sure. I hope he's athletic, smart, funny, and happy. That seems like a reasonable request."

"He?"

"Yeah. Don't you want a boy too?"

"It doesn't really matter to me. You know that."

In truth, it did matter to Sarah, at least a little bit. She had always imagined herself with a little girl she could teach to be a powerful, confident, successful woman. She had an idea.

"Let's make a list of traits we want our baby to have and some traits we want to avoid. Kind of a wish list for our baby. Whaddya think?"

"Okay, I'm game."

Sarah fetched some paper and they took a sheet each. They started with the five traits they would want their baby to have. It took Matt about thirty seconds, but Sarah agonized over her list for several minutes.

"Okay, hon, show me your list," she said eventually.

"No. You show me yours first."

Just like two second-graders. After a little bit of haggling, they agreed to reveal their lists at the same time.

"One, two, three!" counted Sarah.

At three, Matt turned over his list right away, but Sarah kept hers hidden for a few more seconds, yielding to her competitive streak.

Matt's list was no surprise to Sarah:

1. *BOY!!*
2. *tall*
3. *athletic*
4. *coordinated*
5. *smart*

Sarah's list was quite different:

1. *intelligent*
2. *attractive*
3. *confident*
4. *assertive*
5. *friendly*
6. *tall*

"Both of us want our son to be smart," observed Matt.

"Yeah, but I put intelligence first, and you put it last."

"At least it's on my list."

"First things first. Why is it so important to you to have a boy?"

"I want someone to play ball with."

"Girls play ball too!" snapped Sarah.

"Well, I want someone who can talk about guy stuff with me."

"What kind of guy stuff?"

"You know, just regular guy stuff — sports, girls, cars."

"Matt!"

"What's wrong with that? I want a boy and I want him to be just like me."

Although Sarah wanted a girl, gender seemed to be more important to Matt, so this might be something she could concede if it came down to it. She would agree to have a boy if Matt would agree to blue eyes. Sarah caught herself mid-thought. *I'm mentally bargaining the traits of our future child. How weird is that?*

"We haven't even conceived our child yet. Can we refrain from calling our baby a boy, at least for now?" said Sarah, hinting that she might agree to a boy at some point down the road.

"Okay."

"I see we both agree our child should be tall," Sarah continued.

"Yeah. Hey you put it as a sixth trait! I thought we were only supposed to do five."

"Sorry. I added it at the last minute and couldn't decide what to take out. Let's look at the rest of our lists. You want a good athlete, and I want someone who will be successful in her professional and personal life."

"Hey, you just said *her*. I thought we were leaving gender out of this."

"You're right, hon. Sorry."

"Let's do the negative traits," said Matt.

Sarah was pleased to see that he was getting into it now. "Ready, set, go!"

They both wrote as fast as they could.

"Done!" exclaimed Sarah, putting her pen down as if she had just finished the SATs.

"Hey, not fair," said Matt. "You got a head start."

"Did not!"

Second-graders again.

Without waiting for Matt to finish, Sarah grabbed his list:

1. *obesity*
2. *dwarfism*
3. *bal*

"Hey, I didn't have time to finish," said Matt. "So what do you have?"

Sarah held up her list for Matt to see:

1. *cancer*
2. *heart disease*
3. *alcoholism*
4. *mental retardation*
5. *cystic fibrosis*

Sarah frowned down at Matt's list. "What's 'bal'?"

"I was starting to write 'baldness' when you grabbed the paper from me."

"You really are superficial! All you care about is how our child will look."

"Don't you want our kid to be attractive?"

"Of, course, but—"

"You don't want a child who's a fat, bald dwarf, do you?"

Sarah laughed as she thought about giving birth to Grumpy or Dopey.

"See, my list isn't so bad," said Matt triumphantly.

"Fair enough," replied Sarah. "But I listed diseases and conditions that are much worse than baldness—cancer, cystic fibrosis, those sorts of things. We definitely don't want our child to have any of those, do we?"

"But aren't diseases a natural way to cull the herd?" Matt said.

Sarah was aghast. "Are you saying you want to cull our child?"

"Of course not. But aren't we fooling with Mother Nature if we try to eliminate diseases?"

"Is that what you really mean?"

Matt took a deep breath. "Well, wouldn't it be like playing God?"

There, it was out. God versus science.

Creationism versus evolution.

Matt and Sarah had many things in common, but their view on evolution was not one of them. Matt came from a deeply religious background; his parents and grandparents were devout Catholics. Matt believed in Jesus, an almighty God, and heaven and hell. As for evolution, he tried not to think about it.

Sarah and Matt had engaged in the creation–evolution discussion only twice before. The first time was when they had just started dating, when nothing really mattered other than the excitement in the bedroom and the blush of a new romance, and the second time was about a month after their wedding. That discussion led to one of the biggest arguments of their entire marriage. Sarah cited fossil evidence, DNA studies, and Darwin's work with finches, while Matt quoted the Bible, not very accurately, but well enough to make his points.

Matt had called Sarah a heathen, and Sarah had started throwing things—her shoes, a Kleenex box, a large notepad. When things looked hopeless, Matt came up with a solution they could both live with: They would use the term "Mother Nature" when discussing these sorts of things in future. That's how they left it five years ago, and neither of them had ever broached the subject again. Until now.

"I figured this was going to come up sooner or later," said Sarah.

"Me too. If we're going to talk about this, we need to agree to disagree," suggested Matt. "Can we just say Mother Nature, like we agreed a long time ago?"

Sarah was surprised that Matt seemed so conciliatory, but he was right—they really were talking about the same thing. Without saying a word, Sarah gave Matt a full-body hug and held it for what seemed like several minutes.

"Oh no, it's already eleven!" she said, catching sight of the clock over his shoulder. "I've got to get ready. We can finish this later."

Sarah pulled on jeans and a T-shirt and headed out the door. "I'll be back by two thirty. Love you."

"Love you too."

CHAPTER 8

Sarah arrived at the Cheesecake Factory first and took a table in the very back corner of the large dining room. After a few minutes, an attractive woman with shoulder-length red hair approached her table. She was wearing a cute green sundress that Sarah had seen in the J. Crew catalog.

"Hi, Sarah," the woman said, smiling.

"Dr. Markowitz?" said Sarah, unable to hide her surprise. "I'm so sorry. I didn't recognize you."

"No worries. A lot of people don't recognize me when I'm not in court."

"I'm so sorry," Sarah repeated.

"That's fine. And please, call me Candi."

As Candi Markowitz eased into her chair, she motioned for the waitress standing over by the bar. "We'd like a pitcher of strawberry margaritas and some chips."

"Thank you so much for meeting me today," Sarah said while they waited for their drinks. "As I told you over the phone, what I want to talk about is rather personal."

"That's fine with me. You've sent lots of business my way."

"I'm not sure how to begin. You see, Matt and I are trying to have a baby and — well, to make a very long story short, we're going to a fertility clinic."

"Which one?"

"New Beginnings. Do you know it?" asked Sarah.

"Yes, I've heard of it."

"Matt and I have been trying to have a baby for years. We've tried artificial insemination, IVF, ZIFT, and probably something else I can't remember right now."

"Wow, you two have been through a lot. I can't imagine how hard this must be for you," said Candi.

"About a month ago, Matt and I met with Dr. Svengaard at New Beginnings —"

"Dr. Bjorn Svengaard?"

"Yes," said Sarah cautiously.

"How long have you been working with him?"

"He's been our fertility doctor for three years. Why?"

"Bjorn is famous, internationally famous. He's also known for pushing boundaries."

"What exactly do you mean?"

"Well" — Candi paused — "Why don't you tell me what he's told you?"

Now Sarah was worried. "When we met with him last week, he told us we had one option left — intracytoplasmic sperm injection."

"Sure," said Candi. "That's where they take one of Matt's sperm and inject it directly into one of your eggs. Generally very successful. And very expensive. So what's your question?"

"Well, it seems Dr. Svengaard has added a twist. He's been genetically engineering the embryos during the procedure."

Candi's eyes widened. "Go on."

"He told us the reason we can't get pregnant is because our fertilized embryos are not properly implanting in my uterus, and he suspects that the problem is not with me or my uterus, but with the embryos. He thinks our embryos are genetically defective, which prevents them from implanting."

"That's plausible."

"I know. I've been reading up on this, and I've learned that if an embryo is severely genetically defective or malformed it may not implant, or if it does implant it might spontaneously miscarry within a few weeks, thus sparing the mother a useless pregnancy. Sort of nature's way of culling the herd."

"Well, I guess you could say that," said Candi, surprised by Sarah's choice of words.

Sarah tried to explain that she and Matt had been talking about evolution and Mother Nature and God and they had used that term in their discussion of diseases.

"That's okay," interrupted Candi. "I understand," though she clearly didn't.

"Dr. Svengaard told us that he can correct a defective gene—I think he called it the BS1 mutation—so that the embryo has a greater chance of implantation. Is that true?"

"To be honest with you, I've never heard of the BS1 mutation."

"Does that mean it doesn't exist?"

"Not necessarily. It may just mean that Bjorn hasn't published his findings yet. Although human genetic engineering is illegal in the US, a couple of fertility clinics overseas are experimenting with it. One of those clinics is in Sweden, where he received much of his training early in his career. He splits his time between that clinic and New Beginnings."

"I didn't know that. But that explains a lot," said Sarah.

"Explains what?"

"Why it's so hard to get an appointment with him. We usually have to wait two or three months for our next appointment. So, Candi, do you know anything about how this procedure might work?

"Not really. There are several ways to engineer animal embryos, but none of them have been tried on humans."

For the next half hour, Candi gave Sarah a quick tutorial on genetic engineering. She started simply, probing what Sarah already knew about genetics and cell division, and then dove into more complex topics such as gene splicing and gene delivery strategies. Most of what she talked about went far beyond the simple summary that Dr. Svengaard had given them five weeks earlier.

Throughout the impromptu genetics lecture, which Candi clearly relished, Sarah took lots of notes and asked more than a few questions. At one point, she found herself raising her hand before posing her inquiry, making both of them chuckle. Sarah felt like she was back in college, only this time she was sipping margaritas during the lecture.

But then she started to lose focus. Maybe it was the complexity of the topic or maybe it was the margaritas. Most likely it was a combination of the two. She understood the gist of what Candi was saying, but she wasn't processing all the details.

"So is genetic engineering safe? Does it work?"

"The short answers are maybe and maybe. It's not as simple as just taking a defective gene out and adding a new one in its place. When you do any of these procedures you might affect other genes. For many years, scientists thought that genes operated independently, but now we know that genes interact in very complex ways. Genes interact with other genes, and some genes are responsible for turning others on and off. And, of course, most genes interact with the environment in affecting our behavior. It's incredibly complicated, and our understanding of how it all works is extremely rudimentary right now."

Dr. Svengaard hadn't mentioned anything about the environment, Sarah thought. He'd only talked about genes.

Candi drained her second margarita. "It's these complex interactions that make us who we are. Did you know that humans have fewer genes than a single grain of rice?"

Sarah almost spat out her mouthful of chips. "How can that be?"

"See, it's not the absolute number of genes that matters—it's how they interact with each other and with the environment." Candi's face brightened. "Now that I think about it, one of my ex-boyfriends wasn't much smarter than a grain of rice."

They both laughed.

"So whenever you alter the genetic code of a cell in any way, there could be unintended consequences," Candi added.

"Unintended consequences?" The very term sent shivers through Sarah. "Such as?"

"I can't tell you what the unintended consequences might be in your case, but I can tell you about some genetic experiments on people and animals."

This was what Sarah wanted to hear about.

"The published literature on genetic engineering in humans is very small," Candi continued. "There was one famous case at the University of Pennsylvania back in the 1990s involving a young man with a rare blood disorder. His name was Jesse Gelsinger. Have you heard of him?"

"The name is vaguely familiar," replied Sarah.

"Jesse volunteered to be in a gene therapy trial for a liver disease. Although the disease is usually fatal in infancy, Jesse was eighteen and actually doing pretty well. The researchers injected Jesse with a corrected copy of his defective gene and four days later he was dead."

"Why'd he die?"

"It wasn't the gene they inserted. He died because his immune system reacted to the viral vector they used to transport the gene."

"Huh?"

"In order to insert a new gene into an organism, scientists usually use some sort of virus as a carrier for the gene. That carrier virus is called a vector. Viruses are used because they're really good at invading cells."

"Yes, Dr. Svengaard told us about viral vectors."

"I think the scientists in Jesse's case used an adenovirus, the same type that causes the common cold, to deliver the genes. For some reason, he had a massive reaction to the adenovirus. I don't think they ever figured out exactly what went wrong."

"But what they did to Jesse is different than what Dr. Svengaard told us about, right?"

"Well, yes and no. Did Bjorn tell you about the difference between somatic cell and germ-line genetic engineering?" asked Candi.

"I don't think so," replied Sarah. "If he did, I don't remember."

"Well, they're actually quite different. In somatic cell genetic engineering the goal is to alter the DNA of a group of cells in a living organism. That's the method that was used with Jesse Gelsinger and it's the procedure scientists are using to try to cure diseases such as cancer, cystic fibrosis, and immune deficiency disorders such as SCID. But in your case we're talking about germ-line genetic engineering, which is altering the DNA of the entire organism. Potentially very exciting, but also fraught with danger."

"So how does germ-line engineering work?"

"It alters the genetic code of an egg, sperm, or a very early-stage embryo. The entire organism is impacted by the genetic engineering, and the changes will be passed on to future generations through germ cells — sperm or eggs. As the embryo divides and develops, the early embryonic cells differentiate into all of the many types of cells of the body — skin cells, lung cells, heart cells, and so forth."

"But how can a lung cell and skin cell have the same genetic code?" Sarah asked.

"When the egg is first fertilized by the sperm, the resulting zygote is the parent cell for all the cells that will make up the living organism. In the beginning, as the cells start dividing, they're all the same. These embryonic stem cells can produce any type of cell in the mature organism. Pretty soon, though, the cells in different parts of the developing embryo become specialized. Some become skin cells, some bone cells, and so on."

"Huh? I'm lost," admitted Sarah. "I thought all the cells in the embryo have the same exact DNA."

"They do. In fact, with a couple of exceptions, all of the cells in your body have the exact same DNA. What makes a skin cell a skin cell instead of a lung cell is the fact that there are genetic switches that turn genes on and off. So hair-related genes are switched on in hair cells and off in lung cells." Candi paused. "I've simplified things greatly here, but you get the idea."

Simplified greatly? What's the complicated version?

"This is why germ-line engineering is potentially so dangerous," Candi continued. "Let's take a simple case of an embryo in which the eye color is changed to blue through germ-line genetic engineering. If the procedure is successful, the child will be born with blue eyes, but she will also carry the altered eye-color gene in every cell in her body. When the eye-color gene was originally altered, the genetic engineering process may have affected other genes in the embryo's DNA. That seemingly simple germ-line engineering of an eye-color gene could cause her to lose her sense of smell, for example, or have purple hair, or grow a third arm. We just don't know enough about genetics yet to predict any of this with any degree of certainty. Hence the possibility of unintended consequences."

The term sounded even worse the second time.

"I know you and Matt are desperate to have a baby," Candi said, "but you should think very carefully before proceeding with even the simplest forms of germ-line genetic engineering. You wouldn't want to be a guinea pig in one of Bjorn's experiments."

That's a funny way to put it, thought Sarah. We aren't volunteering to be part of any experiments. We just want to have a baby.

"Thank you so much, Candi. I really appreciate your help," she said. Sarah looked down at her watch. She could still make it home by two thirty.

"Miss, one more pitcher of margaritas please!" Candi shouted over the din of the restaurant. "So Sarah, how's life in your law firm?"

"Pretty good. Busy as usual."

"I heard you got the baby-killer case!" Candi spoke so loudly that the man at the table behind them turned around.

"My client is innocent unless she's proven guilty!"

"I'm sorry," said Candi, blushing ever so slightly. "I should know better. Can you tell me about it?"

"It's a tough one. The baby died of carbon monoxide poisoning. My client was found unconscious in her running car in her garage with her baby strapped in the car seat in the back. It seems pretty cut and dried."

"So what's your defense?"

"I don't really have one. My client—her name is Lexi Conway—says her baby was already dead before she pulled into her garage. She claims she went home to kill herself to join her baby in heaven. Trouble is, all of the medical evidence points to carbon monoxide poisoning as the cause of death. I want to believe that it was just a terrible accident, but Lexi has been very uncooperative. The more I've talked with her, the more evasive she's become, and that's making it really hard for me to help her. And she's got quite a temper. I'm not saying it's bad enough to cause her to kill her own child, but she can be explosive at times."

"Have you thought about insanity?"

"I had a psychiatrist appointed and he said there's no evidence that Lexi is insane."

"How about a plea bargain?"

"I haven't asked the DA about that because Lexi says she won't go for it." Sarah stopped. "Perhaps I've said too much."

"That's okay. I always consider our communications to

be privileged," Candi assured her.

"This case has been really hard on me. Matt and I have been trying so hard to have a baby and here I am representing someone who is accused of killing hers." Sarah stood up. "It's getting late. I better go. Thanks again for meeting me today. Is it okay to get in touch if I have any further questions?"

"Hang on—I think I might have an idea about your case," Candi said suddenly.

"Oh?"

"It might be a little crazy, but hear me out."

"All right," said Sarah, sitting down again. "But I promised my husband I'd be home by two thirty."

"Just give me five minutes." Candi filled both of their glasses with fresh margaritas. "You say your client has quite a temper?"

"That's right."

"Does she seem out of control when she gets mad?"

"I guess."

"Scientists have started looking for genetic markers of aggression. Some of the studies seem quite promising."

"I don't see how this can help Lexi," Sarah said.

"What I'm suggesting is that you might be able to argue that Lexi's aggressive behavior was somehow caused by her genetic makeup, just like some people are genetically predisposed to schizophrenia, obesity, or alcoholism. In fact, one line of research just might apply to Lexi. I'm not that familiar with it, but it's worth looking into. A couple of studies have identified a specific gene in humans that's associated with increased levels of violence. I think it has to do with MAOA, an enzyme that breaks down certain neurotransmitters in the brain. There's a gene responsible for the production of MAOA and it has several variations, each of which produces different levels of MAOA. The basic idea is that people with one of the variations have very low levels of MAOA and are more likely to be violent than those with high levels. Some people call this genetic variant the Warrior Gene."

"But what are the chances that Lexi has this Warrior Gene?"

"Better than you might expect. I think it's about thirty or forty percent."

"Wow! But if this Warrior Gene causes violence and it's so common, why aren't people killing each other left and right?"

"Well, first of all, I didn't say it always led to *killing*, just to violence. Lots of people are violent. Also, I think there has to be some sort of environmental trigger for the gene to activate."

"Like what?"

"I don't know. This isn't really my area of expertise."

"I must admit, it sounds pretty far-fetched to me."

"Maybe so, but what if Lexi has this gene? What if she has the Warrior Gene?"

"I guess that means she would be more likely to be violent."

"What if you take that argument one step further?"

"I'm not sure I'm following you, Candi."

"What if you argue that Lexi killed her baby because she was genetically programmed to do so?"

"What? Like a robot?" Sarah was incredulous.

"Sort of, but not exactly."

"Who's going to buy that?"

"That's *your* job, Sarah. You can convince a jury of anything! All you have to do is raise a reasonable doubt."

"Hmmm."

"In any event, I'd be happy to consult with you about the Warrior Gene if you think it's worth pursuing."

"Why not." Sarah paused. "Of course, we still have a big if. We don't know if Lexi has this Warrior Gene. Odds are she doesn't."

"But if she does, we could make legal history!" Candi said brightly.

"Let's go for it. I've got nothing else at this point." Sarah shrugged. "I'll ask the court to appoint you on Monday morning. So what should we do now?"

"First, we need to look into the research about the Warrior Gene to make sure it says what I think it says. Second, we need to find out if Lexi has any DNA samples floating around that we can have access to. Can you do some digging on that?"

"Sure, but why don't we just get a swab from her cheek?"

"The jailers would never let us do that without a court order. And a court order will make the DA suspicious. We need to find another way to get a sample of her DNA."

"Who might have a sample of Lexi's DNA?" asked Sarah.

"You'd be surprised how often people give biological samples. They usually give blood samples when they get arrested, but we don't want to try to access Lexi's booking sample so we don't tip off the DA. Also people routinely give urine samples when they apply for jobs. Has Lexi applied for any jobs recently?"

"I think she applied for a couple right before she got pregnant."

"It's probably been too long ago, but let's see if any of those samples still exist. Keep in mind that this is really a long shot. We don't know if Lexi has the Warrior Gene, and even if she does, this defense has never been tried in court before, as far as I know — it'll be quite a feat to convince a jury to acquit your client of killing her baby just because she's got some bad DNA."

"Still, it's worth a shot," said Sarah.

"Wouldn't it be something if we could pull this off?"

Sarah looked at her watch and let out a little yelp. "Yikes. It's past three! I've got to go. Can I call you later this week?"

"Sure." Candi took out a business card and scribbled her

cell number on the back. "Call me any time."

As Sarah walked out to her car she called Matt. She was almost an hour late, but she figured he would understand.

Matt picked up on the first ring, and he didn't wait for Sarah to say hi. "Where are you? It's way past three. You said you would be back by two thirty. Are you okay?"

"I'm fine, hon. I just finished talking with Candi."

"Who?"

"Dr. Markowitz."

"So what'd she say?"

"She told me I might have a defense for Lexi!" Sarah could feel her enthusiasm growing. "It seems there's this genetic marker for aggression called the Warrior Gene, and if Lexi has it I might be able to convince a jury — "

"But what about our baby?" interrupted Matt. "Didn't you ask her about the genetic engineering?" Matt shouted so loudly Sarah had to hold her phone away from her ear.

"Calm down. Yes, I asked her. It's just that I'm excited about this new defense."

"Aren't you excited about our baby?"

"Of course I am," said Sarah. "Candi gave us lots to think about. We can talk about it when I get home."

"Did she say that genetic engineering was safe?"

"She told me it was theoretically possible to engineer an embryo so it is more likely to implant."

"But?"

"But what, hon?

"I know you, Sarah. I can tell there's a but."

"Well, she said that whenever scientists try genetic engineering there's always the possibility of unintended consequences."

"Such as?"

"She didn't really know because this is such a new procedure."

"What advice did she have about the extra genetic engineering — you know, all of the positive and negative stuff Dr. Svengaard told us about?"

"Well, I didn't exactly ask her about that."

"What do you mean you didn't ask her? I knew I should have come along." Now Matt sounded angry.

"I told her that Dr. Svengaard wanted to genetically alter the embryo so that it would be more likely to implant, but I never got around to the other stuff. We got off track and started talking about Lexi's case. I'm just so excited about—"

Matt hung up before she could finish. She would have a bit of making up to do when she got home.

When Sarah reached her car, she realized that she felt a bit woozy—the margaritas had been stronger than she'd thought—and she decided to walk off some of the alcohol before driving home. There wasn't really anywhere to go, so she just did some slow laps around the Cheesecake Factory parking lot. By the time she finally started up the car it was almost four o'clock. Matt was going to be livid, but there was nothing she could do about that now.

When she got home she opened the front door as quietly as she could and stepped slowly down the front hallway. She could hear the television on in the den. It sounded like Matt was watching a game.

"Hon, I'm home," Sarah called out.

There was no reply. Matt just turned up the sound on the TV.

CHAPTER 9

Sarah slept in on Monday morning, and by the time she got to the office it was almost ten o'clock. Although the lobby of 17 West Regency Avenue was buzzing, she dipped her hand in the waterfall as she did every day. She felt like she needed all the luck she could get.

Friday was going to be a big day for her. She and Matt had their appointment at New Beginnings in the morning, and Lexi's next court appearance was in the afternoon. She was excited about both, but her excitement about the DNA defense was mixed with anticipation while her excitement about genetic engineering was laced with fear.

She pulled out her notes from her conversation with Candi Markowitz, turned on her computer, and began searching the Internet for everything she could find on the Warrior Gene. There wasn't much to find.

The story began several decades ago with a Dutch schoolteacher who had tried to determine why so many men in his family had been violent over the years. His carefully constructed family tree helped researchers identify a gene that seemed to be linked to aggression. They discovered that this gene controls the production of monoamine oxidase-A—MAOA—an enzyme that helps break down certain neurotransmitters in the brain, such as dopamine, serotonin, and norepinephrine, that help regulate aggression in humans and other animals.

Sarah learned that there were several variants of the

gene, some that produced low levels of MAOA and some that produced high levels. At this point she had to skim the technical explanations concerning how the gene governs the production of MAOA, but she was able to glean an important fact—it was one particular variant of the gene, one that produces very low levels of MAOA, which had been linked to aggressive behavior.

She was surprised at how common the Warrior Gene was. About one-third of Caucasians had the Warrior Gene variant, but all the studies made the same point that Candi had explained on Saturday: having the Warrior Gene wasn't enough in itself to make someone act aggressively. It had to be activated by some sort of environmental trigger to lead to violence.

Virtually every study on the link between the Warrior Gene and aggression had focused on one type of environmental influence—childhood trauma or abuse. These studies suggested that the predisposition to violence in some men sprung from the Warrior Gene, and that childhood trauma could activate the gene. That helped to explain why not all men with the Warrior Gene were aggressive, and why not all men who were abused as children turned out to be violent adults. It took both to be present—Warrior Gene and childhood trauma—a classic example of the interactive effects of nature and nurture on human behavior.

Although no one seemed to understand exactly how the Warrior Gene worked, that wasn't a problem for Sarah's defense. All she needed was for the theory to be plausible. She didn't have to prove that the Warrior Gene caused Lexi to kill her baby; she just had to present a *reasonable possibility* that it did.

As she continued her research, she discovered something important about the Warrior Gene that Dr. Markowitz hadn't mentioned: the gene lay on the X chromosome, which meant that men were more likely to be affected by it than women. Men only have one X chromosome, so if a male has the Warrior Gene, there is no other variant to cancel its effects. But females have two X chromosomes, and if a woman has the Warrior Gene there is a good chance that it would be negated by a good variant of the MAOA gene.

This revelation dimmed Sarah's enthusiasm for the Warrior Gene defense somewhat. Lexi wasn't male, so it was less likely that it would affect her. In fact, there hadn't been a single study on women, so it wasn't even clear that the Warrior Gene affected women at all. On top of this, there was no evidence that Lexi had been abused as a child. Maybe the Warrior Gene defense was not going to be the panacea she hoped for.

She browsed through the research articles one more time. In the middle was a short article she had skipped over earlier. This time Sarah's gaze landed on a single important word in the abstract — *experiment*. This study was an experiment!

Indeed, this was a carefully controlled examination of whether men with the Warrior Gene were more aggressive than men without it, but it was one of those artificially contrived studies that psych professors love to run. Male participants were allowed to earn money based on their performance in a simple vocabulary task. Then an anonymous male partner, linked only by computer, could take some money from the original participant's earnings. Afterwards, each participant was given an opportunity to punish his partner by forcing him to ingest a really hot, spicy sauce.

The findings *were* interesting — at least Sarah thought so. Males with the low-activity MAOA gene — the Warrior Gene — exhibited more aggression than the high-activity MAOA group, and the effect was much greater when the males were provoked — that is, when their partner took money from them. So in this experiment, the provocation interacted with the Warrior Gene to produce aggression. The provocation acted as an environmental trigger. Sarah's excitement was tempered by the fact that, as is often the case in psychology studies, plenty of deception was involved in the experiment — there was no "male partner," just a computer, and it didn't have to eat any hot sauce. The entire setup was carefully controlled to see how the participants would react.

Male college students sitting at computers deciding whether to give imaginary hot sauce to imaginary people — it was a far cry from a nineteen-year-old girl killing her own baby in real life. But it was a step in the right direction.

* * *

On Wednesday, Sarah called Candi.

"I've been doing lots of reading about the Warrior Gene," she explained, "and I'm not so sure it's going to help Lexi after all."

"What? I disagree. I think we can pull this off!" Candi was almost breathless in her enthusiasm.

Sarah winced at Candi's *we*. "Maybe so, but I found a couple of potential problems."

"Like what?"

"First off, this Warrior Gene is located on the X chromosome, right?"

"Correct."

"That means men only have to have one copy of the Warrior Gene to be affected by it."

"Yes, because men have one X chromosome and one Y."

"But women need two copies of the gene, right?"

"Maybe, maybe not. That's true for most recessive sex-linked X chromosome disorders, because the recessive gene on one X chromosome is nullified by the dominant gene on the other one. Women need the recessive genes on both Xs in order for the phenotype to reflect the recessive traits. That's why male pattern baldness is much more common among men than women. Same thing is true about hemophilia. Women can have hemophilia, but because it's caused by a recessive gene on the X chromosome it's much less common among women than men."

"So that would be true about the Warrior Gene too, right?"

"That's not altogether clear. I couldn't find any studies on the Warrior Gene that have been conducted on women."

"Me neither."

"Also, it's not clear that this is a true recessive gene. Maybe women need two copies of the low-activity gene to prevent normal levels of MAOA from being produced or maybe they just need one. We just don't know. What's the second problem?"

"As you mentioned on Saturday, the gene doesn't actually cause aggression by itself. It has to be activated by something in the environment. As far as I can tell, almost all of the studies on the Warrior Gene have focused on childhood abuse as a possible environmental trigger. But it seems that Lexi had a loving, supportive family when she was growing up and didn't experience any sort of childhood trauma or abuse, so I don't think those studies are going to help us."

"You may be right," said Candi. "But I found another study that might hold more promise for us."

"You mean the hot sauce study?"

"Exactly!"

"But Lexi didn't give anyone any hot sauce. She killed a defenseless baby. Hardly the same thing."

"True, but the hot sauce study suggests that if someone with the Warrior Gene is provoked they might react more violently than someone without the Warrior Gene."

"But how could a baby provoke an adult?"

"How about with a really stinky diaper?" Candi

laughed, but Sarah didn't share her amusement.

"You're kidding, right?"

"Of course, but you get the idea. You can argue that almost anything could be a trigger. Remember, all you have to do is raise a reasonable doubt. You can do it, Sarah."

"I guess so. But we still don't know if Lexi has the Warrior Gene. I've run into one dead end after another trying to get a sample of her DNA. There are no job application samples, nothing from her high school. I even tried her family doctor. Nothing. I don't know where else to look. We may have to get a court order after all."

"Actually, that won't be necessary." There was a hint of mischievousness in Candi's voice.

"How come?" Sarah asked, feeling a little uneasy.

"I already got a sample."

"How? From where?"

"From Lexi. I've already submitted it for testing and we should have the results in about four or five weeks. Until then, we need to—"

"You did what?" Sarah was furious. "I didn't give you permission to do that. When did you talk to Lexi? How could you have done that without telling me?"

"I'm sorry. I thought you would be excited about this."

"Well, you thought wrong!"

Neither of them said anything for what felt like a long time, which gave Sarah time to calm down a little.

"How did you do it? Did you get a court order?" she asked.

"No. I just visited Lexi at the jail yesterday morning and took the sample myself. Used a cheek swab. Only took fifteen seconds."

"But how did you do it without a court order? I can't even shake Lexi's hand when I see her at the jail. The sheriffs are standing right there outside the interview room and it's all glass."

"Let's just say I used my feminine charms."

"What?"

"I figured the jailers would be mostly male, even in the women's section, so I used that to my advantage."

"I don't understand."

"When I went to see Lexi, I told her who I was and explained that I was working for you. We made some small talk for a few moments, and then I stood up, leaned waaaay over the table, and swabbed Lexi's cheek. The sheriff was more interested in looking at me than in watching what I was doing. It was over in an instant."

While Sarah admired Candi's chutzpah, she was offended that a female professional would use her appearance in that way.

"Doesn't it bother you that the sheriff was looking at your ass?" she said.

"Whatever it takes, Sarah. It's a sexist world out there, and it usually works against us. Every once in a while, we girls get to use it to our advantage, and that's all I did. Don't you feel like turning the tables on the guys every once in a while?

"No. That's stooping to their level and it just makes it worse."

"Anyway, you have to admit I was pretty clever."

"I guess."

"And we've got our DNA sample."

"That *is* good," Sarah admitted. "But what about the chain of custody of the sample? How will we establish that?"

"I'll just testify about it at trial. I personally delivered the sample to the lab myself. No one else ever had it."

"What will you say about how you got it?"

"The truth."

"Won't you be embarrassed?"

"Not at all, but I bet that sheriff's deputy will be!"

Candi was right. She hadn't done anything illegal in

obtaining the sample. She might have bent a few jailhouse rules, but that was more of a problem for the jailers than for her.

After hanging up, Sarah stared out the window. She had been fighting all her life for gender equality in a male-dominated profession, determined to get people to respect her for her brains instead of her legs, and she was more than a little mad at Candi. *It's women like her who ruin it for the rest of us. How can I be taken seriously when she's shaking her ass to get what she wants?*

Sarah still had to figure out how to present her Warrior Gene defense. She could argue that Lexi's DNA caused her to have diminished capacity, making her guilty only of manslaughter, not first-degree murder.

But that wasn't what Sarah wanted. She wanted a verdict of not guilty — complete absolution — and she wasn't going to settle for anything less. She wasn't going to argue that Lexi's faulty DNA caused her to be *less* culpable. No, she was going to claim that Lexi's DNA excused her completely — that she had no choice, no free will when she killed her baby. No *mens rea*, no crime.

* * *

It was Thursday morning and only one more day until Lexi's court appearance and the appointment at New Beginnings.

Since she was ready for Lexi's arraignment, Sarah decided to do a little more online research about genetic engineering. Most of what she found concerned somatic cell engineering, the type used by scientists in an effort to cure cystic fibrosis and other diseases, the type of genetic engineering that had killed young Jesse Gelsinger.

She learned that somatic cell engineering had been used on humans since the early 1990s. Probably the most notable studies involved a gene therapy regimen designed to treat

Severe Combined Immunodeficiency, or SCID. Scientists inserted healthy genes into SCID patients' blood in the hope that the inserted genes would express normal enzymes, which the SCID patients could not produce on their own. Some of these attempts actually worked, and a four-year-old girl named Ashanti DeSilva gained notoriety as the first human to be treated successfully with gene therapy.

More than a dozen other patients were treated with similar procedures, but unfortunately complications developed. A significant percentage of them developed cancer and the gene therapy trials were stopped. It turned out that the retrovirus used to insert the healthy gene into the patients' blood cells had somehow activated an oncogene, a type of gene responsible for many cancers. What struck Sarah was the apparent unpredictability of the side effects. It wasn't the altered target gene that had caused the problem; it was a different gene that had been activated by the viral vector. Now she really understood what Candi Markowitz meant by "unintended consequences."

Sarah turned back to her search for germ-line studies. No matter how hard she looked, she couldn't find a single legitimate scientific study on germ-line engineering in humans, other than a few attempts to demonstrate that such procedures were possible. If germ-line genetic engineering was indeed being done, as Dr. Svengaard claimed, the results had not yet seen the light of day. She did find a few scattered claims about engineered human embryos, two from South Korea and another from Italy, but none of those studies had been verified by the international scientific community.

So Dr. Svengaard is a pioneer, Sarah thought. He's willing to take risks that others won't. That's how science advances — on the backs of pioneers. But am I willing to let him be a pioneer with my baby?

* * *

Sarah and Matt had just finished a quiet dinner and were chatting over their decaf coffees.

"Hon, our fertility appointment is tomorrow. What are we going to do about our baby?"

"The more I think about it, the more scared I become," said Matt. "I'm leaning toward not doing any of it."

"Not even to correct the BS1 mutation? If we don't do that, we may never have a baby of our own. I *really* want a baby."

"Me too, but what if something goes wrong?"

"Life's full of risks. I know genetic engineering is risky, but I want a baby, and I'm willing to take some risks to get one."

"Tiger, do you really think it's safe?"

"I can't really answer that question, hon. Dr. Svengaard's techniques are so advanced that there hasn't been much research on whether they're safe or not." Sarah decided not to mention the possibility of unintended consequences.

"*Not much* research?"

"Actually, not any."

"That's what I thought. Case closed. I'm not willing to do it."

"But I am, hon. I want to have a baby." Sarah was not going to give up yet. Matt didn't call her Tiger for nothing. "Remember those lists we made last Saturday? The ones with all of the baby traits?"

"Sure."

"I thought it was kind of fun. Let's do it again."

"I don't know. I don't want to think about it anymore."

"C'mon, it'll be fun. This time, let's not make separate lists — let's make one master list together."

And that's exactly what they did. They made long lists,

short lists, realistic lists, fantasy lists. They wrote and scribbled, crossed out and started over. They made a game of throwing their discarded lists into the trash can on the far side of the room, which, by the end of the evening, was surrounded by dozens of paper balls, with only a few finding the intended target.

They talked about hair color and eye color, height and weight, athletic ability and intelligence. Then it got kind of crazy.

"Since we're making a super-baby, let's give him some super powers," suggested Matt.

Sarah started another list. "How about the ability to fly?" she began.

"Sounds good. Also, super strong and super fast."

"How about super smart?"

"Tiger, I've never heard of a superhero who was super smart. What would he do? Solve crosswords faster than anyone else?"

"I see your point."

"I've got one more," said Matt. "X-ray vision."

"You pervert!" Sarah laughed and hit Matt with a large cushion.

Sarah had been right. It was fun to make the list together. After six hours of writing and revising, laughing and squabbling, Sarah and Matt had their final list. Sarah wrote it out as neatly as she could.

Sarah and Matt's Baby

Boy
Brown hair
Brown eyes
Tall (over 6 feet)
Athletic (enhanced slow-twitch and
*   fast-twitch muscles)*
Smart (enhanced cognitive processing
*   speed)*

To close the deal, Sarah had acceded to virtually all of Matt's preferences. This wasn't her dream baby; it was Matt's. But that was fine with her. They were going to have a baby.

"You know what? We've created a mini version of you," said Sarah. "Look at it. That's you! We're going to have a little baby Matt. Maybe we should just clone you and be done with it," Sarah said with a yawn.

"There's one more thing I'd like to add to the list," said Matt. He picked up the pen and wrote:

Ten fingers and ten toes

Sarah smiled. "I love you, Matt."

"I love you too, Tiger. Let's go to bed. I'm exhausted."

She looked at the clock. "I'm just going to stay up. It's almost three fifteen and I'll never be able to get up in the morning if I go to sleep now. I'll wake you at eight so we've plenty of time to get ready for our appointment."

He kissed her tenderly on the top of her head and shuffled into the bedroom.

Sarah made some tea and settled in for an all-night marathon of *Sex and the City*. After the second episode, she closed her eyes for just a moment.

CHAPTER 10

"Sarah, Sarah! It's eight thirty! Wake up!"

Exhausted and stiff from sleeping on the couch, Sarah stretched and rubbed her eyes. "What? What happened?"

"You overslept! *We* overslept. We've got to go in a half hour!"

"Shoot!"

Sarah leaped up and threw on her clothes, quickly checking in the mirror that she looked presentable. Then she grabbed her briefcase, and stuffed her makeup and brushes into a large purse.

"Hon, can you drive?" she asked Matt. "I can do my hair and makeup in the car." She was fully alert now, the grogginess swept away by the excitement of the day ahead.

They arrived at New Beginnings with five minutes to spare. Almost immediately they were ushered into Dr. Svengaard's office where he was waiting for them. He motioned for them to sit down.

"So, Mr. and Mrs. Wong, what have you decided to do?"

"We've decided to do that genetic engineering stuff you told us about last time," said Matt.

"Which part?" inquired Dr. Svengaard.

"We want you to fix our embryos so they'll plant in Sarah's uterus."

"You mean *implant*?"

"Yes, sure," said Matt. "We might want to do some of that other stuff too."

Dr. Svengaard's face lit up. "Great!"

Sarah jumped in. "I've been doing some reading about all of this, and I'm curious why you don't use CRISPR instead of the genetic engineering you've told us about."

"I see you've done your homework, Mrs. Wong. CRISPR has certainly got a lot of attention recently, but it's really more hype than reality. My method is much more promising."

"But I thought CRISPR was easier to do than other types of genetic engineering," said Sarah.

"In some ways it is. But the problem is that the CRISPR technology is controlled by a few big biotech companies, and there's a lot of patent litigation about who actually owns the rights to it. It's all very messy. That's why I've been innovating on my own. I want to serve people like you and your husband, not the big biotechs."

"But if CRISPR is better, maybe we should find someone who would be willing to try it," said Sarah.

"It is NOT better!" Dr. Svengaard said forcefully. "There is nothing better than what I am doing here. Nothing!"

He spun around, got up, and strode over to the large filing cabinet. After unlocking the top drawer, he pulled out two sheets of paper. They looked like the lists of genetic procedures they had seen before, only these sheets had a small square box to the left of each item and room for two signatures at the bottom of the page, "Mother" on the left and "Father" on the right. There was no place for a date, and no place for Dr. Svengaard's signature.

Sarah was struck by the informality of the forms. They didn't even have the name of the New Beginnings Fertility Clinic on them anywhere. They certainly didn't look like most legal documents she had ever seen, and she was about to inquire about their validity when Dr. Svengaard started talking about them in a rapid-fire delivery reminiscent of the TV pitchmen for the Ab Roller, Veg-o-Matic, and ShamWow.

"All right. Here are the two lists I showed you last time. Let's look at diseases and conditions first." The doctor put the sheet on his desk so it faced Sarah and Matt. "Are there any conditions you don't want to get rid of?"

"No. Of course we want to get rid of them all," said Sarah. "Who wouldn't?"

"You'd be surprised. Some people want to leave these things to chance."

"Really?"

"Not cancer or Huntington's, but things like baldness."

"Well, we want to get rid of them all. Right, hon?"

"Yep. All of them," agreed Matt.

Dr. Svengaard checked all twenty-two boxes on the "Diseases and Conditions" list and circled the first defect on the list, BS1, in a big blue swirl. He handed his pen over for Matt and Sarah to sign at the bottom.

"The first thing I'll do is test each embryo to see if any of these alleles are present," the doctor explained while they signed.

"That's the pre-implantation genetic diagnosis procedure you told us about last time, right?" said Sarah.

"Right. We already know that some of your embryos are likely to have the BS1 mutation, but I don't know if I'll have to do any additional genetic engineering to get rid of any of these others. Given your family history, I'd say it's about fifty-fifty."

Sarah scanned the list one more time and stopped at item fifteen. She didn't remember seeing that entry last time, but now it stood out from the others:

MAOA Low-Activity Variant

"Dr. Svengaard, was number fifteen on the list you gave us last time?"

"Yes, this list is exactly the same as the one I showed you before. Why do you ask?"

"The low-activity variant of the MAOA gene—that's what some people call the Warrior Gene, isn't it?"

"Yes, it is. How do you know about that?"

"I must have read about it somewhere. Do you know much about it?"

"Not really. But it's easy to identify and correct, so I've included it on my list."

Dr. Svengaard took the signed "Diseases and Conditions" list from Sarah and positioned the "Genetic Enhancements" form in front of them. "Now, let's move on to the positive genetic engineering. As I told you before, you can pick four items from this list."

"What? I don't remember you saying that," said Sarah, feeling a little alarmed.

"Oh, I'm sure I told you. As I explained last time, these procedures are very complex, and I have to do all of the genetic engineering within seventy-two hours of harvesting your eggs, so four is the absolute most I can do. Even four is pushing it."

"You never told us about the four-item limit," Sarah said testily.

Dr. Svengaard ignored Sarah's barb and pressed on. "So, what gender do you want again? A girl is it?"

Sarah looked at Matt and smiled. "No, we've decided we want a boy."

"Are you sure, Tiger?" Matt asked.

"I'm sure."

"A boy it is." Dr. Svengaard made a note in their folder. "Now I need you to choose four traits on this form."

Sarah pulled out the list she and Matt had made just a few hours earlier. "We've got six traits on our list—seven if you count gender. It took us a long time to come up with this list. I don't know how we're going to choose four of them in just a few minutes."

"Can I see your list? Maybe I can help," said the doctor.

"I don't know … Is that okay with you, hon?"

"I guess so," Matt said reluctantly.

Sarah pushed the list across the table to Dr. Svengaard, who studied it for less than a minute.

"The way I see it, two of these — hair color and eye color — are purely aesthetic. The other four — height over six feet, enhanced fast-twitch muscles, enhanced slow-twitch muscles, and enhanced cognitive processing speed — are all functionally relevant to success in sports, school, and life. If it were me, I would choose these last four."

Sarah's mind was racing and she was breathing so hard it was difficult for her to hear Dr. Svengaard clearly. "But it's not up to you, is it?" she snapped.

"Of course not, I'm sorry."

"We really had our mind set on all six of these. Can't we do them all?" she said.

"I'm sorry, but four is the absolute maximum I can do. If you've changed your mind about going through with this, there are many other couples who will jump at the chance to participate in my study."

Why did he refer to it as a study, Sarah wondered. Maybe Candi Markowitz was right. Maybe they were just guinea pigs for this mad scientist.

Dr. Svengaard went to take the forms, but Sarah pulled them back out of his reach. "No, we're going ahead with this," she said.

She turned to Matt. "What do you think, hon? Maybe Dr. Svengaard is right. Who really cares about hair color and eye color anyway? Besides, our son can always dye his hair or wear colored contacts."

"Okay, I'm fine with that."

Sarah checked the four boxes on the "Genetic Enhancements" form, signed on the line that said "Mother" and then pushed the form toward Matt for him to sign.

"What's this at the very bottom of your list?" Dr. Svengaard asked, pointing at Sarah and Matt's handwritten list. "Ten fingers and ten toes. What's that about?"

"Nothing," said Matt. "Just an inside joke."

"I don't get it," replied Dr. Svengaard.

That figures, thought Sarah. If there's a gene for humor, this guy doesn't have it. She handed the "Genetic Enhancements" form back to the doctor, who glanced at it and gave it right back to her.

"I forgot to tell you – you need to rank your four choices from one to four," he said.

"How come?" Sarah could feel herself growing more annoyed by the minute.

"In the event that I have to use genetic engineering to eliminate one or more of the diseases or conditions on the other page, I'll only have time to do three, or maybe even just two of these enhancements. So you need to rank them from one to four, with one being your first preference and four your last."

Sarah had had enough. "Maybe we should just call this off," she said. "I don't like being pressured like this. Let's go, Matt."

"Come on, Tiger. I really want to have a little boy," said Matt. "Let's just get this done."

She really wanted a baby too, but she hated feeling like she was buying a used car. "Dr. Svengaard, would you mind leaving us alone for a few minutes so we can talk about this?"

"I'm afraid I can't do that," he said. "But I tell you what, I'll answer some emails while you two talk. Will that do?"

Sarah nodded, and the doctor swung around to his computer keyboard.

"The highest priority is easy," Sarah whispered to Matt.

"I agree," said Matt. "Fast-twitch muscles."

"What? I was going to say enhanced cognitive

processing speed. Do you really think that sports are more important than academics?"

"Of course not. Okay, let's put cognitive processing speed first, fast-twitch muscles second, slow-twitch muscles third, and height last."

Sarah thought about Matt's suggestion for a moment. "But height is really important to me, hon. Being short has always been a real disadvantage for me and I don't want our child to go through the same thing."

"I guess you're right," said Matt. "So we'll switch the order of the last two — height then slow-twitch muscles."

"Can't we put height second? Please? For me?"

"Oh all right. We might not have an Olympic athlete in the family, but at least we'll have a tall, smart son," he said. "I never can win an argument with you."

"Thank you, honey!" Sarah leaned forward and kissed him right on the lips, catching him by surprise. "Dr. Svengaard, we're ready," she said.

"So what's the order then?" asked the doctor.

"Cognitive processing speed first, then height, fast-twitch muscles, and slow-twitch muscles, in that order," said Matt.

While Dr. Svengaard added the numbers next to the boxes on the "Genetic Enhancement" form, Sarah kissed Matt again. This time he was ready.

Then Dr. Svengaard put both forms in a plain manila folder, folded his hands on the desk, and looked directly at Sarah. "I have one more form for you to look at. It's something new I've just started, and it's completely optional. Would you like to see it?"

Isn't *all* of this completely optional? thought Sarah. "Sure."

The doctor pulled a single sheet of paper from a drawer in his desk and placed it gently on the desk in front of Sarah.

"So what do you think?" he asked, looking up at her.

Project Beta
- Enhanced sense of smell (*Canis lupus*)
- Enhanced hearing (*Mus musculus*)
- Enhanced visual acuity (*Morphnus guianensis*)
- Enhanced nocturnal vision (*Tyto alba*)

Sarah wasn't sure what she was looking at. "Are these additional genetic enhancements you can do?"

"Yes, but I must concede that they are somewhat experimental at this point."

"Have you done these for anyone else?"

"Yes, two other couples."

"What were the results?"

"I can't reveal that information due to the privacy agreements we have with our study participants."

There was that phrase again: "Study participants." Sarah liked it even less this time.

Matt pulled the form closer. "Now THIS is what I'm talking about! Tiger, remember when we joked about super powers? That's what these are!"

"How come flying isn't on here?" inquired Sarah, her tone dripping with sarcasm.

"I can tell you're not interested," the doctor said snippily, "I'll just take this back and we can—"

"Hold on a second." Sarah slapped her hand on the sheet of paper. "What are these Latin words next to each trait? … These are animal species!"

"Very perceptive, Mrs. Wong."

"This is transgenic engineering!" Sarah shouted. "You want to put ANIMAL GENES in my baby!" Then she screamed at the top of her lungs, "Why don't you just make him GLOW GREEN like a jellyfish!"

"Calm down, Mrs. Wong. I told you this was optional. I'll just take the form back."

"Damn right it's optional. This whole thing is optional.

I'm out of here, and this time I mean it!"

Sarah stormed out of the room.

Matt looked at Dr. Svengaard and asked if it was okay for him just to sit there. "I've been married to Sarah for over five years, and I know it's best to just leave her alone when she's like this. She'll come back in a few minutes."

"That's fine," said Dr. Svengaard.

After a minute or so, Matt broke the silence. "By the way, doc, just out of curiosity, what animals are these?"

"You really want to know?"

"Sure. Why not?"

"It's a gray wolf for sense of smell, a common mouse for hearing, a crested eagle for visual acuity, and a barn owl for night vision. Would you like me to tell you how I do it?"

"No, that's okay. I wouldn't understand anyway," Matt answered honestly.

While Matt was sitting there, Dr. Svengaard's phone rang twice. Both times he told the person on the other end he was running late and the other patients would just have to wait.

It was a full thirty minutes before Sarah returned to the doctor's office. She sat down and took Matt's hand.

"I'm still in," she said quietly. "I really want a baby. But we are NOT going to do ANYTHING on this last sheet! Is that clear?"

No one disagreed.

Dr. Svengaard tried to apologize, but Sarah would have none of it. She just wanted to finish up and get going.

"Are there any more forms?" she asked wearily.

"Yes, there's one more. It's our standard consent and privacy agreement."

Dr. Svengaard went to the filing cabinet, pulled out what looked like a small booklet and handed it to Sarah.

"This is our standard privacy and consent form," Dr. Svengaard said in an understated monotone. "You know —

releases for me to conduct the agreed-upon procedures, privacy information, confidentiality information — that sort of stuff. Basically it says that I won't tell anybody about what you do here and you won't tell anyone either. It also gives me permission to do the genetic engineering procedures we've talked about."

To say that the privacy and consent form contained a great deal of legalese was an understatement. The font size was small, the paragraphs long, and the language dense and technical. Sarah had seen many a consent form in her career, but none were as complex and convoluted as this one. It contrasted sharply with the informal forms they had signed a few minutes earlier.

"Just sign on the last page, and we'll be all set to go," said Dr. Svengaard brightly.

"Do you mind if I take time to read it? I like to know what I'm signing," she said.

"Of course. I don't think you'll find much of interest, but take your time."

Sarah really didn't have the energy to read the entire form, even though she knew she should. Instead, she pretended to study the voluminous document, staring at each page long enough to save face with Matt, and she got through the entire thing in less than five minutes.

"Looks okay to me, hon," she said when she got to the last page.

She scribbled her name on the signature line and pushed the document toward Matt. He signed without hesitation.

Smiling, Dr. Svengaard put the form in a plain manila folder. "Congratulations! We're ready to go. Mrs. Wong, when was your last period?"

"Umm. I think I started about September eighth — or maybe it was the ninth."

Dr. Svengaard looked at his calendar. "Perfect, you can start your Lupron shots on Tuesday. That's the thirtieth." Dr. Svengaard counted silently for a moment under his breath. "That means I'll harvest your eggs about the twenty-fourth or twenty-fifth of October, give or take a day or so. We'll be doing the usual protocol. Lupron for about eleven days, then FSH injections for another eleven or twelve days. Your HCG shot will be about October twenty-fourth. I'll retrieve your eggs thirty-six hours after that. Then it will be about five more days until I transfer the engineered embryos back into you."

Sarah hadn't been prepared for it all to start so soon. It usually took months to schedule IVF procedures with Dr. Svengaard, but now he was ready to begin in just a few days.

"Are you sure you can fit us in that quickly?" she asked.

"Absolutely," said the doctor. "No time like the present!"

Sarah and Matt had been going to New Beginnings for almost three years and this was the happiest they'd ever seen Dr. Svengaard.

"Any other questions?"

"I have one," said Matt. "We've only been talking about one baby, but you said embryos — plural."

"As I explained last time, I'll transfer two embryos to increase our chances of success. Anything else?"

"I think we're good," replied Sarah, her trepidation slowly ebbing away as her excitement mounted.

"Great. Allison will set you up with all of your supplies for the injections."

Dr. Svengaard stood up, thrust out his hand, and shook Sarah's hand so vigorously she almost lost her balance. "See you in a couple of weeks."

New Beginnings had an in-house supply of drugs and medications, obviating the need for clients to get prescriptions filled at regular pharmacies, which often didn't stock some of the more exotic fertility drugs. As Allison carefully counted out the vials and disposable syringes, it suddenly occurred to Sarah that these were cutting-edge procedures and were likely to cost tens of thousands of dollars.

"We completely forgot to ask Dr. Svengaard about the cost of all of this," she said. "Is there a fee sheet you can give us?"

Allison looked puzzled. "Didn't you sign the consent form? It's all in there."

Sarah *knew* she should have read the form more closely. "I ... I ... I must have missed that part," she said sheepishly.

"It's all free," Allison explained. "Every bit of it."

"What?"

"You don't have to pay a penny."

"But why?" asked Sarah.

"If it were up to me, Dr. Svengaard should be paying you," was all Allison said.

* * *

Sarah and Matt shared their excitement as they sat in their car.

"I can't believe we're going to have a baby boy!" exclaimed Matt.

"I'm excited too, hon, but I'm not pregnant yet. We've still got a long way to go."

"But Dr. Svengaard said it was going to work this time for sure, and I believe him."

"Me too," said Sarah.

Matt started talking about baby names. "I've always liked strong names for a boy, like Duke, Jake, or Magnus."

"Are you kidding me? Magnus? That sounds like the name of a gladiator."

"Maybe. How about Matt Junior?"

Sarah smiled. "I'll have to think about that one." She glanced at her watch and swore. "It's already past twelve thirty. I'm going to be late for court! Go, go, go!"

Matt broke every speed limit on the way to court while Sarah brushed her hair and reapplied her makeup, making the forty-minute drive in less than thirty minutes. As soon as he came to a stop in front of the courthouse, Sarah bolted from the car.

"This shouldn't take more than a half hour. Can you wait?" she yelled back as she dashed up the steps.

"Sure!" Matt shouted as Sarah disappeared through the courthouse doors.

After clearing security, Sarah took the elevator up to the fourth floor and walked briskly to Department H, a small utilitarian courtroom tucked away in the farthest corner of the top floor of the courthouse. Just outside the courtroom doors she stopped, smoothed her skirt, and glanced at her watch: one fifteen. *Not too bad, all things considered.* She walked briskly into the courtroom and apologized to Isabel, the court clerk, for being late.

"You're in luck," said Isabel. "The judge isn't back from lunch yet. Just take a seat."

As Sarah turned, a tall, smartly dressed man strode toward her and stuck out his hand. "Renaldo Sepulveda. I'm the DA on the Conway case. Are you Sarah Wong?"

"The one and only," she said, shaking his hand.

She knew Renaldo's name, but had never tried a case against him. He was inexperienced, having been with the District Attorney's Office for only eighteen months, but he was one of their rising stars. The word handsome did not do him justice. Six foot one, maybe six foot two, with dark-brown eyes and dark hair that was neither too neat nor too messy, Renaldo was so striking she wondered if he'd ever done any modeling. Standing there talking with her, he exuded a quiet energy, coupled with a dynamic spark.

"Quite a case you've got there," he said.

"I can handle it," replied Sarah. "How about you give me an involuntary manslaughter with three years tops, and we can get rid of this case today." It wasn't true, but Sarah wanted to test the waters.

"Afraid not. Word from the top is that this one has to go to trial. No deals at all."

So Renaldo wasn't calling all the shots on this case, noted Sarah. He was just the face of the prosecution in court. Behind the scenes, other DAs would be planning strategy and making important decisions.

Isabel interrupted them. "Judge Sandoval will see you now. You can go in."

Renaldo held the door for Sarah, but she insisted he go first.

"Good afternoon, counselors," said the judge. "Have a seat."

A rotund man of fifty-five, Burt Sandoval had been a judge for eleven years. His bushy eyebrows contrasted with the almost complete absence of hair on his head. He often looked disheveled, and on occasion he didn't even bother to zip up the front of his black judicial robe. His reading glasses usually sat on top of his bald pate, but sometimes they slipped all the way down to the tip of his nose while he was talking.

His cramped chambers looked much like Sarah's office — files and papers everywhere, mostly in large stacks. She had to clear away a pile of folders from one of the chairs just so she could sit down.

"Quite a doozy we've got here," said Judge Sandoval. "Mom kills her own baby. I can never understand why this sort of thing happens. Just makes no sense to me."

"Your Honor! My client hasn't been convicted of anything yet," Sarah protested. "I've half a mind to file a motion to recuse you right now."

"Calm down, Mrs. Wong. Don't get your knickers in a twist. I'm just saying these sorts of cases are always heart-wrenching, that's all. Of course, I've got a completely open mind." He turned to Renaldo. "Any chance of settling, Mr. Sepulveda? Maybe second degree?"

"Sorry, Judge, I can't offer anything. Got to go to trial."

"I see we've got a death penalty letter here. Any chance of backing off that so we can get a deal?"

"No, Your Honor, the state's position is that—"

"No need to be so formal in here, Mr. Sepulveda. You're saying there's no possibility of a plea bargain and you're going for the death penalty. I get it. Any pretrial motions, Mrs. Wong?"

"Not yet, but I'm going to file some within the next few weeks. Change of venue, a motion to exclude evidence, and probably a couple of others."

"Which evidence?" asked the judge.

"The 911 call and my client's statement to the police."

"The written confession?"

"It's not really a confession, Your Honor."

"Then why are you trying to exclude it? Sounds like it might help you."

"Maybe so, but some jurors might think parts of it are incriminatory, so I may try to exclude it. I haven't made a final decision yet."

"Any other motions?"

"Like I said, a change of venue motion. And I'm sure I'll think of some others before trial begins."

"I have no doubt about that, Mrs. Wong," said Judge Sandoval, smiling. "All right, let's set some dates." He pushed the button on his intercom. "Isabel, can you come in please?"

Isabel came in and stood in front of the computer on the table behind the judge's chair.

"I'm thinking we set the trial for the first week of December, right after Thanksgiving," said the judge. "How long do you think the trial will last?"

"At least a month," said Sarah.

"A week and a half," Renaldo said at the same time.

"One at a time, please. Renaldo?"

"About a week, maybe ten days tops, Your Honor."

"It's going to be at least four weeks, probably more like six," Sarah butted in. "Jury selection alone will probably take two weeks."

"Hmmm. Let's go after the holidays then. I don't want to have a jury working through Christmas and New Year's. That's never a good thing. Isabel, how do we look in January?"

"Not great, Judge. We've already got the Lopez matter starting on the twelfth, and it's estimated for three weeks. Let's go into February."

"Okay. Give me a date."

Isabel peered at the computer for a bit longer. "Friday, February sixth," she said eventually. "The Lopez case should be done by then."

"How's that look for the two of you?" asked Judge Sandoval.

"Fine with me, Your Honor," said Sarah.

"And for me," added Renaldo.

"Okay, let's set pretrial motions for the first or second week of December."

Isabel had already picked a date. "Wednesday, December tenth," she said, looking up.

Sarah and Renaldo nodded.

"Let's go out into court and put this all on the record," said the judge.

When they went into the courtroom, Lexi was already seated at counsel table, but Sarah didn't even get a chance to say hello to her.

"The court calls the State of California versus Lexi Conway," announced Judge Sandoval. "Lexi Conway, is that your true name?"

"Yes, Your Honor."

"You are charged with one count of first-degree murder. The prosecution is alleging that you killed Anna Conway. In addition, they have alleged a special circumstance, which means that you could receive the death penalty if you are convicted. Do you understand the charges against you?"

"Yes," Lexi said quietly.

"How do you plead?"

Sarah jumped in. "My client pleads not guilty."

"Very well. Pretrial motions are set for December tenth at nine a.m. and jury trial is scheduled for February sixth. All parties are ordered back for both of those dates. Pretrial motions will be held in this courtroom, but the jury trial will be held in Courtroom 201 on the second floor. Because of the extensive pretrial publicity, I'm issuing a gag order. Neither of you may discuss any aspect of this case with the press. Is that clear, Mrs. Wong?"

"Yes, Your Honor."

"Mr. Sepulveda?

"Yes."

"Anything else, Mrs. Wong?" the judge asked.

"Yes, Your Honor. I ask the court to set bail for Ms. Conway at twenty-five thousand dollars. My client has no prior criminal record and has very strong ties to our community. Ms. Conway has lived in Santa Felicia all her life and—"

"Your motion is denied. This is a capital murder case. There will be no bail. We are adjourned."

Sarah wanted to put on more of a show for Lexi. "But Your Honor ..."

But Judge Sandoval had already risen from his seat and was heading back into chambers.

Sarah turned to speak with Lexi, but she too had left the courtroom, escorted out through the inmate door by the bailiff. Even the reporter from the Santa Felicia Observer had left.

Suddenly Sarah felt very alone.

* * *

On Tuesday, September 30 the fun began. Matt and Sarah knew the fertility treatment routine by heart. Each day for the next three weeks, Matt injected Sarah in the thigh with drugs that would prepare her ovaries for their big task ahead. Because he had to be at work by six thirty each morning, he gave Sarah her daily shot—alternating between her left and right thigh—at about six. Sometimes he would sneak up on her before she was even awake.

Everything went according to plan. Matt started the FSH shots on October 12, and it looked like Sarah would be ready for her HCG injection about October 24.

Amid all the visits to New Beginnings, Sarah tried to work on Lexi's case, but it was difficult to make any meaningful progress. The hormones wreaked havoc on her emotional state, and the constant driving to and from the clinic took a substantial physical and mental toll. Instead, she spent some time reading up on genetic engineering so she could learn more about what Dr. Svengaard was going to do and how he was going to do it.

Over the course of the three-week injection cycle Matt and Sarah talked about genetic engineering almost every day. As the egg-retrieval date drew near, Sarah grew increasingly nervous about the risks. There was so little scientists knew about it, and what they did know scared her. Now she and Matt were heading in opposite directions. Where once she had been enthusiastic about it, she was growing more hesitant with each passing day and he was becoming more enamored with the idea of creating a designer baby—a tall, smart, strong, good-looking kid who could run incredibly fast.

Then Sarah's nightmares started.

Although the details varied, the basic theme was the same: she would give birth to some sort of genetically altered monster, which sometimes was a sci-fi alien and other times looked like Frankenstein's monster, all stitched together from a patchwork of body parts.

She blamed the potent cocktail of fertility hormones she was getting for the nightmares, and she knew they didn't really mean anything, but deep inside, they bothered her greatly.

* * *

On Thursday, October 23 Sarah went in for her blood work and ultrasound.

The ultrasounds were not the tickly kind done with goopy gel placed on Sarah's stomach. These were invasive and uncomfortable. Grace, the nurse, inserted a long, thin, white probe directly into her vagina to conduct a transvaginal ultrasound. Sarah had long ago abandoned any sense of modesty at New Beginnings. Now she hopped up on the examining table without any hesitation, slipped off her underwear, and placed her feet in the stirrups.

When Grace was finished, she wiped off the probe and told Sarah she would probably be ready for the HCG shot the next day. That meant that egg retrieval would be scheduled for eight a.m. on October 26, a Sunday—fertility cycles paid no heed to weekends and holidays.

"We'll call you this afternoon with the blood test results," Grace added. "That'll tell us for sure whether tomorrow is the day. Will you be at home or work?"

"At home, staring at the phone."

That afternoon, Sarah carried her phone with her everywhere—into the kitchen, the bedroom, even the bathroom. When it finally rang, she didn't wait to say hello.

"Are we all set, Grace?"

"Yes we are!" said the nurse cheerfully. "Have Matt give you the HCG shot at exactly eight tomorrow evening, and then we'll see you at eight on Sunday morning. The shot needs to be exactly thirty-six hours before Dr. Svengaard does the egg retrieval. Get here by seven fifteen on Sunday, so we can begin the egg retrieval promptly at eight."

Sarah was so excited she hung up without even saying goodbye. It was going to work this time. She knew it.

The next morning, Sarah and Matt were both awake by six fifteen, too excited to sleep. Almost immediately, though, Sarah's excitement turned into panic — she felt trapped with no escape. She knew right then that she didn't want to engineer little Duke, Jake, or Magnus. She wanted to leave everything up to chance. Or Mother Nature. Or maybe even God.

"Matt, I don't want to do this anymore."

"Do what?"

"All the genetic engineering. I'm too scared."

"C'mon Tiger, you're just getting last-minute jitters, just like when we got married. Remember what you told me then?"

"No."

"Actually, I don't either. But I'm pretty sure you got cold feet the day before our wedding."

"See! Wasn't I right about that?"

Matt turned quickly to look at her, and he broke into a broad grin when he saw her smiling.

"How about this? Let's just take the day off from all of this fertility talk," he said. "I'll call in sick and we can go to a movie or something. We'll have a nice dinner, get a good night's sleep and then see how we feel about everything tomorrow."

Sarah liked the idea of a day off — a day off from fertility worries, genetic engineering, and Lexi Conway. They went for a couple of walks; she had a long nap, and they watched an afternoon movie on the couch with Chloe. Neither of them felt like going out to dinner, so they had Chinese food delivered. All in all, a peaceful day.

After dinner, Sarah relaxed on the couch with Chloe while Matt put away the leftover Kung Pao chicken. Suddenly she jumped off the sofa with a loud squeal, sending Chloe tumbling out of her lap.

"My shot! We forgot about my shot!"

"Oh my lord," yelled Matt. "What time is it?"

"Eight fifteen! Grace said the shot had to be given at eight. Exactly at eight!"

Matt gathered his composure along with the syringe and the vial of HCG.

"We'll be fine, Tiger. A few minutes won't matter."

Working quickly, he got everything ready, and five minutes later the shot went in. This time it hardly hurt at all.

That night, Sarah had the worst nightmare of all. In it, she gave birth to a glowing green monkey. As she tossed and turned in bed, Matt woke her gently, trying not to frighten her further. Then she sat up straight, fully awake, dripping sweat and breathing rapidly. She told him about the glowing green monkey.

"That's it, hon. I can't go through with the genetic engineering. I just can't," she said.

Matt didn't try to change Sarah's mind. He really wanted to do the genetic engineering, but he respected her decision. He loved his wife and merely wanted her to be happy. It was a loving concession that Sarah would remember for a long time.

* * *

In all their visits to New Beginnings, Sarah and Matt had never been there on a Sunday. As they drove in for their eight a.m. appointment, they relished the thought of having the place all to themselves. They were astounded when they saw seven or eight cars parked near the entrance when they pulled into the lot. Sarah wondered why so many nurses and technicians had shown up for a simple egg retrieval.

When they walked hand in hand through the front door, she quickly realized that the cars didn't belong to staff members but to patients—the office was in full swing. A receptionist was behind the glass window, and there were two other couples in the waiting room.

Within minutes, Sarah and Matt were called into Procedure Room 3. When Grace met them at the door, Sarah told her immediately that they needed to talk to Dr. Svengaard. She wanted to make sure she had enough time to tell him about their change of heart.

"No problem," replied Grace. "If you have any questions, you can ask him in the procedure room."

"But we need to talk to him before we start. It's really important."

"I'm afraid that won't be possible. He's with another couple right now. You can see him when he starts your procedure."

"But we've changed our minds," said Sarah forcefully.

"Changed your mind? You don't want to do the egg retrieval?"

"No, we're fine with that. We just don't want to do any of the genetic engineering."

"None of it? Not even to correct the BS1 mutation?"

"That's right. None of it."

"Dr. Svengaard isn't going to be very happy about this," said Grace.

After Sarah changed out of her clothes and into the gown, Rebecca, the nurse who usually drew her blood, put Sarah on an IV, and Sarah and Matt sat in silence holding hands.

After a few minutes, Dr. Svengaard strode in, fully clad in surgeon's scrubs, facemask, cap, and gloves. Grace followed closely behind. He pulled his mask down.

"Grace tells me you've had a change of heart?" he said to Sarah.

"That's right. We've decided not to do any genetic engineering at all. Not even to correct the BS1 mutation."

"Can I ask why?"

"Doc, all we need is ten fingers and ten toes," said Matt. "We'll just leave the rest up to God."

"Or Mother Nature," added Sarah giving Matt a quick smile.

"If that's what you really want," said the doctor curtly.

"It is."

"But you still want to go forward with the ICSI, right?"

"Yes."

"All right then, let's get those eggs."

"Aren't there any new papers to sign?" asked Sarah.

"No, you've signed everything we need."

"What about the cost?"

"The forms you signed said it would be free and I'm a man of my word, so this round is on me." Dr. Svengaard made it sound like they were talking about a couple of beers instead of a $10,000 fertility treatment.

Sarah wondered why the doctor was taking this so well, but she didn't have the energy to figure it out. She just felt relieved that she and Matt had decided to forego the genetic engineering.

Less than thirty minutes later, he was done. The egg retrieval had gone flawlessly — seven mature eggs, all healthy.

Suddenly, Matt bellowed, "Oh no! I forgot to produce a sperm sample at home before we left!" He thought for a moment. "It'll take me about two hours to get there and back. I'll have the sample here by eleven."

"I'm sorry, but that won't do," said Dr. Svengaard. "We've got to wash your sperm immediately and fertilize the eggs this morning. That needs to be done by ten at the latest."

"I can't possibly make it home and back in that time!"

"Just produce your sample here then."

Matt swallowed hard. "But ... but I've never been able to do that."

"Well, there's a first time for everything."

Sarah could sense Matt's panic. While he paced back and forth, she turned and whispered something to Grace.

"Normally it's against our policy," said Grace, "but I don't see why not. Just this one time."

Rebecca removed the IV and Sarah slid off the procedure table. Still in her gown, she smiled at Matt, took him by the hand and led him silently to the Production Room, closing the door behind them.

For the first time ever, Matt was able to give a sample in the Production Room at New Beginnings.

* * *

As usual, Sarah wasn't very good at waiting. Even though she knew there would be no news for at least a day or two, she called New Beginnings later on Sunday. She left a message, but no one called her back. Each day after that, she called the clinic as soon as it opened in the morning. She never reached Dr. Svengaard directly, so she had to be content with Grace's second-hand progress reports. The nurse was evasive each time Sarah called, saying things like "everything's going along fine" or "we should know more tomorrow." Sarah took this as a bad sign, figuring that none of the eggs had fertilized.

By Wednesday morning, after getting the same equivocal response from Grace, Sarah knew it was over. She had been through these cycles enough times to know that if the eggs weren't fertilized by the third day there was no hope. After hanging up she thought about calling Matt, but she couldn't bring herself to pick up the phone. She'd just give him the bad news in person when he got home that evening. She lay down on the bed and cried while Chloe kept her company.

Then shortly after lunch, Grace called. Four of Sarah's eggs had been fertilized, and two were dividing normally. Everything was a go! Sarah was ecstatic. Grace told her that

Dr. Svengaard wanted to wait another couple of days before he transferred the embryos into Sarah, so she needed to come in at the end of the day on Friday for the transfer procedure. Usually embryo transfers were done three days after the egg retrieval, and Sarah asked why the doctor was waiting longer this time.

"Dr. Svengaard knows this is probably your last attempt, and he wants to do everything possible to make sure you have a baby this time," Grace explained.

Friday couldn't come soon enough for Sarah and Matt. The transfer took less than twenty minutes. Before she got up off the procedure table, Matt leaned over and kissed her stomach, then her lips. Grace gave them a picture of their two embryos, which had been taken through a microscope the day before. They were the cutest embryos they had ever seen.

When Sarah woke up on Saturday, she didn't feel pregnant—not that she knew what pregnancy felt like. It had only been one day, but already she was worrying that the embryos wouldn't implant. She couldn't help but feel a twinge of regret that they hadn't agreed to correct the BS1 mutation—without it, this fertility cycle had no greater chance of success than any of their previous ones.

Sarah followed all of Dr. Svengaard's instructions: she stayed in bed as much as she could, and avoided strenuous activities and stressful situations. She only went in to the office twice the following week, and then only for a few hours at a time. She told Nick she had some sort of flu bug and needed to work from home.

She was supposed to wait ten days before trying a home pregnancy test, but of course she couldn't hold out that long. On Friday, November 7, she took the first one. It was negative. She repeated it on Saturday—negative again.

Sunday—negative.

Monday—negative.

Tuesday—two tests, both negative.

Then on Wednesday, an hour after Matt had left for work, Sarah saw a deep-blue line on the indicator stick.

Before calling Matt, she raced in to New Beginnings to take a pregnancy test there, just to be absolutely, positively sure. She only had to wait ten minutes after giving her urine sample. Grace burst in to the room and gave Sarah a big hug.

"You're pregnant!" she announced.

Sarah could barely contain herself. "When will we know whether we're going to have one or two babies?"

"We have to wait a few more weeks before an ultrasound will tell us anything," said Grace.

Sarah was shaking as she called Matt from her car in the parking lot at New Beginnings.

"Hon, are you sitting down?"

CHAPTER 11

Sarah did nothing the next day except read about pregnancy and prenatal care. For three years she had been dutifully ordering books and saving magazines and catalogs about pregnancy and babies in case she needed them some day. Now that day had arrived, and she immersed herself fully, reading about prenatal vitamins, exercise, and birth classes.

She forced herself to go into the office on Friday, not so much because she had a lot of work to do, but because she felt guilty about having been away from the office. They had done just fine without her, but that bothered her. Wasn't she supposed to be indispensable?

Sarah and Matt had decided to wait a month before telling anyone about her pregnancy, but Sarah couldn't hold it in.

"I'm pregnant!" she announced as soon as she walked in the office door.

Nick, Conrad, and Maggie came rushing toward her to offer their congratulations. Nick told her to sit down.

"I didn't even know you were trying!" said Maggie.

"Yeah, Matt and I have been trying for a while, but it wasn't really a big deal."

All four of them sat in the reception area talking about baby clothes, maternity leave, and the best preschools in Santa Felicia. After a few minutes Conrad excused himself to prepare a motion he was filing that afternoon. Sarah was pleased he had stayed even for a little while. After a few more minutes, she shooed Maggie and Nick back to their desks and headed toward her own office.

"There wasn't much mail for you, just a couple of letters," Maggie called after her. "They're on your desk."

On the way, Sarah went into the small bathroom next to her office. She closed the door and took a long look at herself in the mirror above the sink.

Am I really pregnant? I don't look pregnant. Maybe I should go back for another pregnancy test. Maybe it didn't really work. Maybe I'm about to have a miscarriage. Maybe ...

She was in for a long nine months of worry and anxiety, but there wasn't much she could do about it. That's just who she was.

By the time she settled in her office, it was almost ten thirty. She looked at the pile of mail on her desk — a thank-you note from a client, an invitation to a bar association meeting, and ... a letter from The DNA Group with the results of Lexi's genetic test!

On the second page of the letter was an array of numbers and letters, with several cryptic notes about the genetic testing procedures. Sarah was unable to decipher exactly what the results meant, and the term Warrior Gene appeared nowhere on the form. However, the third line of the computerized printout started her heart racing.

MAOA Low-activity/Severe-deficiency variant—*Positive*

Then she saw the same line repeated further down the page.

MAOA Low-activity/Severe-deficiency variant—*Positive*

She knew immediately what this meant — or, at least, she hoped she did. Lexi had the Warrior Gene, and it looked like the lab had tested the sample twice to be certain. She quickly called Candi for help interpreting the report.

Candi hadn't opened her mail yet and put the phone down to go and look. After a few moments Sarah heard a shriek, not sure if it was one of pain or joy.

"She's got it!" yelled Candi when she returned to the phone. "She's got the Warrior Gene!"

"That's what I thought," said Sarah.

"But it's even better than that," said Candi cryptically.

"What do you mean?"

"She doesn't have just one copy of the Warrior Gene — she's got two!"

Sarah joined Candi in whooping and hollering.

Nick stuck his head around the door to see if Sarah was all right.

Grinning, she covered the mouthpiece of the phone. "Lexi's got two copies of the Warrior Gene!" she told him.

Nick gave her a thumbs-up and disappeared while Sarah picked up her conversation with Candi. "Now all we've got to do is find the environmental trigger that set her off."

"It may not be that simple," said Candi.

"Why not?"

"It might not be a single environmental trigger. It might be several, or even many. Genetic-environment interactions are often very complex, sometimes involving feedback loops in which changes in the environment alter the effects of certain genes. I recommend we look for multiple triggers."

"Any ideas about where to start?"

"Why don't we start with environmental factors that are known to cause aggression in humans?"

"Like what?"

"I'll leave that to you — you're the psych major, I'm the geneticist. You start looking for environmental triggers and I'll stick to the genetic analyses."

"Sounds like a plan," replied Sarah.

"I'm testifying on a case in Iowa next week, and I'll be out of the office the week after that. How about we talk again when I get back?"

"You got it. By the way, thanks for everything."

"No problem. We're in this together."

Just as she was about to hang up, Sarah blurted out, "I'm pregnant!"

"You are? That's great! So the genetic engineering worked after all. I must admit I had my doubts."

"Actually, Matt and I chickened out at the last minute. We decided not to do any genetic engineering. We just had a typical ICSI procedure. Nothing fancy."

"Good for you. That was the right choice."

* * *

Over the next couple of days, Sarah read everything she could about the causes of human aggression. In less than two days, she came up with a comprehensive list of environmental factors associated with aggressive behavior in humans.

Environmental Causes (Triggers?) of Aggression in Humans
- Competition for resources
- Competition for land
- Competition for food
- Competition for mates
- Protecting family members
- Protecting offspring
- Frustration
- Provocation
- Heat
- Crowding
- Annoying noises
- Noxious smells
- Sports competitions

- Violent movies and TV
- Video games
- Dysfunctional family dynamics

Her next step was to match her list to the facts in Lexi's case. She read through all the police reports again and looked at the notes from her interviews with Lexi. She divided the factors into two groups.

Factors Possibly Present on August 11
- Frustration
- Provocation
- Heat
- Crowding
- Annoying noises
- Noxious smells
- Postpartum stress/depression

Factors Possibly Present Prior to August 11
- Physical or sexual childhood abuse
- Violent movies and TV
- Violent video games
- Dysfunctional family dynamics
- Pregnancy hormones
- Pregnancy stress

She thought the first group of factors held more promise than the second, but she would ask Lexi about all of them the next time they talked.

* * *

As Lexi's trial date approached, Sarah pawned off more and more office responsibilities on Nick, Conrad, and Maggie. She had the most difficulty delegating tasks to Conrad. She knew he was a talented attorney, yet for some reason she had never grown to trust him. But now she had no choice. At first she handed over just depositions and pretrial motions, but soon it was entire cases. Nick handled almost everything else in the office, especially matters that required an empathetic bedside manner.

Sarah even started trusting Maggie with more than just typing, filing, and answering the phones. She let Maggie conduct screening interviews with prospective clients and allowed her to assemble trial binders for some of Conrad's court cases. To Sarah's delight, Maggie responded enthusiastically to her new responsibilities, invigorated by her new sense of purpose. Although she asked for help when she needed it, she worked more and more independently as the weeks wore on and even began dressing more professionally and coming in early.

However, Sarah still didn't allow Conrad and Maggie to work on Lexi's case, and even though Nick proved invaluable during the months of trial preparation, he was relegated mostly to witness interviews and field investigations. Sarah did all the heavy lifting herself—working with the expert witnesses, conducting the bulk of the legal research, writing the pretrial motions, and preparing for her direct and cross-examinations. She wasn't about to let anyone else muck up her big case.

As the weeks wore on, she became increasingly anxious about the trial, and the tension level in the office rose along with hers. Her patience grew thin, not that she was very patient to begin with, and everyone started steering clear of her.

* * *

After a perfunctory Thanksgiving dinner—the turkey was fresh but everything else was frozen, canned, or out of a box—Sarah told Matt she was going to visit Lexi the next day to talk about the Warrior Gene defense. Matt was furious. Neither of them had ever worked the day after

Thanksgiving since they'd been married. But Sarah was determined to see Lexi.

So on Black Friday, while Matt stewed by himself at home, Sarah headed off to the New Jail to talk with Lexi. She had visited Lexi only twice since their mid-September meeting, and both visits had only lasted long enough for her to let Lexi know she was still working on her case. It was time to tell her about the Warrior Gene strategy and get more information to bolster their defense.

Sarah grilled Lexi about her childhood, her family, her use of alcohol and drugs, her TV viewing habits, and what kind of video games she used to play, but none of the factors usually associated with the development of an aggressive personality were present in Lexi's childhood.

While not perfect, Lexi's upbringing had no red flags, nothing Sarah could latch onto.

Then she asked Lexi about the course of her pregnancy, her prenatal care, her prenatal checkups, her diet and exercise, and whether she had experienced any problems at all during the nine months. Although Lexi was vague about many of the details, it appeared there was nothing unusual about her pregnancy. There certainly wasn't anything that might have been a potential trigger for homicidal behavior.

Finally, Sarah asked Lexi to go through the events of August 11 once more, and this time she probed her incessantly about environmental factors that may have been present that day. Had it been hot? Were any of the stores or roads crowded? Was Lexi frustrated in any way? Were there any loud noises, noxious smells? Did anyone yell at her or make her mad?

Lexi provided lots of useful tidbits. It *had been* really hot that day. Even in her tank top and shorts, she had felt overheated. And the road between the Donut Shoppe and Pete's Market *was* jammed with cars because of the construction on 23rd Street, and the jackhammers outside of Pete's Market *were* awfully loud.

"Anything else you can think of? Anything at all?"

Lexi stared at the ceiling in the small interview room, trying hard to think back. After a few seconds she shrugged. "Not really, ma'am. I do know I wasn't feeling great. I'd had a cold for about a week. Nothing serious, just a stubborn drippy cold. I think I took some Tylenol, but I stopped because my mom said it might hurt my baby 'cause I was breastfeeding."

"Anything else?"

"Not really. How come you're asking about the weather and stuff?"

"Here's the deal, Lexi. For the past two months I've been working really hard on your case, and I think I may have come up with a defense."

In less than thirty minutes Sarah explained the DNA defense, the Warrior Gene, the whole thing. She told Lexi what Dr. Markowitz was going to say on the stand and what she was going to argue to the jury. She wanted Lexi to be ready for everything.

"So what do you think?" Sarah asked her. "Can we give the Warrior Gene defense a try?"

"I don't want a defense. I just want to get this over with so I can go see my baby in heaven."

* * *

Sarah was having trouble setting aside time to attend her weekly prenatal visits at New Beginnings, partly because of her increasingly hectic work schedule and partly because the clinic was so far away. She also wanted to go to a regular obstetrician. Dr. Svengaard tried to convince her to keep coming to New Beginnings where they were equipped to provide prenatal care all the way up to and including delivery. But Sarah had made up her mind; she transferred to Valley Obstetrics, which was only ten minutes from her home. She liked the fact that all their doctors were women, and she hit it off immediately with Ellen Sadler, one of the most experienced obstetricians at the practice. She had found her baby doctor.

Sarah's first ultrasound with Dr. Sadler was on Monday, December 8. This was the type of ultrasound Sarah had been looking forward to ever since she and Matt had talked about having children. Dr. Sadler rubbed the slippery gel all over Sarah's stomach, placed the ultrasound wand directly on her belly, and worked it in slow circles. As she moved the wand around, Sarah and Matt stared at the grainy black-and-white picture on the ultrasound monitor, neither of them able to make out much of anything amid all the pulsating dots. Then Dr. Sadler directed their attention to a couple of oblong marks in the lower half of the screen.

"Congratulations! You're having twins!" she announced.

* * *

When Sarah arrived at Judge Sandoval's courtroom at eight forty-five on Wednesday, he was already on the bench chatting with Brian, who had been the judge's bailiff for four years. Slightly paunchy with thinning hair on top, Brian looked like he could be the judge's younger brother. He was courteous to everyone, even the most unruly prisoners.

"Come on in and have a seat, Mrs. Wong," bellowed the judge when he spotted Sarah walking in. "The DA's not here yet. We'll get started as soon as he arrives."

Sarah was taken aback by the informality of the courtroom. Brian's feet were propped up on his desk in the corner, and the judge hadn't even bothered to don his black judicial robe. Pretrial motions were usually informal, but this was much more relaxed than Sarah was used to.

Brian went downstairs and brought Lexi up, and just as

she took her seat Renaldo walked in.

"Let's get this show on the road," said the judge. "I've got another pretrial conference at ten. Mrs. Wong, I've read all five of your motions and I'm prepared to rule on them now. Let's take them one at a time."

Sarah had filed five pretrial motions, all fairly standard, and had prepared formal arguments on each one. "If it please the court, I would like to summarize my arguments on the motions here in court."

"That won't be necessary, Mrs. Wong. I don't need to hear any additional arguments. I've got all the information I need."

The first motion was Sarah's request for a change of venue. In her written brief, Sarah had argued that it was impossible for Lexi to receive a fair trial in Santa Felicia, and she had asked the judge to move the trial to Los Angeles, where pretrial publicity had been far less intense.

Judge Sandoval denied Sarah's motion. "In my opinion, the fine citizens of Santa Felicia County can put aside whatever they've heard about this case and give Lexi Conway a fair trial," he stated for the record. "I'm sure you agree with me, don't you, Mrs. Wong?"

Sarah remained silent. There were two reporters in the courtroom; she couldn't allow the local newspapers to run a story that Lexi Conway's defense attorney believed the jurors of Santa Felicia County could not be fair and impartial.

Her second motion was to ban cameras in the courtroom. As was his style, Judge Sandoval steered away from any complex legal analyses, stating that those issues were better litigated at the appellate level than in a trial court. To no one's surprise, he denied Sarah's motion, noting simply that the defendant's right to a fair trial would not be compromised by the presence of cameras in the courtroom. *Burt Sandoval just doesn't want to miss his chance to perform in front of TV audience,* thought Sarah cynically.

Next was her motion to suppress Lexi's statement to the police. Although it appeared the cops had done everything right — giving the required Miranda warning and avoiding any undue pressure or intimidation — she filed her boilerplate motion anyway. Judge Sandoval denied it without comment. This was followed by a motion to exclude the 911 call from evidence. Judge Sandoval ruled that since Lexi made the call herself, Miranda warnings were not required. Motion denied.

In her final motion, Sarah requested that the jury be sequestered throughout the entire trial, including jury deliberations. She argued that the extensive pretrial publicity, as well as the expected media attention during the trial, would make it difficult for jurors to avoid media coverage of the case over the four or five weeks the trial was expected to take.

Judge Sandoval indicated that that motion had more merit than the other four, and he agreed that there might be minor benefits to sequestering the jury during trial, but he stated that the cost of sequestration would place a heavy burden on Santa Felicia County, which was already in dire financial straits. He denied Sarah's motion to sequester the jury during trial, but as a small concession he said he would reserve ruling on her motion to sequester during jury deliberations until they reached that point in the trial.

"Anything else, Mrs. Wong?"

"No, Your Honor"

Judge Sandoval looked at Renaldo. "Mr. Sepulveda, has the DA changed its position on the possibility of a plea negotiation?"

"No, we haven't."

"Very well. The trial is set for the previously selected date of February 6 in Courtroom 201 of this building. The defendant is remanded back into custody without bail, and all parties are ordered to return on February 6 at nine a.m. We are in recess."

Before Brian reached Lexi, she turned to Sarah and asked, "Why did the judge refuse everything you asked for?"

Sarah's reply was more flippant than it needed to be. "Lexi, you better get used to it, because that's going to happen a lot during trial."

* * *

Sarah barely noticed as Christmas came and went. All too soon, it was only a month to the start of the trial.

There was still one weak link in her Warrior Gene defense. How was she going to prove that Lexi acted without free will when she killed her baby? What about Lexi's statement in the 911 call that she was afraid this might happen? That didn't sound like someone who had no idea what she was doing. If Sarah couldn't establish that the Warrior Gene caused Lexi to act without free will, the entire defense would fail.

Over the next two weeks, she read as much as she could about free will and determinism. She scanned books, articles, and monographs, perusing works written by philosophers, theologians, historians, psychologists, and neuroscientists. Sarah was bright and well educated, but this free will stuff was tough, even for her. Incompatibilism versus compatibilism; causal determinism; logical determinism; theological determinism; metaphysical libertarianism. Even philosophers couldn't agree on what the terms meant. She was in over her head, and she gave it her best shot, but eventually she gave up in frustration. If she was having so much trouble understanding all of this, how on earth was she going to explain it to a jury?

Throughout January, Sarah spoke with Candi Markowitz frequently. They discussed genetics, environmental triggers, and trial strategy. Almost every time they talked, Sarah sought help with the free will question. How was she going to prove in court that the Warrior Gene led Lexi to act without free will when she wasn't even sure herself what free will was? Candi usually replied, "Don't worry, Sarah, you'll figure it out," which did nothing to calm Sarah's fears.

There was one other tiny hitch with the Warrior Gene defense: Sarah didn't believe it herself.

In the past, that had never bothered her. Like most defense attorneys, she was adept at arguing for interpretations of the facts that flew in the face of common sense. It was simply part of the job. If she didn't believe her client, it was no big deal. "Let the jury decide" was the rallying cry of defense attorneys everywhere.

But this case was different. The Warrior Gene defense was inconsistent with Sarah's own beliefs. She didn't believe in determinism or in any of its incarnations — logical determinism, theological determinism, and certainly not genetic determinism. Hard work and perseverance were why she had been successful in life; it hadn't been because of a string of genetic code. Sure, genes played a role, she thought, but it was free will — human choice — that ultimately determined who people were and how they behaved.

Yet now she found herself in the position of having to convince a jury that Lexi had no free will — that she killed her baby while on automatic pilot.

Sarah was open to the proposition that Lexi's violent behavior had a genetic basis. After all, some people did seem to be naturally bad, even evil — Hitler and Osama bin Laden came to mind — while others were supernaturally good, like Mother Teresa and her Aunt Bethany. But she was not willing to assign *all* the blame for Lexi's horrible crime to her DNA. It was one thing to say that some people are evil by nature, but it was quite another to say that their behavior was completely determined by their DNA.

The seeds of doubt had been planted weeks ago, but now they had germinated and were growing rapidly. Even if she could figure out how to make the Warrior Gene–Free Will argument, could she look the jurors in the eye and convince them that Lexi had no free will, no choice when she killed her baby?

* * *

It was less than two weeks before trial, and Sarah was winding up her final preparations.

Nick knocked softly on her door. "I think you ought to read this," he said.

She waved him in.

"I was doing some Internet searches about the Warrior Gene, looking for anything that might help you, and I found this." Nick handed Sarah a printout of an article from a small-town paper in Tennessee. It was only a couple of paragraphs long, and the headline read "His Genes Made Him Do It."

"It looks like someone's used the Warrior Gene as a defense before," Nick said.

Sarah grabbed the article and started reading. Her heart sank—Nick was right, somebody *had* used it before. Why hadn't she come across this herself?

In 2006, Bradley Waldroup had shot his wife's friend eight times, hacked her with a machete, and then turned the machete on his wife, almost killing her too. The attacks had been brutal and gory. It turned out that Waldroup had the Warrior Gene and had been abused as a child. The judge in the case had allowed a defense expert to testify that the combination of the Warrior Gene and the history of child abuse may have contributed to Waldroup's violent behavior, and the jury had agreed, at least in part, convicting the defendant of voluntary manslaughter instead of first-degree murder.

"Oh no," Sarah said out loud as she set the paper down.

"I thought this was *good* news," Nick said, looking puzzled. "A judge has already allowed a defense attorney to use the Warrior Gene defense. Isn't that legal precedent? Doesn't that help you?"

He was right—it did help. Sarah could cite this case when she asked Judge Sandoval to allow the Warrior Gene defense. Although it was a single ruling by a small-town judge in another state, it would indeed bolster her argument. But instead of feeling excited at this discovery she felt deflated, and then she realized why: someone had beaten her to the punch; her novel DNA defense wasn't so novel after all.

Am I trying this case for Lexi or for me?

"Yes, it helps a lot, Nick. Thanks so much," she said, quickly recovering her composure.

After Nick left, Sarah read the article more carefully. The defense had argued that the Warrior Gene made Bradley Waldroup more likely to be violent, but they hadn't claimed he had lacked free will. Instead, they had argued that his genetic makeup had *reduced* his culpability, not eliminated it. And when all was said and done, the judge had sentenced Mr. Waldroup to thirty-two years in prison—certainly better than the death penalty, but hardly a slap on the wrist. And best of all, thought Sarah, the Waldroup case had garnered virtually no media attention.

Maybe this obscure case was good news for both Lexi *and* Sarah.

* * *

By the beginning of February, Sarah still hadn't come up with a convincing argument for the Warrior Gene–Free Will connection. Even if the judge allowed her to present evidence that Lexi had two copies of the Warrior Gene, her defense would be doomed if she couldn't convince the jury that Lexi had no free will.

She'd been working on this for months, and she still couldn't fully grasp the distinction between free will and determinism. Neither could anyone else she'd asked. She needed something simple, something jurors could understand. Maybe some sort of metaphor or analogy. Or how about a diagram? Jurors love diagrams.

She affixed a huge poster board to the wall of her office and wrote WARRIOR GENE in block letters right in the middle. Around the periphery she listed all the possible environmental triggers—heat, provocation, noxious smells. Then she drew lines and arrows connecting all the factors to each other and to WARRIOR GENE in the middle. Dr. Markowitz said the relationships might be complex, so she made more connections with lines and arrows. Every few minutes she stepped back, hoping for inspiration.

Feedback loops. She had forgotten about feedback loops! She examined the triggers from a different perspective and drew in some simple loops, but when they didn't bring any clarity, she created larger loops and added more swirls. For over an hour she worked on the board, scribbling out connections and drawing in fresh ones.

And still nothing.

Her frustration mounting, Sarah drew bigger and bigger swirls on the board, pressing harder and harder, until finally her pen sank into the board, leaving a ragged trail behind as she drew. But that didn't stop her; she swirled and swirled some more, until the words were no longer legible. When her pen ran out, she plopped down, physically and mentally exhausted. Swiveling slowly from side to side, she viewed her artwork with disdain. The poster board was a mess—a meaningless jumble.

That's not a defense for a murder trial—it's a damn hurricane, she thought. Then it came to her. She threw her pen on the table.

"It's a damn hurricane," she said out loud. "Or maybe it's a perfect storm!"

That was it! It was a perfect storm of genetic and environmental factors. Something so catastrophic, so powerful, so unpredictable, that Lexi couldn't control what she was doing. It wasn't that she'd been crazy when she killed Anna, it was just that she'd had no control, no choice—no choice but to ride out the storm until it subsided.

So Lexi had no choice, no free will!

Sarah knew she wouldn't be able to explain the exact mechanisms involved, but that didn't matter. She'd simply tell the jury that a perfect storm of genetic and environmental factors had ensnared Lexi, and she had had no choice but to hang on tight and go along for the ride. It wasn't Lexi's fault that Anna had died; it wasn't anyone's fault.

This was an argument jurors could understand and accept!

CHAPTER 12

As she sat in the packed courtroom on Monday, February 23, an unfamiliar feeling washed over Sarah. A veteran of over forty jury trials, including brutal robberies, sordid sexual assaults, and unspeakable murders, she didn't get nervous in the courtroom anymore. But now she was terrified, excited, and exhilarated all at once, and it caught her by surprise as she waited for Judge Sandoval to emerge from his chambers.

If everything went right, this case would make Sarah Wong a household name in California, maybe even across the entire country. But she was heading into unchartered legal territory, with no signposts or familiar landmarks to guide her. This was going to be a treacherous journey indeed.

An expectant hum resonated throughout Courtroom 201. It was by far the largest, most attractive courtroom in the Zerr Courthouse. It was often used for ceremonial proceedings, such as enrobing new judges or swearing in new citizens, and occasionally for high-profile cases. Just last year it had been completely renovated, replete with all the newest technological bells and whistles—a computer on the judge's desk, Internet connections at both counsel tables, and three large monitors so that attorneys and jurors could view documents and evidence.

The front of the spacious courtroom was dominated by an oversized judge's bench flanked by two large flags—the

American flag on the left and the California one on the right. The ceilings were high, at least twenty feet, and the walls were covered with mahogany paneling.

Instead of the typical government-grade tables and chairs that were standard issue in most of the public facilities in Santa Felicia County, the counsel tables in Courtroom 201 were polished cherry, each accompanied by three plush leather chairs. The witness stand was in the usual place, adjacent to the judge's bench on the side nearest the jury box. The customary swinging half-doors separated the front of the courtroom from the public gallery, where the long benches were padded and comfortable, a rarity in a courtroom.

For a trial of this magnitude, there were often two attorneys, sometimes three, seated at the defense and prosecution tables. But right from the start Sarah knew she wanted to fly solo. She had done all the hard work herself, and she didn't want anyone else messing things up during trial or sharing the credit when she won. However, as it got closer to the trial, Matt tried to convince her to enlist Conrad or Nick to assist her, and she had spurned him at every turn. But then, with only days to spare, he got through; Sarah agreed that another set of eyes and ears would be helpful. But whose?

Although extremely bright, Conrad was a bit of a loose cannon and Sarah didn't want to risk getting into an argument with him at counsel table during the trial. Nick was clearly the safer choice. He had been with Sarah from the beginning, and he was loyal and dependable. He wouldn't challenge Sarah's decisions and, most importantly, he wouldn't claim any of the credit when the trial was over. Besides, Sarah liked Nick a lot more than Conrad. In the end, it was an easy decision.

When Sarah broke the news to Conrad, he was extremely upset and even threatened to quit. He knew this case was a potential career changer and he wanted to be a part of it. After a while he calmed down, but he stopped offering to help on the case.

Sarah leaned back in the tall leather chair at the defense table thinking how nice it would be to have this chair in her office. To her left was Lexi, and on the other side of Lexi was Nick. Sarah glanced over at him and he gave her his usual reassuring smile. Lexi, meanwhile, sat looking straight ahead, clearly nervous, and she appeared to be on the verge of tears. Sarah was worried Lexi might have a meltdown in front of the jury. But at least she looked nice.

Nick and Sarah had chosen Lexi's outfits for her, settling on three that would be rotated throughout the trial. They all projected the same youthful but subdued look: a knee-length skirt (tan, beige, or gray) and a white or cream blouse, coupled with a neutral-colored cardigan. All three blouses were long-sleeved with high necklines to conceal Lexi's tattoos.

For the first day of trial Sarah had chosen a beige skirt and cream blouse for Lexi. Her hair had grown out during her time in jail, and her jet-black dye job had given way to a natural, softer, mousy brown color. Her hair was pulled back in a ponytail, a look that made her appear younger and more naive. Though Sarah was irritated by sexism in the legal system, this was one time she could make it work in her favor. Jurors tended to be sympathetic toward young girls — sugar and spice and everything nice — and sweet young girls didn't commit horrific crimes. Or if they did, it wasn't their fault.

Sarah had thought carefully about what she would wear herself during the trial, the most important of her career. She decided to go mostly with power suits in dark shades of gray or blue. As she was almost four months pregnant and her baby bump was starting to show, she had to reposition the zippers and add a section of elastic at the side of each skirt. If she kept her jacket on, she figured she could make it through the trial without anyone noticing.

No one in the courtroom other than Nick knew she was pregnant, and she wanted to keep it that way. What might jurors think about a pregnant lady representing an accused baby killer?

She gazed at the large video monitors that allowed jurors a close-up view of documents and other pieces of evidence. It wasn't long ago that bloody knives and flattened bullets were passed among the jurors in a macabre show-and-tell; now they had to be satisfied with viewing DNA printouts and PowerPoint presentations on large screens. One thing that hadn't changed over the years were the six crescent-shaped grease stains adorning the paneled wall behind the top row of juror chairs, where drowsy jurors leaned their heads while attorneys droned on.

Growing impatient, Sarah went over to the clerk's desk to see if she could find out what was causing the delay.

"Isabel, do you have any idea what the holdup is?"

"Nope. The judge told me he would be out in a few minutes."

"Thanks." Sarah returned quickly to her seat at the counsel table, taking care not to look out over the packed courtroom lest it made her even more nervous than she already was.

Finally, just after nine thirty, the jury filed in. Eight women and four men — plus four female alternates. All in all, Sarah was satisfied with the jury, especially given how challenging jury selection had been.

Jury selection had taken two full weeks. The original pool of two hundred and fifty prospective jurors had been reduced to two hundred and two after forty-eight jurors had been excused because they were against the death penalty. After that initial death-qualification stage, jury selection was more like a game of chess than an exercise in choosing the fairest, most impartial jurors.

Sarah knew how to play the game, and she played it

well. She usually won jury selection, but she had met her match in Renaldo Sepulveda. He might not have been the best technician or the sharpest on the law, but he was good-looking and smooth-talking, and he oozed charm. Jury selection had turned into a warm and fuzzy love fest, with Sarah and Renaldo falling over each other as they tried to curry favor with the jurors who would decide Lexi's fate.

They took turns probing the prospective jurors. Many of Sarah's inquiries were designed to assess what the jurors knew about the case — whether they had already formed an opinion based on what they had heard or read. Questioning jurors about pretrial publicity is tricky business because a single juror's answer can taint the rest of the jury pool, which is exactly what happened while Sarah was questioning the very first prospective juror.

"Have you heard about the Lexi Conway case?"

"Yes, I have."

"What have you heard?"

"That she's a baby killer."

A knowing murmur swept through the courtroom.

Sarah replied, "She's not a baby killer, just an accused baby killer." Sarah winced at her own choice of words, which were not much better than the juror's.

Sarah had been in a quandary as to what type of juror to choose. Would women be sympathetic to Lexi, or would they judge her more harshly because she was a woman? In the end, she had decided she did want mostly women on the jury, but she would avoid those with young children as they might not be able to judge Lexi fairly. Her background as a psychology major had helped her immensely. She knew not to rely solely on what the jurors said, and she looked for nonverbal cues while they were talking. That was when it really helped to have a second set of eyes in the courtroom, and she told Nick to watch all the jurors closely, not just the one being questioned. She explained that body language is very leaky, especially when the spotlight is on someone else.

Since this was a death penalty case, Renaldo and Sarah had twenty peremptory challenges each, allowing them to excuse jurors without having to give a reason. Sarah knew it was never wise to use her last peremptory challenge, because the next person might be even worse.

As they neared the end of jury selection, Renaldo had two peremptories left. Sarah had only one. A few quick questions revealed that Juror 125, a white male construction worker, would be problematic for the defense — very conservative with several police officers in his family — and Sarah had exercised her final peremptory challenge. She knew it wasn't wise to do that because the next person might be worse, but she felt she had no choice. And indeed, her worst fears were realized when Isabel pulled the card for Juror 72. An ex-marine, he was as law-and-order as they came. In his world, cops never lied and bad guys should be locked away forever. Sarah did her best to have him excused him for cause, but to no avail. She was stuck with Juror 72, and Renaldo had quickly accepted the jury as constituted.

"All rise. Department H of the Superior Court of Santa Felicia is now in session, the Honorable Judge Burt Sandoval presiding," Brian announced to the packed courtroom, jolting Sarah out of her reverie.

Before he could finish, Judge Sandoval burst through his chamber door and ascended the two steps to his elevated seat at the front of the courtroom.

"Please be seated. Good morning, everyone," he said. "The court calls the case of the State of California versus Lexi Conway. Ms. Conway is charged with one count of first-degree murder, and the prosecution has alleged a special circumstance that the murder was especially heinous, atrocious, or cruel. This special circumstance makes the defendant eligible for the death penalty." The judge quickly added, "If she's convicted, of course."

Sarah winced. Although his last statement was meant to emphasize that her client had not yet been convicted of anything, she feared it would have just the opposite effect.

Judge Sandoval continued. "As everyone has undoubtedly noticed, there are three cameras in the courtroom — one pointed at the witness chair, one at the counsel tables, and one at *me*." He straightened up in his chair, a smile twitching at the corners of his mouth. "This case has drawn quite a bit of interest from the local and national media, so portions of the trial may be shown on television. These cameras will never be pointed at the jury box, so as to protect the identity of the fine ladies and gentlemen who have been chosen to sit on this jury."

Many of the jurors smiled at the judge's acknowledgment of their role in the case.

"To be honest with you, I don't like having cameras in the courtroom. Not one bit. But the law in California is clear — cameras are allowed if there is a compelling public interest in a matter, and this case has generated just such public interest."

Judge Sandoval is probably ecstatic the cameras are here, thought Sarah. He had been a superior court judge for eleven years and was probably hoping to be elevated to the Court of Appeals. The Conway case was the perfect opportunity for him to make a name for himself. His robe was zipped, she noted, his glasses were on his desk instead of on top of his head, and he looked like he meant business.

"Let me add a warning for those of you operating the cameras," the judge went on. "If any of you cause any disturbance whatsoever, I will banish you all from the courtroom for the remainder of the trial. Still cameras, TV cameras, I don't care. MSNBC, CNN, Wolf Blitzer, Nancy Grace or whoever can appeal me all the way to the Supreme Court if they want to. I will do everything in my power to ensure that the State of California *and* Lexi Conway get a fair trial." He looked around the courtroom.

"Let's begin. Are both parties ready?"

"Yes, Your Honor," chimed Renaldo and Sarah in unison.

"Mr. Sepulveda, you may make your opening statement."

There was another district attorney at the table with Renaldo — Joe Jimmerson. Sarah knew him well. A veteran prosecutor, he was knowledgeable and highly skilled, but he had none of Renaldo's flair. Joe would probably be formulating the overall trial strategy and attending to technical details, Sarah thought, while Renaldo would be the public face of the prosecution — questioning witnesses, making objections, and delivering the closing argument.

Renaldo stood up tentatively. Sarah was surprised — he seemed nervous. He was not accustomed to the glare of the media spotlight, and it showed. Gone was the easygoing, charming style he had exhibited throughout jury selection. He began his opening statement cautiously and spoke in a monotone throughout what was a long, boring, and tedious presentation.

After first explaining that Lexi was charged with a single crime — first-degree murder with a special circumstance — Renaldo told the jury that he had to prove four things, and he listed them in bullet-point format in a PowerPoint presentation, complete with the district attorney's logo on each slide, visible on the large monitors throughout the courtroom.

"Objection, Your Honor," shouted Sarah as soon as the list appeared on the screens. "None of these have been proven. Mr. Sepulveda has presented them as if they are facts. They are just his fanciful ideas about what happened, nothing more."

Judge Sandoval looked directly at Sarah. "Mrs. Wong, I do not have a hearing problem, so there's no need to shout. Your objection is overruled. You may continue, Mr. Sepulveda."

"Of course, I haven't proven any of these yet," Renaldo said uncertainly. "That is what I will try to do during the trial."

Sarah smiled. Although her objection had been denied, the interruption had thrown Renaldo off his stride. He said he was going to "try" to prove these things; an experienced attorney would have said they were "going" to prove them. Right then, Sarah decided to employ a strategy she had learned from watching football on Sunday afternoons with her dad: Blitz rookie quarterbacks constantly from the first play of the game. She was going to object loudly and often to keep Renaldo off balance. If Renaldo was allowed to stand still in the pocket, he might win. But if he had to constantly scramble, he would probably make some critical mistakes.

Renaldo went through each of his four points in order, sticking closely to his script. For each point he had prepared several PowerPoint slides. Sarah objected to each and every slide, but she asked Nick to watch the jury closely. Sometimes juries appreciated aggressive lawyering and sometimes not. There was a fine line between aggressively protecting Lexi and obstructing the judicial process, and she wanted to get as close as possible to that imaginary line without going over, at least not too often.

After her fifth objection, Nick pushed a hastily written note in front of her:

Keep going. The jury's still with you.

Sarah objected to the next two slides, and even though Judge Sandoval summarily denied her objections, Renaldo eventually stopped showing his PowerPoint presentation and just read from his notes. Without the colorful signposts up on the large monitors, Renaldo's opening statement grew murkier by the minute. He tossed around dozens of legal definitions and talked about facts, inferences, and credibility. His voice settled into a low mumble, and as he droned on it seemed like even he was losing interest.

While he rambled on, Sarah had plenty of time to study the jury, and she caught their gaze whenever she could. For the most part, they seemed like a nice enough bunch, save for that last juror she had had to accept. But what would they make of her defense? Would they have the courage to buy into her Warrior Gene argument? Only time would tell. It appeared most of the jurors were bored by Renaldo's long-winded presentation, and two of them started to nod off toward the end. Sarah was determined she would not make the same mistake when her turn came.

Renaldo concluded with a desultory "That's all I have, Your Honor."

"Thank you for that *very comprehensive* opening statement," said Judge Sandoval. "Mrs. Wong, do you care to make an opening statement at this time?"

"No, Your Honor. I'd like to reserve that right."

"Very well. Mr. Sepulveda, you may call your first witness."

"The prosecution calls Miriam Connelly to the stand."

As soon as she heard the name of their first witness, Sarah knew who was calling the shots at the prosecution table. Most rookie DAs would have started with the arresting officer. Beginning with the operator who took the 911 call was a shrewd move, designed to get Lexi's own words in front of the jury at the very beginning of the trial. Joe Jimmerson was clearly in charge on the other side of the aisle.

Renaldo had Ms. Connelly authenticate the recording of the 911 call. Then he played it for the jury while a transcript was displayed on the video monitors throughout the courtroom. The transcript scrolled on the monitors in sync with the audio recording.

911 Operator:	*Hello, this is the 911 operator. Do you have an emergency?*
Female Voice:	*Not really. There's nothing you can do now. It's probably all for the best anyway.*
911 Operator:	*What do you mean?*
Female Voice:	*I was afraid this might happen.*
911 Operator:	*Ma'am, I don't understand.*
Female Voice:	*That's okay. There's nothing you can do. Just tell Ryan I love him.*
911 Operator:	*Do you need any help?*
Female Voice:	*Not anymore.*
911 Operator:	*Do you want me to send an ambulance? The police?*

[Nineteen seconds of a constant rumbling sound]

911 Operator:	*Ma'am. Do you need any help? Shall I send the police?*
Female Voice:	*If you want.*

[End of recording]

Although Sarah had read the transcript dozens of times, she had only heard the audio once before. She still couldn't tell if Lexi's voice sounded like she was grieving, desperate, or indifferent. Was it the voice of a heartless killer, a depressed suicidal mother, or someone on automatic pilot? In any event, she had no questions for Ms. Connolly on cross-examination.

"The prosecution calls Officer Hector Clemente to the stand."

Officer Clemente, dressed smartly in his gray patrol uniform, approached the witness stand, turned toward Isabel and raised his right hand without being asked. Clearly he had testified hundreds of times during his long career. Once he was sworn in he took his seat in the witness chair and smiled at the jurors.

After a long set of introductory questions covering Officer Clemente's training and experience, Renaldo walked him through the events of August 11 in painstaking detail, leading him question by question instead of letting him tell the jury what had happened. Sarah could see that Renaldo was reading from a script, and she wondered whether he or Joe Jimmerson had prepared it.

During the officer's testimony, she kept one eye on the jury. At first all twelve jurors scribbled furiously, but one by one they put down their pens and just stared ahead. The trial was less than two hours old and already the jurors were bored.

Renaldo took pains to establish facts that seemed irrelevant to the case. Every once in a while, Sarah would object simply to break the boredom (and to play with him a little bit). When he asked the officer to describe what the weather was like on August 11, she couldn't help but jump in.

"Officer Clemente, what was the weather like on August 11?"

"It was sunny and very hot."

"Objection," Sarah said in an even tone. "The term 'very hot' is a conclusion beyond the expertise of the witness."

Judge Sandoval peered down at her over his glasses. "Overruled."

She continued to interject petty objections over the next few minutes to signal that she was bored with the tedious, irrelevant testimony, but Renaldo didn't take the hint. The final straw was when Renaldo asked Officer Clemente to explain the difference between the duties of a patrol officer and a homicide detective.

"Objection, boring," said Sarah leaping to her feet.

She braced herself for a fusillade of criticism from Judge Sandoval. Instead, she was pleasantly surprised.

"Mr. Sepulveda, this is a little tedious. Please move on."

Around eleven forty-five, just as the morning session was coming to a close, Renaldo started to home in on the germane facts of the case. Sensing that they were about to get to the important portion of the officer's testimony, Judge Sandoval jumped in.

"That will be enough for now, Mr. Sepulveda. This is a good time to take our noon recess." Turning to the jury box, the judge smiled. "Ladies and gentlemen, we are going to take our noon recess. Please return to the courtroom no later than one thirty. Remember that you are not to form any opinions about the case or discuss it with anyone, including other jurors, until the case has been submitted to you at the end of the trial. Have a nice lunch."

Judge Sandoval swiveled his chair until his eyes locked on the camera at the back of the courtroom. "The court stands adjourned until one thirty p.m. All parties are ordered back at that time."

Sarah and Nick found a shaded bench at the far end of the courtyard to eat and talk about the morning's proceedings.

"I thought that went pretty well," Nick said as he extracted sandwiches for them both from his bag.

"Mmmmm, I guess so," said Sarah. "Do you think I was too heavy-handed with all the objections?"

"Maybe a little. I'll keep a close eye on the jury and let you know if they start to turn against you."

"Thanks, Nick. What would I do without you?"

"You'd do just fine."

The rest of the time they chatted about anything except the trial. There wasn't really much to talk about in the way of strategy at this point. They both knew what the afternoon held—a drawn-out description of what the officers had encountered on August 11. After they finished eating, they sat quietly soaking up the warm February sun.

"What a nice warm day," Sarah observed.

"Objection," Nick said in an officious tone. "Beyond the expertise of the witness."

Laughing, they picked up their bags and made their way back to the courtroom.

The afternoon session began the same way the morning session had ended. Led by Renaldo's relentlessly detailed questions, it took most of the afternoon for Officer Clemente to describe how he and his partner, Officer Leon Keller, had rescued Lexi from certain death. He layered on a patina of heroism not apparent in his original police report, but most of the embellishments were harmless, so Sarah decided not to interrupt. Officer Clemente told the jury that they had tried forcing the garage door open, first with their hands and then with a crowbar, but had to give up. Then they jumped in their squad car and rammed the garage door. On the second attempt the door had collapsed onto the hood of their car. Covering their mouths with their uniform shirts, they had raced into the garage. While his partner struggled to turn the car off, Officer Clemente had dragged Lexi out of the driver's seat and onto the driveway. He said that her skin was pale, but not completely devoid of color—it had a slight pinkish tinge.

For the most part, Officer Clemente's testimony was consistent with his report, but there were many minor deviations. Without being asked, Nick followed along on his annotated copy of the report as Officer Clemente testified, and he affixed a bright green sticky note to the report each time the officer's testimony varied even slightly from the report. It wasn't long before dozens of lime green stickies had transformed the report into a two-dimensional Chia pet.

In most trials, Sarah would have hammered away at

these discrepancies in her cross-examination. Make the cops look forgetful and untrustworthy. That was her usual tactic.

But the outcome of Lexi's trial hinged on whether the jurors would buy into Sarah's novel defense. Knowing that her likability would be critically important, she decided not to worry about minor discrepancies and inconsistencies. This strategy was challenging for her, as she was used to fighting and scrapping over even the tiniest issues. Now she had to sit on her hands and let these things slide by.

Officer Clemente described in dramatic detail how he had to revive Lexi by performing CPR for several minutes before she regained consciousness. He described how Lexi coughed and sputtered until the paramedics arrived.

When Renaldo asked Officer Clemente to describe what paramedics do, Sarah heard at least one juror groan. To the relief of almost everyone, Judge Sandoval jumped in.

"Mr. Sepulveda, I think everyone knows what paramedics do. In any case, this is a good time to stop for the day." He turned toward the jury. "Ladies and gentlemen, I will see you back here tomorrow morning at nine a.m. sharp. We are adjourned."

CHAPTER 13

When court convened on Tuesday morning, everyone seemed more relaxed. A good night's sleep had done Sarah some good, and she took her seat at the defense table with a renewed vigor.

Officer Clemente began the morning session by recounting how he and Officer Keller had secured the scene and started their investigation while the paramedics attended to Lexi. After about ten minutes, most of the fumes had dissipated from the garage, but the officers proceeded cautiously, for they knew that pockets of carbon monoxide could still be lingering in the recesses near the back. Clemente testified that he took pictures while his partner jotted down notes about the scene.

They began to make an inventory of the contents of the car, keeping an eye out for anything that might indicate this was an attempted suicide, such as sleeping pills or a suicide note. It was at this point that Officer Clemente opened the rear passenger door and made a grim discovery — a baby, now identified as Anna Conway, was strapped into an infant car seat and appeared to be lifeless. Officer Clemente said he didn't realize at first that it was a baby, mistaking the tiny figure for a doll. Only when his hand brushed against her cool, smooth skin did he fully comprehend what he had found.

He unbuckled the baby as quickly as possible, tearing her tiny yellow sleeper on the metal latch of the car seat, placed her body on the concrete driveway, and began CPR.

As he described his efforts to revive her, he paused and looked at the jury. He told them he knew there was nothing he could do, but he kept going anyway.

"I've got two daughters of my own," he added, "and I'd want someone else to do the same for them."

"Objection. Immaterial and irrelevant," Sarah said in a calm, measured tone. She had to stop this maudlin performance, but she needed to be careful how she did it.

"Overruled. The witness is just telling the jury how he felt at the time." Judge Sandoval turned to face the officer. "I'm sure you love your daughters very much. You may continue."

"As I was saying, I kept trying to revive that little girl, but it was no use. She was already gone."

Silence enveloped the courtroom when Renaldo asked his next question. "How did you know she was dead?"

"I just knew."

While Renaldo paused to look at his notes, Officer Clemente kept going. "One thing was weird though. Usually dead people are bluish-gray, but this little girl was almost pink. That's why I kept trying to revive her for so long."

Renaldo couldn't find his next question, so he used the standard default prompt: "What happened then?"

"Well, Officer Keller and I were really upset. We had already called for another ambulance, but it hadn't gotten there yet. So we just sat down and wrapped the baby in a blanket we found in the car."

"What color was the blanket?"

"It was pink with small white flowers."

Renaldo retrieved a small receiving blanket, pink with white flowers, from a large evidence bag under the prosecution table. "Is this the blanket?"

"Yes, that appears to be the one."

Renaldo waved the blanket with a flourish. "Your

Honor, I would like to offer this baby blanket, which has been identified by Officer Clemente, as state's Exhibit E."

Sarah shot to her feet. "May we approach, Your Honor?"

"For what purpose, Mrs. Wong?"

"I'd like to discuss an objection."

"No, let's do it here in open court."

"As you wish, Your Honor. I object to the introduction of this blanket on the grounds that it's irrelevant and immaterial to any issue in the case. Furthermore, the probative value of this item is clearly outweighed by its prejudicial impact."

Sarah didn't want the jurors to be able to see and touch the blanket that had cradled little Anna Conway as she lay dead on the driveway six months ago. If it were admitted into evidence, the jury would have that blanket in the room with them as they deliberated Lexi's fate and be constantly reminded of the lifeless little girl who had once been wrapped in its embrace.

To no one's surprise, Judge Sandoval overruled Sarah's objection.

Next Renaldo produced an infant car seat.

"Officer Clemente, is this the car seat in which Anna Conway was sitting on August 11, when you discovered her lifeless body?"

"Objection," said Sarah. "Irrelevant, immaterial, and —"

"Overruled."

This same scenario played out numerous times over the remainder of the day as Renaldo repeatedly introduced items that had little or no relevance to the case but were calculated to arouse the sympathy of the jury. Although she knew it was futile to object, she did so anyway to preserve the issues as possible grounds for appeal. Over her objections, Judge Sandoval admitted the infant car seat, two small baby rattles, another baby blanket, three stuffed animals, even a box of baby wipes.

Renaldo pulled from the evidence bag a tiny yellow sleeper with a big white bunny on the front and a ragged tear on the right side.

"Officer Clemente, is this the outfit Anna Conway was wearing on August 11, the day she died?"

"Objection. Irrelevant and immaterial. Any probative value is far outweighed by the prejudicial impact."

"I admire your persistence, Mrs. Wong. Overruled."

Renaldo stood holding Anna's yellow sleeper, the last outfit she ever wore. He waited as long as he could to make sure each juror got a lasting view of it. When Officer Clemente confirmed its identity, Renaldo walked slowly over to Isabel to give her the sleeper as evidence, holding it in his arms as if it still enclosed little Anna Conway.

"That's all I have for Officer Clemente," he said.

"Thank you, Mr. Sepulveda." Judge Sandoval glanced up at the clock. "I'm sure Mrs. Wong will have a lengthy cross-examination, so this looks like a good time to break for the day."

Sarah stood up quickly. She wanted to get her cross-examination in before the jurors went home for the night. "You honor, my cross-examination will take no more than five minutes — probably less. Can we just finish up with Officer Clemente so he won't have to come back tomorrow?"

"Really? That's all you have? Then go ahead."

"Thank you."

She didn't bother to walk to the podium, instead addressing the officer from behind her seat at the defense table.

"Officer Clemente, you said you have two daughters?"

"Yes."

"I assume you love them very much."

"Of course."

Judge Sandoval jumped in, not waiting for Renaldo to object. "Mrs. Wong, I don't see the relevance. Please move on to a different line of questioning."

"But Your Honor, Officer Clemente brought this topic up and you allowed him to talk about it. It's only fair that I be allowed to ask him a couple of follow-up questions."

"Very well, but just a few more. Then move on."

Sarah continued quickly before Judge Sandoval changed his mind. "Officer Clemente, I assume you would do everything in your power to protect your daughters from harm."

"Absolutely."

"Would you risk your life for them?"

"Yes, without even giving it a second thought."

"Mrs. Wong, I've already warned you," said the judge, sounding irritated. "Move on to another topic."

"Nothing further, Your Honor." Sarah glanced at the jury and quickly sat down.

"Any redirect, Mr. Sepulveda?" asked Judge Sandoval.

"I don't think so, Your Honor," replied Renaldo, clearly stunned by the brevity of Sarah's cross-examination.

"Is that a yes or a no, Mr. Sepulveda?"

Renaldo glanced over at Joe Jimmerson, who shook his head. "It's no. I have no further questions."

Judge Sandoval smiled and turned to face the jury. "Ladies and gentlemen, we are going to stop for the day. Do not discuss the case or form any opinions until it has been submitted to you. Court is adjourned."

* * *

On the third day of trial, Sarah decided to dress in a slightly more feminine way, going with a maroon silk dress and a dove-gray blazer instead of the dark conservative suits she had worn the first two days.

The morning began with the testimony of Officer Leon Keller, Hector Clemente's partner. Sarah couldn't figure out why Renaldo had called him. He had got everything he needed from Officer Clemente, and she had no idea what Officer Keller could possibly add.

From the start, Leon Keller seemed nervous and uncertain, in contrast to his partner's polished style. Renaldo covered much of the same ground with him as he had with Officer Clemente. Officer Keller testified about how they broke down the garage door, rescued Lexi Conway, and found little Anna Conway. Although the big picture was the same, there were numerous inconsistencies between the two officers' testimonies.

Lexi had hardly said anything to Sarah during the first few days of the trial, and had spent most of the time just staring down at the counsel table. Sarah had given her a pad of paper so she could write notes, hoping that would get her more involved in her defense. So far she had barely written anything at all, but while Officer Keller was testifying, Sarah noticed that Lexi had started to scribble on the pad. She hoped that Lexi's notes would prove to be useful at some stage.

During the course of his six-hour excursion through the events of August 11, Officer Keller frequently asked Judge Sandoval for permission to look at his police report to "refresh his memory" before answering a question. Of course, the judge granted every request. Sarah thought about objecting to the frequent memory-refreshing interruptions, but decided the uncomfortable interludes reinforced the inadequacy of Officer Keller's memory. In contrast to the rapid-fire objection strategy she employed on the first two days of trial, Sarah did not utter a single objection during Officer Keller's testimony. Renaldo frequently turned around and looked at the defense table, waiting for Sarah to object. Much to her delight, the mere possibility that she might interrupt seemed to be enough to throw him off his game.

Sarah's no-objection strategy paid off in a surprising way at the end of the officer's testimony. To maximize the focus on Lexi's culpability, Renaldo saved the identification of the defendant until the very end of his questioning of Officer Keller.

"Officer Keller, I have just a few more questions and then we will be done. You have testified extensively about the woman you and Officer Clemente pulled from the car on the morning of August 11. Do you see that woman here in court today?"

"Yes, I do."

"Could you point her out for the jury please?"

Officer Keller pointed toward the defense table. "That's her."

"Your Honor, may the record reflect that the officer pointed to the defendant in the case, Lexi Conway?"

Without looking up from his desk, Judge Sandoval said, "The record will so reflect."

"How do you know that's her?" Renaldo continued.

"Well, it must be her because she's seated at the defense table."

A few of the jurors snickered.

Officer Keller continued. "I must admit she looks a little different today than she did six months ago."

"How so?"

"Well, she looks nice in her maroon dress and gray jacket today. Back in August she looked ... well, almost dead."

Sarah immediately realized that Officer Keller had identified her as the defendant! Because she hadn't said a word during his testimony, Officer Keller didn't know which woman at the defense table was the defendant and which was the attorney. Lexi had been writing sporadically on her notepad during his testimony and Sarah had just been sitting there listening. Officer Keller had guessed, and he had guessed wrong. Sarah could keep silent no longer.

"Your Honor, may the record reflect that Officer Keller pointed at me and described me when he was asked to identify the woman the officers dragged from the car on August 11."

"The record will so reflect," the judge replied automatically, still staring down at his desk.

Renaldo asked the judge for a moment while he looked over his notes and consulted with Joe Jimmerson. The pause gave the jurors plenty of time to take in what had just happened.

Finally Renaldo turned to face the judge. "I have no further questions, Your Honor."

It appeared Judge Sandoval was still oblivious to the fact that Officer Keller had identified Sarah as the defendant.

"Your witness, Mrs. Wong."

"No questions, Your Honor."

"You are excused, Officer Keller," said Judge Sandoval.

Then, just as Leon Keller stepped down from the witness stand, Sarah said, "I'm sorry, Your Honor, I do have one question."

"Very well, Mrs. Wong, but make it brief."

"Officer Keller, are you as certain about the accuracy of the rest of your testimony as you are about your identification of the defendant here in court today?"

The officer, standing a few feet in front of the jury box, shifted awkwardly from one foot to the other.

"No," he said quietly after a pause.

A perfect answer, thought Sarah.

* * *

Over the next five days, Renaldo paraded almost a dozen technical, forensic, and medical witnesses through Courtroom 201. Popular TV shows like CSI and its many spin-offs had led jurors to expect ever-increasing amounts of forensic evidence, and Renaldo was going to great lengths to satisfy them, even if the evidence had little or no relevance to the case.

He started with the detective who had taken the crime scene photographs. She identified pictures of the exterior and interior of Lexi's car and the inside of the garage. Most of the photographs were in color, but a few were taken in ultraviolet light to reveal fluids and other details not visible to the naked eye. None of the pictures depicted Anna's body because it had been taken away before the photographer arrived.

Next Renaldo called two fingerprint witnesses. The first one testified about how he had collected latent fingerprints at the scene. He explained in great detail the methods used to lift fingerprints from all sorts of surfaces — glass, metal, wood, even cloth. He told the jury he obtained seventy latent prints from Lexi's vehicle and from various items inside the car.

The second fingerprint expert, Jenna Rice, testified about comparing the latent prints taken from the scene with known exemplars from Lexi Conway. Her testimony was filled with technical explanations of friction ridge impressions, swirls, and whorls. All told, she was able to match forty-seven latent prints from the crime scene to exemplars taken from Lexi.

Sarah had no questions for the first fingerprint expert and only a few for the second.

"Ms. Rice, did any of the latent fingerprints taken from the scene not match my client?"

"Yes."

"How many?"

"Either twenty-two or twenty-three, I believe."

"So those fingerprints belonged to someone else?"

"Yes."

"Were you asked by the detectives to compare those latent prints to any other known exemplars — say from other family members or other possible suspects?"

"No."

Although the fact that other people's prints had been found at the crime scene was not germane to her Warrior Gene defense, Sarah wanted to keep everyone guessing, especially Renaldo. With a wave of her hands, and a dramatic spin, she headed back to her seat, signaling that she had scored an important victory for the defense.

Next, Renaldo called five health professionals to the stand. He started with the two paramedics who attended to Anna. They testified that she was already dead when they arrived, but they continued to work feverishly to try to revive her. Knowing there was going to be a criminal investigation, they called their supervisor to ask for permission to transport her body directly to the county morgue instead of the hospital, which they did. Both paramedics testified that Anna's body was slightly pink. This was unusual, they told the jury, because dead bodies are usually grayish. Despite repeated prodding from Renaldo, neither paramedic was able to explain why Anna's body was pink instead of gray.

The next two witnesses were the paramedics who treated Lexi and took her to Memorial Hospital. The first was confident and self-assured, and her memory of the event was exceptional, as she testified about tiny details that were not in the written report. Her partner was far less impressive. He had been a paramedic for almost fifteen years, and gave his testimony with an air of indifference, even becoming downright surly on occasion.

All in all, Renaldo's direct examination of the four paramedics was disjointed and confusing. By calling them out of sequence, their accounts were difficult to follow. Sarah wondered why Renaldo kept calling unnecessary witnesses — two police officers, two paramedics. Almost always, the second witness added little new information, and more often than not there were inconsistencies between the two. She passed on cross-examining the first three paramedics, but thought she would give it a go with the last one.

"Mr. Wasserman, did my client say anything before you transported her to the hospital?"

"Yes. She kept asking what had happened."

"What did you tell her?"

"I told her I didn't really know."

"Why did she ask about what had happened?"

"I don't know."

"Could it have been because she actually didn't know what had happened?"

Renaldo jumped up. "Objection, calls for speculation."

"Sustained. Move on, Mrs. Wong."

Sarah nodded. "How would you characterize the tone of my client's voice, Mr. Wasserman?"

"It wasn't really that emotional, especially considering everything that had happened. It was sort of flat, almost like a monotone."

"Sort of like a robot?" probed Sarah.

"Yeah, I guess you could say that."

"Like a robot on automatic pilot?"

"Yeah, sort of."

Sarah had everything she needed, so she sat down.

The final medical witness was the emergency room doctor who had treated Lexi at Memorial Hospital. It took Renaldo almost half a day to walk Dr. Taylor through his description of Lexi's condition and treatment.

Using technical language filled with jargon that few in the courtroom understood, Dr. Taylor explained that Lexi was in a very serious condition when she was brought in to the emergency room. She displayed all the classic symptoms of acute carbon monoxide poisoning, and she was given pure oxygen to breathe until her blood gas levels returned to normal, the usual treatment in such cases. Extensive neurological testing indicated she had suffered no permanent brain damage.

More than once Judge Sandoval tried to hurry Renaldo along, but eventually he gave up. Renaldo was determined to plow ahead with his methodical examination of each witness. Technically there was nothing wrong with his approach — his questions were to the point, clear, and unambiguous — but he seemed to have forgotten that being a good trial attorney was as much art as it was science, and there was nothing artistic about his performance.

Renaldo pressed Dr. Taylor several times about any statements Lexi may have made when under his care, and initially the doctor refused to answer the questions, citing the sanctity of the physician–patient relationship. After Judge Sandoval ruled that the physician–patient privilege did not apply in this situation, Dr. Taylor told the court that Lexi had made several mumbled references to her baby, but nothing that could be construed as either an admission or denial of guilt.

Sarah had no cross-examination for Dr. Taylor. Just as Dr. Taylor was leaving the witness stand, Lexi showed Sarah a note she had written on her pad.

> *I'm tired of all of this. Can't I just plead guilty and get it over with?*

After reading the note, Sarah asked Judge Sandoval for an extra-long afternoon recess so she could talk with her client. The judge readily agreed, as he needed a break from the increasingly mundane testimony, and he decided to adjourn for the day.

After Lexi had been escorted back to the holding cell at the courthouse, Sarah went to see her. Brian moved to the other end of the hallway outside to give them a modicum of privacy. The cell, eight by eight with a bench on one side, was not designed for lengthy attorney–client discussions. Sarah had to stand by the lockup door, which was solid steel on the bottom and steel bars with reinforced wire mesh on the top. Though their faces were only inches apart, she could barely see Lexi as they talked.

"I just want to plead guilty and get this over with," said Lexi, her voice sounding tired and filled with emotion.

"But Lexi, the DA hasn't offered any sort of plea bargain. If you plead guilty, the judge might give you the death penalty."

"That might not be so bad. Why are we even having this stupid trial anyway?"

Sarah chose her words very carefully. "I want to help you. We might even be able to win."

"But what if I don't want to win?"

* * *

On Thursday, Renaldo began by calling two clerks from the Donut Shoppe, who both testified they saw Lexi and Anna on the morning of August 11.

Most of Renaldo's direct was aimed at establishing when Lexi and Anna entered and left the Donut Shoppe. Right in front of the jury box Renaldo and Joe set up a large poster board that depicted the hours of eight a.m. to noon on August 11 divided into fifteen-minute segments. James Bayne, the first clerk from the Donut Shoppe to testify, indicated on the outsize timeline that Lexi and Anna arrived at 8:50 and left at 9:10. The second Donut Shoppe clerk confirmed James's time estimates.

Next up was Lou Gordon, a cashier at Pete's Market. He said Lexi spent about forty-five minutes in Pete's, coming in about 9:05 and leaving at 9:50. He made his own entry on the huge timeline, slightly overlapping the one made by James Bayne. While the Donut Shoppe clerks had interacted with Anna—James remembered Lexi holding Anna up so they could see her—Lou Gordon testified that Anna stayed in her baby carrier the entire time Lexi was in the market.

Sarah decided it was time to be a little more aggressive in her approach and put on more of a show. Jurors expected defense attorneys to be fighters, especially for clients they believed in. After more than a week of doing very little, some of the jurors might have concluded that Sarah didn't believe Lexi was innocent. Besides, a headline in the *Santa Felicia Observer* that morning had asked "Has The Baby Killer's Defense Attorney Given Up?" Sarah didn't want to risk losing public support or the jurors' sympathy.

She cross-examined all three of the timeline witnesses vigorously and was able to elicit widely disparate descriptions of Lexi's appearance from them. James Bayne said that Lexi had been wearing a sundress, while the other clerk from the Donut Shoppe said it was a miniskirt. Only Lou Gordon testified correctly that Lexi had been wearing shorts and a tank top, although he was mistaken about their color. Numerous other inconsistencies were sprinkled throughout their testimonies, and Sarah drew attention to each one. Although none of these details really mattered, she noticed that many of the jurors started taking notes again, something that hadn't happened in days.

When she was done with Lou Gordon, she felt exhilarated as she always did after a successful cross-examination. Her heart was racing and her palms were clammy. As she shuffled through her notes in preparation for the next witness — the manager of the Sunoco station — she suddenly felt lightheaded and disoriented. Everything slowed down and the courtroom started closing in on her, getting darker and darker.

"Your Honor, I'm not feeling ..."

* * *

"Mrs. Wong, can you hear me?"

"Sarah? Are you okay?"

The lights in the emergency room made her squint. She knew one of the voices was Matt's, but she didn't recognize the other one.

"Are my babies okay?" Sarah tried to sit up, but Matt held her down gently.

"They're fine, Mrs. Wong. Your obstetrician is on the way, and she'll do a full exam when she gets here. It shouldn't be long. 'Til then, just try to get some rest."

"Hon, what's going on?"

"You fainted in court, Tiger. Right in front of the jury. I heard it was quite a show. They took you out on a stretcher and everything. You really do have a flair for the dramatic."

Matt's lighthearted tone helped Sarah relax, but she was still worried about her babies.

"Do you think our babies are okay?"

"I'm sure they are," Matt assured her. "Let's just take it easy until Dr. Sadler gets here."

She closed her eyes for what seemed like a few seconds, but Matt told her later that she slept for forty-five minutes.

When Dr. Sadler finally arrived, she quickly said hello and started right in. The doctor worked on Sarah for a full half hour, prodding and poking her before conducting an ultrasound with a portable machine that had been wheeled into Sarah's room.

"I've got great news, Sarah. Both babies look fine," she announced at long last. "One of them has a bit of an elevated heart rate. Nothing to worry about, but I do want to keep an eye on it."

"That's good," Sarah said with relief.

"But you're not going to want to hear what I'm about to tell you," said the doctor.

Sarah frowned up at her.

"I'd like you to stay off your feet for the rest of your pregnancy," Dr. Sadler continued.

"You mean bed rest?"

"That's exactly what I mean."

"But I can't! I'm in the middle of a huge trial — a murder trial, my biggest case ever. I can't stop now!"

Matt jumped in. "Can't Conrad take over for you?"

"Absolutely not. He's never tried a capital case before, and he's not even familiar with the facts. It would take him weeks to get up to speed."

"Couldn't the judge just postpone the trial until after you give birth?" suggested Dr. Sadler.

"Not possible," replied Sarah. "We're almost halfway through."

"How much longer is the trial likely to last?"

"Probably two or three weeks."

"I'll tell you what—if you agree to wear a dual-channel fetal heart monitor for an hour every evening and send me the data before you go to bed, I'll let you keep going in the trial."

How nice of you, Sarah thought to herself.

"But if I see any problems, I'm going to order you into bed. I'll call the judge myself if I have to."

"Okay, that's a deal," said Sarah. "But please don't call the judge. Nobody in court knows I'm pregnant and I'd like to keep it that way."

"I think that's a compromise I can live with," said the doctor. "Matt, can you come by the office today and pick up the heart monitor?"

"Sure thing."

"I think that's everything," said Dr. Sadler, "but I have one more question for you."

"What's that?"

"I noticed the sex of your babies while I was doing the ultrasound. You want to know?"

Sarah turned to Matt and grabbed his hand. "What d'ya think, hon?"

"It's up to you, Tiger. Whatever you want."

Sarah paused for only a second or two. "Go ahead. Tell us."

"You're going to have a boy and a girl!"

CHAPTER 14

After Sarah had fainted in the courtroom, Judge Sandoval had adjourned the trial until the following week. Sarah stayed in bed for the next three days with her fetal heart monitor on all the time, and she sent readings to Dr. Sadler four times a day. She ate properly and slept well, and on Sunday Dr. Sadler reluctantly kept her end of the bargain and gave Sarah her permission to keep going in the trial.

The following Monday, Sarah and Nick were already seated at counsel table when Brian brought Lexi in to court at nine fifteen.

"Mrs. Wong? Are you okay? I was really worried about you. I kept asking about you all weekend, but the guards wouldn't tell me nothing."

"I'm fine, Lexi. I just fainted, that's all. Thanks for asking."

"Are you feeling better today, Mrs. Wong?" asked Judge Sandoval, sounding genuinely concerned.

"Yes I am, Your Honor. I don't think I've been eating well enough over the past few weeks and I just got a little lightheaded. Thank you for giving me a couple of days to rest. I'm much better now."

Judge Sandoval nodded and turned to Renaldo. "Mr. Sepulveda, you may call your next witness."

The manager of the Sunoco gas station on the corner of Lassiter Street and 18th Avenue testified for almost an hour about the station's surveillance cameras and the manner in

Death by DNA

which the videotapes were recorded and stored. Renaldo had the manager identify and authenticate the videotape from August 11, and he moved it into evidence. He then asked Judge Sandoval for permission to show the tape to the jury, which Judge Sandoval granted, without objection from Sarah — the tape wasn't going to hurt her case, as it didn't really show much.

But as soon as the tape started to play, she realized it was not the same video she had seen before. The video she had in her possession had shown the driver's side of Lexi's car, but this video was focused on the passenger side. Thinking the difference was no big deal, Sarah didn't object right away. Soon enough, though, she realized it was indeed a big deal. With her eyes glued to the oversized video monitor near the jury box, Sarah watched Lexi open the rear passenger door, lean into her car and shake Anna violently. For at least a minute Lexi slapped, hit, and shook her little girl repeatedly. Sarah was so dumbfounded she couldn't object. When Renaldo turned off the tape, she got up and blurted out, "Your Honor, may we approach?"

Without waiting for a response, she strode briskly to the judge's bench. Renaldo and the court reporter scurried after her.

"Your Honor, I move for a mistrial," Sarah began. "This is the first time I've seen this tape. I filed a discovery motion months ago and the prosecution gave me a different tape, nothing like the one we just saw in court. This is clearly prosecutorial misconduct and I demand a mistrial."

"Mr. Sepulveda?"

"Your Honor, in all honesty this tape is new to me too. The other tape shows Ms. Conway from the other side of the car leaning in. You can't really see what happens in the car."

"Mrs. Wong, I'm inclined to believe Mr. Sepulveda, and I'm going to allow the tape into evidence. In my opinion, this is no different than a witness's testimony varying from what was expected. I'll give you plenty of latitude to cross-examine the witness about the tape. Trials are full of surprises and you're just going to have to deal with this one. Your objection is overruled."

"Your Honor, in view of the completely unexpected nature of this videotape, I need some time to talk with my client. May we have a half-hour recess?"

"That seems fair." Judge Sandoval turned toward the jury. "Ladies and gentlemen, it's time for our morning break. We will be in recess for a half hour."

By the time Sarah reached the holding cell she was fuming. Lexi's actions at the gas station didn't look like those of someone who was on automatic pilot, acting without free will. She looked like she knew exactly what she was doing.

"Why the hell didn't you tell me the truth about what happened at the gas station?"

"I did, ma'am."

"No you didn't," exclaimed Sarah, doing her best not to yell. "You told me you shook and poked your baby to see if she was okay. You didn't tell me you slapped her and hit her!"

"I didn't really hit her," Lexi said, her head bowed.

"Yes you did!" Now Sarah was shouting. "Didn't you watch the videotape in court? What did it look like to you?"

Sarah's chest was heaving in and out, and she was shaking. Nobody said anything. Sarah stared at Lexi and Lexi stared at the floor. Eventually Lexi broke the silence.

"I don't want to talk about this anymore."

"What do you mean you don't want to talk about it? You never want to talk about it. How am I supposed to help you?"

"I told you, I don't want your help. I just want to plead guilty and get this over with."

"It's too late for that. Let's just go out and finish the trial."

Sarah had no intention of giving up now. Despite the new videotape, she still thought she could win.

"Brian, we're done in here," she yelled down the hall.

When everyone had returned after the recess, Renaldo told the judge he had no further questions for the gas-station manager.

"Very well. Your witness, Mrs. Wong."

Sarah was still steaming from her confrontation with Lexi. It was hard for her to think clearly, and she was worried her anger might show during questioning, so she quickly decided on the safest course of action.

"I have no questions for this witness, Your Honor."

"Please call your next witness, Mr. Sepulveda."

"The prosecution calls Dr. Vijay Prakeesh."

Sarah quickly rose to her feet. "Your Honor, the defense will stipulate as to the cause of death. We stipulate that Anna Conway died of carbon monoxide poisoning on August 11."

"Mr. Sepulveda, do you accept this stipulation?" asked Judge Sandoval.

Renaldo was clearly caught off guard. He had probably been expecting Sarah to battle with him tooth and nail over the cause of death since carbon monoxide poisoning can be difficult to diagnose, as it sometimes looks like other forms of asphyxiation. She knew that Renaldo had three experts lined up to testify about the cause of death. If he accepted the stipulation, none of them would get to testify.

Renaldo looked over at Joe who shrugged and, after a moment's pause, Renaldo agreed to the stipulation.

"Very well," said Judge Sandoval. "Ladies and gentlemen of the jury, the defense and the prosecution have agreed that Anna Conway died of carbon monoxide poisoning on August 11. This stipulation means that the cause of death has been proven beyond a reasonable doubt and the prosecution does not have to present any evidence about it."

This was a huge gamble for Sarah — probably the biggest risk she had ever taken in a trial — but there was no turning back now. She looked at Lexi to see how she had reacted to the stipulation, but Lexi just stared straight ahead, no discernible emotion on her face.

"Mr. Sepulveda, you may call your next witness."

"Unfortunately my next witness is not available today. I had three witnesses ready to testify about the cause of death and I thought their testimony would take the entire day, if not longer."

"I understand, Mr. Sepulveda. I'm also surprised by Mrs. Wong's stipulation."

Sarah almost objected to the judge's editorializing, but stopped herself just in time. She preferred judges who stayed out of the way and let the attorneys try their cases with little interference. That clearly wasn't going to happen with Judge Sandoval.

The judge took off his glasses and swiveled so that he was directly facing the jury. "Ladies and gentlemen, I know it's only eleven fifteen, but it looks like Mrs. Wong has brought today's session prematurely to a close. Enjoy your time off today, and remember not to form any opinions about the case until it has been submitted to you. See you tomorrow at nine sharp."

Damn him! Why is it my fault? Renaldo was the one who wasn't ready to proceed.

Sarah kept smiling until the last juror was out of sight and then turned back to Lexi to explain what had happened, but Lexi and Brian were already halfway to the lockup door.

Sarah tried to visit Lexi in the courthouse lockup, but Lexi refused to see her.

* * *

Judge Sandoval began Tuesday morning with an apology to the jury that quickly transformed into another barb at Sarah.

"Ladies and gentlemen, I want to apologize for these delays. I know how frustrating it is to spend so much time waiting. I've asked Mrs. Wong to avoid any future delays, and I'm hopeful she will comply with my request."

"But Your Honor ..."

"Call your next witness, Mr. Sepulveda," the judge continued.

Renaldo called the detective who had taken Lexi's written statement in the hospital. Lexi had been semi-conscious for almost two days after the events of August 11, and Renaldo took great pains to establish that she was clearheaded by the time she gave her statement to the detective. After many preliminary questions, Renaldo handed the original copy of Lexi's statement to the detective.

"Detective Stenhouse, do you recognize this document?"

"Yes, it's the defendant's written statement I obtained from her on Wednesday, August 13."

"Your Honor, with the court's permission I would like to display a slightly larger version of the statement for everyone to see."

"Go ahead, Mr. Sepulveda."

"Slightly larger" was not an accurate description of the display Renaldo actually produced. From behind Isabel's desk he retrieved a gigantic blowup of Lexi's statement, while Joe set up a wooden tripod next to the jury box. Together they positioned the image on the stand so everyone in the courtroom could see it. Sarah had to admit she was impressed with the crystal-clear reproduction, including Lexi's signature at the bottom.

"Detective Stenhouse, is this an exact copy of the written statement you obtained from the defendant on August 13?" Renaldo asked.

"Yes, it is."

"And is that Ms. Conway's signature at the very bottom of the statement?"

"Yes."

"Could you step off the stand and approach the poster board, please."

"Sure."

"Could you please take the red marker and circle the paragraph that begins with 'I didn't know what to do'."

Very carefully, Detective Stenhouse drew a neat red line around the fourth paragraph on the board.

> *I didn't know what to do. For sure, I wasnt going to tell Ryan. He would never ever ever understand and he would be mad at me forever. I was panicy. I knew it was my fault that Anna was dead.*

When the detective sat back down, Renaldo had one final request. "Could you please read the last sentence of the paragraph you circled."

"I knew it was my fault that Anna was dead."

"Nothing further, Your Honor."

"Your witness, Mrs. Wong."

Two could play this game, thought Sarah.

"Detective Stenhouse, I'm sorry to inconvenience you, but could you approach the poster board one more time."

Once the detective was back in front of the board, Sarah asked him to take the red marker again.

"Would you please put a neat red box around the words in the statement where it says that Lexi killed her baby."

"But I've already done that, counselor."

"No, you haven't. You just circled the paragraph in which she said it was her fault. I'm talking about the words where Lexi explicitly admits to killing her baby."

Detective Stenhouse stared at the giant poster board for

at least a minute. "I'm sorry, counselor, but I don't see those words anywhere."

"That's because they're not there," Sarah said, turning to face the jury.

Her cross-examination was done.

"Any redirect, Mr. Sepulveda?"

"No, Your Honor."

"Very well. Is your next witness ready?"

"No, Your Honor."

"Why not?" asked Judge Sandoval impatiently.

"Because we don't have any more. The prosecution rests."

"Thank you, Mr. Sepulveda. Mrs. Wong, are you ready to begin the defense case?"

"Your Honor, I have a motion for dismissal."

"Very well. Ladies and gentlemen, the prosecution has rested their case. We will be in recess until tomorrow at nine a.m."

As the jurors filed out of the courtroom Sarah watched them closely, trying to glean some indication of which way they were leaning, but she came up empty.

"Let the record reflect that the jury has left the courtroom," said the judge when the last juror had gone. "You have a motion, Mrs. Wong?"

"Yes, Your Honor." Sarah moved over to the podium with a stack of papers. "Your Honor, I move to dismiss the charges pursuant to Section 1118.1 of the California Penal Code on the grounds that the evidence is not sufficient to sustain a conviction on appeal."

Renaldo stood up. "Your Honor, the State has proven every element—"

"Sit down, Mr. Sepulveda," Judge Sandoval said curtly. "Do you really think I'm going to grant Mrs. Wong's motion? You need to learn when to keep your mouth shut."

Judge Sandoval turned to Sarah. "Motion denied."

CHAPTER 15

"Mrs. Wong, do you wish to make an opening statement?"

"Yes, Your Honor."

"You may proceed."

Sarah stood up and spoke from her place at the defense table. "Good morning, ladies and gentlemen." As she spoke, Sarah made eye contact with each of the twelve jurors and four alternates.

"Good morning," the jurors responded in unison.

"My opening statement will be very brief," she began, unable to resist getting in a dig at Renaldo's rambling opening statement. "Over the next few days, I'm going to show you that Lexi Conway is neither legally nor morally responsible for the death of her daughter, and I will ask you to find her not guilty of the charges against her."

With that, she sat down.

"You may call your first witness, Mrs. Wong."

Over the course of the next two days, Sarah called four character witnesses to the stand: Lexi's mother, her sister Lisa, her cousin Julie, and Peg Bassi, her best friend from high school. She asked all four the same set of questions.

She began by asking them to describe Lexi's childhood, upbringing, and personality. They all described her as a happy, carefree child who loved to play with animals, and each shared a sentimental animal story — when Lexi adopted a homeless cat, the time she stopped to help a dog that had been hit by a car, and when she nursed a bird that had damaged its wing. Then Sarah asked about Lexi's love for her baby and her boyfriend. Was she a kind and loving person? Did she want her baby? Did she love her baby? Did she love Ryan? To a person, each of her friends and family members explained that all Lexi had ever wanted was to have children and be a mother. They all painted the same picture—Lexi was a caring mother who loved Anna more than anything in the world.

For each witness, Sarah finished by asking if they could think of any reason why Lexi would kill her own baby. All of them answered quickly and confidently: No.

Renaldo's cross-examinations of these witnesses were lengthy, energetic, and pointed. Without much difficulty, he got each of them to concede that they had no firsthand knowledge of what had happened on the morning of August 11. In one of his more inspired moments, he asked Peg Bassi, Lexi's high-school friend, if she thought it was possible for a nice person to commit murder. Peg could only muster, "I suppose so."

On Friday morning, Sarah called her final character witness, Madeline Truex, one of Lexi's neighbors on Windmere Place. Her testimony was especially important because she was the only character witness who was not a good friend or family member, and she had seen Lexi on the morning of August 11.

Mrs. Truex told the jury that Lexi was a nice, kind person. She described how Lexi and Anna used to go for walks almost every day and how Lexi would show off Anna to everyone she encountered.

Sarah directed Mrs. Truex's attention to the morning of August 11. Mrs. Truex said she remembered it well, because that was the day two ambulances came roaring up to Lexi's place. She had seen Lexi and Anna as usual that morning while she was out walking her dog, Henry, and nothing seemed out of the ordinary. She remembered that Lexi had a bad cold and little Anna had the sniffles, but other than that they both seemed okay.

It was about eleven forty-five when she heard the first ambulance, Mrs. Truex said. She thought she had seen Lexi pull into her garage about a half hour or so before that, but she wasn't absolutely certain about the time. She also saw a police car, but couldn't remember if it arrived before or after the ambulance. She had walked over to Lexi's place to see what was going on, but one of the officers told her to go back home, which she did. There was a second ambulance siren sometime later, but she didn't go back out because the officer had told her to stay away.

On cross-examination, Renaldo probed Madeline Truex's memory for details of the morning of August 11 and demonstrated that her memory was far from perfect. He got her to concede that all her time estimates could be off by as much as a half hour or so, and he established that she had no direct knowledge of what happened in Lexi's garage that morning.

To wrap up his cross-examination, Renaldo asked Mrs. Truex the same question he had posed to Peg Bassi: did she think it was possible for a nice person to commit murder? Her reply was direct and heartfelt: "I guess it's possible, but I'm certain that Lexi Conway would never have hurt her beloved Anna, may she rest in peace."

When Madeline Truex stepped off the stand, Sarah felt that this part of the defense case had gone better than she had expected. All five of her character witnesses had painted the same portrait of Lexi, though with slightly different brushstrokes — she was a kind, caring person who loved her baby, and there was no apparent reason why she would intentionally hurt little Anna. To Sarah's relief, none of the witnesses mentioned Lexi's temper and occasional flashes of anger, or said anything about her regretting having Anna.

After the lunch break on Friday, Sarah stood up and announced that she wanted to offer another stipulation.

"Counsel, please approach the bench," said Judge Sandoval swiftly.

Sarah, Renaldo, and the court reporter went to the side of the bench furthest from the jury. Once everyone was in place, Sarah jumped right in. "Your Honor, I would like to stipulate that my client killed her baby," said Sarah.

"What? Did I hear you correctly?" asked Judge Sandoval.

"Yes, you did, Your Honor."

"Mr. Sepulveda, I assume this stipulation is fine with you. Is that right?"

"I guess so, Your Honor, but I have no idea what Mrs. Wong is up to. I need to think carefully about this. Can I have a one-hour recess?"

"I think we all need a recess, especially Mrs. Wong. Let's take a two-hour break and come back at three thirty. I'll meet with the two of you in chambers at that time, and then we'll bring the jury back in at three forty-five. Mrs. Wong, I hope you know what you're doing."

Judge Sandoval dismissed the jury, telling them to return to the court at three forty-five.

Before Brian took Lexi back into the lockup, she leaned toward Sarah and asked what was happening.

"Nothing much, Lexi. Just some technical legal stuff. I'll see you in a bit."

Sarah had only decided to propose the second stipulation the night before, and she needed to explain to Lexi why she was doing it. But first she needed to talk with Nick.

* * *

"You're going to do what? Are you crazy?" Nick couldn't believe what he was hearing.

"Hear me out," Sarah said. "You know I'm not contesting the manner of death, right?"

"Yeah."

"And you know I'm not claiming that someone else killed Anna, right?"

"Yes."

"Well, I've already stipulated to the cause of death. Why not stipulate as to the killer? I figure the jury will see that I'm sincere and honest, and they'll be more likely to believe me when I explain what the real defense is."

"It sounds reasonable when you explain it like that, but I just don't know. Why don't we get Conrad's opinion?"

"No."

"Why not?"

"I know what he'll say. He'll say it's a terrible idea."

"Well, maybe he has a point ..."

"My mind's made up."

Nick took a deep breath and stared at Sarah. "If it's okay with you, I'd like to run some errands. I'll see you back in court at three thirty," he added before rushing off.

Sarah knew he wasn't running any errands; he was going to see Conrad. But that was okay—nothing they could come up with would change her mind.

She still had Lexi to deal with and she went down to the courthouse holding cell to see her. She expected a huge battle, but Lexi barely looked up when Sarah explained the stipulation and why she was doing it. It was clear that Lexi had given up long ago.

* * *

By three twenty, all the attorneys were back in court, and a third attorney from the DA's office had appeared and was sitting next to Renaldo and Joe.

Isabel waved everyone back into chambers.

"Let's get started," said Judge Sandoval. "Mrs. Wong, are you still offering the stipulation?"

"Yes, I am."

219

"Please repeat it slowly so I can write it down."

Sarah obliged, speaking slowly and clearly. "The defense will stipulate that Lexi Conway killed Anna Conway on August 11."

Judge Sandoval read it back. "It is stipulated that Lexi Conway murdered Anna Conway on August 11."

"NO, Your Honor! I did not say *murder*. I said *kill*. We are only stipulating that Lexi Conway *killed* Anna Conway."

"Is that wording fine with you, Mr. Sepulveda?"

Renaldo turned to Joe and the third DA, both of whom nodded. "Yes it is," he said.

Judge Sandoval glanced at the clock. "All right, let's go back out and put the stipulation on the record and then adjourn for the day."

As they returned to the courtroom, Nick and Sarah conferred in hushed tones. He told Sarah what Conrad had said, and Sarah assured him that she knew what she was doing, that everything would be fine.

When they got back to the courtroom, Lexi was at the defense table and the jury was seated in the jury box.

"Welcome back, everyone," Judge Sandoval said once he had taken his seat. "I trust you enjoyed the extended recess." He turned toward the jury and put on his reading glasses. "Ladies and gentlemen, the prosecution and the defense have entered into another stipulation, and this one's a biggie."

Sarah thought about objecting, but what would be the point. It *was* a biggie.

"Let me read it to you," the judge went on. He looked down at his notepad. "It is hereby stipulated by the defense that the defendant, Lexi Conway, killed Anna Conway on August 11."

The jurors' faces, a collective mixture of disbelief and confusion, confirmed that it was indeed a biggie.

CHAPTER 16

The Conway case went on a two-day hiatus at the beginning of the following week while Judge Sandoval attended a judicial conference in San Francisco. Sarah could imagine him holding court in the hotel bar as he regaled his colleagues with tales of the baby killer's case.

When the trial resumed on Wednesday the eighteenth, after three weeks of testimony, the real defense was about to begin.

"The defense calls Dr. Markowitz to the stand."

Judge Sandoval dispatched Brian to the hallway to ask Dr. Markowitz to come in. As she walked down the center aisle to the front of the courtroom, sashaying like a runway model, no one could take their eyes off her. Even the judge scrutinized her progress with interest. She was wearing a sleeveless crimson silk top and a short black skirt, and her shoulder-length auburn hair gleamed in the sunlight streaming through the windows. She stood next to the witness stand and looked around the room.

Sarah was a little alarmed at this display of coquettishness. It showed a lack of respect for the court and it made her distinctly uncomfortable.

"Please state your name for the record," said Isabel.

"Candi Markowitz."

"I'm sorry, what is your first name?"

"Candi. C-A-N-D-I."

"Thank you, you may have a seat."

Judge Sandoval turned to Sarah. "Mrs. Wong, you may proceed."

Sarah approached the large wooden podium and stood to one side, keeping both her and the witness in full view of the jury.

"Good morning, Dr. Markowitz."

"Good morning, Sarah."

Sarah winced. She didn't like the casual way Candi was treating courtroom proceedings, and feared she was going to have a rough time with her star witness.

"Dr. Markowitz, what is your occupation?"

"I am an expert in DNA analyses and DNA fingerprinting."

"Can you describe your education, training, and experience for the jury?"

"After majoring in biology at Oberlin College, I obtained a masters and a Ph.D. in behavioral genetics, and an M.D., all from the University of California at Berkeley. After completing my M.D. and Ph.D., I was awarded a two-year postdoctoral fellowship at Stanford University, where I studied advanced techniques in gene splicing and other forms of genetic engineering. After my postdoc at Stanford, I worked at the FBI crime lab in Quantico, Virginia for four years, mostly doing DNA fingerprinting. After that, I established my own practice with offices in Los Angeles and Santa Barbara. I currently spend most of my time analyzing DNA samples and doing consulting work for attorneys on criminal and civil cases. I also serve as an adjunct professor at the University of California, Los Angeles, where I teach a graduate seminar in DNA fingerprinting."

"What exactly is DNA fingerprinting, Dr. Markowitz?"

"Simply put, it involves comparing the DNA from a tissue or fluid sample, such as semen, blood, or saliva obtained from a crime scene or a victim's body, with the DNA from a known sample, often from a suspect in a criminal case. Conceptually, it's not that different than making regular fingerprint comparisons. The goal of both procedures is the same – to examine whether the DNA or fingerprints of a suspect match the DNA or fingerprints left at a crime scene. Would you like me to go into more detail about how DNA fingerprinting is done?"

"That won't be necessary. Would you say that you're skilled in conducting DNA analyses?"

"Yes. I've been qualified as an expert in almost every county in California, in seven other states, and in several federal jurisdictions. At the risk of sounding immodest, I think I'm very good at what I do."

Sarah anticipated that Renaldo would want to make an issue out of the fact that Dr. Markowitz was a paid defense expert, and she decided to raise it herself to undercut his argument.

"Are you being paid for your work on this case?"

"Of course."

"Who hired you?"

"You did, Sarah."

"And who is paying you?"

"My checks come from the Superior Court of Santa Felicia County."

"Is your pay conditioned on what conclusions you reach?"

"I'm not sure I understand."

"What I mean is, are you paid the same whether or not you reach conclusions that are favorable to the defense?"

"Of course. My remuneration is never dependent on what I find. I believe that would be illegal, and even if it's not illegal, it would certainly be unethical."

Sarah paused and looked at the jury. So far they seemed accepting of Dr. Markowitz.

"Did you perform any DNA fingerprinting in this case?"

"No, you told me it wasn't necessary."

"What *did* you do?"

"I acted as a consultant for the purpose of exploring whether there might be a genetic explanation for Ms. Conway's behavior."

Renaldo jumped up, almost knocking his chair over. "Your Honor, may we approach?"

"Yes."

As soon as Renaldo, Sarah, and the court reporter were at the bench, Judge Sandoval asked, "Mr. Sepulveda, is this a discovery matter?"

"Yes it is, Your Honor."

"Let's take this in chambers then." While Sarah and Renaldo were still at the side bar, Judge Sandoval addressed the jury. "Ladies and gentlemen, we are going to take a thirty-minute recess. Please retire to the jury room and we will let you know when we are ready for you again."

Back in chambers, the judge poured himself a coffee and sat down. "Mr. Sepulveda, I don't see the problem. Dr. Markowitz is on the witness list provided by the defense."

"Yes she is, Your Honor, but she's only listed as a DNA expert. There's no indication that she would be testifying about the genetic causes of behavior."

"Mrs. Wong?"

"Your Honor, I didn't know I was required to say *exactly* what she was going to testify about. Dr. Markowitz is a DNA expert and she's going to testify about matters relating to DNA and genetics."

"So what exactly *is* she going to testify about?"

"Just as she said a few moments ago — the genetic causes of behavior."

"Mrs. Wong, when I saw the witness list last week I came to the same conclusion as Mr. Sepulveda. I assumed that this expert was going to testify about DNA fingerprinting or something like that. In my opinion, listing her as a DNA expert was misleading."

"Also, I have no written reports from Dr. Markowitz,"

added Renaldo. "I demand that counsel turn those reports over to me before Dr. Markowitz is allowed to testify."

"Dr. Markowitz did not prepare any written reports for me, so I have nothing to hand over to the prosecution. Also, let me remind you that this is very similar to the failure of the prosecution to provide the defense with all the videotapes from the Sunoco gas station. You allowed Mr. Sepulveda to present that videotape to the jury despite the fact that I had never seen it before, and you imposed no sanctions at all on Mr. Sepulveda."

"I see your point, Mrs. Wong, but this is quite different. Mr. Sepulveda was unaware of the existence of the second videotape, whereas you knew ahead of time exactly what Dr. Markowitz was going to testify about. I am inclined to allow Dr. Markowitz to testify, but I am going to give the prosecution ample time to prepare for their cross-examination. Let's go out in court and put this on the record."

When Sarah walked back into court the jury was absent, but everyone else was still in place, including Dr. Markowitz. This was going to be a bit embarrassing, but at least it would be over quickly.

Judge Sandoval summarized what he had discussed with counsel in chambers. "I find that Mrs. Wong has violated the spirit, if not the letter, of the California discovery law for criminal cases, specifically Section 1054.3 of the California Penal Code." Sarah cringed. "Therefore, I find Mrs. Wong in contempt of court and I fine her $100."

What? Contempt? The judge hadn't said anything about contempt in chambers. For a moment Sarah was speechless. But she quickly recovered and took a deep breath.

"I apologize for my oversight, Your Honor," she said, trying to sound like she meant it. "I accept your punishment, and I will pay the fine first thing in the morning."

"Mrs. Wong, the fine is payable forthwith. In cash."

Sarah quickly searched through her briefcase. "Your Honor, I've only got $80 with me. Can I give the rest to the court clerk tomorrow?"

"No. If you can't pay now, I will have to sentence you to one day in jail."

"Judge, I've got $20," piped up Isabel. "Sarah can pay me back tomorrow."

"This seems a little irregular," said Judge Sandoval, "but I guess I'll allow it. Brian, bring the jury back in."

As the jury filed into the courtroom Sarah smiled broadly at Isabel and mouthed, "Thank you."

As the jurors took their places, Sarah knew that a bigger problem lay ahead. She had not given Renaldo a copy of the Warrior Gene test conducted by The DNA Group, and that was a clear violation of California discovery rules. She had decided weeks ago that she was willing to risk a contempt fine in order to keep her defense a secret from the prosecution as long as possible. Originally, she figured the fine would be a couple of hundred dollars at most, but given that the judge had just fined her $100 for a minor violation, she realized that the fine for a second violation would be much larger.

Judge Sandoval thanked the jury once again for their patience and turned to the witness stand. "Dr. Markowitz, let me remind you that you are still under oath. Mrs. Wong, you may continue your direct examination."

"Thank you, Your Honor. Dr. Markowitz, have you reviewed the facts involving the death of Anna Conway?"

"Yes. I've read all the reports and documents at least three or four times each. I wondered why this young girl had done such a horrible thing. That's when it occurred to me that there might be some sort of genetic cause for what she did. At first it was nothing more than a hunch, but the more I looked into it, the more plausible it seemed."

"Let's not get ahead of ourselves, Dr. Markowitz. Before we turn to your expert opinion about this case, could you give us a quick summary of the research on genetics and aggression?"

"As you know, all behaviors, whether human or animal, are the result of complex interactions between genes and the environment. And it's clear that environmental factors often play a large role in aggressive behaviors, especially in humans. For example, someone is much more likely to get into a fight in a hot, crowded bar than while sitting in an air-conditioned office at work. Heat, overcrowding, and alcohol intoxication are all environmental factors that can lead to aggressive behavior."

"But most people in hot, crowded bars don't get into fights, so it isn't all due to environmental factors, is it?"

"No. Some people are more likely to be aggressive than others."

"How come?"

"Some people seem to be innately aggressive. We've known this for quite some time. Numerous studies have linked testosterone levels with aggression in both males and females. The more testosterone, the more likely the person is to be aggressive. The neurotransmitter serotonin has also been linked to human aggression—the more serotonin, the less aggressive the person is. Other neurotransmitters and hormones such as dopamine and epinephrine also seem to be involved. In sum, the biological causes of aggression are numerous and quite complex."

"What about genetic causes? Are any genes responsible for aggressive behavior in humans?"

"Most of the research on the genetic bases of aggression has been done on animals. Numerous studies have demonstrated that some individuals within a species are more aggressive than others, and that behavior seems largely inherited—that is, due to the animal's genetic makeup. An interesting example of selective breeding has been going on in Siberia for decades. Researchers there have been able to eliminate aggressive behavior in wild foxes by breeding only the tamest foxes in each generation. This shows that aggression has genetic underpinnings."

"Are there any studies that show a genetic basis of aggression in humans?"

"Yes, one line of research suggests that there may be a gene that is responsible for human aggression in certain specific circumstances. It is the gene that regulates how much of a certain enzyme people produce. Unfortunately, some members of the media have labeled it the Warrior Gene, which oversimplifies how it works."

"Can you tell us about the Warrior Gene?"

"I prefer not to use that term."

"Sorry, Dr. Markowitz."

"No problem, Sarah. What we are talking about is actually a variant of the MAOA gene, which controls the amount of monoamine oxidase-A, or MAOA, a person produces. MAOA is an enzyme that helps break down certain neurotransmitters in the brain, such as dopamine, serotonin, and norepinephrine. As I said earlier, several of these neurotransmitters are involved in the regulation of aggression in humans. Most people have the normal variant, or allele, of the MAOA gene and therefore have normal levels of the MAOA enzyme. There are several other variants, though, one of which produces especially low levels of the MAOA enzyme. This low-activity variant is the one that has been called the Warrior Gene."

"So when I say Warrior Gene, I should really be saying the low-activity variant of the MAOA gene?"

"Exactly."

"If it's okay with you, can I just say Warrior Gene?"

Sarah drew a few chuckles from the jury, but not as many as she had hoped.

"I also need to point out that the MAOA gene lies on the X chromosome," Dr. Markowitz continued before Sarah had a chance to ask her next question.

"Why is that important?" asked Sarah, playing along.

"As you know, males have one X chromosome and one Y, while females have two Xs. Because the MAOA gene lies on the X chromosome, males only have one copy. When a male has the low-activity variant, there is no normal variant to cancel out its effects."

"What about females?"

"Since females have two copies of the MAOA gene, it is possible for them to have no copies of the low-activity variant, one copy of the low-activity variant, or two copies. So far, there have been no studies on females, so no one really knows the effects of one copy of the low-activity variant in females."

"What if a female has two copies?" Sarah asked in a matter-of-fact tone, hoping Renaldo wouldn't guess its significance.

"Two copies of the Warrior Gene?" deadpanned Dr. Markowitz. "That would be a potent combination indeed."

Sarah was surprised she had gotten this far without much trouble, and she moved on quickly.

"So how does the Warrior Gene cause violence in humans?"

"Objection," interrupted Renaldo. "Assumes a fact not in evidence, specifically that the Warrior Gene does in fact cause aggression in humans."

"Sustained."

"Dr. Markowitz, is there any evidence that the Warrior Gene is linked to aggression in humans?"

"Yes."

"Could you *briefly* summarize that research for us?"

Despite Sarah's pointed instruction to be brief, Candi Markowitz dove into a detailed explanation of genetics, enzymes, and neurotransmitters and quickly lost everyone in the courtroom.

Sarah jumped in to redirect her. "How many people have this Warrior Gene? Is it common?"

"Keep in mind that we are talking about variations of a gene. We call these variations alleles."

"So how many people have this particular allele?"

"It's actually quite common. About one-third of Caucasians have the low-activity allele of the MAOA gene, and the proportion is even higher in some other populations."

"Then why aren't all these people who have the Warrior Gene running around acting aggressively?"

"That's an excellent question, and it highlights an interesting aspect of the way the Warrior Gene works. It appears that having the low-activity variant of the MAOA gene is not enough, by itself, to cause aggressive behavior. There also has to be some sort of environmental trigger to activate the low-activity variant."

"What do you mean by environmental trigger?"

Dr. Markowitz launched into a comprehensive description of the Warrior Gene studies, beginning with the ones demonstrating that childhood abuse was a potential environmental trigger. Renaldo objected frequently, but each time his objection was overruled. Was Judge Sandoval interested in learning more about the Warrior Gene or was he just interested in Candi Markowitz, Sarah wondered.

"The take-home point from this line of research is that the Warrior Gene does not by itself cause aggression in humans," Dr. Markowitz concluded. "It needs to be activated by some sort of environmental trigger, such as an abusive or traumatic childhood. It is a classic case of gene–environment interaction where the interplay of genes and the environment leads to a specific behavior."

"Are there any other environmental triggers that can activate the Warrior Gene?" Sarah asked.

"Yes, in 2009 scientists from UC Santa Barbara identified a different type of environmental trigger—direct provocation from another person. In sum, all of these studies demonstrate the same principle—there is a low-activity variant of the MAOA gene that is associated with increased levels of aggression, but the gene needs to be activated by some sort of environmental trigger. Although we only know about a few triggers so far, it is likely — indeed very likely — that there are many more."

"How long will it take to identify all of the factors that can activate the Warrior Gene?"

"Maybe ten years, maybe twenty years — maybe never."

"I was afraid you were going to say that." Sarah paused, hoping for some laughter. There was a little from the audience, but none from the jurors. "Since we can't wait that long, I'd like to ask you whether you think there are other possible environmental triggers."

"Objection. Speculation," interrupted Renaldo.

"Mrs. Wong, where are you going with this?" asked Judge Sandoval.

"If you can bear with me, Your Honor, it will become clear soon. First, I need to ask the witness if she has any hypotheses about possible environmental triggers for the Warrior Gene."

"All right, but you are on a short leash here. A very short leash."

"Thank you, Your Honor." Sarah turned back to Dr. Markowitz. "Where would you start looking for environmental triggers?"

"I would look for factors that are already known to be associated with aggression in humans."

"Such as?"

"Heat, crowding, loud noises, noxious smells. Those sorts of things."

"What makes those good candidates as possible triggers of the Warrior Gene?"

"Their association with human aggression is strong, but far from perfect. Not everyone gets more aggressive in hot weather — some people do, some don't."

"What does that suggest to you?"

"It tells me that hot temperatures cannot be solely responsible for increases in aggression. The heat must be interacting with some other factor to cause an individual to be aggressive."

"Such as the Warrior Gene?"

"Objection," barked Renaldo.

"Overruled. You may answer the question, Dr. Markowitz."

"Yes."

"Are there other factors that might trigger the Warrior Gene?"

"Alcohol, drugs, maybe even hormone levels."

"Hormones?"

"Yes. As I explained before, testosterone has been linked with aggression in humans, as have other hormones and neurotransmitters."

"What happens to a woman's hormone levels when she's pregnant?"

"They're all over the place. In the early part of the pregnancy, HCG stimulates the ovaries to produce very high levels of estrogen and progesterone in order to sustain the pregnancy. By the fourth month—"

"That's enough, Dr. Markowitz," Judge Sandoval said, holding up one hand. "Where are you going with this, Mrs. Wong?"

"I'm just trying to lay some groundwork for Dr. Markowitz's testimony."

"Let's skip the preliminaries."

"Very well, Your Honor. Dr. Markowitz, can fluctuating hormone levels during pregnancy affect a woman's behavior?"

"Indeed. In fact, falling hormone levels after birth have been cited as a primary cause of postpartum depression."

"Is that what we're talking about here?"

"No. Lexi did not suffer from postpartum depression. She had no clinical signs whatsoever. But she did go through the same hormonal changes experienced by all women during pregnancy and after birth."

"What other possible environmental triggers are there for the Warrior Gene?"

"Noxious smells. I mentioned this before, but it bears repeating. Strong smells can trigger basic animal-like behaviors in humans. Certain odors can act as cues for sexual activity, while others can precipitate aggressive behavior."

"Any other possible triggers?"

"Yes, frustration and provocation. Time and time again, research has shown these factors to be two of the most potent triggers of human aggression."

"Sort of like the experimental study on the Warrior Gene you told us about a while ago?"

"Yes."

With that, Renaldo jumped up. "I object to this entire line of questioning, Your Honor. These studies are completely irrelevant to this case. There is no evidence that the defendant had an abusive childhood and no evidence that little Anna Conway provoked the defendant. And all of these other triggers are mere speculation on Dr. Markowitz's part. In fact, there's not one scintilla of evidence that the defendant even has this warrior thing."

"Mr. Sepulveda has a point," said Judge Sandoval. "I don't see the relevance of all this. Dr. Markowitz has been on the stand for over a day, and although her testimony has been quite interesting, we haven't learned anything that will help the jury decide this case. I'll give you just a couple more minutes to get to your point, Mrs. Wong. That's it."

Sarah looked down at her notes and took a deep breath. "Dr. Markowitz, were you able to determine whether Lexi Conway has a copy of the Warrior Gene?"

"Yes."

"How did you do that?"

"I obtained a sample of Ms. Conway's DNA and submitted it to The DNA Group for analysis."

"OBJECTION! May we approach?"

It was not Renaldo's voice. Sarah turned to see Joe Jimmerson on his feet.

"Mr. Jimmerson, did Mrs. Wong provide you with a copy of a lab report from The DNA Group?" the judge asked him.

"No, Your Honor. She did not."

Judge Sandoval's face grew beet red, and for a moment he looked like he might explode. When he spoke to the jury he sounded like he was choking.

"Ladies and gentlemen, there is an allegation that Mrs. Wong has acted unethically. We are going to excuse you while we hold a hearing on this matter. Brian, please take the jury back into the jury deliberation room. Dr. Markowitz, please step down from the witness stand and wait in the hallway."

By the time the last juror was gone, Judge Sandoval had calmed down a little.

"We are now conducting an evidentiary hearing outside the presence of the jury," he said, the color subsiding in his cheeks. "The purpose of this hearing is to determine whether Mrs. Wong has violated Section 1054.3 of the California Penal Code."

He turned toward the prosecution table. "Mr. Jimmerson, let me ask you again. Did Mrs. Wong give you or anyone in the District Attorney's Office a copy of any reports from The DNA Group?"

"No, Your Honor."

"Mrs. Wong, please take a seat on the witness stand."

Sarah walked stiffly to the witness stand, thinking carefully about what she was going to say.

Once Isabel had sworn Sarah in, the judge turned to look directly at her.

"Mrs. Wong, I am conducting a hearing to determine

whether you are in contempt of court because you violated Section 1054.3 of the California Penal Code. You have the right to be represented by an attorney at this hearing. Do you wish to have an attorney assist you?"

Sarah was surprised by the formality of the proceedings. Nevertheless, she didn't feel she needed an attorney for a simple charge of contempt. "No, Your Honor."

"You also have the right to remain silent. Do you give up that right?"

"Yes, Your Honor."

Joe Jimmerson stood up, but Judge Sandoval waved him back to his seat. "Mr. Jimmerson, I'm going to conduct this examination myself."

He read the relevant portion of the California law on discovery into the record and then turned to Sarah. "Mrs. Wong, do you understand your responsibilities under this statute?"

"Yes, Your Honor."

"In the course of your investigation of the case against Lexi Conway, did you ask Dr. Markowitz to obtain a DNA sample from Lexi Conway for the purpose of genetic testing?"

"No, I did not. It was Dr. Markowitz's idea."

"But you knew about it, correct?"

"Yes."

"And you approved of it, correct?"

"Sort of."

"Is that a yes or no?"

"It's a yes, Your Honor."

"At some point did you receive a written lab report from The DNA Group containing the results of a genetic test conducted on the DNA sample from Lexi Conway?"

"Yes."

"When did you receive that report?"

"I believe it was about November thirteenth or fourteenth."

"So you have been in possession of that report for almost four months?"

"Yes, Your Honor."

"Do you have a copy of that report with you today?"

"Yes."

"Please retrieve it and hand it to the bailiff."

Sarah was about to step down from the witness stand when Nick waved the report in the air. "I've got it right here, Your Honor."

"Please give it to the bailiff."

Brian took the two-page report from Nick and handed it to Judge Sandoval, who donned his reading glasses and studied it for a minute or two.

Judge Sandoval removed his glasses and looked out over the courtroom.

"For the record, I have now read the two-page report from The DNA Group," the judge said. "Mrs. Wong, when you received this report, did you anticipate that you would be seeking to introduce it into evidence at trial?"

"Yes, Your Honor."

"Did you realize that you had a legal obligation under Section 1054.3 of the California Penal Code to provide a copy of the report to the District Attorney's Office?"

Sarah swallowed hard. "Yes, Your Honor."

"Understanding that you had a legal obligation to give the report to the prosecution, did you transmit a copy of the report to Mr. Jimmerson, Mr. Sepulveda, or anyone else in the District Attorney's Office?"

"No I did not, Your Honor."

"Did you even inform the District Attorney's Office about the existence of this report?"

"No, Your Honor."

"Mrs. Wong, I'm done with my questioning. Do you want to say anything on your own behalf?"

"Just that I'm sorry, Your Honor."

No matter what she said, Sarah knew the judge was

going to find her in contempt and give her the maximum fine of $1,000. The best thing she could do was keep quiet and accept her punishment with dignity. She stepped down from the witness stand and took her seat at the defense table next to Lexi.

"I find Sarah Wong in contempt of court in that she willfully failed to comply with Section 1054.3 of the California Penal Code," Judge Sandoval announced. "Because this violation was willful and intentional, I am sentencing Mrs. Wong to five days in jail and a $1,000 fine, the maximum sentence allowed under California contempt laws. This sentence is to be served forthwith."

Sarah leaped to her feet. "What? You're sending me to jail? How can I represent my client from jail?"

"You should have thought about that before violating the law," snapped the judge. "Today is Thursday. We will resume the trial next Tuesday, five days from now. At that time I will decide whether to allow Dr. Markowitz to continue her testimony. The court will appoint a genetics expert for the prosecution. Mr. Sepulveda, please give the name of your expert to Isabel tomorrow morning."

"Your Honor, I respectfully request that I be allowed to serve my sentence under house arrest so I can continue working on Ms. Conway's defense," Sarah protested.

"Your request is denied."

"Well, then, would you allow me to serve my sentence when the trial is over?"

"Denied."

Sarah had no choice but to play the pregnancy card, her last chance at avoiding jail. "Your Honor, I ask for leniency because of my medical condition."

"What medical condition?"

"I'm four and a half months pregnant."

For at least fifteen seconds, no one said a word. Based on everyone's shocked expressions, Sarah had done a good job of concealing her pregnancy.

Renaldo broke the silence. "Given the circumstances, the state has no objection if Mrs. Wong serves her sentence under house arrest."

"That's very kind of you, Mr. Sepulveda," said Judge Sandoval, "but Mrs. Wong committed an egregious, intentional violation of California's discovery law. These rules are in place to ensure that both the state and the defendant receive a fair trial. Therefore my sentence stands. However, I will order the sheriff to house Mrs. Wong in the hospital wing of the New Jail. I hear it's very nice there. I'm sure they'll see to it that she gets her prenatal vitamins and whatever else she needs. Brian, take Mrs. Wong into custody."

Brian spoke up quickly. "Your Honor, I need to call for backup since I have to escort Ms. Conway to her cell too."

"Very well. Everyone remain in their places until the second bailiff arrives."

While they waited, Sarah instructed Nick to call Conrad and tell him to file a writ of habeas corpus to get her out of jail as soon as possible, and to tell Matt that she was okay. Nick raced out of the courtroom, taking Sarah's briefcase with him, and he was accosted by a few reporters on the way out. All Sarah heard was Nick shouting, "What do think my reaction is? The judge just put a pregnant defense attorney in jail. Put THAT in your paper!"

Sarah turned to Lexi and attempted a bit of humor. "Maybe we'll be cell mates."

But Lexi was crying. "I'm so sorry. This is all my fault."

"Don't worry, Lexi, I'll be fine."

When Brian's backup arrived, he led Lexi into the lockup, and Sarah followed with Brian, doing her best to hold her head high.

After Brian returned, Judge Sandoval asked him to bring the jury in. As soon as they were seated, Judge Sandoval addressed them in a somber tone. "Ladies and gentlemen, while you were gone from the courtroom, we held a hearing concerning Mrs. Wong's conduct in this case. I won't bore you with all of the technical details, but I found that Mrs. Wong acted unethically and unlawfully. I held her in contempt of court and sentenced her to five days in jail. She is beginning that sentence today."

Several jurors gasped audibly, and many of them looked at Sarah's empty chair.

"We will resume trial on Tuesday at nine a.m. Enjoy your extended break. The court is adjourned."

* * *

Nick and Conrad worked all afternoon and through the night to get Sarah out of jail. Maggie stayed up with them, mostly offering moral support, snacks, and drinks. By six thirty Friday morning, they had completed three writs, one each for the Appellate Court of California, the Supreme Court in California, and the United States Supreme Court.

Exhausted from their all-nighter, Nick and Conrad asked Maggie to file the writs. It took Maggie a while to navigate the electronic filing systems of the three appellate courts, and she didn't get the last writ filed until almost ten thirty. Then they waited, slumped in their chairs. Nick wanted to go visit Sarah, but he knew he should stay in the office in case one of the courts called with a decision.

By one that afternoon, they'd heard nothing. Nothing from the California Appellate Court, nothing from the California Supreme Court, nothing from the United States Supreme Court.

Maggie ran out to grab some lunch, and when she came back she could see on Nick and Conrad's faces that there was still no news.

At two, still nothing.

By three, Nick started to worry that Sarah might spend the entire weekend in jail, and he couldn't remain seated. He wandered all through the office, staring at each phone as he ambled by. Conrad and Maggie preferred to sit, their eyes following Nick on his never-ending loop.

At four fifteen the phone finally rang, and Conrad got to it first. It was Isabel and she asked for Nick. Nick grabbed the phone from Conrad and asked Isabel what was happening.

"Get your butt down to the New Jail immediately. Sarah's going to be released, but you better get down there right away before somebody changes their mind."

"But how? We filed three writs and we've heard nothing."

"Don't worry about how, just get down to the jail right now."

The New Jail was a little over four miles from Sarah's office, but Nick navigated the Friday afternoon traffic in less than ten minutes. He pulled up to the main visitor entrance, turned off his car, and raced inside. He must have looked slightly deranged as he entered, breathing heavily and talking rapidly, and three sheriffs converged on him within seconds. He spit out what he was there for, and the deputies told him that the inmate release door was outside, at the rear of the jail.

As he ran back out, Matt was coming in. Nick grabbed Matt's arm. "She's going to be released out back. Let's go."

Once outside, they slowed to a fast walk.

"I've been trying to visit Sarah all day," said Matt, "but they wouldn't let me see her because she's in the hospital wing. Judge Sandoval's clerk just called me and said that Sarah's going to be released. Is she really getting out?"

"I think so," sputtered Nick, still out of breath. "We'll know soon enough."

Just as Nick and Matt rounded the corner, they saw Sarah exiting through the lone metal door at the back of the jail. They all came together, merging into a trembling pile of arms and shoulders. Sarah asked to sit down, and they plopped down right there on the curb. Matt could tell that

Sarah was shaken and upset, but otherwise she seemed okay.

Exhausted, Sarah could barely speak. "Thanks so much for getting me out, Nick."

"But we never heard from the appellate court about our writ."

"Then why was I released?"

"I don't know. The court clerk called me about a half hour ago and told me that you were going to be released and that I needed to get down here as fast as I could."

"I don't understand."

"Me neither, but you're out now and that's all that matters."

Sarah started sobbing uncontrollably. Matt stroked Sarah's hair gently and asked her if she was okay.

"I don't want to talk about it. I just want to go home," Sarah replied quietly.

And they never did talk about Sarah's night in jail. Not that day, not ever.

CHAPTER 17

Sarah was so relieved to be back in her own bed that she slept until almost noon on Saturday. Chloe was purring next to her ear when Matt woke her up, telling her that Dr. Sadler was on the phone.

When Sarah picked up the phone she was expecting words of comfort and support, but instead Dr. Sadler was furious with her.

"You are not to go back into that courtroom under any circumstances, Sarah. Do you understand?"

"But I'm fine, Dr. Sadler. Just a little tired, that's all."

"No buts, no complaining. Do you want to lose your babies?"

"Of course not."

"Then you do what I tell you."

"But the trial's almost over. I can't withdraw now. Besides, even if I wanted to, the judge would never let me off the case this late in the game."

"We'll see about that. I want you in bed with your fetal monitor on 24/7 over the next few days. If everything looks good, then you can start some limited activity next week. But you are not to go anywhere near that courtroom. Is that clear?"

"Yes, Dr. Sadler," replied Sarah in her best second-grade voice.

But Sarah had no intention of staying away from court on Tuesday, and she suspected Dr. Sadler knew that. As a compromise, she stayed in bed most of the weekend and kept the fetal monitor on all the time, sending readings to Dr. Sadler's office every few hours.

On Sunday, Matt brought Sarah her breakfast in bed, along with the Sunday paper. She turned to the local news section. Across the top of the page was the sensational headline: "Baby Killer's Pregnant Lawyer Thrown in Jail."

She read the article carefully. The jurors would be able to read it too and she wanted to know what had been said about her. Fortunately, there was very little detail about why she had been held in contempt—most of the piece focused on California contempt law and included reactions from several local attorneys—and it turned out not to be damaging either to Lexi's case or Sarah's reputation.

Sarah never gave a second thought to staying away from court on Tuesday, despite Dr. Sadler's vociferous admonition. She would be as careful as she could, but she had a trial to finish.

* * *

On Tuesday morning, Sarah arrived at the courthouse an hour before the trial was set to resume so she could talk to Lexi in the lockup.

"Are you okay, Mrs. Wong? I worried about you all weekend."

"I'm fine, Lexi. They let me out on Friday afternoon, so I only spent one night in jail."

"I still can't believe you went to jail for me."

"I told you I'm doing my best for you."

"I believe you now."

"Thanks, Lexi. That means a lot to me."

"You know what? I think I've been wrong about a lot of things."

"Like what?"

"Maybe it wasn't my fault that Anna died after all."

Sarah was stunned. "What do you mean? You've been telling me all along that it was your fault."

"Well, maybe it was my fault, but I just want you to know that I didn't kill her."

"Well then, who did?"

"Nobody."

"What do you mean nobody?"

"I mean nobody."

Sarah was more confused than ever. "So why did you say it was your fault?"

"Because that's what I believed. I really felt everything was all my fault. But maybe it wasn't. Maybe I should testify and tell them I didn't kill my baby."

"But we've already stipulated that you DID kill your baby! We can't change our minds now. Why didn't you tell me this a few months ago?"

"I didn't trust you. Besides, I really did think it was my fault. I still do, sorta."

"Lexi, we've got to keep going with the Warrior Gene defense. The trial is almost over and we can't change our defense now."

"Does that mean you're going to keep saying in court that I killed my baby?"

"Not really," replied Sarah carefully. "It just means that your bad DNA killed your baby. It wasn't really your fault."

Lexi was silent for a few moments. "You know what else?"

"What?"

"I don't want to die anymore. That won't bring Anna back. I'm tired of being in jail and I want to go home."

"I can't promise you anything, Lexi, but I think we've got a chance if we keep going with the Warrior Gene defense. Are you willing to give it a go?"

"We don't really have a choice, do we?"

"No, we don't. And there's no guarantee we're going to

win. We're still in for quite a battle, I'm afraid. I don't know if the judge is going to let Dr. Markowitz testify about the Warrior Gene."

"I know you'll do just fine, ma'am."

Sarah arrived at the courtroom right at eight forty-five, just as Brian was opening the doors.

"Morning, Sarah. How are you doing?"

"Much better than last Thursday."

"I'm glad you're okay."

"Thanks." Sarah gave Brian a hug, but pulled away quickly in case anyone saw her. She didn't need any more allegations of improper behavior.

As soon as she saw Isabel, she broke into a huge smile. She almost sprinted up to her desk to thank her for getting her out of jail on Friday.

"Thank you, thank you, thank you!" Sarah gushed. "I know you're the one who got me out of jail. How on earth did you do it?"

"Don't thank me," said Isabel quietly. "Thank the judge."

"What? Judge Sandoval was the one who got me out?"

"You didn't hear it from me."

"But why?"

"All he wanted to do was scare you a little bit. In fact, he tried to get you released Thursday night but the sheriff said it was too late. He put the release order through first thing on Friday morning but it took the Sheriff's Office all day to process the paperwork. Sarah, don't you EVER let on to the judge you know he was the one who released you from jail."

"My lips are sealed," said Sarah, drawing an imaginary zip across her mouth. Maybe she had misjudged Burt Sandoval.

Gradually the courtroom filled with reporters and spectators, even more than there had been before. Nick came in just before nine, sat down next to Sarah, and gave her a quick nod. He looked tense and worried, but Sarah assured him she had no intention of returning to jail for any reason.

Lexi came out, and she and Sarah exchanged big smiles. Then Brian called the court to order without the jury present, and Judge Sandoval took the bench.

"Mrs. Wong, I trust you learned your lesson last week."

Sarah stood up. "I did, Your Honor."

"Do you have any more surprises in store for us today?"

"No, Your Honor."

"Good. I've read the report from The DNA Group, as well as an offer of proof filed by the defense."

What offer of proof, wondered Sarah as she sat down again. She hadn't filed anything over the weekend. She looked over at Nick who slid a folder in front of her. Inside was a formal offer of proof, complete with cogent arguments and all the relevant legal citations. She looked at Nick. "How did you ...?"

"I didn't do it all by myself," Nick whispered. "Conrad and I worked on it together."

First, she had misjudged Burt Sandoval, and now she'd misjudged Conrad. "Thank you," she mouthed.

"Would you like to respond, Mr. Sepulveda?" Judge Sandoval asked.

Renaldo got to his feet. "Your Honor, the state vehemently objects to Dr. Markowitz testifying about the Warrior Gene, and we strenuously object to any testimony from The DNA Group about the analysis of Ms. Conway's DNA. Furthermore—"

Judge Sandoval held up his right hand. "Although your vehement and strenuous objections are duly noted, I'm going to overrule them for the time being. I believe that Mrs. Wong's offer of proof is sufficient for her to proceed at this point. You'll have ample opportunity to cross-examine all of Mrs. Wong's witnesses." He shifted his gaze to Sarah. "Mrs. Wong, if either you or Dr. Markowitz start speculating or conjecturing instead of sticking to scientific facts, I will strike all of her testimony from the record and I just might hold you in contempt again. Is that absolutely clear?"

"Yes, Your Honor."

"Good. I'm glad we understand each other. Is there anything else before I bring in the jury?"

A female voice rose from the back of the courtroom. "Your Honor, I'd like to say something."

Sarah turned around. It was Dr. Sadler!

"Ma'am, you may not know this, but I've already issued two contempt citations during this trial," said Judge Sandoval sternly. "I don't want you to be the recipient of a third one. I would advise you to sit back down and be quiet."

"But Your Honor, I need to talk with you."

"About what?"

"About Sarah Wong's health."

"What do you know about her health?"

"I'm Dr. Ellen Sadler, Sarah's obstetrician. I request that the trial be postponed until after the birth of her babies."

By now everyone in the courtroom was looking at Dr. Sadler.

"I can't possibly do that, Dr. Sadler," said the judge impatiently.

"Well then, I request that Sarah Wong be allowed to withdraw from the case for health reasons."

Judge Sandoval turned to Sarah. "Mrs. Wong, are you asking to withdraw from this case?"

"No, Your Honor."

"But I insist that she be removed from the case," the doctor said loudly.

"Dr. Sadler, you have no legal standing here. Either sit down and be quiet or leave the courtroom immediately."

Without another word, Dr. Sadler pushed her way through the other spectators and stomped out of the courtroom.

Judge Sandoval looked out over the packed courtroom. "I hesitate to ask, but does anyone else want to say anything before we bring in the jury?" he said with a smile.

When the scattered laughter died down, Judge Sandoval instructed Brian to get the jurors, and once they were seated in the jury box, he addressed them.

"Welcome back, ladies and gentlemen. I trust you enjoyed your long weekend. I am hopeful that we will be able to proceed to the end of the trial without any further interruptions. Mrs. Wong will now continue her direct examination of Dr. Markowitz."

Sarah decided to backtrack a bit — it had been five days since the jury had heard about the Warrior Gene — and she asked Dr. Markowitz to recap her testimony about the Warrior Gene and how it was activated by certain environmental triggers. After Renaldo's objection, which was overruled by Judge Sandoval, Sarah asked Dr. Markowitz to repeat the list of possible environmental triggers. Then she turned to the most critical testimony of the entire trial.

"Dr. Markowitz, did you obtain a sample of DNA from Lexi Conway?"

"Objection," shouted Renaldo.

"Grounds, counselor?"

"Lack of foundation."

"Overruled. You may answer the question, Dr. Markowitz."

"Yes. I obtained a cheek swab from Ms. Conway in the interview room at the New Jail."

"Did you verify that the person was actually Lexi Conway?"

"Yes. I asked her several questions, including her full name, date and place of birth, and the full names of both of her parents."

"Is the person from whom you took the cheek swab in court today?"

"Yes, that's her sitting at the defense table," said Dr. Markowitz as she pointed at Lexi.

"May the record reflect that the witness has identified Lexi Conway?"

"So noted," said Judge Sandoval, without looking away from Candi Markowitz.

Over the next hour, Sarah elicited a detailed description from Candi Markowitz about what she did with the cheek swab after she obtained it from Lexi. She explained that the sample never left her possession as she drove directly to The DNA Group. She accompanied her explanation with meticulous handwritten records (which Nick had turned over to the prosecution on Monday) about the chain of custody from the time she obtained the sample until she placed it directly into the hands of Keira Miller, the head lab technician at The DNA Group. Sarah's questioning was painstakingly thorough, as she wanted to leave no doubt in the jurors' minds that The DNA Group had indeed analyzed cells obtained from Lexi Conway.

When she was done, Sarah asked Judge Sandoval how he wanted her to proceed. "I can keep going with Dr. Markowitz and ask her about the results of the DNA testing or, if the court wishes, I can interrupt Dr. Markowitz's testimony now and re-call her after the testimony of Keira Miller from The DNA Group."

"Mr. Sepulveda?"

"Your Honor, I insist that Ms. Miller testify before Dr. Markowitz goes any further."

"I agree with Mr. Sepulveda. Mrs. Wong, how long will it take you to get Ms. Miller into court?"

"About five seconds, Your Honor. She's waiting out in the hallway."

Judge Sandoval smiled. "That's more like it, Mrs. Wong. You may call your next witness."

Renaldo jumped up. "But Your Honor, what about my cross-examination of Dr. Markowitz?"

"Can't it wait until the end of the second portion of her testimony?"

"No, Your Honor. I'd like to begin my cross-examination now and finish it after she completes her testimony."

"Very well. You may cross-examine."

Renaldo walked slowly to the podium, bringing a huge stack of notes with him. After fidgeting with his papers and giving the jury a weak smile, he turned toward Candi Markowitz.

"Good morning, Dr. Markowitz."

"Good morning, counselor," she replied calmly.

"May I call you Candi?" asked Renaldo.

"I prefer to be called Dr. Markowitz," she said without missing a beat, drawing chuckles from most of the jurors.

"All right, let's get started. Almost all of your training and experience is in DNA fingerprinting. Correct?"

"Yes, that is correct."

"Forgive me, but I'm a little confused." Renaldo gave her a patronizing smirk. "I didn't think this case involved DNA fingerprinting. We all agree that Lexi Conway killed her baby."

Dr. Markowitz was ready. "Counselor, the question in this case is not *who* killed Anna Conway, but *why* she was killed."

Sarah couldn't have said it better.

And so it went for the next day and a half — punch and counterpunch, thrust and parry. Although Candi Markowitz didn't win every battle, she won most of them. Renaldo tried going toe to toe with Candi about the science behind the Warrior Gene, but each foray only helped cement the extent of her expertise and depth of her knowledge. It was readily apparent that she was a highly trained, accomplished scientist and Renaldo was not.

In addition to besting Renaldo on the technical aspects of her testimony, Candi even out-charmed him, which was no easy task. Several times she drew laughs and chuckles from the jury while Renaldo only elicited a few polite smiles. When he concluded his cross-examination just before noon on Wednesday, everyone—including Renaldo—knew that Candi Markowitz had come out on top, at least for this round.

After the lunch recess, Sarah called Keira Miller from The DNA Group to the stand. Although she was a skilled laboratory technician, Keira was nervous and unsure of herself on the stand. She had only testified a handful of times before, and it showed. She delivered her testimony in a halting cadence, frequently pausing and looking at Sarah to seek assurance that she had said the right thing.

After Sarah established Keira's credentials—a master's degree in molecular biology from Northwestern and five years' experience working in three different genetics labs— Sarah questioned her about the analysis of Lexi's DNA sample. Keira explained that she was the only person at the lab who had handled Sample 17-485, the number she assigned to Lexi's cheek swab, and that she had performed all of the testing herself.

Then Sarah moved on to the description of the genetic tests Keira conducted. This part proceeded very slowly, as Renaldo objected to almost every question. Just as she was about to get to the results of the DNA testing, Judge Sandoval decided to recess for the day. Sarah was disappointed about the timing—Renaldo would have all night to prepare his cross-examination of Keira the next day.

Sarah felt nauseous as she drove home from court. She pulled over twice, thinking she was going to throw up, but each time she swallowed hard and pulled back into traffic. When she finally got home, she headed straight for the bathroom and got there just in time.

Before strapping on the fetal monitoring equipment that evening, she knew something wasn't quite right. Sure enough, the digital readout confirmed her suspicions — one heartbeat was fine, but the other was faster and outside the acceptable range. She quickly sent the data to Valley Obstetrics and anxiously awaited Dr. Sadler's call.

By the time Dr. Sadler called thirty minutes later, the aberrant heartbeat was back to normal and Sarah's frayed nerves had calmed down considerably. But she still spent some time on the phone with Dr. Sadler. Mostly she listened, throwing in a "yes" or "uh-huh" every minute or so. She promised to eat better, get lots of sleep, and go on walks whenever she could. Dr. Sadler had given up trying to dissuade Sarah from finishing the trial, so the doctor settled for dispensing common-sense advice to Sarah about taking care of herself and her babies. Sarah made a final promise to be good and hung up. When she placed the phone on the table in front of the couch, Matt came and sat down beside her.

"Hon, I'm going to take care of myself. I promise," she said.

"We've come a long way to have these babies. I don't want to jeopardize all of that now." Matt's voice revealed a mixture of concern and irritation.

"I know, I know. I want them to be healthy just as much as you. I've just got a couple of hours of work to do to get ready for tomorrow and then — "

"Oh no you don't." Matt put his hand on her shoulder. "As soon as you eat dinner, it's off to bed."

* * *

The following day, Keira seemed more confident in the witness stand as she explained how she tested Sample 17-485 for all known variants of the MAOA gene.

At last Sarah had reached the scientific and emotional apex of her entire defense. She took a deep breath and handed the lab report containing the results of Lexi's DNA test to Keira. "Do you recognize this lab report?"

"Yes, I do."

"Is that your signature at the bottom of the page?"

"Yes, it is."

"Does this lab report contain the results of your genetic analyses of tissue Sample 17-485?"

"Yes, it does."

Sarah turned and looked at the jury as she asked her next question. "After conducting all of these analyses, were you able to determine whether the DNA contained in Sample 17-485 had the low-activity variant of the MAOA gene?"

"Yes. Sample 17-485 contained two copies of the low-activity variant of the MAOA gene, one on each X chromosome."

Sarah didn't take her eyes off the jury. "Two copies of the low-activity variant?"

"That's right. Two copies."

"Not just one copy, but two copies?"

Renaldo jumped up. "Asked and answered."

"Sustained. Move on, Mrs. Wong."

"Are you absolutely certain that Sample 17-485 contained two copies of the low-activity variant of the MAOA gene?" Sarah asked and turned around to face the witness.

"Yes, I am."

"Nothing further, Your Honor."

After his ineffective attack on Candi Markowitz, Renaldo launched into a vigorous cross-examination of Keira Miller, a grueling experience not only for Keira but also for everyone else in the courtroom. He began by trying to belittle Keira's AA degree in biology from Santa Felicia Community College.

"Mr. Sepulveda, I'll have you know that I started my college studies at Santa Felicia Community College, just like Ms. Miller," Judge Sandoval interrupted. "And I'll bet some of our fine jurors attended SFCC as well." Three jurors nodded their heads. "I think it would be best if you moved on."

Renaldo did move on, but he never regained his balance. Keira soon realized that she knew much more about DNA testing than he did, and her confidence grew with each response. As Keira's confidence waxed, Renaldo's waned. In the end, after hours of tedious cross-examination spread out over two days, Renaldo had been unable to discredit the only part of Keira's testimony that really mattered: the DNA in Sample 17-485 contained two copies of the low-activity variant of the MAOA gene — one on each X chromosome.

* * *

On Friday morning, Sarah recalled Candi Markowitz.

Despite Sarah's entreaties to dress more conservatively for her second session on the stand, Candi waltzed up in a short electric-blue sundress that could only be described as provocative.

"Dr. Markowitz, I'm handing you Defense Exhibit Q. Do you recognize this document?"

"Yes. It's the lab report from The DNA Group."

"Have you reviewed this report before?"

"Of course. You and I have talked about it many times."

"In plain language, what does this lab report say?"

"It indicates that Lexi Conway has two copies — "

"Objection." Renaldo stood up quickly. "The lab reports says nothing about Lexi Conway. It just talks about Sample 17-485."

"Overruled," intoned Judge Sandoval. "Mrs. Wong has established a sufficient chain of custody for the sample."

Sarah breathed a sigh of relief. "Dr. Markowitz, you may answer the question. What does the lab report say?"

"The results in the lab report indicate that Lexi Conway

has two copies of the low-activity variant of the MAOA gene."

"The Warrior Gene?"

"Yes, the Warrior Gene."

"What percentage of Caucasian women have two copies of the Warrior Gene?"

"It's hard to say exactly, since most of the clinical studies have been conducted on men, but my best estimate is that it's about nine percent, give or take a few percentage points. Roughly about one in eleven Caucasian women."

"During your earlier testimony, you told us about several research studies on the Warrior Gene. Were any of those studies conducted on women?"

"To my knowledge, no."

"So all of the studies have been conducted on men with only one copy of the Warrior Gene, correct?"

"That's right."

"And only women can have two copies of this genetic defect, correct?"

"That's right. Only women have two X chromosomes, which is where the Warrior Gene is situated."

"Dr. Markowitz, based upon your many years of training in behavioral genetics, as well as your extensive experience in DNA analyses, do you have an opinion about whether the effects of two copies of the Warrior Gene might be stronger than the effects of just one copy?"

"Objection! Calls for speculation," Renaldo called out loudly and forcefully.

Before Sarah got the chance to speak, Candi turned toward Judge Sandoval and locked eyes with the jurist who was twenty years her senior. She slowly crossed her legs, tossed her hair, and smiled seductively. For fifteen seconds or so Burt Sandoval seemed to forget where he was and returned Candi's smile with a sheepish schoolboy grin.

Sarah broke the spell. "Your Honor—"

"The prosecution's objection is overruled," said the

judge without shifting his gaze. "I believe this expert witness is sufficiently qualified to testify about this issue. Candi, you may answer the question." As soon as he uttered Dr. Markowitz's first name, he realized how inappropriate it sounded. "Continue, Mrs. Wong. We don't have all day," he said gruffly.

The judge's rulings were finally going in Sarah's favor, but she was incensed that Candi Markowitz had once again used her sexuality to get what she wanted.

"Mrs. Wong, let's get moving," the judge repeated.

"Sorry, Your Honor." Sarah took a moment to regain her focus. "Dr. Markowitz, based on your many years of training in behavioral genetics, as well as your extensive experience in DNA analyses, do you have an opinion about whether the effects of two copies of the Warrior Gene might be even stronger than the effects of just one copy?"

"Well, we don't know for sure, but it's reasonable to expect that two copies of the Warrior Gene might be more likely to lead to aggression than a single copy."

Renaldo jumped up. "Your Honor, I'm going to renew my objection."

"And I'm going to renew my ruling. Overruled."

"Dr. Markowitz, why might two copies of the Warrior Gene be worse than one?" Sarah continued.

"Two reasons. First, it's reasonable to assume that MAOA levels might be lower for women with two copies of the Warrior Gene than for men who have only one copy. Second, there is reason to believe that environmental factors such as heat and noxious smells might have stronger interactive effects with two copies of the Warrior Gene because they would activate aggression more readily and cause more extreme aggressive actions."

Though Sarah knew the logic behind the first point was faulty, the second explanation *was* plausible. She moved on quickly before Renaldo could object.

"Let's talk a little more about the role of environmental

triggers," Sarah said. "When you were on the stand yesterday, you told us about some possible environmental factors that might trigger the Warrior Gene. Can you list those factors again?"

"Sure. Heat, crowding, provocation, frustration, noxious smells, hormonal imbalances."

Next, she turned to the topic of free will, but this was when her luck ran out. She had hoped to ask Dr. Markowitz about the possibility that two copies of the Warrior Gene, when triggered by outside factors, might cause someone to act aggressively without any choice, without any free will. But no matter how hard she tried, Judge Sandoval would have none of it.

Renaldo objected to each attempt to talk about free will, and after a while Judge Sandoval didn't even wait for his objection. Sarah kept trying until Judge Sandoval signaled he had had enough, so she gave up and moved on to the final part of her direct examination.

"Dr. Markowitz, I have one final topic to cover and then we'll be done. You have testified that the Warrior Gene, when triggered by certain environmental factors, can lead to aggression. Is there any way to predict who might be a target of such aggression?"

"Based on everything we know about genetics, evolution, and natural selection, there are two likely targets of aggression caused by the Warrior Gene—one obvious and one quite surprising."

"Let's start with the obvious."

"As with any other type of animal aggression, likely targets include other organisms that might get in the way of survival and reproduction."

"Such as?"

"Competitors. Competitors for food, territory, or mates."

"Seems logical enough," Sarah said. "And the surprising target?"

"The organism itself."

"I don't understand," said Sarah, feigning ignorance. "What do you mean the organism itself?"

"I mean that an organism with a defective gene might try to get rid of that gene by killing itself."

"But I thought the goal of all organisms is to survive, reproduce, and pass on their genetic material to future generations?"

"Generally speaking, that's true. But sometimes nature builds in safeguards to prevent the spread of maladaptive traits."

"Go on."

"For example, do you have any idea how many women miscarry in the first twenty weeks of pregnancy? About ten to twenty percent."

Sarah played along for dramatic effect. "Wow. I had no idea."

"And do you know the primary cause of most of these early miscarriages?"

"Genetic abnormalities?" suggested Sarah, as if she were guessing.

"Exactly. The best estimate is that about fifty to seventy percent of early miscarriages in humans are due to fetal genetic abnormalities. When a fetus has a substantial genetic defect, it often miscarries spontaneously. This prevents the mother from spending a great deal of time and energy on an inferior fetus, and it helps reduce the incidence of severe abnormalities across an entire species."

"So how is that relevant here?" asked Sarah.

"I was going to ask the same thing," added Judge Sandoval wryly.

"It may be that the Warrior Gene, which is quite common among humans, has started to mutate, thereby causing the host organism to kill itself so that the gene can't spread any further. We are just beginning to understand such self-destructive genetic behaviors."

"Let me make sure I understand this, Dr. Markowitz," Sarah said. "Are you saying that someone with the Warrior Gene might commit suicide so as to get rid of the Warrior Gene itself?"

"Yes, that is a distinct possibility."

Sarah gathered up her papers and headed back to the defense table. In a move she had practiced several times the night before, she started to sit down and then stood straight up again.

"I'm sorry, Dr. Markowitz, but I have one more question," she said. "Is there any other way the Warrior Gene might try to stop its own spread?"

"Yes."

"What's that?"

"It could program its host to eliminate any living progeny." Candi paused. "In other words, the Warrior Gene could cause someone to be aggressive against their own offspring."

"You mean it could instruct someone to kill their own baby?"

"Yes."

"Thank you, Dr. Markowitz. I have nothing further," Sarah said after a few moments and sat down.

"Your witness, Mr. Sepulveda," said Judge Sandoval.

Renaldo got to his feet and approached the stand.

"Dr. Markowitz, have there been any studies on women who have one copy of the Warrior Gene?"

"No."

"Have there been any studies on women with two copies of the Warrior Gene?"

"No."

"Have there been any studies on heat as a possible trigger for the Warrior Gene?"

"No."

"Any studies on overcrowding as a possible trigger?"

"No."

"Any studies on hormones as a possible trigger?"

"No."

"Any studies on stinky smells?"

"No."

"In fact, there have been no studies on any of these, have there?"

"Not to my knowledge."

Renaldo should have stopped right then. He knew it, Sarah knew it, and Candi Markowitz knew it. But he asked one more question.

"So there's no hard science — none at all — to back up any of your claims, is there?"

"That's not quite true. A new study from Finland published just a few weeks ago suggests that intoxication caused by alcohol or other drugs might trigger the Warrior Gene."

Sarah was floored. She hadn't seen this study, but then she realized she'd stopped doing research on the Warrior Gene during trial. But Candi Markowitz had seen it.

Renaldo didn't seem to know about it either, but he recovered quickly.

"But there's no evidence that the defendant was drunk or high on the day she killed her baby daughter, isn't that correct?"

"I'm not aware of any evidence that Lexi Conway was drunk on August 11."

"So this study from Sweden ..."

"Finland."

"So this study from Finland isn't relevant to our case here, is it?"

"If you say so," replied Candi sharply.

"I do say so," shot back Renaldo. "Let me try this again, Dr. Markowitz. So there is no hard science — none at all — to back up your claim that the Warrior Gene caused the defendant to kill her defenseless little baby. Isn't that correct?"

"You are correct, Mr. Sepulveda. Such studies have not yet been conducted. But that doesn't mean my opinions are incorrect. There have been no empirical studies proving that God exists, but does that mean that God does not exist? Of course not. Can I prove that God exists with one hundred percent certainty? No, I can't. But is it a reasonable possibility? Yes, it is. Can I prove with one hundred percent certainty that a woman with two copies of the Warrior Gene killed her baby because her genetic code was triggered by a panoply of environmental factors? No, I can't. But is it a reasonable possibility? Absolutely."

Sarah offered no redirect. She didn't need to.

"You may call your next witness, Mrs. Wong," said Judge Sandoval, watching Candi Markowitz walk down the center aisle of the courtroom one last time.

"The defense rests, Your Honor," Sarah said. She smiled at Lexi, who smiled back.

"Very well. Mr. Sepulveda, do you have any rebuttal witnesses?"

"No, Your Honor."

Sarah was shocked. She'd assumed that the prosecution would put on at least one, maybe two, genetic experts to counter Candi Markowitz's testimony. Why hadn't they called their own DNA expert? Did Renaldo think the Warrior Gene defense was so absurd that it didn't deserve a response? Sarah started second-guessing her strategy. *Maybe I've missed something. Maybe I've overlooked a fatal flaw in my Warrior Gene defense. Maybe …*

Sarah was jolted back to reality by Judge Sandoval's booming voice.

"Ladies and gentlemen, both sides have rested, so that concludes the presentation of the evidence in the case. Closing arguments will begin promptly at nine on Monday morning. Have a nice weekend."

After the jurors left the courtroom, the judge invited Sarah and Renaldo back into chambers to talk about jury instructions.

"Your Honor, before we do that I'd like to remind you about my motion to sequester the jury," Sarah said.

"Let's take that back in chambers, Mrs. Wong," said the judge as he left the courtroom, Sarah and Renaldo following close behind.

"Your Honor, I'd like to renew my motion to sequester the jury during deliberations," said Sarah after they were all seated.

"Mrs. Wong, I've thought carefully about this issue, and there's nothing in the record that leads me to believe that the jurors need to be sequestered. I will admonish them not to read the newspapers or watch TV during their deliberations. That should be enough. Motion denied."

Then they discussed the instructions to be given to the jury. For almost the first time during the five-week trial, Sarah and Renaldo agreed about something: There would be no instructions about insanity and no instructions about lesser-included offenses such as manslaughter or second-degree murder.

It was going to be all or nothing for both Renaldo and Sarah.

And for Lexi.

CHAPTER 18

On Monday morning, Sarah was calm and confident. This was the day she had been planning for during the past seven months — the day when she would make her DNA argument for all the world to hear.

"Welcome back, ladies and gentlemen," announced Judge Sandoval.

Sarah couldn't tell if he was addressing the jury of twelve in the courtroom or the jury of millions watching on TV.

"We are ready for closing arguments. First up will be Mr. Sepulveda. Then Mrs. Wong will have her turn. And then Mr. Sepulveda will have an opportunity to respond to Mrs. Wong's arguments. Mr. Sepulveda, you may begin."

Renaldo delivered a powerful and effective closing argument, even if it was a little too long. He laid out all the elements of first-degree murder and went through a detailed description of the evidence in the case. He used every single piece of physical evidence, holding up Anna's little yellow sleeper for what seemed like an eternity, before placing it gingerly at the edge of the prosecution table for everyone to see. He told the jury that he spoke for Anna Conway, who could not speak for herself. He asked for justice for little Anna. Everyone was crying, especially Lexi.

He harped on the complete lack of scientific evidence about how the Warrior Gene might affect women, and he repeatedly reminded the jury that all the testimony about the Warrior Gene was nothing more than speculation. Then he homed in on the one glaring weakness in Sarah's defense — even if the Warrior Gene had caused Lexi to kill her baby daughter, there was no evidence that she had done so without free will, without any choice. He reminded the jury of two very important pieces of evidence — evidence provided by Lexi herself in her 911 call: "It's probably all for the best anyway," and in her police statement: "I knew it was my fault that Anna was dead."

His voice rose as he reached the apex of his closing argument.

"Ladies and gentlemen, this was no mistake, no tragic accident, no Warrior Gene mumbo jumbo. The defendant said in her own words that it was her fault and that it was all for the best. Yes, Lexi Conway wanted little Anna dead. For what twisted, horrible reason? Maybe she regretted having her, maybe it was something else. We'll probably never know. But the prosecution doesn't have to prove why Lexi killed Anna. All we have to do is prove that Lexi killed her baby intentionally. And we have done just that. Lexi may also have intended to kill herself, but that doesn't matter here. What matters is that Lexi killed her baby intentionally, which is murder in the first degree."

In many ways Renaldo's closing argument was outstanding, just the right blend of facts and law. The perfect balance of passion and reason. It was polished and professional, and he delivered it flawlessly. Yes, it was a superb closing argument. That is, until the very end. Not more than thirty seconds before he finished, Renaldo looked at Sarah and offered a challenge.

"And finally, I challenge defense counsel to explain how this Warrior Gene could have caused the defendant to act without any free will. As I'm sure you've noticed throughout the trial, Mrs. Wong is a very talented lawyer, but not even she will be able to explain that to you, because it's simply not true. That is why you must find Lexi Conway guilty of first-degree murder with a special circumstance."

That was just the opening Sarah needed. Within seconds of Renaldo's final words, before he had even moved away from the podium, she stood up.

"Good afternoon, ladies and gentlemen," she began, pausing to look at each of the twelve jurors and four alternates. "I accept the district attorney's challenge. I am going to show you why all the evidence in this case points to a single logical conclusion—that Lexi Conway had no free will, no choice, when she killed Anna Conway on that hot summer day last August."

Sarah approached the podium taking nothing with her—no notes, no papers.

"The district attorney took almost two hours to summarize the evidence that Lexi Conway killed her daughter. But I've already stipulated to that fact, so we don't need to go over that again. This is not a case of *who* did it. This is a case of *why* Lexi Conway did it." Sarah paused. "So why did Lexi kill Anna? Let's look at the possibilities.

"Is Lexi crazy? No. There's no evidence of that.

"Is Lexi a homicidal maniac? No. There isn't one scintilla of evidence that Lexi is a mean, horrible person. In fact, everyone who knows her, from her own family members and friends to the clerks and cashiers at Pete's Market and the Donut Shoppe told you what a kind, loving person she is. Even the detectives who took her statement commented on her politeness.

"Did Lexi want some sort of revenge? Was she trying to get back at someone? Again, based on all of the evidence, the unequivocal answer is no."

Lexi had been sobbing quietly while Sarah spoke, and now her crying became clearly audible throughout the cavernous courtroom. Sarah glided quickly behind Lexi's chair and put her hands on her shoulders. Lexi flinched slightly when she felt the pressure of Sarah's fingers, but she didn't look up, instead burying her sobs in her cupped hands while Sarah kept going.

"The DA has speculated that Lexi didn't want her baby, but that's all it is—speculation. You heard from five defense witnesses how much Lexi loved her baby, how much she celebrated her daughter. No one has loved their baby more than Lexi Conway loved her precious Anna.

"So what about Lexi's statement to the 911 operator, 'It's probably all for the best anyway'? Lexi wasn't talking about her baby's death. She was talking about her own."

Renaldo jumped up. "Objection! Assumes facts not in evidence."

"Overruled. Move on, Mrs. Wong."

"In fact, the district attorney has not been able to prove why Lexi Conway killed her baby. That's because there was no motive. And without a motive, you cannot possibly conclude that Lexi killed Anna intentionally."

Sarah moved back to the podium, keeping her eyes glued on the jury.

"So why did Lexi kill Anna Conway?" Sarah paused again. "I'll tell you why." She nodded at Isabel, who dimmed the lights in the courtroom. A PowerPoint slide with a single phrase appeared on every monitor in the court.

One Warrior Gene

It was accompanied by the sound of distant thunder.

"Lexi doesn't have just one copy of the Warrior Gene," Sarah said.

Then a second slide appeared, and this time the thunder was much louder.

Two Warrior Genes

"Lexi has two copies. That fact is not in dispute. So, what does that mean? Did this genetic defect cause Lexi to kill her baby? Not by itself. There was more. Much more."

One by one, more phrases appeared on the screen:

Postpartum Hormonal Changes
Extreme Heat
Lack of Sleep
Excessive Noise

They formed a circle around the perimeter of the PowerPoint slide, with a noticeable gap for one more.

"All of these contributed to Lexi's actions that day," Sarah went on. "But there was one final trigger that activated Lexi's two Warrior Genes — the smell of gasoline."

The words "Smell of Gasoline" appeared on the screen, completing the circle of words around the perimeter.

"That horrible, noxious smell of gasoline. You've all smelled it before, when gasoline gets on your hands at the filling station. And there is nothing more noxious than the smell of gasoline on a hot summer day. In fact, some people say that the smell of gasoline makes them feel woozy, even sort of drunk. Remember how Dr. Markowitz testified about a recent study from Finland that demonstrated that intoxication can trigger the Warrior Gene? Could Lexi have been intoxicated from the smell of gasoline that morning?

"Look carefully at the video from the Sunoco gas station and you'll see a puddle of liquid right where Lexi was standing. It wasn't water — it hadn't rained for weeks — it was a puddle of gasoline."

Then Sarah reached under the defense table and pulled

a large red plastic container out of a black canvas bag. It had a single word in block letters on the front— GASOLINE.

"Ladies and gentlemen of the jury, I'm going to open this container to remind you just how terrible gasoline smells."

"Objection!" yelled Renaldo and Joe, leaping up in unison.

"Sustained," ruled Judge Sandoval. "Mrs. Wong, you are going to do no such thing. Do you want to make us all sick to our stomachs?"

"No, Your Honor," replied Sarah. She turned back to the jury. "Judge Sandoval is a very wise man. He won't let me open this gas can here in the courtroom because the smell of gasoline is so powerful, so foul, that it would probably make most of us nauseous. It might even make some of us vomit. Back on August 11, the horrible smell of gasoline was the final trigger that set Lexi in motion."

With a click of the remote, Sarah sent the words on the monitors swirling and flashing around in big circles while the sound of thunder grew louder and louder. The intense visuals and deafening sounds were overwhelming, especially in the cavernous courtroom, and Judge Sandoval eventually yelled for Sarah to stop the presentation, his booming voice barely audible above the din.

Sarah obliged.

"Pretty annoying, isn't it?" Sarah looked directly at the jurors. "Just imagine how Lexi Conway felt back on August 11. She was caught up in a storm—a perfect storm—of genetics and environmental factors. She tried to resist the intense power of the storm, and for a while she was successful. You saw her begin to slap and shake Anna in the car at the gas station, but then she was able to stop. With what little energy she had left, she got back in her car and drove home, hoping she'd be able to escape the storm. But she couldn't.

"When she pulled into her garage, there was that smell again—that noxious, intoxicating smell of gasoline—only this time it was mixed with the smell of car exhaust. The perfect storm was relentless. It had become even more overpowering, and Lexi could resist no longer. She had no choice but to let nature take its course. Lexi and Anna sat in her car while the carbon monoxide filled the tiny garage, killing Anna and almost taking Lexi herself. Anna Conway was the ultimate victim of that perfect storm, and there was nothing Lexi could do about it."

Sarah turned to the jury.

"Do you remember how Mr. Wasserman, one of the paramedics who treated Lexi, described her voice? He said it sounded like she was a robot on automatic pilot. And that's exactly what she was. Her two Warrior Genes had manufactured her robot circuitry, and the perfect storm of environmental triggers had flipped the switch.

"But why did Lexi kill Anna? Why not kill a stranger, like one of the clerks at the Donut Shoppe? Dr. Markowitz told us why. She testified that the Warrior Gene could program an organism to kill its own offspring to prevent the Warrior Gene from spreading further. That wouldn't be accomplished by killing a stranger.

"Somewhere deep inside, in a way she couldn't really understand, Lexi had a premonition that this might happen, that her two Warrior Genes would make her commit this horrible act. But there was nothing, absolutely nothing, she could do about it."

Sarah paused to catch her breath.

"Can I prove to you absolutely, with one hundred percent certainty, that Lexi had no free will back on August 11? I don't think I can. Can I prove it to you beyond a reasonable doubt? Probably not. But that's not my burden, it's the state's. The prosecution has to prove beyond a reasonable doubt that Lexi *did* have free will on August 11. They have to prove beyond a reasonable doubt that she acted voluntarily and with purpose. But they have failed to do so. Why? Because the only reasonable explanation, indeed the only *possible* explanation, is that she was caught in a perfect storm of genetics and environmental factors that deprived her of any choice, any free will. And that is why you must return a verdict of not guilty."

Sarah returned to her seat. She was exhausted but exhilarated, and she barely heard any of Renaldo's rebuttal argument. As best as she could tell, Renaldo simply went back over the case and focused on the cause and manner of death, facts about which there was no dispute—a little baby had died, killed by her own mother. Renaldo just kept repeating how horrible the crime was and how horrible Lexi was.

While Renaldo spoke, Sarah fixed her eyes on the jury. Right away she noticed that a few of them were looking not at Renaldo but at her and Lexi. As he droned on, more and more of them turned their attention to the defense table until it seemed that none of them were paying attention to Renaldo.

And then it was over.

Renaldo sat down, and Judge Sandoval, his glasses perched on the end of his nose, began to read the jury instructions. He read each one carefully and slowly, enunciating every word, occasionally looking at the jury and frequently peering into the cameras.

"You shall now retire to the jury assembly room and begin your deliberations," he said, adding, "Good luck and Godspeed," as if the jury were embarking on some kind of heroic mission.

As the jury left the courtroom, Sarah stood and pulled Lexi up with her, doing her best to smile as they filed out.

"What happens now, Mrs. Wong?" Lexi whispered.

"We wait."

CHAPTER 19

On the drive home from the courthouse, Sarah replayed the entire trial in her mind, reliving every choice, every decision, every mistake, worried that her Warrior Gene defense would turn out to be some huge, ill-conceived gamble.

She had promised Matt they would go out for dinner as soon as the trial was over, but she just felt like ordering takeout and watching an old movie on TV. When she got home, though, Matt was dressed up and ready to go. He had been so supportive throughout the trial and she couldn't let him down. They went to Ocean Cove, the restaurant where they had made their pregnancy pledge four years before, and despite Sarah's complete physical and mental exhaustion, dinner actually turned out to be fun. They shared an appetizer, two entrées, and two desserts. As they walked out to their car in the cool Santa Felicia evening, they even shared a kiss.

The next morning, Matt had already left for work when Sarah woke at seven fifteen, and she enjoyed having the place to herself. She took her time having breakfast and read the newspaper while the twins kicked and jostled for position inside her expanding belly. An hour later, she got dressed for work. With her due date less than four months away, most of her regular clothes didn't fit anymore, but since she wouldn't be needed in court during the first day of jury deliberations on such a complex case, she could wear something more casual and comfortable than the suits she'd been buttoned up in for the past two months.

When she got to the office, she was surprised to find it completely empty. She had forgotten that she had told everyone to take the day off as a reward for all their hard work over the previous few months. Maggie and Conrad had kept her law practice going during the trial, and Sarah had been pleasantly surprised by Conrad's willingness to pitch in and handle her other clients.

She was in the middle of sorting through hundreds of unanswered emails when the phone rang. It was Isabel.

"Judge Sandoval asked me to call you because the jury has a question," she told Sarah.

"Already?" Sarah was surprised. The jury had been deliberating for less than two hours. She did her best to get Isabel to read the question over the phone, but Isabel refused and told her that the judge wanted the attorneys in court at one p.m. sharp.

Luckily enough, Sarah always kept an extra set of court clothes — a gray suit, white blouse, and black shoes — in her office for just this sort of situation. But it wasn't until she slipped off her jeans that she remembered that the garments on the door weren't maternity clothes. They were petite, size zero — perfect for a five-foot two-inch, one-hundred-pound lawyer — but not so good for one who had added twenty-five pregnancy pounds in the past couple of months. She quickly switched to Plan B.

She figured she could make it home to change and get back to court in time. At home, she put on the same dark-gray suit she had worn the day before, pulled on a fresh blouse, and snatched her travel makeup kit from the bathroom counter. She pulled into the courthouse parking lot at twelve fifty, and as she freshened her makeup and brushed her hair she thought about the jury's question. Questions were almost always a good sign for the defense — it meant the jury was thinking carefully about the case. But this question came awfully quickly. What could the jury possibly want to know so early in their deliberations?

When she arrived in Courtroom 201, Isabel told her to go straight back into the judge's chambers. But Sarah said she'd rather wait out in court until Renaldo arrived—it wouldn't be right for her to meet with the judge without the DA.

"Actually, Renaldo's already in chambers with the judge."

Sarah could barely contain her anger as she stomped past Isabel and pushed through the closed door without knocking. When she entered the large room, Judge Sandoval and Renaldo were sitting on the dark-brown tufted-leather couch laughing heartily.

"Come on in," said the judge.

"Your Honor, I don't think it's proper for you and—"

"Don't worry, Mrs Wong. We weren't talking about the case. We were just talking about the Lakers. You know—guy stuff."

Sarah took a deep breath. Was this a battle worth fighting right then? Probably not. After a moment or two, she said, "The Lakers are toast. Watch for the Clippers to finish strong and make the playoffs."

Renaldo and the judge fell silent and just stared at her, their mouths slightly agape. Sarah hoped she had made her point.

"All right, let's get down to business," Judge Sandoval said as he went and sat down behind the large desk, empty except for a small lamp and a single piece of paper. "Why don't you both pull up a chair so you can look at the jury's note."

As Sarah and Renaldo sat down, Judge Sandoval pushed the paper across his desk so they could see it. There were two questions printed neatly on the yellow paper.

1. Has Mrs. Wong been charged with obstruction of justice or some other crime because of her unethical conduct in the case?
2. Can we take Mrs. Wong's unethical conduct into account in deciding the case?

Sarah didn't know whether to be angry or embarrassed. In truth, she felt both. This couldn't be worse. The jury was focusing on *her* conduct instead of thinking about the defense. Then she realized it *was* worse. The note was signed "Robert Bergmann, jury foreman." Of the twelve jurors, he was the absolute worst choice for foreperson. She immediately ran through in her mind possible grounds for appeal — prosecutorial misconduct, jury misconduct, maybe even defense attorney misconduct.

"I need to formulate a response to the jury's questions," said Judge Sandoval. "Any suggestions?"

Sarah jumped right in. "Your Honor, the answers are easy. No and no."

She turned and looked at Renaldo.

"Your Honor, I am inclined to agree with Mrs. Wong," he said, much to Sarah's surprise. "Although her conduct in this case has been reprehensible —"

"Hold on, Renaldo," said Judge Sandoval. "I think we need to get this on the record. Mrs. Wong, could you ask the court reporter to come in?"

Sarah delivered the message to Savannah, who came in promptly, carrying her dictation machine. The judge and Renaldo watched Savannah intently as she walked quickly across the room in her tight-fitting plaid skirt, in much the same way as they had stared at Candi Markowitz during the trial. Sarah couldn't stay quiet any longer.

"Gentlemen!"

Both men knew immediately why Sarah had spoken up, and they quickly looked away from Savannah, who sat down between Sarah and Renaldo.

Judge Sandoval began. "We are here in chambers discussing a note sent to me from the jury. Mrs. Wong and Mr. Sepulveda, have you both read the jury's note?"

"Yes, Your Honor," they chimed in unison.

"We need to answer their questions. Any suggestions?"

"Your Honor, I believe you should simply tell the jury that the answer to both questions is no," Sarah said.

"Do you agree, Mr. Sepulveda?" asked Judge Sandoval.

"I'm afraid not, Your Honor. Mrs. Wong's behavior has been reprehensible, and the jury should be told that they can consider her misconduct in their deliberations."

Sarah was livid. Less than five minutes earlier Renaldo had agreed to Sarah's suggested responses. Was he retaliating because she had caught him ogling the court reporter?

"Your Honor, my conduct is completely irrelevant to the issue of guilt or innocence and the jury should be told that."

"I must disagree with you, Mrs. Wong," said Judge Sandoval. "I found you in contempt twice during the trial—hardly a spotless record. Therefore, your conduct is indeed relevant."

Everyone sat in silence for a few moments while Judge Sandoval pondered what to do.

"After further consideration, I think the prudent thing is to tell the jury that they should only consider those aspects of Mrs. Wong's behavior that are relevant to an issue in the trial, such as the credibility of Dr. Markowitz. Any objections to this approach?"

"Yes, Your Honor," Sarah said, "I strenuously object because—"

"Your objection is noted for the record."

"But Your Honor—"

"Mrs. Wong, I said that your objection has been recorded. Let's go into court and bring the jury out."

"Your Honor, shouldn't we send back a written response instead of bringing the jury out into court?" asked Sarah.

"I don't think that's necessary, Mrs. Wong. I'll just tell the jury what I said here."

"Don't you think we should write down a statement for you to read?"

"That won't be necessary either," said Judge Sandoval firmly. "I know what to tell them." Then he shouted loudly toward the closed chamber door. "Isabel, ask Brian to bring the jury in!"

Sarah rushed out to the courtroom to speak to Lexi before the jury came in, but it was already too late. Judge Sandoval walked out of his chambers and smiled broadly at the jurors.

"Good afternoon, ladies and gentlemen. I trust you had a nice lunch."

"Your Honor —" interrupted Sarah.

"I'll get to you in a moment, Mrs. Wong."

Sarah stood up. "Your Honor, my client is not present!" she exclaimed.

"Mrs. Wong, we don't really need her, do we? We're just responding to a question from the jury."

"I insist that Ms. Conway be present, Your Honor. As you know, she has a *Constitutional right* to be present during all phases of her trial."

"Yes, I suppose you're right," conceded Judge Sandoval. "Brian, can you bring in the defendant?"

"It'll take me about ten minutes, Your Honor. She's in the holding cell in the basement."

"That's fine. Take your time."

While Brian went to get Lexi, Judge Sandoval made small talk with the jurors. It was hard for Sarah to listen while the judge joked with them. He told stories of past cases and even answered questions posed by some of the jurors. It was all highly inappropriate while a trial was going on, but it was another battle not worth fighting, especially in front of the jury. But she made a mental note that she could raise his behavior on appeal.

At last Lexi walked in, escorted at the elbow by Brian. She was wearing her bright orange county jail jumpsuit, with all her tattoos clearly visible.

Sarah jumped to her feet. "May we approach the bench?" she shouted.

"About what, Mrs. Wong?"

Sarah walked briskly to the bench. By the time Renaldo and Savannah caught up with her, she was already speaking excitedly to Judge Sandoval.

"Your Honor, my client is in her county jail clothes. I move for a mistrial."

"Calm down, Mrs. Wong. I'll take a brief recess so the defendant can change clothes." Judge Sandoval turned to the jury. "Ladies and gentlemen, we will take a brief recess so that the defendant can change into her courtroom clothes. See you back here in about ten minutes."

The judge didn't have to tell the jury *why* they were taking a recess, thought Sarah. As usual, his comments had only made matters worse. The sweet, innocent image of Lexi that Sarah had worked so hard to craft over the past five weeks had been shattered in a matter of seconds. She slumped back down in her chair.

Without the jury to entertain, Judge Sandoval sat in silence while they waited for Lexi to reappear. Sarah's mind began to race. What would the judge say about her conduct to the jury? What would the reporters have to say about her? Would they say that she was unethical ... or worse?

Suddenly the side door opened and Lexi walked back in. As soon as Sarah saw her, she knew she had made the right decision to have Lexi change into her trial clothes. In her brown tweed skirt and tan cardigan, and her hair pulled back into a loose ponytail, Lexi looked more relaxed, softer, and maybe a little less guilty.

"Is everything to your liking now, Mrs. Wong?" Judge Sandoval asked with a hint of sarcasm.

Sarah looked down at the papers in front of her. "Yes, Your Honor."

"All right. Let's try again. Brian, bring in the jury."

After the jurors were seated, Judge Sandoval began. "Welcome back, ladies and gentlemen. Thank you for your patience. I have a note signed by Robert Bergmann. Mr. Bergmann, are you the jury foreman?"

"Yes, I am."

"Congratulations, Mr. Bergmann, that is quite a show of respect from your fellow jurors."

"Actually, we drew straws and I got the short one," replied Mr. Bergmann.

Several jurors giggled.

Sarah exhaled audibly. Although Robert Bergmann was a horrible choice for foreperson, at least the other jurors hadn't elected him, which would have been a clear signal that the jury was going to be trouble for the defense.

"Mr. Sepulveda, Mrs. Wong, and I have all read your note," Judge Sandoval continued. Sarah's entire body clenched up. She had no way of knowing what Judge Sandoval was going to say, and she prepared for the worst. "The answer to your first question—about whether Mrs. Wong has been charged with obstruction of justice or some other crime—is no."

Sarah relaxed a little.

"Not yet, anyway," the judge added.

Sarah almost objected, but thought better of it.

He sat up and looked directly at the jury. "Keep in mind that Mrs. Wong is not on trial here. Lexi Conway is. Therefore, the answer to your second question is that you should not be concerned about whether or not Mrs. Wong has done anything wrong"—Sarah held her breath—"unless her misconduct is relevant to an issue in the case."

All Sarah could do was look down at the counsel table.

Judge Sandoval continued, "Ladies and gentlemen, please return to the jury room to continue your deliberations."

As the jury filed out, Sarah sank into her chair, making eye contact with no one. After a while she realized Lexi was tapping her on the shoulder.

"Ma'am, are you all right? What just happened? Are you in some sort of trouble again? Are you going back to jail?"

"No, I'm fine," Sarah replied. "Everything's fine."

Depressed and disappointed, she drove straight home and fell fast asleep on the couch. Matt was sitting right next to her when she woke up.

"What time is it? What day is it?" she asked.

"Wednesday morning, eight forty-five."

"What?!" Sarah's screech startled Chloe, who arched her back and hissed.

Sarah tried to get up off the couch, but Matt gently pushed her back down.

"You're not going in to work today. I've called Nick and told him you're sick and won't be in for a couple of days."

Sarah stayed home for the rest of the week. Wednesday and Thursday passed without a single word from the jury, as did Friday morning. No notes, no questions, no signs of progress.

At three p.m. on Friday, confident there would be no verdict or jury questions before the weekend, Sarah thought she might go for a walk and get some fresh air. But as she was about to head out the door, Isabel called to tell her that the jury had another question and Judge Sandoval wanted her to get to the courthouse as soon as possible. Her walk would have to wait.

She had an outfit for court laid out in the bedroom so she could get ready at a moment's notice and it took her only a few minutes to get dressed. She packed her briefcase quickly and got down to the courthouse within a half hour, arriving at the same time as Renaldo.

"Hey Renaldo, any guesses what the jury's question is about?" she asked, doing her best to be civil.

"Maybe this time they think *I* committed misconduct," Renaldo replied with a high-pitched laugh.

Sarah rolled her eyes. She was beyond getting mad about the misconduct questions from Tuesday. "Maybe we'll end up spending the weekend in jail together."

"That would be fine with me," replied Renaldo with a smile.

Was Renaldo hitting on me, Sarah wondered, a little flattered but mostly shocked.

When they walked into the courtroom, Isabel waved them back to the judge's chambers.

"Come on in. Have a seat," said Judge Sandoval briskly. It was apparent he wanted to finish up quickly so he could start his weekend early. "The jury wants to know if they can convict the defendant of a less serious charge, such as second-degree murder."

"No," Renaldo and Sarah said at the same time.

"We've already discussed this issue," Sarah continued, "and we all agreed that the jury would only be instructed as to first-degree murder. Our defense is not consistent with any lesser charge, and frankly neither is the prosecution's case. It's either first-degree murder or not guilty — there's nothing in between."

"I think we should give instructions for lesser includeds," said Judge Sandoval. "Maybe second degree or even manslaughter. Otherwise we might get a hung jury and we'll have to try this case all over again. Nobody wants that."

"Actually, I wouldn't mind," Sarah said halfheartedly. "Your Honor, we need the court reporter in here before we go any further."

"Not possible, I'm afraid. I let her go home already."

"But it's only three forty-five."

"I didn't think we would need her any more today."

"Well, I won't proceed without a court reporter present," Sarah said emphatically.

"Mr. Sepulveda, what do you think?" the judge asked.

"Maybe we can get a court reporter from another courtroom."

The judge instructed Isabel to find a court reporter, but she returned only five minutes later.

"Judge, there are only two court reporters in the whole building and they're both tied up in trial."

"Okay, I guess we'll just tell the jury to go home," said Judge Sandoval, walking to the door with his briefcase in hand. "We'll handle their question on Monday at nine. Have a nice weekend."

Sarah went down to the holding cell in the basement of the courthouse to tell Lexi that the jury had another question.

"Is that a good thing or a bad thing?" asked Lexi.

"I'm not really sure."

"This waiting is really hard."

"For you and me both, Lexi. I'll see you on Monday when we answer the jury's question."

Just as Sarah was about to leave, Lexi blurted out, "I sure am glad I never had to testify during the trial."

"Why's that?"

"What if they'd asked me about my other baby?"

"Your what?"

"My other baby."

"What do you mean *your other baby*? You never told me you had another baby! Why didn't you tell me this before? Where is it now? Did you place it up for adoption?"

"No, he's dead too."

"What do you mean *he's dead too*?"

"He died just like Anna."

Sarah's chest tightened and she gasped for air. She didn't know what a heart attack felt like, but she was convinced she was having one right there and then.

"Mrs. Wong, are you okay?"

Sarah was unable to respond. Her throat felt like it had closed off completely.

Lexi waved frantically at the sheriff standing outside by the door. "Guard! Guard! We need some help in here!"

The sheriff burst in and headed toward Lexi.

"It's my attorney. I think she's sick."

"I'm okay. I'm okay. I just need a few minutes," Sarah said when he reached her.

"Would you like some water, counselor?" the sheriff asked.

"Sure, that'd be great."

While the sheriff was gone, Sarah glared at Lexi and hissed, "Why didn't you tell me?"

Lexi was about to reply when the sheriff reappeared with a small paper cup full of water and handed it to Sarah. She took a few sips, thanked the guard and told him he could leave.

As soon as the door closed behind him, Sarah lit into Lexi.

"Why didn't you tell me about this before?" Sarah had her voice back now, and it was filled with anger and disbelief.

"You never asked me."

"Didn't you think I should know about your other baby?"

"Maybe, but I was scared."

"Scared of what?"

"That you might tell someone."

"Was it a boy or a girl?"

"A boy—Jacob."

"And how did Jacob die, exactly?"

"Just like Anna. One day he just didn't wake up from his nap in the car."

"How old was he when he died?"

"Three days old."

"How old were you?"

"Seventeen."

Sarah's questions came fast and furious.

"What did you do with Jacob after he died?"

"We buried him."

"Where? Who helped you?"

"Me and Ryan. We buried him in the woods behind my grandma's house. That's where I was living then."

"Who else knows about the baby?"

"Just me and Ryan. Nobody else."

"What about your mom? Your sister? Your grandmother?"

"None of them knew anything. I moved out of my mom's house as soon as I found out I was pregnant with Jacob. Her and me weren't getting along so good back then. I moved in with my grandma, and she let Ryan live with us too. Ryan and me just hung out together until the baby was born, and my grandma left us alone."

"Are you sure nobody else knows about the baby except Ryan?"

"Absolutely."

"Why didn't you tell me before?"

"I didn't trust you before."

"So how come you've decided to tell me now?"

"Now I trust you. You're not going to tell anyone, right?" Lexi looked directly at Sarah. "That's what the attorney privilege thing is for, right? So I can tell you anything I want and you can't tell anyone."

"Yes, Lexi, that's right. I won't tell anyone."

"You promise?"

"I promise."

* * *

Less than two days went by before Sarah broke her promise to Lexi. She couldn't hold it in any longer. It just sort of spilled out while she and Matt were having breakfast on Sunday morning.

"Lexi killed two babies."

"What d'ya say, Tiger?"

"Lexi killed two babies."

"What? What do you mean?"

"She had two babies and she killed them both."

"How do you know?"

"She told me."

"When?"

"Friday, right after we were done in court."

"And you've kept it to yourself since then?" Matt looked shocked.

"I promised her I wouldn't tell anybody. Not even you."

"But I'm your husband."

Sarah didn't say anything.

"Does anyone else know?"

"Only Lexi's boyfriend. Nobody else."

Matt flung his fork down on the table. "How can you represent someone who killed *two* babies?" he shouted.

"I don't have a choice. I'm her attorney. Besides, until Friday I only knew about one of them."

"Oh, that makes it *much* better."

Matt walked off, leaving Sarah alone at the table, and she sat there, crying softly. A few minutes later, he reappeared with his jacket on.

"I'm going out. I'll be back tonight," he announced and slammed the door shut on his way out.

CHAPTER 20

When Brian opened the courtroom doors at eight forty-five on Monday morning, Sarah walked in briskly and took her place at the defense table. Renaldo arrived not long afterwards looking tense and exhausted.

Sarah felt a bit sorry for him. What had begun as a straightforward baby-killer case had morphed into a high publicity referendum on Sarah's Warrior Gene defense. Lexi's case had attracted a huge amount of attention all over the world. Talking heads of all sorts—a few true experts, some pseudo-experts, and quite a few blowhards—were debating genetics, free will, crime, and punishment. There was even a Facebook group— FreeLexi—that had attracted over ten thousand members.

Just after nine, Isabel told them the judge was ready for them, and Sarah and Renaldo walked back to chambers together. Savannah was already there.

Judge Sandoval greeted them cheerfully and got straight down to business. "The jury sent me a note on Friday asking if there are lesser charges they might consider. I showed the note to Mr. Sepulveda and Mrs. Wong, and we all agreed to take the matter up this morning."

Sarah jumped right in. "Your Honor, as I said on Friday, I strenuously object to giving the jury any instructions on second-degree murder, manslaughter, or any other charges. Our contention is that Ms. Conway is completely innocent of the charges against her, and the DA has only argued that she is guilty of premeditated first-degree murder. Neither of us has even mentioned the possibility of lesser-included charges to the jury, so it would be reversible error for you to give such instructions now. As he indicated during our conversation on Friday, Mr. Sepulveda agrees with me on this point."

"Actually, Your Honor, I gave this issue more thought over the weekend," said Renaldo looking sheepish.

"But Your Honor, on Friday —"

"Mrs. Wong, this is Monday, not Friday. Let me hear what Mr. Sepulveda has to say."

Renaldo continued. "Your Honor, it is our position that Ms. Conway deliberately killed her baby with malice aforethought and therefore is guilty of first-degree murder. However, we acknowledge that there is a slim possibility that Ms. Conway's state of mind was consistent with second-degree murder, so we ask you to instruct the jury that they have the option of convicting the defendant of second-degree murder."

"Is that your opinion or Joe's?" Sarah asked, her voice dripping with sarcasm.

Renaldo kept his composure. "Both Mr. Jimmerson and I support this position."

"Your Honor, because Mr. Sepulveda agreed with me on Friday I assumed this issue was settled and I didn't do any research on it over the weekend. I'd like a day to review the applicable case law before you rule on this."

"Mrs. Wong, you should know better than to assume anything during a trial. I agree with Mr. Sepulveda, and I'm going to instruct the jury on second-degree murder. I'm also inclined to throw in an instruction on voluntary manslaughter. Anything else?"

"But Your Honor —"

Isabel burst into the judge's chambers without knocking. "Your Honor, I have some news. The jury buzzed."

"Another question already?" exclaimed Judge Sandoval.

"No, Your Honor. They buzzed three times."

Three times? The jury had reached a verdict!

"But, Your Honor, we haven't answered their question yet," said Renaldo.

"I wouldn't worry if I were you, Mr. Sepulveda," replied Judge Sandoval, ignoring Sarah's icy stare. "Let's get ready for prime time! Isabel, make sure all members of the press know we have a verdict and verify that the TV reporters are here. They might want to interview me after we're done."

As Sarah and Renaldo rose to go back out into the courtroom, Judge Sandoval disappeared into his private bathroom.

Renaldo appeared just as stunned as Sarah. When the jury went home on Friday they had been asking about lesser charges, yet now they had a verdict. So what had happened over the weekend? The jury had been deliberating for only ten minutes this morning before signaling they had a verdict. But which verdict?

Sarah made her way to counsel table rapidly mulling over the various possibilities in her head. Sometimes when juries inquired about lesser-included charges it meant they believed a lesser charge was appropriate, but more often than not it meant there was a split in the jury and they were trying to reach a compromise. Nick had arrived while she had been back in chambers, and seeing his familiar face reassured her.

The side door opened and Lexi entered the courtroom wearing the same outfit she had worn the previous Tuesday. "Hi Sarah, what's going on? Are we going to answer the jury's question now?"

"Actually, it sounds like they've reached a verdict," Sarah told her as calmly as she could.

"What does that mean? Is that good or bad? Am I going home today?"

"I don't know, Lexi. I don't know."

Everyone was ready, but Judge Sandoval had still not appeared. Sarah walked over to Isabel to ask when they'd be starting.

"In a bit," replied Isabel evasively. "Judge Sandoval isn't quite ready yet."

"I'm sure he's had time to comb his hair by now — what little there is of it." Sarah's impudent comment made Isabel giggle.

"C'mon, Isabel. What's the holdup?"

"The judge doesn't want to start because all the reporters aren't here yet," she whispered.

Sarah and Isabel smiled knowingly at each other. This was Burt Sandoval's big moment, and he wanted to make sure every reporter was in place and all the cameras were rolling.

Sarah returned to her chair at the defense table. Lexi leaned over and asked her if anything was wrong.

"No. We're almost ready to start," replied Sarah.

"I'm really nervous, Mrs. Wong."

"Me too."

Sarah was just about to tell Nick what was going on when Judge Sandoval emerged from chambers. It was nine forty-five.

Brian sprang to his feet. "All rise. Department H of the Superior Court of Santa Felicia is now in session, the Honorable Judge Burt Sandoval presiding," he announced with more gusto than usual.

Judge Sandoval took the bench and smiled broadly.

"Good morning, everyone. Please be seated." He looked directly at the camera stationed at the back of the courtroom. "Mr. Sepulveda and Mrs. Wong, I understand we have a verdict. Are you both ready to proceed?"

"Yes, Your Honor."

Sarah grabbed Lexi's hand beneath the defense table and squeezed it.

"Brian, please bring in the jury."

After the jury had been seated, Judge Sandoval shifted his gaze from the camera to the jury box. "Good morning, ladies and gentlemen. Does the jury have a verdict?"

"Yes, we do, Your Honor," replied Robert Bergmann, rising from his seat in the middle of the back row.

"Very well. Mr. Bergmann, please hand the verdict form to the bailiff."

Brian retrieved the verdict and took it to Judge Sandoval.

The judge put on his glasses, unfolded the form, and studied the verdict silently. After a few moments, he peered at the jury over his reading glasses and then looked down at the form again. Sarah thought something might be wrong with the form, and her spirits lifted. That would present a fertile ground for appeal.

"The clerk of the court will now read the verdict into the record," Judge Sandoval said somberly as he handed the verdict form to Isabel. He looked at Sarah and Lexi. "Will the defendant please rise."

Lexi and Sarah stood up as one, holding hands. Lexi seemed to be taking this much better than Sarah, who closed her eyes as Isabel read out the verdict.

"In the case of the State of California versus Lexi Conway we the jury in the above entitled cause find the defendant, Lexi Conway, not guilty of the charge of first-degree murder. The verdict form is signed Robert Bergmann, Jury Foreman."

Did Isabel say NOT guilty? Startled, Sarah opened her eyes and looked at Isabel.

Isabel turned to the jury. "Is this your verdict, so say you one, so say you all?" she asked, her voice breaking with emotion.

A chorus of yeses, some louder than others, emanated from the jury box. Sarah turned to the jurors and could see that many of them were crying. Two women had buried their heads in their hands, and one of them was sobbing uncontrollably. Sarah's gaze fell on Robert Bergmann who gave her a big smile.

Overwhelmed by emotions and wondering if she had heard the verdict correctly, Sarah turned to look at Lexi, who had tears running down her cheeks — but were they tears of joy or sadness? Maybe Sarah had misheard.

"I'm going home," Lexi said quietly. "I'm going home," she repeated more loudly. "I'M GOING HOME!"

Sarah and Lexi hugged each other tightly. Both of them were crying now. But Sarah didn't care. They had won!

While the courtroom descended into chaos, Renaldo stared ahead stony-faced.

"Order please. Order in the courtroom," Judge Sandoval yelled while he banged his gavel angrily. "Everyone be seated," he ordered with one more blow of the gavel.

Renaldo got to his feet. "May I have the jury polled, Your Honor?" he asked politely.

"Of course. Madame clerk, please poll the jury."

Isabel stood. "As I call your juror number, please respond to my question in a clear voice. Juror Number 1, is this your verdict?"

"Yes."

"Juror Number 2, is this your verdict?"

"Yes."

It was the same reply each time until she reached Juror 10.

"Juror Number 10, is this your verdict?"

Juror 10, a woman in her 60s, did not respond. She simply looked down at her hands, which were folded in her lap.

"Juror Number 10, is this your verdict?" Isabel repeated.

Juror 10 still did not respond, so Judge Sandoval interrupted brusquely. "Ma'am, is this your verdict?"

Startled by the judge's tone, Juror 10 managed a barely audible, "Yes."

She must have been a holdout, thought Sarah, and

changed her mind over the weekend. That's why the jury reached a verdict so quickly this morning.

Isabel finished polling the final two jurors and sat down.

Sarah could see that Judge Sandoval's face was almost purple, as if he had been holding his breath for several minutes. Yet he spoke in a measured, somber tone.

"Ladies and gentlemen of the jury, thank you for your hard work. You are released from further service on this case. The court will stand in recess for one hour. Brian, please remand Ms. Conway back into custody."

Lexi gasped audibly. "I … I thought I was going home!" she said loudly.

Judge Sandoval ignored her. "Counselors, I will see you in my chambers immediately. Savannah, you don't need to come back with us."

Brian grabbed Lexi lightly by her elbow and asked her to stand up. She turned to Sarah, her face still damp from all the tears.

"What's happening? The jury said not guilty! I want to go home now!"

"Don't worry, Lexi. You *are* going home. We just have to fill out some paperwork. I'll come see you as soon as I've finished talking with the judge."

But Sarah *was* worried. Why hadn't Judge Sandoval released Lexi immediately? And why did he want to talk to the attorneys in chambers off the record?

When Sarah and Renaldo entered chambers, Judge Sandoval was seated at his desk writing furiously on a pad of paper.

"Sit down," he said without even looking up. "I'm sure you both know that the jury's verdict is contrary to the facts and law in the case. I have no choice but to vacate the jury's verdict and order a retrial in the case. I will set the date for a new trial one month from today."

"What? Your Honor!" Sarah shouted. "This is completely and utterly unfair and contrary to the laws of the State of California! What about double jeopardy? The jury has spoken. They found my client not guilty! I demand that you release her immediately!"

"I will note your objection for the record."

"But, Your Honor, we don't have the court reporter in here. I'll go get her." Sarah got up quickly and went to the courtroom door.

"That won't be necessary, Mrs. Wong. I've written your objection down on my notepad."

Sarah spun around and shouted at the judge from the doorway. "I am going out this door and I'll tell the reporters what you're doing! I will explain that you have usurped the jury's duty and that you are violating the basic principles of fairness and due process delineated by the Constitution of the United States of America. After that, I will call the Judicial Conduct Board of the State Bar and report your conduct. I'm sure a State Bar reprimand will look good on your appellate court application!"

"Do not threaten me, Mrs. Wong."

"I am not threatening you, Your Honor. I am asking you to enforce the law and to uphold the Constitution."

"May I remind you, Mrs. Wong, that I instituted a gag order for the duration of the trial. If you say anything to the press, even one word, I will hold you in contempt and have you remanded immediately."

"May I remind YOU that you just released the jury, which means that the trial is over," she shot back. "I can say anything I damn well want to and there's nothing you can do about it."

Sarah was right and Judge Sandoval knew it. She moved to open the courtroom door.

"Stop!" the judge shouted. "Let's try to be reasonable."

Sarah was in control now and she wasn't going to let up. "Release my client immediately or I walk out this door and talk to the press."

"Let's see if we can reach some sort of compromise."

"No compromise. Release my client now!" Sarah stood with her hand on the brass doorknob.

Renaldo hadn't said a word during the entire exchange.

Judge Sandoval finally broke the silence. "I'll release your client tomorrow morning."

"No, release her now!" Sarah turned the knob and pulled the door toward her.

"Okay, okay. Let's go out in court and get this done."

Judge Sandoval picked up the phone and rang the bailiff's desk. "Brian, bring the defendant back into the courtroom."

Sarah opened the door and went directly to the defense table. Renaldo followed quickly and took his seat. The courtroom was almost empty, as the reporters had gathered outside the courthouse waiting to hear from Sarah about her triumphant defense.

Brian brought Lexi in and directed her to sit down at the defense table.

Lexi looked at Sarah with fear in her eyes, but Sarah smiled broadly. "Lexi, you're going home today!"

Judge Sandoval emerged from chambers and took the bench. "In the matter of the State of California versus Lexi Conway, the defendant is released from custody."

"Thank you, thank you!" Lexi shouted.

"This matter is continued until tomorrow morning at nine a.m.," the judge continued. "The attorneys and the defendant are ordered back into court at that time. We are adjourned for the day."

"Why do we have to come back to court tomorrow?" asked Lexi.

Sarah was confused too. "I'm not sure," she told Lexi. "But the important thing is, the jury found you not guilty and you can go home now!"

"This way, Ms. Conway," said Brian in a kind tone. Seeing the apprehension on her face, he quickly added, "Don't worry. We just have to go through proper procedures and release you downstairs. It'll only take about twenty minutes."

Lexi looked at Sarah.

"He's right," Sarah assured her. "The Sheriff's Office won't allow you to be released directly from the courtroom. They have to do that downstairs. Everything's fine. The judge's order was clear. You're going home today."

Lexi and Sarah embraced.

"One more thing, Lexi," Sarah said. "There are lots of reporters and TV cameras outside the courthouse. They want to talk with me about the case. Do you want to say anything to them?"

"No, I don't want to talk. I just want to go home."

"That's fine. I'll see you tomorrow. Be sure to get to the courthouse no later than eight forty-five. We don't want to be late."

Sarah stuffed her papers into her briefcase and started toward the door.

"Mrs. Wong?"

Sarah looked up and saw that Lexi was crying again. "What's wrong?" she asked.

"Thank you. Thank you for saving my life."

With that, Lexi disappeared through the side door on her way to freedom.

Sarah turned her thoughts to the throng of reporters waiting outside the courthouse. This was going to be her big moment, the press conference that would transform her from a local trial lawyer into an international celebrity.

She asked Isabel if she could use the judge's bathroom to freshen up. Once Isabel checked that the judge had gone, Sarah pushed through the heavy wooden door and went into the private bathroom at the far side of his chambers. She closed the door, leaned forward on the counter, and took a deep breath.

I did it. I really did it!

The enormity of what had just happened started to sink in. She had won the case nobody thought she could win.

Now it was time for her coming-out party. In the weeks to come there would be interviews and talk shows, possibly even a book deal. She wondered whether she would have time to practice law anymore. Maybe she would be offered a job as a legal analyst for CNN or TruTV.

First things first. What was she going to say to the press? She had drafted a statement a couple of weeks ago but couldn't find it anywhere in her briefcase, so she decided to just wing it. After all, she was used to thinking on her feet.

She looked in the small mirror above the sink and let out a little yelp. Streaks of makeup and smudges of eyeliner lined her face, and she looked a bit like a circus clown. She turned the faucet on full blast and threw water on her face. But that only seemed to make things worse.

There was a soft knock on the door. "Need any help?"

There stood Isabel with a large box of tissues in one hand and a small black zippered bag in the other.

"I thought maybe you could use something in here." Isabel dumped the contents of the makeup bag on the counter — eyeliner, foundation, lipstick, hairspray ... Sarah marveled at how much she had crammed in there.

"Isabel, you're a lifesaver!"

After fifteen minutes of repair work, Sarah was ready. She gave Isabel a big hug, careful not to smudge any of her newly applied makeup, and took the elevator down to the lobby. She stopped just short of the revolving door of the courthouse, took a deep breath, straightened her suit jacket and headed out to face the media throng.

When she emerged from the courthouse, the blinding sun disoriented her momentarily. Her instinct was to reach for her sunglasses, but that wouldn't do at all. She'd look more like a celebrity leaving rehab than a trial lawyer who had just won a big case. There were even more reporters than she had expected. Some of them she knew by sight, like Donna from Channel 10 and Felipe from the *Santa Felicia Observer*, but most of them were strangers.

There were television cameras and tripods everywhere. A podium had been positioned at the base of the courthouse steps, with several microphones taped to the front. Sarah walked down the steps carefully lest her first appearance on the national news be punctuated by a pratfall. She stepped up to the podium and tried to adjust the microphones, but before she said anything, the questions started coming.

"Have you ever been held in contempt before?"

"What was it like spending a night in jail?"

"Why didn't your client testify?"

"Do you feel good about getting a baby killer off?"

Sarah was caught off guard. *Why aren't they asking me about my brilliant trial strategy, my Warrior Gene defense?* She pointed at the friendliest face she could find in the crowd — Sharon, a mousy reporter from Channel 7 in Santa Barbara.

"How is Lexi doing?"

Sarah had to stand on tiptoe to reach the mics. "She's doing fine. She's very excited to be going home." *That was easy enough.*

Sharon continued. "Since she's crazy does she understand what's going on?"

Sarah bristled. "Lexi Conway is not crazy. She's not insane. She killed her baby because she had no choice, no free will."

Sarah pointed to another reporter, a tall, thin man from a newspaper in Northern California.

"Is Lexi going to have any more babies? If she does, will she kill them too?"

Sarah was stunned. She hadn't thought about that. She might kill again — after all, she'd already killed two babies.

"As you heard the judge say, we will be back in court tomorrow for some minor housekeeping matters," she said.

"I'll be available afterwards to answer all your questions. Right now, I need to go see my client."

She walked back into the courthouse, turning once to wave to the assembled reporters before disappearing into the building.

She hadn't planned on seeing Lexi again that morning, but it was the perfect exit line. Despite all their disagreements, she had grown fond of her during the trial. In any case, Sarah was curious. What was Lexi going to do now that the trial was over? Was she going back to her boyfriend? And what about kids? Was she going to have more babies? If so, what then? The reporter's question still rang in her ears: *If Lexi has any more babies, will she kill them too?*

Sarah went straight to the attorney interview area and asked to see Lexi.

"She's almost finished being processed, so we can't bring her in now," said the deputy on duty. "You can see her when she's released."

Sarah headed to the inmate release door in another part of the building. It was a small, unmarked metal door with no handle. She took a seat on an adjacent bench and waited.

After about thirty-five minutes, Lexi emerged wearing the same clothes she had worn in court and holding a single piece of paper.

Sarah stood up slowly. "Hi, Lexi."

"Mrs. Wong!" Lexi ran up to her and gave her a big hug. "What are you doing here? I didn't think you'd be here when I got out."

"Neither did I," admitted Sarah. "I just wanted to make sure you're okay. See you tomorrow at eight forty-five. Remember, don't be late!"

"I won't, ma'am. Thanks again for everything!"

Sarah turned to walk back to the elevator and heard Lexi's footsteps a few feet behind. She whirled around.

"Where are you going?"

"I don't know. I'm just following you."

"Aren't you going home?"

"Yeah."

"How are you going to get there?"

"I'll walk. It's only a couple of miles."

"Can I give you a ride?" In all of her years of practicing law, Sarah had never once invited a client into her car — not the real estate developers, not the slip-and-fall plaintiffs, not even the cute college boys charged with DUI. But here she was, about to give a ride to a baby killer.

"Thanks so much, but I'll walk. It's not a big deal."

"C'mon, Lexi, I'll give you a lift."

"Are you sure?"

"Yes, I'm sure." Sarah wasn't sure at all, but she couldn't back out now.

Downstairs in the parking lot, they made their way silently to Sarah's blue Infiniti sedan. The passenger seat was piled high with files from Lexi's case, and Sarah scooped them up and threw them in the back seat.

"Are those my files?" Lexi asked as she climbed in. "There sure are a lot of 'em."

"Yes, they're my notes on your case." Sarah started up the car. "Lexi, what was that paper they gave you when you left the courthouse?"

"It's the receipt for all my stuff. I have to go back to the New Jail to get it."

"Do you want to swing by there now?"

"Sure. Do you mind?"

"No. It's only about ten minutes away."

The trip to the jail passed in silence, and when they got there, Sarah waited in the car, glad to have a few moments to herself while Lexi went in to get her belongings. After twenty minutes, Lexi reappeared holding a large white plastic bag.

"Sorry, Mrs. Wong. It took forever to get my stuff. They

made me wait so long."

"I know what you mean. They always make me wait too."

"It was weird walking in to the jail and then being able to leave."

Fifteen minutes later Sarah pulled into Lexi's driveway. There, right in front of her, was the garage where little Anna Conway had died seven months earlier.

"Thanks for the ride, ma'am." Lexi said as she opened the passenger door.

"Uh? ... Sure. You're welcome," said Sarah, pulling her eyes away from the garage. "See you tomorrow."

Lexi grabbed the white plastic bag, shut the car door, and bounded up the short front walk, clearly happy to be home at last.

Sarah couldn't wait to get home either. It wasn't even noon yet, but she was exhausted and planned to take a nap. As she was backing out of the driveway, Lexi came running toward her, waving.

"I don't have my keys!" she yelled.

"What?"

"I don't have my keys. I thought for sure I had them, but they're not in my purse."

"Are you positive?"

"Yeah."

Then it dawned on Sarah. "When you were taken to the hospital, your keys were still in your car, in the ignition. The police probably booked them into evidence. Can you get a hold of Ryan?"

"I don't think so."

"Why not?"

"His mom made him move back home with her."

"How come?"

"She doesn't want him to see me anymore."

I can't blame her. I wouldn't want my son living with a baby killer.

"Is that why Ryan never came to trial?"

"I guess so."

"How about your mom?"

"I think she's pretty sick. Last time I saw her she said all the stress was getting to her. The doctors may have put her in the hospital or something."

Sarah couldn't just leave Lexi on the street with nowhere to go. She only had one option. "Hop back in. You can hang out at my place until you get hold of your mom or Ryan."

"Thank you so much, Mrs. Wong!"

Lexi got back in the car and tossed her stuff in the back seat, amid the jumble of files and papers.

Sarah felt sorry for Lexi. For months she had been longing to go home, and now that she was finally out of jail she couldn't even do that.

* * *

Sarah hunted through her kitchen cabinets, searching for something to eat. She and Matt had been eating a lot of takeout during the trial, and their shopping trips had been scaled back to purchasing only the basics. Sarah found three cans of soup, a package of penne pasta, and a box of macaroni and cheese. Lexi chose the mac and cheese.

As they ate lunch, Lexi suddenly asked, "Do you think I did it?"

"What do you mean?" said Sarah, trying to sound casual.

"Do you think I killed Anna?"

"Well, it's kind of complicated," Sarah said meekly.

"No, it's not. Either I killed her or I didn't. What do you think?"

"I think you're not guilty, just like the jury said."

"I know what you said in court, and I'm really grateful and all, but I need you to understand that I didn't kill my baby."

"Lexi, the trial is over. You're free. What I think really doesn't matter."

"It matters to me."

Just then the back door opened and Matt burst in.

"Where's the hotshot attorney?" he asked, a big grin on his face.

"Hi, honey. This is ..." Sarah's reply was drowned out by Matt's enthusiastic praise.

"I just heard the news! I'm so proud of you, Tiger. I can't believe you got the baby killer off!"

Matt saw Lexi sitting at the table with Sarah. "Oh, hi! I'm Matt, Sarah's husband. And you are?"

"Lexi Conway."

Sarah watched as horror spread across Matt's face. He grabbed her by the elbow and pulled her into the bedroom.

"What is SHE doing here?"

"Hon, I'll explain later."

"No, explain NOW. I want her out of my home."

"She has nowhere to go."

"Yes she does. She can go anywhere but here."

"But Matt—"

"Have you forgotten? She's killed two babies! She's unstable, she's crazy!"

Without waiting to hear what Sarah had to say, Matt went back into the kitchen. "I'm sorry, but you're going to have to leave now," he said.

But Lexi had already gone. Sarah watched her through the window walking down the street. She wanted to chase after her, but she knew she'd better stay with Matt.

"You're right, hon. She'll be fine," Sarah said, feeling a little relieved.

That afternoon, Sarah had a chance to relax at last. She stretched out on the couch while Matt fed Chloe and puttered around the kitchen. She should have been ecstatic, but she wasn't. She should have felt like dancing and shouting, but she didn't. She had just won the biggest case of her life, with a defense that was going to make her famous, but all she felt was uneasy and apprehensive about what was going to happen tomorrow.

Judge Sandoval had threatened to overturn the jury's verdict, and although he had let Lexi out of jail he still wanted her back in court tomorrow. Why? She guessed that he wanted to put on a big show for the press. He would state that although he disagreed with the jury's verdict he was bound by fairness and due process to honor their decision. He would tell Lexi that he did not approve of what she had done, and he would let the nation know he was not soft on crime. That would surely get him appointed to the Appellate Court.

Comforted by her analysis and filled with macaroni and cheese, Sarah fell asleep.

Matt woke her at six to have something to eat, and while he worked his gastronomical magic on a can of minestrone, Sarah shuffled off to check her email. When she discovered she had two hundred and eighty-seven new emails she shut the computer down and walked away.

CHAPTER 21

When Sarah got into her car the next morning, she saw Lexi's bag of stuff lying on the back seat. She must have forgotten about it when she left yesterday. Sarah would give it to her after court that day.

She arrived at the courthouse at eight thirty. As she exited the elevator on the second floor, she could see Lexi, wearing the same clothes she had on the day before, lying on the wooden bench outside Courtroom 201 with a stack of newspapers under her head.

"Morning, Mrs. Wong. Sorry about yesterday. I never should have gone to your place," Lexi said.

"That's okay."

"Is everything good between you and Mr. Wong?"

"He'll get over it. He was just being a big baby. Where did you sleep last night?"

"I didn't. I just wandered around. I walked back home, hoping Ryan would show up, but he never did. I tried calling his mom's house twice, but both times she hung up as soon as she heard my voice. I went down the street and knocked on a few doors, but nobody answered. I walked down to Route 315 and went in a couple of coffee shops. One guy let me stay until closing time. Then I went to an all-night diner, but the waitress recognized me from TV and screamed at me to leave. After that I just wandered around. I'm pretty tired. Do you have anything to eat?"

"Nope, sorry. Want something from the vending machine?"

"Sure. Can I have some chips?"

"Whatever you want. Let's go see what they have."

Lexi tore through a large bag of chips and a bottle of Sprite while they waited. At eight forty-five, Brian opened the doors to the courtroom. Sarah went up to Isabel's desk to see what she could find out.

"Hi, Isabel. What's on tap for today?"

"Honestly, I don't know what's on the judge's mind," Isabel told her. "One thing is curious, though. The judge ordered an extra bailiff to stand near the doors at the back of the courtroom. It's like he's expecting some sort of protest or disruption."

In sharp contrast to the past few weeks, the courtroom was nearly empty. The TV cameras were gone and there were only three reporters, all from local news outlets. Most of the reporters had probably assembled outside waiting for Sarah's promised appearance after the hearing was over.

Renaldo and Joe took their seats at the prosecution table, and Sarah was just going to chat with Lexi at the back of the courtroom, when Brian called out, "Please rise. Department H of the Superior Court of Santa Felicia County is now in session, the Honorable Judge Burt Sandoval presiding."

"Just stay here, Lexi. I don't think you need to come up front," Sarah said before rushing up to the counsel table, barely making it before Judge Sandoval emerged from chambers.

"Please be seated," the judge said sternly.

The expression on the judge's face made Sarah extremely uneasy.

"I call the case of the State of California versus Lexi Conway. Mrs. Wong, where is your client? I ordered her back at nine sharp. If she's not here in five minutes I'm going to issue a bench warrant for her arrest."

"Ms. Conway is here, Your Honor. She's sitting in the

audience. I assumed we wouldn't need her up front."

"You assumed wrong, Mrs. Wong. Ms. Conway, step forward to counsel table."

Lexi scurried up front quickly and stood next to Sarah.

"After hearing all of the evidence in Ms. Conway's trial, I have determined that there is probable cause to evaluate the defendant pursuant to Section 5150 of the California Welfare and Institutions Code on the grounds that Ms. Conway is a danger to herself and a danger to others. Pursuant to Section 5150, I am placing a seventy-two-hour hold on Ms. Conway, and I am setting a hearing under Section 5300 for three days from now, on Friday at nine a.m. A court-appointed psychiatrist will examine Ms. Conway to determine if she should be detained further. Both sides are ordered to be ready to proceed at that time. The defendant is remanded into custody."

"Your Honor, what are you doing? My client is innocent! I object! I OBJECT!" shouted Sarah.

Judge Sandoval ignored Sarah's objection. She combed her memory for what little she knew about mental health laws.

"Your Honor, I believe my client is entitled to an initial hearing under Section 5150 or 5200."

"Technically that's true, Mrs. Wong, but I don't see a need for all of those procedural hearings. I heard all the testimony in the trial, and there is ample evidence to proceed directly to a 5300 hearing. It would take several more weeks if we had all of those other hearings. You're not asking for a delay, are you? I'm sure your client would like this matter heard as soon as possible. Isn't that right, Ms. Conway?"

"Yes, Your Honor. I want to go back home now."

"See, Ms. Conway doesn't want any unnecessary delays. That's why I'm proceeding directly to a Section 5300 hearing on Friday. The court stands in recess."

Without making eye contact with Sarah, Lexi, or even

Renaldo, Judge Sandoval left the bench quickly and retreated into his chambers.

Brian moved toward Lexi, as did a second bailiff, who had been standing at the back of the courtroom. Brian held Lexi by her left elbow and tugged her gently toward the side door. "This way, Ms. Conway."

"Mrs. Wong, what's happening?" Lexi screamed. "Am I going to jail again? I DID NOT KILL MY BABY!" There was abject fear in her eyes.

"Don't worry, Lexi. I'll get this straightened out," Sarah called out, but her assurances did nothing to calm Lexi's fears. Or her own.

She turned to Renaldo. "Did you —?"

"I had nothing to do with this. I promise," he said. "I'm just as shocked as you are. I thought the judge just wanted to lecture Ms. Conway today. I had no idea. Honestly."

Sarah bolted out of the courtroom and raced down the courthouse steps. The media were out in force again, waiting for Sarah to appear. As soon as they saw her they started shouting out questions.

"To hell with Judge Burt Sandoval! And you can quote me," Sarah shouted before heading back to the parking garage.

Sarah jumped into her car and sped off with a squeal of her tires to her office. When she burst through the door of Suite 805, she slammed it so hard the pictures rattled on the wall. An elderly couple who were waiting to see Conrad about an estate matter looked frightened out of their wits.

Sarah didn't acknowledge Maggie's hello as she stormed into her office, slamming that door too. After a few seconds, she yelled for Nick. They probably heard her in the lobby seven floors below.

Nick rushed into her office without knocking.

"You okay?" he asked.

Sarah was so mad she couldn't speak. Then she started spitting out numbers.

"5150, 5200, 5300—that bastard! That son of a bitch. I can't believe he did that!" She quickly explained to Nick what had happened. "I'm still so mad I can't see straight. Judge Sandoval set a mental health detention hearing for Friday and he remanded Lexi into custody! Can you believe it? Yesterday the jury found her not guilty and she got out of jail. Today she's back in. I still can't believe it."

"I'll bet you raised hell in court!" Nick said with a smile.

"I did my best."

"Is there anything I can do?" he asked.

"You bet. We've got less than three days to prepare and we may have to work straight through until Friday. Can you do that?"

"Sure. You know I'm always up for a challenge. What shall we do first?"

"First, let's read the statutes. I haven't done one of these since my public defender days."

Having a plan of action was helping her to calm down. She turned on her computer and got out a pad of paper. "Pull up a chair and let's get started."

She flicked through some files on the screen.

"Here it is. Welfare and Institution Code Section 5150." She swiveled the screen around so Nick could see it better. "Cops use these laws to get crazy people off the streets for a couple of weeks. They take them in under Section 5150 if they consider them to be an immediate danger to themselves. Then they can be held for fourteen days. In many cases the homeless don't mind—three hots and a cot."

Nick frowned at Sarah.

"Three meals and a place to sleep," she explained. "Even if it's in jail. It's often better than being on the street."

Sarah described the three grounds for detention under Welfare and Institutions Code Sections 5150, 5200, and 5300. Someone can be held if they are an immediate danger to themselves, if they are an immediate danger to others, or if they are so gravely disabled that they can't care for themselves.

Sarah and Nick worked together all afternoon reading statutes and case law and debating the finer points of mental health law and preventive detention. Then Sarah pushed back from her desk, stood up, and stared out the window.

"My gut feeling is that Judge Sandoval's going to be able to do whatever he wants with Lexi," she said. "No one's going to care if he locks her up in a mental hospital and throws away the key."

Nick searched for something to cheer Sarah up. "By the way, I loved your gas can stunt during your closing argument! That was a classic! I was hoping the judge would let you open the can so everybody could smell it."

"I'm really glad he didn't."

"How come?"

"It wasn't gasoline. It was only water."

"You devil!"

* * *

On Wednesday morning, Sarah arrived at work earlier than usual and stood at her window watching the sunrise over the hills just beyond Santa Felicia. She knew that the upcoming hearing would have far-reaching implications for how Americans think about crime and punishment. What Judge Sandoval was proposing to do had never been done before. He was threatening to incarcerate Lexi Conway because of her genetic makeup—her DNA.

Before launching into her preparations for Lexi's hearing, Sarah scanned the hundreds of emails in her inbox and listened to some of the dozens of phone messages. The first wave of emails and messages congratulated her on her stunning victory. Many were sent by colleagues and friends, but more than a few came from complete strangers who just wanted to tell her what a good job she had done. The tone of the second wave was very different—those messages mostly expressed outrage at Judge Sandoval's decision to detain Lexi under the mental health laws.

Of course, a fair number of emails were not supportive. Many of them expressed anger that Sarah had helped a baby killer go free, and a few contained threats against Sarah and her family. She put those in a separate email folder, and made a mental note to call the police, or the FBI, or whoever handled those sorts of things.

As news of Tuesday's hearing spread, offers of legal help poured in from around the country. The Chief Public Defender of Santa Felicia County, Sarah's old boss, called, as did public defenders in LA, Santa Barbara, and several cities outside of California. Attorneys from the Legal Defense Fund and the ACLU, along with dozens of private lawyers, sent emails. As politely as possible, Sarah declined each and every offer of help.

There was one person she was willing to listen to, however—Candi Markowitz. On Thursday Sarah called her to see if she had any sage words of advice. Maybe she would be willing to testify at the detention hearing.

"Hi, Candi."

"Hey, Sarah. How're you holding up?"

"Okay, I guess."

"Are your babies doing well?"

"You sound like my obstetrician."

"I'm just looking out for my pal."

"I assume you've heard what happened on Lexi's case," Sarah said.

"How could I not? It's been all over the news. What are you going to do?"

"I'm not sure. That's why I called you."

"What can I do?"

"Could you testify for me at the hearing? Maybe say that Lexi's not a danger to others?"

"I'm afraid not, Sarah. One of the best predictors of future violence is past violence. Just a few days ago we argued that Lexi had no control over her actions. How can we go back into court and say she's fine? What if she has another baby?"

Everybody kept bringing up the what-if-she-has-another-baby issue. Sarah was annoyed with herself for not thinking of that before she made the Warrior Gene argument.

"So you can't help me?"

"I don't know what I can do, Sarah, I really don't. I'm really sorry."

* * *

On Thursday afternoon, the day before the hearing, Sarah still had no idea what her strategy was going to be. She had been staring at the cases and statutes on her computer screen for hours, but the more she read, the more jumbled everything became.

At three, Maggie poked her head in and gave Sarah a letter delivered by courier from a Norman Ponce. Sarah didn't recognize the name, but quickly opened the envelope. At the top of the first page was written "Psychiatric Evaluation of Lexi Conway."

"Nick, Lexi's psych evaluation is here!" Sarah called out.

Nick came flying in through the door and stood behind Sarah reading the evaluation over her shoulder. Sarah grew impatient by the third page, which contained technical summaries of several psychiatric measures, so she skipped all the way to the end. There it was, the final recommendation. She read it out loud.

Conclusion and Recommendation
Based on my in-depth examination of Ms. Conway and my thorough review of the trial transcript in the State of California v. Lexi Conway,

it is my opinion that Ms. Conway is a danger to others and a danger to herself due to a mental defect caused by her genetic makeup.

Therefore, it is recommended that Ms. Conway be detained indefinitely in a maximum-security mental health facility. The outlook for treatment is exceptionally bleak, as there are no known methods for correcting genetic defects such as Ms. Conway's. Given that Ms. Conway will continue to remain a danger to others and to herself for the foreseeable future, it is recommended that her commitment be open-ended, with reviews scheduled every five years.

Sarah dropped into her chair. She had feared the psychiatric report would be bad, but she hadn't anticipated it would be this bad.

"What are we going to do?" she asked Nick, knowing he didn't have any answers either. "Essentially Dr. Ponce is recommending that Lexi be incarcerated for life with no chance of getting out. What are we going to do?"

As Thursday afternoon turned into Thursday night, Nick and Sarah came to the same conclusion: no matter what Sarah did the next day, she was going to lose Lexi's detention hearing. It didn't matter that Lexi wasn't mentally ill, at least not in the traditional sense. The psychiatrist's report was going to give Judge Sandoval permission to do what he had wanted to do from the very beginning — put Lexi away for life.

Sarah couldn't figure out whether the judge really believed that Lexi was a dangerous person who needed to be in jail forever or whether he was just putting on a show for the press so he would be seen as tough on crime. If it was the former, it was a lost cause — nothing she could say would change his mind. But if he was just trying to burnish his public image, maybe there was something she could do.

"Nick, if we can convince Judge Sandoval that letting Lexi go is the right thing to do—the compassionate, moral, and ethical thing to do—then maybe he'll change his mind about sending her to jail indefinitely. He wouldn't be losing face. He'd just be seen as being fair-minded."

"But who's going to let a baby killer back out on the street?"

"Nick, I swear you're starting to sound just like Matt!"

"Still, I don't see what sort of argument we can make."

"Well, it can't be a scientific one," said Sarah. "I'm pretty sure Judge Sandoval doesn't want to hear any more about genetics, or DNA, or the Warrior Gene."

"I agree. What about a plea for mercy?"

"Mercy? Judge Sandoval? The two don't go together."

"What else is there?"

"I have no idea."

Sarah stood up, watching the sky darken over Santa Felicia as the sun set. Nick drew circles absentmindedly on his legal pad.

"I've got it!" he exclaimed suddenly. "It's the only argument that's worked on Judge Sandoval during the entire case."

Sarah beat him to the punch. "The Constitution!"

After a few seconds she added, "The Fourteenth Amendment! I'll argue that preventive detention violates the Fourteenth Amendment. For this to work, we need to pack the courtroom with reporters, cameras, and journalists."

"I'm on it," said Nick. "I'll contact every reporter in the county—in the state if I have to. I'll make sure it's standing room only in court tomorrow. You go home and get some rest."

"I really should stay and do some more research," countered Sarah.

"On the Fourteenth Amendment? C'mon, you know

every due process and fairness argument by heart. What you need is a good night's sleep."

And with that, he turned off Sarah's computer and pushed her toward the door.

CHAPTER 22

When Sarah and Nick arrived at court on Friday morning, Renaldo was already there, accompanied by four other attorneys from the DA's office. Joe Jimmerson was sitting at counsel table with Renaldo, and the others had taken seats in the front row of the audience. Sarah was surprised at this unexpected show of force.

She pulled out her files and laptop, then chatted with Nick about their strategy while they waited for Judge Sandoval to appear. She turned around to look at the audience, but other than the three extra DAs and two bailiffs, Courtroom 201 was empty. Where were the reporters and TV cameras?

"I thought you were going to get lots of press in here today," Sarah said to Nick.

"I thought so too. I called everyone I know and they all said they'd come."

"Then how come nobody's here?"

"I don't know."

"Maybe Isabel knows something. I'll ask her."

Sarah greeted Isabel cheerfully. "Hey, Isabel. I'm surprised there are no reporters in court today. I thought for sure there would be some media interest."

"The judge banned them," Isabel explained. "Banned the cameras, banned the reporters, banned them all."

"What? Why?" Sarah stuttered.

"Don't know. Maybe you should ask him when he takes the bench."

"I'd rather ask him back in chambers. Can Renaldo and I go back to see him?"

"Afraid not. The judge gave me strict orders not to let anyone back today. He wants to do everything on the record out in court. I think he's coming out now."

Despite the absence of an audience, Brian still began with his usual exhortation as soon as the chamber door opened.

"You may be seated," said Judge Sandoval when he had taken his place. "We are here this morning to conduct the 5300 certification hearing for Ms. Lexi Conway. Brian, please bring out the defendant."

Lexi shuffled in dressed in a bright lime green jumpsuit reserved for flight risks, her feet shackled just as they had been the first time Sarah met her seven months ago. Her hair was disheveled, her face drawn, and her eyes dark from lack of sleep. Sarah tried to smile at her, but it was no use. There was nothing to smile about.

Judge Sandoval had carefully orchestrated every detail of the hearing—scheduling it in an impossibly short three days and closing it to the public—all to make sure the proceedings went quickly, smoothly, and without interruption. Sarah was furious with him.

"It is alleged that Ms. Conway is a danger to herself and to others and therefore qualifies for involuntary commitment under Section 5300 of the Welfare and Institution Code," the judge stated. "We are here to determine whether Ms. Conway should be detained pursuant to that section. Are both sides ready to proceed?"

"Yes, Your Honor," said Renaldo.

Sarah rose and spoke as calmly as she could. "Your Honor, I object to this hearing. It is a farce and is just your way of subverting the will of the jury. I demand that the proceedings be terminated and Ms. Conway be released immediately."

"Your objection is noted, Mrs. Wong. We will proceed."

"One more thing, Your Honor, why have you closed this hearing to the public?" Sarah said without waiting for the judge's permission to speak. "Fairness and due process dictate that this hearing be open to everyone, including representatives from the media."

"Mrs. Wong, I have ordered that this hearing be closed pursuant to Section 5200 of the Welfare and Institutions Code."

"Your Honor, Section 5200 does not mandate a closed hearing. I demand that this hearing be open to the public."

"All I'm trying to do is protect your client's right to privacy and dignity, Mrs. Wong. Objection overruled."

Sarah sank down into her seat. The judge had made up his mind and nothing she could say or do was going to make a difference. For the first time in a very long while, she gave up. Lexi Conway, a woman who had killed not one, but two babies, was going to spend the rest of her life in a mental hospital and there was nothing Sarah could do about it. She would make her objections and go through the motions, of course, but Lexi's fate seemed to be sealed.

"Let the record reflect that I was the trial judge in the criminal case of the State of California versus Lexi Conway, which concluded four days ago," Judge Sandoval began. "I hereby take judicial notice of all of the evidence presented during that trial."

He proceeded to summarize all the evidence against Lexi, highlighting Sarah's stipulation that Lexi had killed Anna Conway and describing the scientific evidence, including Dr. Markowitz's testimony.

"I am also in possession of a seven-page psychiatric report submitted by Dr. Norman Ponce," the judge continued.

Sarah objected half-heartedly. "Your Honor, I just received this report yesterday, and I haven't had time to fully digest—"

"Overruled."

Judge Sandoval then read Dr. Ponce's conclusions aloud. The words were just as damning the second time around.

"Mr. Sepulveda, do you have anything to add?"

"It is the people's position that Ms. Conway is a danger to herself and to others as a result of her genetic defect. Therefore, we urge the court to order that Ms. Conway be held indefinitely in a mental health facility until her genetic defect is cured."

Which, everyone knew, was a life sentence.

"Mrs. Wong, would you like to say anything?"

Sarah knew her dramatic invocation of the Constitution would have little effect in the empty courtroom, but she summoned all of her resolve and presented her argument with as much passion as she could muster.

"Your Honor, I assume you are familiar with the Constitution of the United States of America?"

"Mrs. Wong, there are no reporters here today. Just get to your point."

"Yes, Your Honor. What you are doing today is in direct violation of the Fourteenth Amendment. Lexi Conway was acquitted by a jury of her peers and set free. She has been convicted of no crime, and she is not mentally ill. In some countries, governments hold people in jail without cause, but not in the United States of America. At least, that's what I thought before today. I am simply asking the court to uphold the Fourteenth Amendment of the Constitution of the United States of America and let Lexi Conway go home."

It was the best she could do, and she sat down, satisfied with her effort.

Judge Sandoval turned to Renaldo. "Anything else from the state?"

"No, Your Honor."

"Very well, I am ready to issue my ruling." Judge Sandoval took a deep breath. "I fully understand your plea for due process, Mrs. Wong. As you know, this court is always concerned with fairness, and I have done everything in my power to ensure that Lexi Conway has been accorded due process throughout her jury trial and this hearing. I have listened to five weeks of testimony, read numerous scientific and psychological reports, and viewed dozens of pieces of evidence. I have more than enough information to make my decision."

He peered at Sarah over the rim of his glasses before continuing.

"First, I make the following findings of fact. Lexi Conway killed Anna Conway on August 11, as stipulated by the defense during the jury trial. Ms. Conway has two copies of a genetic defect to her MAOA gene, as established by the defense in the jury trial. This genetic defect caused Ms. Conway to kill her child, as argued persuasively by the defense during the trial. Ms. Conway still has this genetic defect and will continue to have it for the rest of her life. As argued by the defense attorney during trial, because of this genetic defect Ms. Conway had no control over her actions when she killed her baby. In essence, she acted as a homicidal robot on remote control. Based on all of these findings, there is only one possible conclusion. As a result of her genetic defect, Lexi Conway is currently a danger to others and to herself. Therefore, in order to protect Ms. Conway and the people of the State of California, I have no choice but to order that Ms. Conway be detained in a locked-down mental health facility for an indefinite period of time. As recommended by Dr. Ponce, we will have a progress report on Ms. Conway's condition in five years."

There was still a tiny bit of fight left in Sarah. "But Your Honor, the Welfare and Institutions Code clearly states that progress hearings should be held every one hundred and eighty days," she argued. "A five-year wait is patently unfair and clearly violates the protections afforded all citizens by the Fourteenth Amendment."

"The Welfare and Institutions Code, written decades ago, originally addressed traditional mental illness," the judge replied. "The drafters of the code did not contemplate genetic defects. As you argued so persuasively during Ms. Conway's trial, this is indeed unchartered territory. Given that genetic defects cannot be cured by therapy or counseling, the outlook for treatment of Ms. Conway is quite bleak. Therefore, in view of all of the circumstances, five years is a reasonable time for a progress report. We are adjourned."

"I'm not going home today, am I?" Lexi asked Sarah as the judge left the bench. It sounded like the fight had gone out of her too.

"No, you're not, Lexi. I'm really sorry."

"Don't worry, ma'am. You did the best you could."

"We're not done yet. I'm going to file an appeal right away."

And that was it. Lexi's trial, in which she had been exonerated by a jury of her peers, had lasted more than seven weeks. This sham of a hearing, in which she was given a life sentence in a mental health facility, had taken all of twenty minutes.

CHAPTER 23

Sarah lay awake in the early hours of Saturday morning, staring at her alarm clock and replaying the entire jury trial in her mind while Matt slept.

How could something so brilliant, so groundbreaking, have turned out so badly? Why hadn't she seen this coming? If she had just stuck to the usual strategies in these sorts of cases — there was reasonable doubt as to how the baby died; reasonable doubt as to who killed the baby; reasonable doubt as to whether the killing was intentional or accidental — she probably could have obtained either a second-degree murder or manslaughter verdict, and Lexi would have got five to ten years in prison, maybe even less.

Instead, Lexi had been sentenced to spend the rest of her life in a locked mental hospital — condemned to a life of mind-numbing medication alongside other killers who were criminally insane. A real-life version of *One Flew Over the Cuckoo's Nest*.

Might Lexi kill again if she were set free? Sarah had no way of knowing, but she had to admit it was a possibility. After all, she had killed twice before. Two helpless infants; two dead babies. Sarah entertained the idea that perhaps it was for the best if Lexi remained in a mental hospital for the rest of her life. Maybe that was where she belonged.

But the defense attorney in Sarah kicked back into gear one more time. Lexi had been found not guilty by a jury, and Judge Sandoval had no right to lock her up for crimes she had not yet committed. Sarah would continue to fight for Lexi and for the principles her cause represented.

* * *

First thing on Monday morning, Sarah started to work a writ of habeas corpus. If she could prevail on a writ, Lexi would be released pending the outcome of the appeal.

In less than a day, Sarah put together a compelling argument that preventive detention was unconstitutional, unfair, and unlawful, violating both state and federal statutes. She filed the writ in the California Court of Appeals, where it was denied summarily two days later without a hearing. In a one-paragraph decision, the Court of Appeals ruled that Sarah had not made a prima facie case that Lexi's confinement was unconstitutional or unlawful. Next she tried the California Supreme Court, with the same result.

As a last-ditch effort, Sarah turned to the federal courts, first the Ninth Circuit Appellate Court and finally the United States Supreme Court. Both of these courts refused to even consider the writ, indicating they had no jurisdiction until all state appeals had been exhausted.

Sarah understood their reticence. What judge would be willing to let a baby killer back out on the streets, possibly to kill again? And they didn't even know about her first baby.

Lexi's first baby.

Sarah needed to know more about Jacob — when he was born, how he died, those sorts of things. She wasn't sure why. No matter what she found, it wasn't going to make her feel any better, and it certainly wasn't going to help Lexi. Still, she needed to know, so she called Nick into her office and shut the door.

"I'm going to tell you something I haven't told anyone else except Matt," Sarah said. "Do you promise you won't tell anyone? I really need your help."

"Of course. You can trust me, Sarah. Wait ... are you and Matt having problems? Did he cheat on you? Or did you ..."

"It's nothing like that! This is about Lexi. You have to promise to keep what I am about to tell you in the utmost confidence."

"Absolutely. You can count on me."

"Okay, here goes—Lexi killed another baby."

"What?! She's been in jail since August. How could she have killed another baby?"

"This was before Anna. Lexi had a baby two years ago and she killed that one too."

"How do you know?"

"She told me."

"When?"

"A week ago or so, while we were talking in the lockup after court. Out of the blue she just blurted out that she was glad she hadn't had to testify during the trial because she wouldn't have known what to say if the DA asked about her other baby."

"What'd you say?"

"I promised her I wouldn't tell anyone else."

"So Lexi told you she killed that baby too?"

"Not in so many words. She said the first baby died the same way Anna died."

"You haven't told anyone else?"

"Only Matt."

"So why are you telling me?"

"I want you to find out about the other baby. I want to know when it was born, how long it lived, how it died—everything."

"Why?"

"I just want to know. Can you do this for me?"

"I can try. Do you have a name?"

"The baby was a boy called Jacob. He was born about

two years ago, just before Lexi turned eighteen. Lexi's lived in Santa Felicia her whole life, so it shouldn't be too hard to find some information about him. I think there are only three hospitals in Santa Felicia with maternity wards. You can't let anyone know what you're looking for or why you're looking. Are you up for this?"

"Sure. You can count on me."

* * *

Over the next few days, Sarah drafted Lexi's notice of appeal, which included many of the usual grounds such as prosecutorial misconduct and the judge's failure to grant her pretrial motions. She knew it would be years before she got a final resolution in Lexi's case.

As quickly as the media attention had begun seven months ago, it tailed off even faster now that the trial was over. No one cared about the complex legal issues raised in Sarah's appeal. After all, Lexi had killed her baby, so maybe everything had turned out for the best. There were new criminal cases to capture the public's attention — horrific crimes, salacious affairs, brutal slayings. Lexi Conway's name faded rapidly from public consciousness.

And now it was time for Sarah to move on too.

She decided to turn the bulk of the work on Lexi's appeal over to Conrad. This sort of thing was right up his alley, and it had the added benefit of making him feel that he was a valuable member of her law firm. Sarah met with Lexi twice in the week following the 5300 hearing, but then Lexi was transferred to Atascadero State Mental Hospital, over an hour's drive from her office, so it was going to be hard to see Lexi regularly from that point on.

In the weeks that followed, Sarah renewed her relationships with her established clients. She even started taking on a few new clients, handpicked from the hundreds of inquiries generated by her newfound notoriety. It didn't really matter that she had lost the 5300 hearing. She had won the jury trial in dramatic fashion, which was what everyone remembered.

Her weekly checkups at Valley Obstetrics were proceeding without a hitch. Ultrasounds, weight checks, blood work — everything was looking good with her pregnancy. At every checkup, Dr. Sadler reiterated her plea for Sarah to stop working and stay in bed — Matt had been telling her the same thing for weeks — and she eventually , acquiesced, working mostly half days, even permitting herself a full day off every now and then.

Although they had talked about baby names before, Sarah and Matt started to get serious about them. They generated their own lists, but there wasn't one single name in common on the two lists. Matt seemed hooked on the idea that the twins should be named after famous couples: Brad and Angelina, Caesar and Cleopatra, Mickey and Minnie, Samson and Delilah, Adam and Eve, Charles and Diana, even Shrek and Fiona.

Sarah figured he was joking about his names, but she couldn't be sure. Her choices were more practical, although she seemed to favor a certain amount of alliteration: Victor and Veronica, Mark and Madeline, Corey and Courtney, Reginald and Rebecca.

They agreed to disagree about baby names, at least for the time being.

* * *

It was almost four thirty on Friday afternoon when Nick knocked on Sarah's door. She waved him in, and he closed the door before sitting down.

"I think I'm done with my investigation about Lexi's first baby," he said.

"And?"

"There's nothing. I couldn't find a single record relating

to Lexi's first baby—no medical records, no hospital records, not even a birth certificate. I searched under Lexi's last name, Ryan's last name, and I examined birth certificates and death certificates in Santa Felicia and all four surrounding counties for every baby born in the three-month time period you gave me." Nick paused for a moment. "It's as if Jacob never existed."

"Are you sure?"

"As sure as I can be. As far as the State of California is concerned, Jacob was never born."

"Do you think Lexi just made the whole thing up?"

"I don't think so."

"How come?"

"After having no luck finding Jacob, I decided to try again to get Anna's birth certificate and medical records to see if they contained any names or addresses that would help me work backward to find the records for Jacob."

"And?"

"Other than her autopsy report and death certificate, there are no official records of Anna Conway either."

"No medical records at all?"

"No hospital records, no pediatrician records, nothing. She doesn't have a birth certificate either."

"What do you mean?"

"I mean, Anna Conway has no birth certificate. I spent almost four days going over the birth records for the entire state of California during the week Anna was born, and there were no birth certificates matching her information."

Sarah was stunned. "So as far as the State of California is concerned, *neither* baby ever existed."

"That's right. At least until Anna died."

Sarah sat in silence for a few moments. "What if Lexi didn't have any babies at all?"

"But we know Anna existed. There are autopsy photos, a detailed autopsy report, the whole nine yards. There's no doubt that baby existed!"

"But what if Anna wasn't Lexi's baby?"

"What do you mean?"

"Maybe she kidnapped Anna from a maternity ward. That kind of stuff doesn't just happen in the movies, you know."

"I don't know. That seems kind of out there to me."

"Sure it is, but it would explain everything. If Lexi had kidnapped Anna, that would explain why she didn't take Anna to the emergency room. It would explain why she didn't take her to a doctor or call her mom for help. She couldn't. It wasn't her baby and if she went to a hospital or a doctor, they'd have found out and she'd have been arrested for kidnapping. That would also explain why Ryan wouldn't talk to me."

"But why on earth would Lexi make up the first baby?"

"Maybe to throw us off track so we wouldn't figure it out."

"You really think so?"

"I don't know what to believe any more. I'd like you to check whether any babies were kidnapped in California about the time Anna was born. On Monday, I'm going to go see Lexi."

* * *

On Saturday morning, Sarah and Matt started getting their home ready for the twins. She had a lot of cleaning to do — something she usually abhorred, but a task she didn't seem to mind now at all. Over the weekend she cleaned every room in the townhouse from top to bottom.

By Sunday afternoon, the only thing left to clean was her car. She extracted granola bar wrappers, loose coins, pens, and paper clips. Underneath the rear passenger seat she found a plastic bag and realized it was the bag Lexi had retrieved from central booking after she had been released from jail. Since she was going to visit Lexi at Atascadero

State Hospital the next day, she could take it with her.

She opened the bag to check its contents in case there was something Lexi couldn't have in the hospital.

Sarah dumped everything out on the kitchen table. Out tumbled two lipsticks, a large brush, a pack of gum, a wallet, and a small gold heart-shaped locket. Sarah opened it and saw two baby pictures, one on each side. In the wallet was a picture of Lexi and Ryan at the beach, Lexi's driver's license, $42 in cash, and a crumpled beige business card. Sarah flattened the card on the table and gasped.

It was a card for New Beginnings Fertility Clinic.

CHAPTER 24

Sarah didn't even bother changing out of her sweats before jumping in her car to drive to Atascadero State Hospital. It was just past two, and it would take her about ninety minutes to get there.' As soon as she got on the highway, she called the hospital to make sure she could see Lexi that afternoon. She was in luck. On Sunday, visiting hours lasted until seven p.m. They would have plenty of time to talk.

Sarah glanced over at the passenger seat where she had placed the card from New Beginnings. She picked the card up and turned it over in her right hand while steering with her left. On the back were five dates: two in May, two in June and one in July. She guessed these were appointments, but for what? Why would Lexi be going to New Beginnings? Surely she wasn't going for fertility appointments—she was only nineteen. Maybe the card wasn't Lexi's. Maybe it belonged to a friend or relative. Or maybe Lexi had applied for a job there.

As her mind raced, so did her Infiniti. Sarah glanced down and gasped when she saw her speedometer almost touching ninety. Fortunately there were no cops around, and she backed off to about seventy-five. The trip to Atascadero passed quickly, but not quickly enough for Sarah. She needed answers and she needed them fast.

Just over an hour later, she pulled into the parking lot at Atascadero. She had never been there before, and it took almost thirty minutes to complete the entrance screening process. In addition to the x-ray machine, the metal detector, and the full-body pat down, Sarah had to complete several forms explaining who she was and why she was there.

In contrast to her usual experience at the New Jail, she didn't have to wait long for Lexi to appear.

"Afternoon, Mrs. Wong! I wasn't expecting you today!" Lexi's voice was bright and cheerful.

"I wasn't expecting to be here myself."

"You got some good news for me? Was my appeal granted?" Lexi's voice rose in excitement.

"Nothing like that, I'm afraid."

Lexi's shoulders slumped visibly. "Well, what is it then?"

"I want to talk with you."

"About what?"

"About New Beginnings Fertility Clinic."

"What clinic?" Lexi's voice quivered ever so slightly.

"New Beginnings," repeated Sarah.

"Never heard of it."

"Is that right?" Sarah pulled the crinkled business card out of her pocket and slapped it down on the small table between them. "I found this card in your wallet. It was in the bag you picked up when you got out of jail."

"Oh."

"Lexi, I've got all day, so why don't you start at the beginning?"

And to Sarah's surprise, that is exactly what she did.

A little over three years ago, when Lexi had just turned sixteen, she met Ryan and fell in love immediately. After just a handful of dates, they started talking about getting married and having kids. Of course, neither of their parents approved of their marriage plans. Instead of just eloping, which Lexi admitted would have been the more sensible thing to do, she and Ryan decided to have kids first and hope their parents would approve of their getting married once they had a baby.

Their plan had seemed like a good one except for one thing—they had no money for prenatal care, not to mention the cost of raising a child on their own. The pregnancy had to be a secret, so they couldn't ask their parents for help. They were both still in school, and although Ryan had a part-time job at the paint store, he had no money saved up.

One of Ryan's friends had heard that a fertility clinic was paying young couples to have babies, so they checked it out. Everyone at the clinic seemed so nice, and they said they would pay for everything—all the prenatal care and the baby's delivery, and Lexi and Ryan would even get a $10,000 bonus once the baby was born. All they had to do was let the doctors try a new type of fertility treatment, some new test-tube baby sort of thing.

"What new technique? Were you having fertility problems?" Sarah asked.

"No, ma'am. I'd had an abortion when I was fifteen, so I knew I could get pregnant."

"What sort of techniques did they try on you?"

"They didn't really tell us much. They gave me and Ryan a bunch of forms to sign, but I didn't read them."

"Did they explain anything at all about what they were doing?"

"Yeah. The Swedish doctor told us they were trying out some sort of engineering stuff and they needed some volunteers to help them out. He said they weren't going to do anything to me or my baby. They just wanted to practice the engineering techniques."

Sarah already knew the answer to her next question. "Do you remember the doctor's name?"

"Yeah, Svengaard. Weird name."

Sarah swallowed hard. "Did Dr. Svengaard ask for your parent's permission?"

"No. That's what was so good about it. They didn't need anybody's permission."

"But you were only sixteen."

"By the time my first baby was born I had just turned seventeen."

In response to Sarah's gentle prodding, Lexi described the course of her first pregnancy — the hormone shots, egg retrieval, and embryo transfer. She had weekly ultrasounds and blood tests throughout her pregnancy, all at no cost to her. Lexi didn't know all of the terminology, but it was fairly easy for Sarah to follow.

"Just so I'm clear on this," Sarah said. "This is your first baby you're talking about, not Anna. Right?"

"That's right."

"So where was your first baby born?"

"At the clinic."

"What? You didn't go to a regular hospital?"

"No."

"Well, that explains it."

"Explains what?"

"Why there's no birth certificate for Jacob. What happened after Jacob was born?"

"Everything was just fine. We brought him home and everything seemed fine."

"What happened then?"

"Ryan and I kept Jacob at Grandma's house, like I told you before. We were just getting ready to tell our parents when Jacob died."

"He was three days old, right?"

"Yep. Like I told you before, everything was fine. I'd taken him out for some errands, and he slept in the car the whole time. When I got home I put him in his crib and he just never woke up from his nap."

"Was he sick?"

"I don't think so. I'm always getting colds, and I had a pretty bad one that day, but he seemed fine to me. He sneezed once or twice, but that was it."

"Did you take him to the emergency room?"

"I couldn't. What was I going to tell them? I had a secret baby with Ryan and now the baby was dead? I couldn't tell anyone anything. Besides, the Swedish doctor told me to never ever tell anyone about the clinic. So I didn't. Like I told you before, Ryan and I just buried Jacob in the woods behind my grandma's house."

"What did you do then?"

"We went back to the clinic and told them."

"About Jacob dying?"

"Yeah."

"What was Dr. Svengaard's reaction?"

"He took a lot of notes and said something like, 'These things happen.' He wasn't very nice. He wouldn't even give us our money because Jacob hadn't lived long enough."

"But that wasn't your fault!"

"I know, but he said it was in the contract." Lexi started to cry softly, and she looked up at Sarah. "Was my locket in the bag? It's gold and shaped like a heart. I really want that back."

"Yes, it was in there. It's got two pictures of Anna in it."

"No it doesn't. One of the pictures is Jacob. It's the only picture I have of him."

Sarah just stared at Lexi.

"Mrs. Wong, why are you so interested in Jacob?"

"I thought it might help you get out of here some day."

"Is there something else? Now it seems like *you're* hiding something."

Sarah decided to come clean.

"Remember when we first met last August and I said you looked familiar?"

"Not really."

"Well I do. And now I know why. My husband and I have been going to New Beginnings for almost four years. I

probably saw you in the waiting room a couple of times.
I've seen several young couples at New Beginnings, and
I've always wondered why young kids would be going to a
fertility specialist. Now I know."

"Don't you want to know about Anna?" Lexi said.

"What do you mean? You ... you went to New
Beginnings for both your babies!"

"Yes."

"After what happened to Jacob, you went back again?"

"We had no choice. We really wanted to have a baby
and we still didn't have any money. It was the only way we
could afford a baby."

"But they didn't even pay you the first time!"

"I know, but this time they said everything would turn
out fine and they promised to give us $20,000 after Anna
was born."

"So what happened with your pregnancy with Anna?"

"It went pretty much the same as Jacob's."

Lexi went on to describe the second round of treatments
at New Beginnings. Sarah did her best to listen, but she
was finding it hard to concentrate. She held up her hand
and stopped Lexi mid-sentence.

"You had two babies, right?"

"Yes."

"And both babies were born after you had undergone
some sort of experimental procedure at New Beginnings?"

"Yep."

"And both babies died suddenly while they were still
infants?"

"Right."

Sarah started crying. "You didn't kill your babies!"

Lexi started crying too.

"Now I understand," Sarah said, choking on her words.
"That's why Ryan wouldn't talk with me, isn't it? That's
why you didn't tell anyone. That's why you told the cops it
was your fault that Anna was dead. That's why you said

that Anna was another big mistake. That's why you tried to kill yourself. Now it all makes sense. I don't know exactly what happened to your babies, but I think it's something Dr. Svengaard did. You said Dr. Svengaard did some engineering. Did he use the term genetic engineering?"

"I'm not sure."

"What did he tell you about the procedures?"

"He told me they were completely safe for me and my baby."

"Anything else?"

"He told me never to tell anyone about them. He said he didn't want anyone to find out what he was doing because his competitors might steal his ideas. It all sounded kind of exciting to me, like we were helping out science and stuff. But then he got really mean and told us that people we loved would get hurt if we ever told anyone about what he was doing."

"Lexi, I want you to think back very carefully. Were there any warnings that your babies were going to die?"

"Not really. They were both fine right up until they died. Like I told you, Anna seemed a little cranky the day she died, but Jacob seemed fine, other than a few sneezes. They both just went to sleep and never woke up."

"I'm going to do my best to get you out of here. I'm going to ask for a new hearing, but I've got lots of investigating to do first. It's probably going to take a couple of weeks. Can you hang in a little while longer?"

"I've been locked up for almost nine months. I guess I can wait a few more weeks."

"Good. While you're waiting, I want you to get some paper and write down everything you can remember about what happened at New Beginnings. Also, write down anything that seemed unusual about your babies, especially the day they died — anything at all, even if it doesn't seem important."

"I'll write as much as I can remember. You're really

going to help me, aren't you?"

"You bet I am. I have one more question before I leave. Why didn't you tell me about New Beginnings before?"

"Well, because the Swedish doctor told us never to tell anyone. He said if we told anyone, horrible things would happen to me and Ryan and maybe even my mom. I was so scared, so I just kept my mouth shut. Besides, I was so ashamed. It's sort of like someone paid me to have my babies. I never should have agreed to any of that stuff. It's my fault and God is punishing me. That's why I tried to kill myself. I figured I should stay in prison forever or get the death penalty. Even though I want to go home now, I still sorta feel that way. It's all so confusing."

"Listen to me, Lexi. It's not your fault that Anna and Jacob died. You did nothing wrong. Do you understand?"

"I guess so."

"And now I'm going to fix everything."

"But you can't bring back Anna and Jacob, can you?"

* * *

Sarah was crying so hard on the way back to Santa Felicia that she had to pull over—twice. Lexi had spent nine months incarcerated for something she didn't do. She might have spent the rest of her life locked up if Sarah hadn't stumbled across the New Beginnings business card. As Sarah raced back to Santa Felicia, she called Nick and told him to meet her at the office right away, and she told Matt what she had just learned. For the first time in a long while, Matt understood why she wanted to work on a weekend.

Nick was already at the office when Sarah burst in.

"Lexi is innocent!" she announced. "She didn't kill her babies! She's actually, honest to God, innocent!"

Nick's eyes grew wide. "How do you know?"

As quickly as she could, Sarah filled him in on what she had learned.

"Let me make sure I've got this right," Nick said. "Both of Lexi's babies were conceived as part of some sort of illicit genetic engineering experiment going on at New Beginnings Fertility Clinic, and you think something went horribly wrong, which led to their deaths. Have I got it?"

"That's it!"

"So if you're right, Lexi really didn't kill Anna."

"I know I'm right."

Sarah and Nick just stared at each other for a few moments.

"Now what?" asked Nick enthusiastically.

"I'm pretty sure Lexi is entitled to a jury trial under the Welfare and Institution Code. I think it's in Section 5302 or 5303. Given this new evidence, it shouldn't be too hard to get Judge Sandoval to grant us a new trial. Before I file the motion, though, we've got to be absolutely certain about all of this. I'm going to arrange for a lie-detector test for Lexi."

"What can I do?"

"I need you to don your private detective hat again. I want you to find out what's been going on at New Beginnings Fertility Clinic. I'm convinced Lexi's babies died because of something that happened there, but I don't know what it is. Talk to as many people as you can, but do it discreetly. You can't let them know what you're looking for, or we may never get any information from them."

"How am I going to do that?"

Sarah smiled. "Turn on the old Fargo charm."

"Maybe I can take some of the staff out for dinner or drinks. That might loosen them up." Nick was smiling too.

"I don't care how you do it, just do it. Meanwhile, I'm going to talk to Candi Markowitz. I have a feeling she knows more about New Beginnings than she's told me."

Nick sprang up to leave, excited about his new assignment.

"One more thing," Sarah added, almost as an afterthought. "Since you're going to be poking around

New Beginnings, you might as well know, because you'll probably find out anyway."

"Might as well know what?"

"That Matt and I are clients there." She looked down and patted her bulging belly. "We've been getting fertility treatments there for over four years."

"Is that how you got …"

"Yep."

"Aren't you worried about all this?"

"Not at all. We didn't do any of the genetic engineering stuff they tried on Lexi."

* * *

Nick tried everything he could think of to get somebody at New Beginnings to talk with him. He prodded, he cajoled, he needled. He even flirted. But all in vain. No one would say a word. Nick was certain something big was going on, but nobody would say what. They all seemed scared of something.

While waiting for Nick to complete his investigation, Sarah did what she could on her end to find out what was happening at New Beginnings. She called Candi, but her secretary said she was in Hawaii and wouldn't be back until the beginning of the following week.

For the lie-detector test, Sarah chose Carl Stewart, a polygraph examiner from Indiana who had been highly recommended by one of her law school classmates. He was booked for months, but he promised Sarah he would try to squeeze Lexi in as soon as he could.

Everything was going so slowly. Nick reported that he was having no luck at New Beginnings, Candi Markowitz was lying on a beach in Hawaii, and Carl Stewart couldn't fly out to California for at least another week. Sarah was growing more frustrated by the day.

On Tuesday morning, Maggie yelled out. "Sarah, there's

someone on the phone who wants to talk to you."

"Can you take a message? Tell them I'm busy and I'll call back tomorrow." Sarah wasn't in the mood to talk with any clients.

"She said it's really urgent."

"What's her name?"

"Angela or Angelina. Something like that."

"Did she say what it's about?"

"No, but she kept insisting that it's extremely urgent."

"Okay. Put her through."

Sarah picked up the phone. "Hello, this is Sarah Wong. Can I help you?"

"My name is Angelina McGowan."

"I'm sorry. Do I know you?"

"I work at New Beginnings and I'd like to talk with you. Can I come see you?"

"Can't we just talk over the phone?"

"I'd prefer not to." Angelina's voice was calm, but her tone was insistent. "I can be there in an hour."

"All right. I'm at 17 West Regency Avenue, Suite 805."

Fifty minutes later, Maggie summoned Sarah to the reception area to greet the mystery caller. She let out an audible gasp when she saw who it was: Angelina McGowan was the technician at New Beginnings who wore the too-tight white blouse.

"Thank you so much for coming. Let's go back to my office." Sarah escorted Angelina back to her office and closed the door.

"I have some information about Lexi Conway that I thought you'd be interested in," Angelina began.

"How did you …?"

"Your cute assistant has been hanging around New Beginnings asking lots of questions. He even took me to lunch a couple of times. New Beginnings has a very strict non-disclosure policy, so I was really hesitant to talk to him. However, he did tell me that he worked for you. I assume you know Lexi Conway had two babies with us."

"Yes, she told me a couple of weeks ago."

"I think I may know why her babies died. Well, not *exactly* why, but I may be able to help you figure out why they died. Lexi was part of an ongoing experiment conducted by Dr. Svengaard."

"What kind of experiment?"

"Bjorn has been paying young girls, most of them no more than seventeen or eighteen, to be guinea pigs in his genetic engineering experiments. He hasn't told them anything at all. He gives them $10,000, sometimes even $20,000, and says he's working on some new techniques. Most of these poor girls just want a baby and are desperate for the money, so they don't ask any questions. Nobody besides Grace and me knows about it."

"How does he pay for all of this?"

"By overcharging people like you and your husband."

Sarah grimaced. "So what exactly has he been up to?"

"He's trying to perfect his techniques for positive and negative genetic engineering."

"What sorts of things has he been doing?"

"All the things he told you and Matt about. In terms of negative genetic engineering, he's trying to eliminate the genes that cause cystic fibrosis, Huntington's disease, and several other conditions. Even male pattern baldness."

"What about on the positive side?"

"Eye color, hair color, fast-twitch muscles, lung capacity. Those sorts of things."

"Why is everything so secretive?"

"Because what he's doing is illegal. If he's caught, he'll probably go to jail and lose his medical license."

"So why is he doing it? Is he trying to push the boundaries of genetic engineering or does he just want to become famous?"

"Neither. All he cares about is money. Bjorn's always telling me that he's going to make millions, maybe billions."

"How?"

"Once he's perfected his techniques, he's going to patent them and sell the rights to big biotech companies like Amgen and Biogen. If that doesn't work, he says he'll just move his practice to some Caribbean island and charge big fees to rich clients from around the world."

"So how do you know the genetic engineering killed Lexi's babies?"

"About half of the babies have died, most of them within three or four weeks. I don't know what it is, but something Bjorn does to the embryos is killing them."

Sarah stroked her bulging tummy and took a deep breath. She was so glad they had decided not to do any genetic engineering. She'd made a lot of bad decisions over the past year, but this was one she'd gotten right.

"So why are you telling me this?"

Angelina gazed down at her hands. "I've always liked you and your husband, so I wanted to help out. And I don't want that poor young girl to spend the rest of her life in prison for something she didn't do.

"Well, she's not actually in prison."

"I know, but a mental hospital might even be worse."

"Does anyone else know you came to see me today?"

"Are you kidding? I'd be fired on the spot if they knew I was talking to you."

"And you still came anyway?"

"I've had it with Bjorn. What he's doing to these young girls and their babies is criminal. If I had enough courage I'd go straight to the police."

"I can help you with that. But let's talk about Lexi's babies first."

"I can do better than that. Would you like to come to New Beginnings to look at the files?"

"Absolutely! When?"

"Right now. Bjorn is out of the country, so we can get into his office without him knowing."

"I'll give you a ride. That way we can talk in the car on the way there."

"Not a good idea," said Angelina. "We've got security cameras everywhere, even in the parking lot, and if someone sees us arrive together it might make them suspicious. I'll go first, and you come about ten minutes later. I'll meet you in the waiting room and bring you back to Bjorn's office."

"You don't know how much I appreciate this, Angelina."

"Actually, I think I do."

* * *

As soon as Sarah walked into the waiting room at New Beginnings, Angelina rushed up to her and guided her back to Dr. Svengaard's office. Sarah was a familiar face at New Beginnings, so her presence didn't raise any suspicions. Glancing around to make sure no one was watching, Angelina unlocked Dr. Svengaard's door and they both slipped in quickly, locking the door behind them.

Angelina opened the top drawer of the large filing cabinet in Dr. Svengaard's office. Only three people had access to those files — Dr. Svengaard, Grace, and herself, she told Sarah, and she went on to explain that Dr. Svengaard kept all his records on paper so there would be no electronic trace of what he was doing. She retrieved almost two dozen folders and fanned them out on the doctor's huge desk.

Sarah immediately noticed there were no names on the files. "How did Dr. Svengaard keep track of who's who?"

"Bjorn used code numbers instead of names. See the number in the upper right corner on the cover? That's the month and day of the mother's birthday."

"What if two women had the same birthday?"

"It hasn't happened yet, but I suppose he would just add another number."

Sarah opened up the first file in the stack. It contained about twenty pieces of paper, most of which were computer printouts full of what appeared to be genetic code. Lots of As, Gs, Ts, and Cs, which she knew stood for the four bases in a DNA molecule—adenine, guanine, thymine, and cytosine. But the first page was different from the others. It was a simple piece of lined paper that contained over a dozen groups of letters and numbers neatly handwritten in block letters.

Sarah held up the first page and waved it at Angelina. "What's this?"

"That's the summary page for the file. It contains all the information about that baby."

Angelina's reply struck an emotional chord with Sarah. Each of those files represented a baby.

Sarah stared at the unintelligible jumble of letters and numbers in front of her. "What does all of this mean? I can't make heads or tails of it."

Angelina pulled a chair up next to Sarah's. "This is Bjorn's shorthand for the genetic engineering he performed on this baby. The number in the upper right corner is the mother's birthday. On this file the number is 0315, which means that this woman's birthday is March fifteenth."

"Got it. But what if someone had two or more embryos engineered? Doesn't Dr. Svengaard usually put back several embryos at a time?"

"That's true for regular fertility treatments, but not for these genetic engineering ones. To keep a tight control on things, Bjorn usually transferred only one engineered embryo into each mom, although he may have transferred two embryos into a couple of women recently, but I'm not sure."

Angelina gave Sarah a quick tutorial about what all the numbers and letters meant. It was a lot for Sarah to take in and she peppered Angelina with questions.

"What sort of engineering did Dr. Svengaard perform on this baby?"

Angelina showed Sarah the code for that.

"Can you tell if this baby was stillborn or born alive?"

Angelina showed her the code for that.

"Do you know if this baby is still alive today?"

Angelina showed her the code for that too.

"Okay, now that I know the basics about how to read these things, let's look for Lexi's files," Sarah said.

"What's her birth date?" asked Angelina.

Sarah thought for a moment. "I've no idea. I think it's in July, but I'm not sure. Isn't there some other way we can figure out which files are hers?"

"Nope. We've got to have her birth date."

"Lexi had two babies. Does that help?"

"It might. Not many women come back a second time. For those women there are two files, one coded with the letter A after their birthday and another with the letter B. Let's see what we can find."

It didn't take Angelina long to find three pairs of files with the same maternal birthday. "I guess there were three of them."

Sarah took a quick look at the birthdates. None of them were in July. She groaned.

"I can't tell which of these are Lexi's. Can I take them home and work on them there? I can bring them back in a day or two."

"'Fraid not," said Angelina firmly. "Too risky. Bjorn could arrive back at any time and he'd know something was amiss."

"How about we make photocopies of the summary pages at the front of each file? That should be enough to help me get going on all of this."

"Nope. All our photocopy machines have memory chips. I think Bjorn checks them frequently to make sure nobody is copying or faxing any of our files."

"Seems awfully paranoid."

"Maybe so. But there's millions of dollars at stake."

Sarah thought about taking pictures of the files with her phone, but she had left it in her car.

"Maybe we should just call the cops or the FBI," she said. "Get a search warrant and do this properly."

"If we do that, Bjorn will have everything shredded before the cops get here, including you and me. The only way to do this is to do it ourselves."

Sarah wondered why Angelina was willing to risk so much to help her solve the mystery of how Lexi's babies died. "Are you sure you're okay with helping me on this?"

"I'm sure."

"Okay. Can I meet you back here tomorrow night, after the office is closed?" Sarah suggested.

"I can't do tomorrow. How about Thursday?"

"Great. Let's meet on Thursday at eight. I think we're going to need reinforcements. Would you mind if I asked Dr. Candi Markowitz to join us? She's an expert in genetics and she might be able to help us figure out what's been killing these babies. And we can definitely trust her to keep quiet about all of this."

"I think that's a great idea," said Angelina. "Come to think of it, Grace might be willing to help. She knows a lot more about the technical stuff than I do. Maybe she can figure out what went wrong."

"Will she agree to help us?"

"I don't know, but I'll find out."

"I'd also like to bring Nick and Conrad from my office. Last time I tried to do everything myself I screwed up royally. I'm not going to make that mistake again."

"Can we trust them?"

"Absolutely. Besides, Nick's the cute guy who took you to lunch."

Angelina smiled. "In that case, bring them with you."

* * *

Thursday evening couldn't come quick enough for Sarah. Just after lunch on Wednesday she was able to get a hold of Candi Markowitz, who readily agreed to help. At dinner with Matt that night, Sarah explained what was going on, and he immediately said he wanted to come too. At first she said no, but he pleaded and pleaded, and eventually she gave in.

When Sarah and Matt arrived at New Beginnings on Thursday evening, Angelina was waiting for them in the parking lot. Sarah told her she'd also invited Maggie, figuring Maggie could help out with organizing and note taking. Then the others arrived—Nick, Conrad, and Maggie, who drove together, followed by Grace, and finally Candi. Angelina gave Nick a big hug, and Nick smiled sheepishly at Sarah, who wondered just how friendly the two of them had become during his visits to New Beginnings.

Angelina opened the side door at New Beginnings and guided everyone back to Dr. Svengaard's cavernous office, which seemed cramped with everyone in it.

Sarah called the ersatz meeting to order. "Thank you all for coming. You don't know how much it means to me that you're all here tonight. I hope everyone is fine with Matt and Maggie joining us. Matt's been to New Beginnings with me dozens of times, so I figured he might be able to help, and Maggie can keep us organized."

"But who's going to post bail if we all get arrested?" asked Angelina with a smile.

Sarah and Nick were the only ones who laughed.

Angelina pulled all the files out of the large filing cabinet. Knowing that Lexi's birthday was November 4, she quickly located her two files, labeled 1104A and 1104B and retrieved the summary information sheet from each file.

"Angelina, can you explain to us what all of this means?" Sarah asked.

With everyone huddled closely together around Dr. Svengaard's desk, Angelina explained that the first three lines on each chart described the mother — her age, general health, and other characteristics — and the next three lines contained the same information about the father. Next were the entries describing the genetic engineering that had been conducted on the embryo. For baby 1104A, there were five notations, all on a single line:

M, EBL, HBR, FT, ST

"Let's see. Baby 1104A was a boy who was ..." Angelina paused for a moment. "He was engineered to have blue eyes, brown hair, and enhanced fast-twitch and slow-twitch muscles."

And for baby 1104B, there were six notations:

F, EBR, HBR, FT, ST, ELC

"This one was Anna," Angelina said. "She was engineered for brown eyes, brown hair, enhanced fast-twitch and slow-twitch muscles, and enlarged lung capacity."

"None of these were negative engineering. How come?" asked Sarah.

"Couple of reasons," Angelina replied. "Maybe these embryos didn't have any genetic defects, at least not the kind Bjorn could correct."

"And the other reason?" asked Conrad.

"Positive engineering is much sexier," said Angelina. "Think of the possibilities. Creating a super race of humans. Brave New World. That kind of stuff."

"It's also more dangerous, isn't it?" added Sarah.

"Yes, it is," agreed Angelina.

"I've always wondered why Dr. Svengaard doesn't use CRISPR instead of all of his viral vector stuff," said Sarah.

"From what I can tell, CRISPR is the technology of the future."

"You're right, but Bjorn doesn't use it for two reasons."

"Let me guess. The first has to do with money."

"You got it. Bjorn has a small operation here and it's easier and cheaper for him to engineer a few viral vectors than pay for the rights to use CRISPR."

"But I thought CRISPR was relatively inexpensive?"

"It is, but it's controlled by a few big biotechs and they want big fees for access to it."

"I remember Dr. Svengaard saying something about that. And the other reason?"

"He wants to do his own viral vector genetic engineering without having to go through any regulatory agencies. If he purchased the rights to use CRISPR, he'd have to notify the FDA and the NIH, and that would raise all sorts of red flags. He wants to fly under the radar and keep everything completely quiet."

"So he can do whatever he wants to?"

"Exactly."

Conrad interrupted. "What do these numbers mean?" Conrad said as pointed at a string of five numbers on the line below the genetic engineering codes.

"I think those might have to do with the vectors Dr. Svengaard used."

"The vectors?" asked Conrad.

Sarah jumped in. "Yeah, I remember Dr. Svengaard talking about them when he was explaining the genetic engineering to Matt and me. He said something about making his own viral vectors. It's the virus that delivers the new gene to the DNA in the embryo."

"He always said that was his big breakthrough," added Angelina.

"So what do the numbers mean?" Conrad asked again.

"I'm pretty sure these are identification numbers for the vectors. Bjorn made three different variations of the hybrid vectors, each slightly different than the others."

Next they turned their attention to Lexi's two pregnancies and the babies' births. Sarah reviewed out loud what they already knew — there was nothing unusual about either pregnancy or delivery. Both births were C-sections, which Dr. Svengaard always performed on the mothers of the genetically engineered babies.

"Why do a C-section?" asked Conrad.

"Just another way that Bjorn exercised absolute control," replied Angelina. "He didn't want to leave anything to chance."

Then they examined the notations describing the two newborns, including their Apgar scores and several other physiological measures. Again, there was nothing remarkable.

They were almost at the end of the two papers when Conrad spoke up. "What do these last two entries mean?"

At the very bottom of the form for file 1104A was written:

DEC?: Y

AAD: 3d

"It means that Jacob died when he was three days old," Sarah said quietly.

The entries were just as chilling for file 1104B, Anna's file:

DEC?: Y

AAD: 22d

"Anna lived for twenty-two days."

"Both babies had basically the same genetic engineering, both pregnancies and births were unremarkable, and both babies died within three weeks of birth," observed Nick.

"Actually, Anna lived for three weeks and a day," added Conrad.

Angelina and Sarah glared at Conrad.

"All I'm saying is that the extra day might be important," he said. "One baby died after only three days while the other lasted twenty-two."

Sarah had to admit that maybe Conrad was right. Maybe it *was* important that Anna lived longer than Jacob.

"Any ideas about why Anna lived longer?" she asked everyone. "If they both had the same genetic engineering, shouldn't they have died at about the same age?"

Her slow glance around the room was met with complete silence.

"So what do we do now?" asked Nick.

"We could make a chart," suggested Angelina. "Anna and Jacob both died, but not all the babies did. Some of them have survived for over a year and are still alive."

She grabbed the rest of the files and dropped them in the middle of Dr. Svengaard's desk.

"If we compare the files of the babies who died with the ones who are still alive, we might find something," she went on. "It's certainly worth a shot." She divided the files into two piles. "I've got nine babies who died and fourteen who are still alive."

"It's got to be the genetic engineering, right?" said Matt.

Everyone nodded except for Candi, who sat off to the side pecking away on her phone.

"Well, let's focus on that," said Sarah. "Let's make a list of all the genetic engineering procedures done on the two groups and see if there are any differences."

It took about a half hour to list the genetic engineering for all twenty-three babies. As Angelina had explained earlier, there were many more positive engineering codes than negative ones.

In fact, there were only three negative engineering codes in their entire list: the replacement of the BS1 mutation for three babies, all three of whom were still alive, the removal of the mutation that causes cystic fibrosis in two babies, one from each group, and the modification of the gene that causes male pattern baldness in seven babies, four who were still living and three who had died.

On the positive engineering side, five types of genetic engineering had been done, and Sarah listed them in a table on a sheet of paper.

	Living babies (14 total)	Deceased babies (9 total)
Eye Color		
Brown	7	3
Blue	5	6
Green	2	0
Hair Color		
Brown	7	1
Blonde	7	7
Black	0	1
Fast-Twitch Muscles	12	5
Slow-Twitch Muscles	5	5
Enhanced Lung Capacity	10	4

Sarah was puzzled. "Dr. Svengaard told Matt and me that he could do lots of other types of positive genetic engineering such as increased metabolism and enhanced cognitive processing speed. Why didn't he do any of those on these babies?"

"Because you can't measure their effects in newborns," Grace explained. "Dr. Svengaard wanted quick and easy proof that his genetic engineering worked so he could start marketing his procedures as soon as possible. So he worked mostly with observable traits such as eye color and hair color."

"But why fast-twitch and slow-twitch muscles?"

"He's devised some simple tests for those infants, and

he knew they would be in high demand from parents who wanted their kids to be super athletes."

"It's all about the money, isn't it?" said Sarah. "So, does anybody see anything interesting?"

"Almost all the babies who died had blonde hair?" suggested Nick.

"But not all of them," replied Sarah. "Besides, half the babies still alive have blonde hair too. Anything else?"

Everyone stared at Sarah's list in silence.

"There's no smoking gun here," said Conrad. "I still don't see the point of all this. It looks hopeless to me."

"Maybe we should look at combinations of traits. Maybe that will tell us something," said Maggie.

Sarah spun and looked at Maggie. "What a good idea! Maybe our approach has been too simple. What do you think, Candi?"

"It's worth a shot, I guess," said Candi without looking up from her phone.

Everyone but Candi pitched in, creating dozens of cross tabulations for the engineered traits for all twenty-three babies. It was tedious work. Proceeding slowly and carefully, it took them over two hours to complete all of the tables. Angelina cleared Dr. Svengaard's desk, and she and Sarah laid out all the cross-tabs and everyone gathered round.

"So we're looking for some sort of pattern that differentiates the dead babies from those that are still alive," said Sarah. "Anyone see anything?"

Almost everyone offered up suggestions, but none of them panned out. A couple of ideas were close, but no combination of engineered traits was present in all of the deceased babies and none of the living ones.

"Arrrrrgh," growled Sarah. "Nothing, nothing, nothing."

"I'm hungry," said Conrad.

"Me too. Let's get some food," suggested Sarah. "Nick

and Maggie, would you do the honors?"

"Sure," said Nick. "We'll be back in no time."

"Why don't we take a break and go outside and get some air," said Matt.

While Candi remained glued to her phone, everyone else went outside. While they waited for Maggie and Nick to return, the others walked around the almost empty parking lot. The cool evening air felt good to Sarah, and the twins agreed — she could feel them jostling around as she waddled around clutching onto Matt's arm. Nick came back with two takeout boxes of coffee while Maggie balanced a large bag of muffins on top of two cardboard boxes, one full of donuts and the other containing assorted juices. Everyone piled back into Dr. Svengaard's office and dove into the snacks.

Fortified by carbohydrates and energized by caffeine, they renewed their search for the baby-killing combination of genetically engineered traits, but after twenty minutes they realized they were at a dead end.

"Is there anything missing?" Maggie asked, looking down at the tables.

"A bit, but not much," replied Angelina. "Some information about the moms and dads, some other technical stuff. That's about it."

"And the vector identification numbers," Conrad reminded her.

"That's right," said Angelina. "The identification numbers for the viral vectors."

"Maybe we should take a look at them," said Conrad. "We've exhausted everything else."

"I'm not sure it will help," said Angelina, "but I guess it's worth a try."

Sarah and Conrad worked on the dead babies while Angelina and Nick looked at the living ones, with Matt taking notes for Sarah and Conrad and Maggie helping Nick and Angelina. Candi just kept tapping away on her phone. Sarah wondered why she had bothered to invite her. Candi hadn't said more than a couple of sentences all night.

Each group made a list of the viral vectors used on their babies.

"We're done," proclaimed Nick. "But I thought Dr. Svengaard used three different vectors."

"He did," said Grace. "I know the identification numbers by heart. It was my job to keep track of them — 31701, 31702, and 31703."

"But we've only got 31701 and 31703 in our group. Ten of our babies were engineered with 01 and four with 03."

Everyone turned to look at Sarah and Conrad, who were staring at each other.

"Zero two," Sarah said. "All our babies were engineered with 31702."

"That's it," shouted Grace. "It's the vectors!"

"But why would the vectors matter?" asked Sarah.

"Remember, he made these himself," said Matt. "Maybe he did something wrong."

"Hon, you're right! Engineering these hybrid viruses is completely uncharted territory. Right, Grace?"

"Yep. As far as I know, he's the only one in the world using them on human embryos."

"So what went wrong?" asked Matt.

"I'm not sure, but let me give it a shot," said Grace. "Candi, please jump in any time if I get any of this wrong."

"Sure," said Candi, her eyes still fixed on her phone.

Sarah was quietly seething that Candi seemed to have no interest in what they were doing, but she held her tongue for the time being.

"Okay, so Dr. Svengaard created his own viral vectors by genetically engineering a harmless adenovirus with genetic material from dangerous retroviruses and parvoviruses," Grace said. "Scientists like to use adenoviruses in genetic engineering because they are generally harmless to the target cells. The trouble is, they're not very precise when they deliver their genetic material. In contrast, retroviruses and parvoviruses integrate themselves directly into the genome of the host cells, which makes them very useful in gene therapy — but also very dangerous. Bjorn thought that by combining the two types of viruses he could have the best of both worlds — precise viral vectors that would deliver their genetic package right where he wanted and without harming the cells he was trying to engineer. He figured he could use these hybrid viruses to insert the new genes with a high degree of accuracy."

"Sounds good in theory," said Sarah.

"So what went wrong?" asked Matt.

"I don't know," replied Grace. "But I do know he was moving way too fast. Usually it takes years, even decades, to develop and test these sorts of procedures. First you start with simple organisms like bacteria, then you move up to mice and rats, then to non-human primates, and only after rounds and rounds of testing and government approval do you move to humans. But Bjorn's research was being done in secret, so there weren't any safety tests, no protocols to complete, no ethics boards to consult, no government agencies to answer to. He just started with humans, proceeding largely by trial and error."

"Why did he want to move so fast?" asked Maggie.

Sarah knew why. "Money," she said. "He thought this would make him rich."

"Okay. So we've got a bad batch of viruses. But how did that kill these babies?" Matt asked.

"It's probably got something to do with the fact that these viral vectors were hybrids," said Grace, "but I don't know exactly why the babies died."

Sarah stood, staring at Candi, the one person in the room who might be able to answer that question.

"Candi! Put that damn phone away and help us!" she shouted. "Have you heard a single word we've said?"

"Actually I have. In fact, I think I may have the answer," Candi said, smiling broadly.

Everyone turned to look at her.

"I'm sorry, Candi," said Sarah, red-faced. "It just didn't look like you were paying attention."

"Sarah, you should know better than to be fooled by appearances. While you've all been gabbing, I've been searching the Web for information about viral vectors, and I've think I've found something that might help us. A while back, there were some gene therapy trials involving SCID, an immune disorder. At first these trials seemed to be a huge success because many of the patients' immune systems were improving. But then a couple of patients developed leukemia, so they stopped the trials. It turned out that the viral vector, which was a type of retrovirus, was triggering an oncogene in the patients, and these newly activated oncogenes were causing some of the patients to get leukemia."

"I remember reading about that," added Sarah.

"How's that relevant to these babies?" asked Conrad.

"I have a feeling the same sort of thing may be going on here. Maybe Vector 31702 alters some genes in the DNA of these babies—not the genes Dr. Svengaard's trying to fix, but other genes on the same chromosome—and those altered genes are somehow killing the babies. Another possibility is that the viral vector itself is causing these deaths. Maybe it incorporates itself into the embryo's DNA and remains dormant in the baby's cells until it's triggered by something."

"But these babies aren't dying of cancer," said Sarah.

"Actually we don't know that for sure," replied Candi. "All we know is that Anna died of carbon monoxide poisoning—at least that's what the coroner said. We don't know why the other babies died. My hunch is that they all died of the same cause, more or less. We just need to figure out what that was."

"Are you saying the coroner was wrong?" asked Conrad.

"Not necessarily. The evidence certainly points to carbon monoxide poisoning. But maybe Vector 31702 causes some sort of genetic defect that mimics carbon monoxide poisoning."

"Or maybe the genetic defect makes the babies more susceptible to carbon monoxide poisoning," suggested Conrad.

"Maybe so," said Candi. "After all, babies are naturally vulnerable to carbon monoxide poisoning because of their high metabolism and immature pulmonary systems. It wouldn't take much to make them even more susceptible to low levels of carbon monoxide, levels that wouldn't kill you or me."

"But how does this help us?" said Conrad. "It still looks like Lexi killed her baby in her garage."

"Maybe, maybe not," replied Candi.

"But Anna wasn't exposed to any other carbon monoxide that day," interjected Sarah.

"Are you sure?" asked Candi. "Did Lexi ever leave her car running that morning?"

"Nope. All she did was run some errands—the Donut Shoppe, Pete's Market, and the gas station. That's it."

"Have you watched the video of the gas station carefully?" asked Candi.

"Only about a hundred times."

"Were there lots of other cars there?"

"Tons. It was packed that day," replied Sarah. "I think Lexi even had to wait a while for a pump to open up."

"With the car running?"

"I don't know."

"How about the other cars?"

"I don't know, but I do know that Lexi kept telling me how bad it smelled that day at the gas station. That was the final trigger for my perfect storm defense."

"You and I both assumed that the smell of gasoline bothered Lexi that day," Candi said. "But maybe it was the car exhaust, the exhaust from all those idling cars waiting for a gas pump to open up—car exhaust that contained carbon monoxide."

"The gas station! That's where Lexi first noticed there was something wrong with Anna!" shouted Nick.

"That's right," said Sarah. "Lexi hit and slapped Anna to try to wake her up." She turned back to Candi. "So you're saying that Anna might have died at the gas station from carbon monoxide poisoning because of some sort of weird genetic defect? Come to think of it, that would explain something that's always bothered me about the coroner's report," said Sarah.

"What's that?" asked Nick.

"Despite all of the evidence that Anna died at about eleven thirty or eleven forty-five, the medical examiner listed the time of death in his report as 'Unknown A.M.' Dr. Prakeesh wrote that the degree of livor mortis suggested that Anna had died between nine and eleven that morning, but he claimed that the discoloration of the skin caused by the carbon monoxide poisoning made it difficult to interpret the livor mortis evidence with any precision, which is why he left the time of death vague. So maybe Anna didn't actually die at eleven thirty or eleven forty-five. Maybe she died earlier that day."

"At the gas station," said Conrad.

"At the gas station," repeated Sarah.

"When were they at the gas station?" asked Conrad.

"About ten or ten fifteen."

"That timing is spot on with what the coroner said in his report," said Nick.

"But Anna had been in Lexi's car many times during the three weeks she was alive," Sarah said. "Lexi said she took her everywhere. Why didn't Anna die before August 11?"

"Maybe there wasn't enough ambient carbon monoxide

any of those times," suggested Conrad.

Matt jumped in. "Most of the babies engineered with Vector 31702 survived for more than a few days. A couple of them even lived for four or five months."

"I think there's one more piece to this puzzle," said Candi. "Sarah, remember when we talked about how genes interact with the environment?"

"Sure. That's how we came up with Lexi's defense. It was a perfect storm of genetic and environmental factors."

"Indeed," said Candi. "But that defense never sat well with me."

"How come?" asked Sarah.

"It was too complex. We scientists prefer simple explanations over complex ones. Parsimony. You know, Occam's razor."

Sarah pretended she knew what Candi was talking about. "Of course."

Candi continued. "I think there may be some sort of trigger, some simple environmental factor that interacts with the genetic defect caused by this hybrid viral vector."

"Do you have any idea what the trigger might be?" asked Nick.

"Environmental triggers can be almost anything. Let's look at some possibilities. Sarah, was Anna given formula?"

"Lexi was breastfeeding, so no formula."

"Anything unusual about Lexi's diet?"

"I don't think so, but I'll check."

"Does Lexi smoke?"

"No."

"Use any drugs?"

"Nope."

"Were there any chemicals or other toxic substances in Lexi's home?"

"I don't think so. She lived in a clean, fairly new apartment."

"I'm not sure what other possibilities there are," said

Candi. "Anna had been alive for only a few weeks and her environmental exposure was fairly limited."

Conrad stood up and waved his arms wildly. "Houston, we have a problem!"

Sarah glowered at him. "Yeah? What is it?"

"I think there's a mistake here," he said, pointing to the list of viral vectors. "One of the babies that's still alive was engineered with Vector 31702. It's right here in this file."

Angelina took a look at the folder Conrad was holding. "I'll be damned. He's right. Nick and I must have missed this."

Sarah's heart sank, and she could feel the excitement in the room dissipate rapidly.

"Another dead end," said Conrad.

"Maybe we should all just go home," said Sarah, feeling utterly dejected.

Just a few minutes before it had all seemed so promising, and now it was suddenly over.

"Not so fast," said Candi, almost shouting. "This just confirms what we've been talking about. Maybe this one baby is still alive because it hasn't encountered the environmental trigger yet, whatever it is."

"Well, let's keep looking for that trigger!" said Matt.

Sarah brightened. "I just remembered something. When I told Lexi we were re-examining her case, I asked her to write down everything she could think of about the days when Anna and Jacob died. I glanced at her notes a couple of days ago and nothing jumped out at me, but maybe there's something in there. I think the notes are in my trunk."

Sarah started to waddle toward the door.

"No you don't, Tiger," said Matt. "I'll get them for you."

Matt returned with an armful of folders, but it only took Sarah a few moments to find the right one.

"Give me a few minutes while I read through this. Lexi's handwriting isn't the neatest," she explained.

"So what we've got here is some sort of genetic defect that's triggered by something outside the person," Nick said while Sarah read her notes. "Just like the Warrior Gene can be triggered by provocation or childhood abuse."

"That's the basic idea," said Candi. "We're looking for a triggering factor. Something baby Anna was exposed to. Something all of the deceased babies were exposed to."

"Ah-choo!"

Maggie's sneeze startled everyone.

"Bless you," said Nick reflexively. He continued with his analysis. "Since so many babies died, the trigger has to be something fairly common, right?"

"Makes sense to me," agreed Angelina.

"Aaaah-chhooo! Sorry folks, this cold seems to be getting worse," Maggie said.

Nick's eyes opened wide. "Hey, aren't colds caused by viruses?"

"Yes," replied Grace.

"Adenoviruses?"

"Actually, yes," said Grace.

"We're talking about the common cold, right?"

Everyone looked at Sarah.

"YES! Lexi had a cold when both Anna and Jacob died!" she screamed.

"Colds that were caused by adenoviruses!" said Nick grinning.

"Adenoviruses that could have triggered a latent genetic defect caused by the hybrid viral vectors!" shouted Angelina, grinning back at him.

Matt stood up and started clapping, slowly at first, then faster and louder. Soon everyone was on their feet, applauding and cheering.

After they had calmed down, Conrad sounded a note of caution. "What if we're wrong about all of this? It's almost four a.m. Maybe none of us are thinking straight."

"If we're wrong, we just start over again," said Sarah.

"But what if we're right?"

Then Sarah asked, to no one in particular, "How will we be able to prove in court that Dr. Svengaard engineered all of these babies, including Lexi's? These teenage moms don't really know what he did, and his notes are probably too cryptic to be convincing to a judge or jury."

Grace piped up. "Ironically, Dr. Svengaard may have helped us on this himself. To make sure that everyone would know that he had engineered these babies, he always inserted a unique genetic code into each of the embryos. Sort of his genetic signature."

"How egotistical!" exclaimed Conrad.

"How helpful!" added Sarah.

To be sure, several big questions remained, dozens of details needed to be worked out, and confirmatory genetic testing had to be done, but they all sensed that this was it. They had finally figured out why the babies had died.

"I don't think there's anything else we can do tonight," said Angelina.

"Then it's a wrap!" beamed Sarah.

They set about tidying the office and gathering their belongings for their journey home while dawn broke on the horizon. Nick, Conrad, and Maggie removed all of the papers from Dr. Svengaard's wall and put them in a large manila envelope. Sarah helped Angelina put the case files back into the large filing cabinet, taking care to return them precisely where they had been before. While she was placing the last stack of files in the bottom drawer, she noticed a small group of folders at the back.

"Angelina, what are these? More cases?"

Angelina glanced at Grace and hesitated before responding. "That's the pending birth group — the babies who haven't been born yet, so you wouldn't be interested in them."

Sarah disagreed. "Don't you think we ought to contact these women and let them know what's happening?

There's only about a half dozen files here, so it shouldn't be too hard to figure out who they are. Maybe they can do something to protect their unborn babies. Besides, I think they have a right to know what Dr. Svengaard did to them."

"I don't think there's anything they'll be able to do," said Grace.

"But shouldn't we at least try to contact them?"

"I really don't think that's necessary," Angelina said, and moved to close the drawer.

But Sarah thrust her hand into it, wincing when the metal slammed against her wrist. She pulled out the files from the back of the drawer and tossed them on Dr. Svengaard's desk. Matt started to look through them one by one. "The numbers in the top corner are the mom's birthdates, right?"

"That's right," confirmed Sarah.

Matt laughed. "Hey, one of these women has the same birthday as you, Tiger. 0-7-2-7. July 27. What are the odds of that?"

"Hon, let me see that file," Sarah said, feeling the hairs rise on the back of her neck.

He slid it across the desk to her.

Sure enough, the code was 0727. She opened the file and saw there were two information sheets.

One was labeled 0727-A and the other 0727-B—a boy and a girl.

"DR. SVENGAARD USED GENETIC ENGINEERING ON MY BABIES!" Sarah yelled.

Nobody said a word.

Sarah looked directly at Angelina. "ANGELINA! Did he engineer my babies?"

Angelina didn't answer.

"ANGELINA!" Sarah screamed again.

"Only one of them," Angelina said quietly.

"What do you mean 'only one of them'?"

"He engineered one of your embryos but not the other."

"WHICH ONE?"

"I don't know. I need to look at the file."

Sarah threw the file at Angelina, its contents fluttering to the floor as the folder hit Angelina in the knee. Angelina scooped everything up and scanned the pages. "The boy. The boy was genetically engineered and the girl was not," she said eventually.

"What exactly did he do?" Sarah asked.

"He engineered four enhancements on your male embryo: increased cognitive processing speed, increased height, enhanced fast-twitch muscles, and enhanced slow-twitch muscles. There's a handwritten note next to these entries—'Requested by subjects'."

"Subjects? He called us subjects? We're not damn guinea pigs, we're people! People who chose NOT to have any genetic engineering!"

"There's something else you should know." Angelina's voice started to tremble.

Sarah glared at her. "What the hell is it?"

"Bjorn also engineered an enhanced sense of smell and enhanced visual acuity."

Sarah realized immediately what Angelina was talking about. "You mean he used genes from other animals? From wolves? From eagles? Transgenic engineering?" Sarah shrieked. "My baby's going to be a HYBRID?"

Sarah felt like she was going to faint, but Matt rushed around the desk and caught her.

"This can't be true. When we arrived for the egg retrieval we told Dr. Svengaard we had changed our minds and didn't want to do any genetic engineering, not even for the BS1 mutation. He said that was fine!"

Matt got Sarah a chair. The color of Sarah's face matched the intensity of her anger. "You were there, Angelina! Why didn't you say anything?"

"I'm really sorry."

Then Sarah remembered the most important detail of all. "Which vector did he use?"

Sarah crumpled to the floor when Angelina whispered "31702."

CHAPTER 25

Groggy, hungry, and disoriented, Sarah rolled onto her left side and searched for her alarm clock. It read 5:19.

It couldn't be 5:19. It was already light out. It must be 6:19, reasoned Sarah. She looked at the display again, but as the numbers came into sharper focus, she realized it was indeed 5:19 – in the afternoon.

She sat up slowly and pushed the covers aside. Instinctively she patted her belly, drawing comfort from its large, taut circumference. It wasn't until she tried to stand that she noticed she was still wearing her clothes from the night before.

Then she remembered the horrible dream. She was at New Beginnings with Angelina, Nick, Conrad, Matt and everybody else. Someone told her that Dr. Svengaard had engineered one of her babies and that he had even inserted some animal genes. She shuddered uncontrollably. She'd had nightmares about her babies before, but none so utterly frightening.

Matt appeared at the bedroom door. "You okay, Tiger? You want something to eat?"

"Yeah, I'm starving. How late did we stay at New Beginnings last night? I don't even remember coming home."

"That's because you were completely out of it when we drove back."

"Why am I still in my clothes?"

"You were so tired I just put you right to bed. You feel like eating in the kitchen, or you want me to bring something in here?"

"Let's go in the kitchen. It'll do me good to get out of bed."

Matt grabbed her left elbow and helped her to stand up, belly first. Feeling lightheaded, she plopped back down and decided to wait a minute or two before giving it another try.

"Hon, I had the strangest dream last night," she said.

"About what?"

"About the babies. I dreamed that Dr. Svengaard used genetic engineering on one of them."

Matt was silent for a few moments. "Tiger, you know that wasn't a dream, don't you?"

"What do you mean?"

"It really happened. He actually engineered our little boy. We found out last night while looking at his files."

Sarah locked eyes with Matt, looking at him in horror. "So now what? I'm seven months pregnant. What are we going to do?"

"I don't know, Tiger."

"There's nothing we *can* do—except wait and hope."

"And pray," added Matt.

"And pray," said Sarah as a tear slid down her cheek.

* * *

When Sarah woke up the next morning, she was in full-blown denial. After all, they didn't really know *for sure* that one of her babies was genetically engineered. Maybe Angelina and Grace had made a mistake. Maybe it was all a big, horrible mix-up and everything would turn out fine. Then her denial transformed into anger.

For a full week, she shouted at everyone and everything. It seemed like she was mad at the entire world. Even Chloe couldn't escape her wrath. She went into work on Monday and Tuesday, and both days she stormed out early, mad about something. She thought about seeing a shrink, but what good would that do? Would that fix her hybrid baby boy?

On Tuesday afternoon, she visited Lexi and yelled at her too. Lexi was excited about the possibility of a new trial, but her bubbling optimism made Sarah even angrier. *Why is Lexi going free while I'm going to be imprisoned in my own private hell?*

Sarah yelled longest and loudest at Matt. She wasn't sure why—he hadn't done anything wrong. She was the one who had read all the documents, done all the research, and ultimately made all the decisions. He didn't deserve her wrath, and deep inside she knew that. But she blamed him anyway. For a day or so, she even contemplated leaving him and moving in with her sister.

On Wednesday, she was thirty minutes early for her weekly appointment at Valley Obstetrics. Dr. Sadler had already heard about the genetic engineering from Matt, and she conducted an exceedingly thorough examination of the twins. When she was done, she assured Sarah that everything appeared to be normal with both babies. Dr. Sadler offered to conduct an amniocentesis to test for genetic abnormalities, but Sarah got angry with her too and insisted that her babies were just fine; she didn't need any more tests.

After getting home from her appointment at Valley Obstetrics, Sarah put her feet up on the couch and slowly sipped a decaffeinated tea. Then she started sobbing. It was quiet and intermittent at first, but became louder and louder as the afternoon went on.

The crying continued for four days.

Finally, at dinner on Saturday night, a week after she had learned that Dr. Svengaard had genetically engineered one of her babies, the crying stopped. There would be no more yelling, no more recriminations. She was ready to move on.

She began praying every once in a while about her babies — maybe not to the same God Matt believed in, but to some sort of higher power.

She also thought about seeing some high-priced genetic specialists about her babies and spent the better part of Sunday morning searching WebMD and websites of the National Institutes of Health and the American College of Medical Genetics looking for a geneticist who might be able to offer her a plan, a way out. Something. Anything.

She toyed with the idea of contacting a geneticist she found in New York. But what use would it be? All he could really do was to confirm the bad news.

However, there was one thing she *could* do: she could sue Dr. Svengaard and New Beginnings for everything they were worth. With a vengeance, she started drafting a civil suit, asking for $108 million in damages to compensate her for emotional distress and pain and suffering. She settled on the exact amount of the damages after seeing the number on a billboard announcing the prize for that week's PowerBall drawing. After working on the pleadings for a couple of days, she filed them away, resolving to finish them after Lexi's case was done.

When Sarah called Angelina to get some background information for her lawsuit, Angelina told her that Dr. Svengaard had still not returned to the country and that New Beginnings was not scheduling any more appointments for him. Sarah guessed he had caught wind of their investigation, and she figured he would never return to the United States. She wanted just one opportunity to tell him face to face what she thought of him, but she knew she'd probably never get that chance.

As soon as Sarah returned to work from her grief-filled hiatus, she placed a call to Carl Stewart, the polygraph examiner from Indiana. He told her it would be at least another week before he could test Lexi, but Sarah explained the whole situation and pleaded with him to come to Santa Felicia sooner than that. In the end he succumbed to Sarah's repeated entreaties and flew to California the following day.

Nobody from Sarah's office attended the polygraph examination; they didn't want to taint the results in any way. At Sarah's direction, Mr. Stewart asked Lexi about both of her babies; Jacob's demise was likely to surface at some point, so she might as well be ready for it. The session was videotaped so Sarah could show it to the judge and the DA. As expected, Lexi passed the polygraph exam with flying colors. She was calm and confident, and she didn't look like someone who had killed her babies.

Sarah asked The DNA Group to conduct genetic analyses on tissue and blood samples that had been preserved from Anna's autopsy and toxicology testing. Not only did they find the signature genetic marker inserted by Dr. Svengaard, but they also confirmed that Anna had the engineered genes described in Dr. Svengaard's meticulous personal notes. Most importantly, The DNA Group noted that there appeared to be some foreign DNA in two of Anna's chromosomes, foreign DNA that was consistent with genetic material typically found in retroviruses.

When Sarah ordered the genetic tests on Anna, she thought about asking The DNA Group to test her own fetuses. It would be easy enough. A quick amniocentesis could obtain the cells needed for testing, and she'd have the results within a couple of weeks. She had been angry when she rejected Dr. Sadler's offer to do an amnio, but this time she decided against the testing for an altogether different reason. She was beginning to trust God or fate or Mother Nature or whatever, and she was willing to just let whatever was going to happen, happen.

Everything was beginning to fall into place on Lexi's case. Her polygraph results confirmed her innocence, the genetic testing verified that Dr. Svengaard had genetically engineered Anna, and Nick was almost finished tracking down and interviewing several other teenage mothers who had gone to New Beginnings. All that was left was for Candi Markowitz to tie everything together.

Two weeks after their all-nighter at New Beginnings, Candi delivered her report in person to Sarah's office. Sarah pored over the lengthy document.

At the beginning of the report, Candi described how carbon monoxide kills, and she reviewed some of the literature on the toxicity of carbon monoxide in humans. Sarah learned that the level of carboxyhemoglobin reported in AccFirst's toxicology report was rarely, if ever, fatal, which should have raised a red flag a long time ago. Candi explained that people who die from carbon monoxide poisoning usually have carboxyhemoglobin blood saturation levels of well over 30%, and often as high as 70% or 80%. Because Anna's level was only 27.2%, Candi theorized that if Anna had died of carbon monoxide poisoning, something must have made her especially sensitive to moderate levels of the gas.

Candi noted that although carbon monoxide occurs naturally in the earth's atmosphere, the amount in the air that people breathe is far too small to cause any health problems. The most common sources of higher, more toxic levels of carbon monoxide are furnaces, heaters, generators, and automobile engines. She explained that although catalytic converters had dramatically reduced the level of carbon monoxide emitted from automobiles, car exhaust could still be a significant source of carbon monoxide in enclosed spaces or in highly congested roads and parking lots, especially on very hot days. She cited one study that found levels of 100 to 200 parts per million generated by automobiles in Mexico City.

Anna could have been exposed to ambient levels of carbon monoxide of 100 ppm, or possibly higher, at the

Sunoco gas station on the day she died since many cars were idling at the station while waiting for a gas pump to open up, Candi noted. Because Lexi's air conditioning was broken, she had her windows down while she was waiting, exposing Anna to all of the carbon monoxide. However, ambient levels of 100 ppm usually lead only to a headache or maybe some dizziness. Ordinarily, death wouldn't occur until the ambient level of carbon monoxide rose well above 1,000 ppm.

Knowing that the report would be read by non-scientists such as lawyers, judges, and jurors, Candi began the penultimate section with a straightforward explanation of how viral vectors are used in genetic engineering. She described how Dr. Svengaard had created his own hybrid viral vectors and how he had used one of them to genetically engineer Lexi's embryos. This section of her report concluded with a description of the genetic testing performed by The DNA Group, which confirmed that Dr. Svengaard had genetically engineered Anna Conway, Lexi's baby, and that some of the DNA from Dr. Svengaard's hybrid viral vector had been incorporated into Anna's genome.

Finally, Candi explained how genetic changes and mutations do not always have an immediate effect on an organism, and that it often takes some sort of environmental trigger to activate a dormant gene. She used lung cancer and skin cancer as powerful examples of gene–environment interactions. She continued on to explain that it was likely that an adenovirus or other similar virus could have activated the changes in Anna's DNA that had resulted from Dr. Svengaard's genetic engineering, and that once activated, the altered DNA would have rendered Anna highly susceptible to carbon monoxide poisoning.

At the end of the report, all of the important points were summarized on a single page.

- The genetic code of Hybrid Viral Vector 31702 was integrated into the DNA of all of Anna Conway's cells, including her red blood cells.

- In utero and after birth, the Hybrid Viral Vector gene (HVV gene) lay dormant in Anna Conway's cells.

- At some point before Anna Conway's death, the dormant HVV gene in her red blood cells was activated by an adenovirus, of which there are 57 known serotypes in humans. Among these is the one that causes the common cold.

- Once activated, the HVV gene diminished the ability of Anna Conway's red blood cells to bind to oxygen, and it increased their affinity to carbon monoxide.

- After the HVV gene had been activated, even small amounts of carbon monoxide were able to bind quickly to the hemoglobin in Anna's blood and prevent her red blood cells from carrying any oxygen, thus leading to rapid death via oxygen deprivation, likely occurring in a matter of minutes.

- Given that both Jacob Conway and Anna Conway died after riding in motor vehicles, with both trips involving multiple occasions of engine idling and, in Anna's case, exposure to other idling gas combustion engines at the Sunoco station, it is likely that exposure to ambient carbon monoxide levels of 100 to 150 ppm led directly to the deaths of Jacob and Anna Conway.

Sarah closed the report, looked up at Candi, and smiled. It was a scientific tour de force. Every piece of information gathered and analyzed by Lexi's defense team, capped by

Candi's extraordinary report, was consistent with their caffeine and sugar-fueled speculations concocted in the wee hours of the morning at New Beginnings Fertility Clinic three weeks earlier: Lexi Conway did not kill either of her babies. Anna and Jacob Conway had been innocent victims of the greedy machinations of Dr. Bjorn Svengaard. Only a couple of questions remained.

"How can we be sure that an adenovirus triggered the genetic defect in these babies?" Sarah asked Candi.

"Well, we don't yet have any direct scientific evidence," Candi replied. "But we can look for indirect evidence of that link. We know Lexi had a cold before Jacob and Anna died, but that may not be enough. It could just be a coincidence. What we need — "

" — is evidence that the other babies who died were also exposed to cold viruses," Sarah interjected.

"And that those babies were exposed to at least moderate levels of carbon monoxide," added Candi. "That would be our smoking gun."

They didn't have to wait long. Nick's report was ready the very next day.

Nick had been able to talk with seven women who had undergone genetic engineering at New Beginnings. Their stories were basically the same as Lexi's. They were all unwed teenagers who wanted money so they could have a baby and raise it on their own. Three of the babies were still alive. The other four — all engineered with Vector 31702 — had died as infants at ages ranging from a week to a month and a half. All four mothers reported having had a cold the day their babies died, and two had noticed cold-like symptoms in their babies. More importantly, three of them recalled their babies spending a lot of time in a car the day they died.

This was the evidence they needed to connect Dr. Svengaard's genetic engineering to Anna's death. At last Sarah was ready to ask for a new trial.

She filed a motion for a jury trial under Welfare and Institutions Code 5303, which states that a trial must be held within ten days of the request. In her motion, Sarah stated her grounds for a new trial in a single sentence: The defendant, Lexi Conway, did not kill Anna Conway.

Judge Sandoval scheduled a hearing on Sarah's motion for nine a.m. on Friday, June 19.

* * *

"Let me get this straight," said Judge Sandoval. "Two months ago a jury found your client not guilty of killing her baby, and now you want to litigate that issue again?"

"That's correct, Your Honor."

"I've been on the bench for over eleven years and I've never heard of such a thing."

"There's always a first time for everything," Sarah said.

"I guess there is," replied Judge Sandoval. "But at the first trial, you stipulated that your client killed her baby."

"That's right, I did," conceded Sarah. "But that was a huge mistake. Probably the biggest I've ever made. I made a lot of blunders in the first trial, mistakes that cost my client her freedom. I'm not going to make those again."

"Do you have any new evidence that Lexi did not kill her baby?"

"Yes, I do, Your Honor."

"Very well. As I read Section 5303, your client is entitled to a jury trial within ten days, so I will schedule jury selection to begin on Monday, June 29 at nine a.m. in this courtroom. Can the District Attorney's Office be ready by then?"

"It's very short notice, Your Honor, but we will do our best. We also have a request."

"What is that, Mr. Sepulveda?"

"We request that Mrs. Wong give us her witness list and all relevant reports and documents as soon as possible —

preferably no later than next Tuesday."

"Do you remember what happened the last time you violated the discovery rules of the State of California, Mrs. Wong?" the judge asked sternly.

"Of course, Your Honor. I can assure you I won't be making those same mistakes this time around."

"I hope not. Just so it's crystal clear, I am ordering you to turn over all your evidence, including your witness list and copies of all reports and documents, to the District Attorney's Office by next Tuesday."

"That won't be necessary," replied Sarah.

"Mrs. Wong, are you challenging my discovery order?" Judge Sandoval said loudly.

"No, Your Honor. I'm just saying that your order is unnecessary because I have everything right here."

Sarah picked up a large bound volume, walked over to Renaldo and handed it to him.

"Your Honor, may the record reflect that I just gave the Deputy District Attorney a bound volume containing three hundred and forty-two pages. In that volume is every single document relevant to the defense case. It includes summaries of my investigator's conversations with all potential witnesses, all my handwritten notes relating to the case, a complete witness list, all hospital and medical records, additional genetic testing conducted by The DNA Group, a detailed report from Dr. Candi Markowitz, and the results of a polygraph examination given to my client a couple of weeks ago."

"Anything else, Mrs. Wong?" asked Judge Sandoval.

"Yes. I have another copy of my discovery materials here."

"Who gets that one? The press?"

"No, Your Honor. This one's for you."

Sarah handed Isabel the judge's copy of the materials.

"That's more like it, Mrs. Wong."

Then Isabel walked quickly over to the judge and

whispered something in his ear.

"One more thing, Mrs. Wong," said Judge Sandoval. "Because of the highly compressed time frame under Section 5303, you will need to file all your pretrial motions within the next day or so. I will hear them on the twenty-ninth, right before we start selecting the jury."

"That won't be necessary, Your Honor. I won't be filing any pretrial motions this time."

"What? No change of venue motion?"

"No, Your Honor."

"No camera-banning or jury-sequestering motions?"

"No, sir."

"Not even a motion to exclude evidence?"

"No, Your Honor. There will be no pretrial motions at all. Ms. Conway and I have nothing to hide."

"Excellent. All parties are ordered back to court on Monday, June 29 at nine a.m. Court is adjourned."

* * *

There was nothing left for Sarah to do in the ten days before trial. This time there would be no tricks, no fancy lawyering, no deception. She had a simple story to tell, and she would do it in a no-nonsense, straightforward manner.

The only battle Sarah fought in the lead-up to the trial was with Ellen Sadler. Sarah had promised Dr. Sadler that she would stay off her feet as much as possible during the last few weeks of her pregnancy, yet here she was, about to embark on another jury trial. Dr. Sadler did everything she could to prevent Sarah from trying the case, even threatening to quit as her obstetrician if she went against her orders.

Not surprisingly, Matt sided with Dr. Sadler. Matt didn't care about Lexi Conway. All he cared about was his wife and their two unborn children. But Sarah had some unfinished business to complete. She had gotten Lexi into this mess, and now she was going to be absolutely sure that she got her out of it.

Sarah promised she would stop going to court at the first hint of trouble and prepped Conrad so he would be able to take over if necessary. She asked the judge to shorten the court sessions to six hours a day so she would have time to rest and eat properly. Dr. Sadler reluctantly agreed to Sarah's plan, but asked Matt to keep a close eye on things; she knew Sarah would plow ahead even if she wasn't feeling well. Matt promised to call immediately if there were any problems.

As the trial drew closer, Sarah had more and more difficulty sleeping. Her belly was so large that every sleeping position was uncomfortable. And her nightmares returned. Months ago, she had dreamed about giving birth to baby Frankensteins and glowing green monkeys. Now she dreamed about babies who flew out of her mouth with eagles' wings, babies with the heads of dogs, sheep, and cows. In one of the most disturbing dreams, twin wolves erupted violently from her abdomen.

On Sunday, the day before Lexi's second trial was to begin, Sarah had an early dinner and went to bed at seven thirty. She was munching on SunChips and drinking apple juice when Nick called.

"I've got good news," he told her. "Actually, it's more interesting than good. They found Jacob's body."

Sarah sat straight up in bed, spilling her juice on the comforter.

"Where?"

"Right where Lexi said it was — in the woods behind her grandmother's house."

"How about that?" exclaimed Sarah. "Everything Lexi's told us has turned out to be true."

CHAPTER 26

On Monday the twenty-ninth, Sarah arrived at court rested and ready to go. The night before, she'd slept better than she had in weeks. No midnight wakening, no frightening nightmares.

This trial was not taking place in Courtroom 201, the grandiose setting of Lexi's first trial. Instead, it was being held in Department H, Judge Sandoval's usual courtroom, tucked away at the end of the hallway on the fourth floor. Although there were no cameras this time, several local reporters were present and the courtroom was almost full.

Renaldo and Joe still represented the prosecution, and Sarah and Nick headed up the defense team. But Sarah had added Conrad to the defense table to help out with trial strategy and cross-examination.

In contrast to Lexi's first trial, when Sarah did everything possible to hide her pregnancy, she now celebrated her impending motherhood and wore fashionable maternity clothes in court despite all the anguish and uncertainty about what was going to happen to her baby boy.

Isabel waved everyone back to chambers for a quick meeting with Judge Sandoval before jury selection commenced.

"Mr. Sepulveda, I trust you've read all of the materials provided by Mrs. Wong?"

"I have, Your Honor."

"So have I. Fascinating stuff."

Renaldo said nothing.

"Mr. Sepulveda, don't you think we can come to a plea agreement here?" the judge went on. "Maybe you could offer involuntary manslaughter. I'd be inclined to sentence Ms. Conway to eight years, which would mean she'd get out in about four, with credit for time served and good behavior. By then no one will remember who she is or what she did. It seems like a win-win for everyone."

"Your Honor, it is the position of the District Attorney's Office that Lexi Conway intentionally killed her baby, and we are ready to proceed."

Judge Sandoval cocked his head to one side. "I'm curious, Mr. Sepulveda. Is that your personal opinion?"

"My personal opinion doesn't matter here, Your Honor. I'm ready to represent the State of California and try this case to the best of my ability."

"All right, I guess we have no choice but to proceed. Mrs. Wong, I'll be honest with you. I'm a little uncomfortable retrying a defendant on a case in which she has already been found not guilty. It just doesn't seem right."

"Well, why don't you just dismiss the case right now, Your Honor?"

"I'm afraid I can't do that. How can I dismiss a case against an accused baby killer when the district attorney still wants to go forward?"

"I understand," replied Sarah, barely able to contain her excitement. The judge just said *accused* baby killer!

Judge Sandoval's demeanor suddenly turned sour. "Let me warn you, Mrs. Wong. If you try to pull some fancy lawyering tricks here, I'm going to hold you in contempt again. And this time you won't get out early. Do you understand?"

"Fair enough, Your Honor. But what if the jury decides that Lexi didn't kill her baby? What then?"

"If that happens, I will release her on the spot. The only reason she is being held under Section 5300 is because you convinced the jury at the first trial that she killed her baby due to some sort of screwy genetic defect. Since we can't change people's DNA, I figured if she killed once, she would probably kill again. Maybe another baby of hers or even someone else's. But if you can prove that she didn't kill her baby, and the jury believes you, I will release Ms. Conway from her hold under 5300."

"Will you put that on the record, Your Honor?"

"No, I will not. Anything else, Mrs. Wong?"

"No, Your Honor."

"Mr. Sepulveda?"

"No, Your Honor."

"All right, then. Let's get this show on the road."

Judge Sandoval began jury selection by questioning the group of one hundred prospective jurors to weed out those who had a legitimate reason to be excused. Then Isabel called twelve names, and one by one they took their places in the jury box. Judge Sandoval interrogated them about obvious biases and prejudice and excused five prospective jurors who said they couldn't be fair in this sort of case and replaced them with five others who passed the fairness test. After he finished his questioning, Judge Sandoval turned to Sarah for her voir dire.

Sarah stood up slowly, losing her balance ever so slightly due to the weight of her twins. She looked at the twelve people in the jury box and saw several she would normally excuse with her peremptory challenges: the ex-cop who was member of the NRA, the Tea-Party activist, and the woman from a military family. But this time she gulped, smiled at the men and women in the jury box, and proclaimed loudly, "Your Honor, I have no questions for any of these fine people. I'm confident they can all be fair to my client. I accept the jury."

Renaldo was stuck. If he started questioning and

challenging jurors, it would look like he didn't think they could be fair. "I guess we accept them too, Your Honor," he said.

After ten more minutes, in which three alternates were seated and accepted by both sides, jury selection was over. Jury selection in Lexi's first trial had taken a full two weeks. In the second trial it took less than an hour.

Renaldo had learned his lesson about opening statements in Lexi's first trial. Given a second chance, he delivered a brief opening in which he simply said that the state was going to prove that Lexi Conway killed Anna Conway on August 11. No PowerPoint slides, no fancy charts. It lasted less than fifteen minutes.

As Sarah listened to Renaldo's remarks, she noticed this wasn't the same Renaldo she had faced two months earlier. That Renaldo was aggressive and combative. This one was quieter and less assertive. Almost reticent.

"Thank you, Mr. Sepulveda. Mrs. Wong, would you like to make an opening statement now or would you prefer to reserve that right for later?"

"I'd like to make one now, Your Honor."

"Very well, you may proceed."

Sarah made her way to the podium slowly. She had no notes, no legal pad, not even a pen. She took a deep breath and spoke from the heart.

"Good afternoon, ladies and gentlemen. Normally I don't give opening statements at the beginning of a trial because I don't know exactly what the evidence will show or how the trial will unfold. But this case is an exception. I know exactly what is going to happen. We are going to show you—no, we are going to *prove* to you—that Lexi Conway did not kill her baby. Every witness's testimony and every single piece of evidence will point to that inescapable conclusion.

"In the papers and on TV they've called my client The DNA Baby Killer. I'm sure you've heard the term. There is indeed a DNA Baby Killer here in Santa Felicia, but it's not Lexi Conway. The true killer is Dr. Bjorn Svengaard, founder and director of New Beginnings Fertility Clinic.

"Lexi Conway has been in jail for almost eleven months for a crime she did not commit. Up until now she has been terrified to tell the truth about what happened to her baby. But now she is finally ready to have her day in court. She is going to get on that witness stand and tell you that she did not kill her baby. The defense will present evidence from over a dozen witnesses—friends, neighbors, nurses, doctors, lab technicians, and genetics experts—who will all say the same thing, loud and clear: Lexi Conway did not kill her baby. Lexi has lost eleven months of her life, but you have a chance to set the record straight. Justice can finally be served. With your verdict of not guilty, you can say the words Lexi has been waiting eleven months to hear: We believe you Lexi. We know you didn't kill your baby."

The emotions of the moment overtook her and when she sat down at the defense table, she almost missed her chair. Lexi pushed a piece of paper in front of her on which she had scrawled "Thank you."

"Mr. Sepulveda, you may call your first witness," Judge Sandoval said.

"May I have a minute, Your Honor?"

"Of course."

Renaldo spent much more than a minute in animated conversation with Joe Jimmerson. Sarah could see that they were arguing heatedly, but she couldn't make out what they were saying.

Eventually Judge Sandoval interrupted. "Do you need more time, Mr. Sepulveda?"

Renaldo stood up to address the court, Joe Jimmerson tugging at his sleeve and motioning wildly for him to sit down. "No, Your Honor, I don't need any more time. I have a motion."

"Would you like to approach the bench?"

"That won't be necessary. The State of California moves to dismiss the case against Lexi Conway."

"Grounds, Mr. Sepulveda?" said Judge Sandoval, remaining surprisingly calm.

"I believe Lexi Conway."

"What was that?" asked the judge.

"Your Honor, I believe Lexi Conway. I believe that she did not kill her baby, and therefore I move to dismiss the charges against her."

No one at the defense table moved. What was Judge Sandoval going to do?

"The court will grant the district attorney's motion. The charges against Lexi Conway are dismissed. Ladies and gentlemen of the jury, thank you for your time. Please report back to the jury assembly room."

There was an uproar in the courtroom, the audience members and reporters all talking at once. A few even leaped to their feet. Everyone seemed to have something to say, except for Sarah and Lexi. They just sat there, holding hands, stunned by what had just happened.

Judge Sandoval banged his gavel twice. "Order in the court. Everyone be seated immediately."

"The record shall reflect that the jury has been excused and has left the courtroom. I see that the next hearing on Ms. Conway's detention under Section 5300 is scheduled for a little less than five years from now."

Sarah couldn't believe what she was hearing. "But Your Honor—"

"Save your objection, Mrs. Wong. This time the court is going to do the right thing."

Judge Sandoval spoke directly to Lexi. "Ms. Conway, please rise."

When Lexi stood, she pulled Sarah up with her.

"In view of the district attorney's motion to dismiss the case, I find that Lexi Conway did not kill Anna Conway, and I order the clerk to enter a complete exoneration in the record, including a finding of factual innocence. Furthermore, I order that the detention pursuant to Section 5300 of the Welfare and Institution Code be terminated immediately and that Lexi Conway be released forthwith."

"Am I going home, judge?" asked Lexi, shaking visibly.

"Yes, Ms. Conway, you are."

Now Lexi was crying. Sarah was crying. Conrad, Nick, and Isabel were crying.

Brian approached the defense table. "Ms. Conway, step this way please. I need to take you downstairs so we can process your release."

"Brian, didn't you hear me?" bellowed Judge Sandoval. "I ordered Ms. Conway released immediately, not twenty minutes from now."

"But Your Honor, the Sheriff's Department regulations clearly state that—"

"I don't give a damn about your regulations. Have Sheriff Donaldson call me if he has a problem with this. Maybe I'll put him in jail and see how he likes it." The judge turned back to Lexi. "Ms. Conway, you may now walk out those doors a free woman."

Before she left, Lexi grabbed Sarah's arm. "Mrs. Wong, aren't you going to come out with me? I'll bet there's reporters and cameras out there, and I need you to help me."

"Lexi, you don't need me anymore. This is your moment of triumph, not mine. Go out there and claim your life back."

Lexi walked slowly toward the back of the courtroom, toward freedom.

After Lexi left, Matt came rushing up and gave Sarah a big hug. "I'm so proud of you, Tiger! Let's go home."

"Hon, I just need to sit down for a second."

Sarah never made it to the chair.

CHAPTER 27

"Mrs. Wong, Mrs. Wong! Last … eat … last time … Sarah … hurt?"

Sarah tried opening her eyes, but the light was too bright. And the noise! The siren was wailing, the ambulance was rattling, and everyone was shouting at her. The noise hurt, the light hurt, the bumpy ride hurt.

"Sarah, I'm here. I'm right here next to you."

Sarah recognized Matt's voice instantly and squeezed his hand, but she couldn't see him because she was strapped tightly into the ambulance gurney.

Seeing her hand move, the paramedic jumped in. "Mrs. Wong? Can you hear me?"

Sarah tried speaking, but her mouth was covered by an oxygen mask. She shook her head, trying to get the mask off, but couldn't dislodge it. The paramedic removed the mask.

"Can you hear me?"

"My babies!" Sarah looked at the paramedic. "Are my babies okay?"

"They look good, Mrs. Wong. I can see two heartbeats on the monitors. You wanna see?"

Without waiting for a response, the paramedic pushed the portable heart-rate monitors toward Sarah. But her vision was so blurry she couldn't see anything, so she turned to Matt. "How do they look, hon?"

Matt's voice was strong and calming. "They look great, Tiger. They look great!"

"Mrs. Wong, when was the last time you ate?" the paramedic asked.

"I'm not sure. Maybe this morning."

"You probably fainted because of low blood sugar. You do know you're in labor, don't you?"

"That can't be. My due date isn't for another couple of weeks. These must be Braxton Hicks contractions."

"No, these are for real," said the paramedic. "They're strong and about twenty minutes apart. You're going to have your babies today."

Just then, the ambulance siren went silent and they pulled into the emergency entrance at Memorial Hospital, not Eleanor Community Hospital, a smaller facility that placed a premium on individualized care with a holistic touch, where Sarah had planned to give birth. Her first instinct was to complain and demand a transfer, but she decided to just let it go. She was here now and it probably wouldn't be a good idea to take another ambulance trip across town. She tried to breathe and relax, but she wasn't quite sure what she was supposed to do because she had skipped almost half of her childbirth classes during Lexi's first trial.

After a bumpy ride on the ambulance gurney into the hospital, Sarah was transferred to a bed in the emergency room. The nurse placed both of the portable heart monitors right next to her and now she could see them clearly. Yes, both babies seemed to be doing well, although one heart was beating a little faster than the other.

After over an hour in the emergency room, Sarah was moved to the maternity ward. Her room was surprisingly large and luxurious—more of a suite than a room, with a large sitting area, a full-size bed for sleepy husbands and partners, and a spacious private bathroom.

But as soon as she got to her new accommodation, her labor ground to a halt. The contractions slowed down and seemed less intense. Every twenty minutes or so, the attending obstetrician checked in on her, and every time she was the same—three centimeters, partially effaced, station minus one.

When Dr. Sadler showed up Matt briefed her quickly.

"How about *you*, Sarah?" Dr. Sadler said brightly. "You actually made it all the way through the trial."

"Just barely," replied Sarah.

"Well, you're here now. Would you like me to help speed things along? I can give you some Pitocin to get those contractions going again."

"No, no, no. Matt and I want to have these babies naturally. No drugs, no nothing. Right, hon?"

"Whatever you say, Tiger."

"Very well," said Dr. Sadler. "Since you seem to be plateauing, I'm going to go upstairs and catch up on some paperwork. The nurses will call me as soon as you've made some progress."

"What do you mean *progress*? I'm doing the best I can!"

"Yes, I know. But try to get some rest. You've got a lot of work ahead of you."

On her way out, Dr. Sadler turned off all the lights in the room except for the small table lamp in the far corner.

Matt kicked off his shoes and jumped onto the guest bed. "I think I'll lay down for a few minutes too."

Sarah wasn't sleepy, so she just lay there quietly, and within a few minutes, she could hear Matt's rhythmic breathing. It gave her some time to herself before the impending chaos. She tried to think about her babies, but her mind kept drifting back to Lexi. Although justice had been served in the end, she couldn't help thinking about all the mistakes, missteps, and miscalculations she had made during the trial, and she fell asleep counting her mistakes as they leaped one by one over an imaginary fence. Although she was still having contractions every fifteen to twenty minutes, she slept soundly, roused only by the strongest ones. A nurse poked her head in every half hour, checking to make sure Sarah and her babies were doing fine.

After a couple of hours of fitful sleep, Sarah woke to the sight of a young male intern hovering over her bed.

"Mrs. Wong, I'm Dr. Manning. I'd like to do a quick pelvic exam to see how you're doing."

"I'm doing just fine, doctor. That won't be necessary."

"Why don't I take a look anyway?"

"No thanks." Sarah sat up. "What's that you're holding? Is that an amnio hook? ... I don't need any help!" she screeched. "I want to do this by myself. No hooks, no drugs, no suction, no nothing. My babies and I are doing just fine, thank you."

"I'm sorry. I just assumed you would want to move this along."

"Well, you assumed wrong."

As Dr. Manning turned to leave, Matt's voice rung out from the far side of the room. "You tell him, Tiger!"

The sound of Matt's voice reassured Sarah, and she slumped back down on the bed. For the next two hours, they made small talk, mostly about their nursery at home and about how much their lives were about to change. Neither of them said a word about genetic engineering or what might happen to their little boy.

Three nurses were assigned to their section of the maternity floor, and Matt tried to make friends with Mollie, the most senior and jovial of the bunch. Every time she came in to check on Sarah, Matt asked about her family and her hobbies, and as the day wore on Mollie checked on Sarah more and more frequently.

After four hours of no further progress, Dr. Sadler and Matt discussed the possibility of sending Sarah home, but in the end they decided it would be best to keep her in the hospital because of her fall at the courthouse.

Then one of the nurses popped into Sarah's room. "Mrs. Wong, you have a visitor."

"Who is it?" Sarah asked, trying to sit up a little more.

"It's your cousin, Lexi Conway."

"My cousin?" Sarah paused for a moment. "Oh! Please show her in."

When Lexi arrived, the two women greeted each other at the same time.

Sarah laughed and began again. "Lexi, how are you doing?"

"The question is how are *you* doing, Mrs. Wong? I was so worried about you. As soon as I heard that you passed out in court I came right over."

"I'm fine, and the babies are fine."

"At first they wouldn't let me up here to the maternity ward, but I talked with one of the nurses—I think her name is Mollie—and she said it would be okay. She told me if anybody asked who I was to just say I was your cousin. Can I sit here with you for a few minutes?"

Lexi pulled up a chair next to Sarah's bed and sat there holding her hand. Sarah broke the silence.

"What are your plans for the future, Lexi?"

"I haven't had much time to think about it. I might move somewhere far away. Maybe Modesto."

"How about further than that?" suggested Sarah.

"Like Fresno?"

"Actually I was thinking more like Florida. Or Maine. Or France."

Lexi laughed, making her green eyes sparkle. "I'll have to think about that. But wherever I end up, next time I'm going to have a child the right way. No science or anything."

"Aren't you worried about your Warrior Gene acting up in the future?" As soon as the words were out, Sarah wished she could pull them back.

"Whaddya mean? I thought you just made up all that stuff for my trial. You mean I've really got this Warrior Gene thing?"

"Yes, you do."

Lexi stared at the monitors by Sarah's bed while she took in Sarah's revelation. "Maybe so, but it isn't going to be a problem. I'm going to be the best mother ever. You just wait and see."

"I believe you, Lexi." And Sarah really did.

After a few more minutes, the head nurse barged in. "I'm afraid that's all, Ms. Conway. You're going to have to go now. Cousins aren't usually allowed, and we're breaking the rules by letting you in here. Mrs. Wong needs her rest."

"I understand. Can I hug her?"

"Yes, but make it quick."

Lexi leaned in, and Sarah could see that she was crying.

"Good luck, Mrs. Wong! I hope you have two beautiful, healthy babies."

Sarah hugged her tightly. "Thank you," she whispered in her ear and then watched Lexi head off to her new life.

Two beautiful, healthy babies. The words crushed Sarah.

"Hon, what's going to happen to our little boy? Is he going to die like all those other babies?"

"I don't know, Tiger."

"Not all the other babies died, right?"

"Right."

"Maybe our little boy will beat the odds."

"Maybe he will, Tiger."

"All we should have asked for was a baby with ten fingers and ten toes," Sarah lamented. "Why did we get so greedy?"

"Aren't you forgetting something? We changed our minds at the last minute. This isn't our fault."

"But it is, hon. It *is* our fault. We shouldn't have even thought about genetic engineering in the first place. Do you think God is punishing us?"

"For what?"

"For being so greedy."

"I don't think God does that."

Matt sat on the side of her bed and stroked her hair. "Everything's going to be fine, Sarah. I just know it."

"But what if it's not? What if our little boy dies? What if both babies die? What if I die?"

"Nobody's going to die. Everyone's going to be fine."

"We really do just have to believe that everything will be okay, don't we?"

"I think so. There are just some things in life we can't control, and this is one of them."

"We just have to have faith, huh?"

"Yes, we do."

"Faith in God?" asked Sarah.

"I'm not sure it matters. God, Mother Nature, whatever you want. The important thing is to just have faith."

"Well I have faith in you," Sarah said quietly as she kissed the back of Matt's hand.

"And I have faith in you too." Matt leaned in and kissed Sarah on the forehead.

"Owww!" screeched Sarah.

Matt pulled back quickly. "I'm sorry! Did I hurt you?"

"No, it's the babies. I think they're ready!"

* * *

"Here comes another one. Now, breathe!" instructed Matt. He was getting good at reading the ultrasound monitor, so good that he could tell when a contraction was coming before Sarah could feel it.

The pain was growing more intense with each contraction. She expected labor to be painful, but she hadn't been prepared for this kind of agony. Even if she wanted to change her mind about having drugs it was too late now.

A shrill beep sounded, easily audible over Sarah's grunts and squeals.

"What's that noise?" she asked.

"It's nothing," said Mollie. "One of the baby's heartbeats got a little fast, but it's settled down now. See?"

Sarah tried to focus on the heart-rate monitors by the side of her bed, but it was difficult to see them. Then the beeping stopped, and Matt assured her everything was fine.

But five minutes later, the alarm sounded again and this time it didn't stop.

"I'm going to get Dr. Sadler," said Mollie and she hurried out of the room. The urgency in her voice worried Sarah, and she could see that Matt was worried too.

Dr. Sadler arrived within minutes and huddled in the corner of the room with Matt, Mollie, and another nurse. The doctor quickly tore off the paper printout trailing from the beeping fetal monitor, and returned to the hushed discussion with Matt and the two nurses.

"What are you guys talking about? What's going on?" Sarah yelled at them.

Matt came over and grabbed her hand. "One of the babies is in trouble and they're going to do a C-section."

"Can't they wait a little bit to see if the beeping stops?" pleaded Sarah. "It stopped last time."

"Dr. Sadler said she's got to do this now," Matt said, looking worried.

Mollie lifted the metal rails on both sides of Sarah's bed and started wheeling her down the hallway, Matt running alongside holding her hand.

"But I want to do this on my own! I can do it, I can!" yelled Sarah as they passed the nurses' station.

"Tiger, sometimes we all need help, and this is one of those times."

Matt was right. Sarah had received help from the unlikeliest of sources during the past eleven months—from Conrad, Maggie, and Angelina. Even from Judge Sandoval. Now she needed help delivering her babies.

"You're right, hon. It's finally time for me to let go. Finally time for me to have faith."

* * *

Mollie pushed Sarah through the double doors into the operating room where Matt could see four or five people buzzing around getting ready. One looked like Dr. Sadler, but he couldn't be sure because of all the commotion.

As Matt walked alongside Sarah's bed, he felt a vise-like grip on his right shoulder.

"I'm sorry, sir, but you can't go in there," said a towering female nurse with a deep voice.

"But that's my wife — those are my babies!"

"Sir, it's a sterile operating room. Please step back."

Matt let go of Sarah's hand and tried to kiss the top of her head, but it was too late — she had already gone through the swinging doors in a tangle of IV lines.

"I love you, Sarah!" he yelled as the doors swung closed behind her.

He ran back to the nurses' station and pleaded to be let into the operating room.

"I'm sorry, Mr. Wong. Your wife is undergoing an emergency C-section and your presence could distract the doctors. Please return to your room and wait there."

"Like hell I will. I'm going in there whether you let me or not!"

"Thank you, Katy. I'll handle this."

Matt turned and saw Mollie who had just returned from the operating room. "Mr. Wong, could you follow me please?"

Mollie led him down the hall and through a small door next to the operating room. She motioned to the neatly folded scrubs on the bench in front of the lockers.

"Change into these scrubs. Be sure to put on the shoe covers, the hairnet, and the gloves. Then get your face mask in place. When you're done, I'll take you in."

Matt changed as quickly as he could, leaving his clothes in a heap on the floor. Mollie guided him into the operating room and positioned him against the wall, telling him not to move or get in the way.

As soon as Matt entered, he heard Sarah screaming and crying.

"Sarah, I'm right here," he called out. "Are you okay?"

Gasping for breath between her plaintive wailing, she was eventually able to deliver the horrible news. "We lost a baby! We lost a baby! They won't tell me which one."

"I'm right here, Sarah. Everything's going to be all right."

Sarah drifted in and out of consciousness. Nurses and doctors were running around frantically, yelling out terms Matt had only heard on TV medical shows. The operating room was noisy, and the din was getting louder by the second. Doctors were barking orders; metal instruments were crashing to the floor. Matt was terrified. No one would tell him what had happened to the baby, and he didn't even know if Sarah was going to be okay.

Then one solitary noise rose above all the others and made all the pain and fear disappear.

A baby's cry.

"We have a baby! We have a baby! We have a baby!" yelled Matt.

"Is it a boy or a girl? A boy or a girl?" screamed Sarah.

Matt knew how important this question was. If it was the boy, engineered with the deadly hybrid viral vector, he would almost certainly die within days or weeks. And even if he survived, he might turn out to be some sort of freakish animal hybrid.

But if it was the girl, everything would be fine.

Matt looked carefully at the baby. It was so hard to tell amid all the blood and mucous. Finally, he grabbed Sarah's hand.

"We have a baby girl!" he cried out. "Ten fingers and ten toes—she's perfect!"

ACKNOWLEDGEMENTS

I'd like to thank my editor, Averill Buchanan, for her expertise and her skilful, tireless work in editing *Death by DNA* and also for her keen advice about navigating the world of publishing. Thank you to Andrew Brown and his team at Design for Writers for the striking cover design. Thanks to many former students who read and commented on early versions of *Death by DNA*, including Jennifer Isher-Witt, Elizabeth Blake, Eliza Woolford, Amanda Spinner, the students of VaST 254, and too many others to mention.

Most of all, thank you to my wife, Carolyn, and our children, Carson and Kendall, for their love and support.

ABOUT THE AUTHOR

John S. Shaw, III is a psychology professor and former public defender. He lives in Bucks County, Pennsylvania, with his wife, Carolyn, and their two children, Carson and Kendall. *Death by DNA* is John's first novel.

Made in the USA
Coppell, TX
22 April 2021